Circle of Fire

'Part One of the CIRCLE OF FIRE trilogy'

Riva Shaw

Published in 2010 by YouWriteOn Publishing

First Edition

British Library C.I.P.

A CIP catalogue record for this title is available from the British Library.

Cover design by Jennifer Shaw

With love to
Andrew, Jennifer and Karen.

Chapter One

'Are they still behind us?'

'I cannot tell.' Nick Trayer turned awkwardly in the saddle. The rain fell in sheets, obscuring everything but a few paces of road around them. 'I do not think so but we are nearly there. You must feign sleep as we planned.'

He adjusted Catherine's cloak against the rain, trusting his horse to find the way.

Without warning the stone walls of the town appeared in front of them. Nick brought the horse to a stop beside the water trough and let him drink while he shouted for the watchman. He patted the animal on its neck.

'Good boy, Ransom, good boy.'

Above them, in the gatehouse, a window opened and the watchman appeared. Nick could just about make out his features. He had a friendly face but his voice was sharp with mistrust.

'What do you want? The city is closed.'

He lifted a lantern so that he could see them clearly. Nick raised an arm to shield his eyes. He wore no cloak himself and the rain had soaked his shirt and dripped now from his sleeve.

‘I’m sorry. I know it’s late but my wife is sick. I must find a bed for her.’ He hoped that his voice had not betrayed his fear.

Instinctively the watchman recoiled.

‘What’s wrong with her? Not a fever, is it? We don’t want the Scorge here.’

‘It’s not the fever. See for yourself.’ Resting his hand on the hilt of his knife, Nick chanced that his bluff would work. ‘She is with child. We’ve travelled a long way and she is wet through and exhausted. Please, I must find the inn and let her rest.’

The man lowered his lantern. His expression had softened and he grunted and disappeared from sight. Like an omen, a flash of lightning lit the sky and Nick prayed that the Fates would forgive him the lie. There was no baby but the treasure he guarded was even more precious. He shivered as the rainwater clung, cold against his skin.

A low rumble of thunder accompanied the grating of the bolt and the massive town doors swung open.

Nick urged the horse forward again.

Ransom had belonged to him since he was a foal and Nick not much more than a foal himself. There was a deep love and mutual trust between them, and he knew the horse would have carried him and Catherine to the ends of the earth. Even so, Ransom was clearly reluctant to go forward into the darkness. The buildings one on top of each other and the jumble of smells were completely alien to the animal, used as he was to the comfort of soft grass or the dust of open roads beneath his feet.

Nick understood his fear. Ever since they had begun their flight, the feeling of dread had been heavy in his heart.

‘Come on, Ransom. Come on. Not much further.’

Even the rain seemed different here. It raced along the cobbles and formed small puddles, splashing against the horse's legs. Ransom snorted, and shook his head trying to clear the moisture from his face. Again Nick patted his neck and tried to sound reassuring.

'Good boy. Nearly there.'

The streets of the town were deserted, the wooden houses shuttered firmly against the rain and the night. Nick waited briefly to see the gate slam shut. At least then, he knew that no-one had entered behind them.

He led the horse into a side street and very slowly headed towards an arch in the wall where two thick wooden doors were firmly closed. A tiny chink of light appeared, the same explanations were made and one of the doors creaked open. Finally, in the calm welcome of the inn yard, Nick allowed himself a sigh of relief

***

By morning, the rain had cleared and the sky was an unbroken blue. Nick stood at the window of the tiny room, high in the roof of the inn. He could see the last of the mist lingering over the distant high ground. In some ways, he would have preferred the sun not to shine. It was too painful a reminder.

He gazed across the muddle of rooftops, to the vineyards and wooded hills beyond but in his mind he could see further than that; far away to his beloved farm and across his fields to the mill that Catherine's father worked.

He wished it was still raining and that he could not see the sun. Yesterday he had watched it rise on a very different day, his wedding day.

He could still see it reflecting off the white of Catherine's dress and dancing in the golden highlights of her hair.

How could he ever have guessed that duty, loyalty and honour would bring him here, less than twenty four hours later, to this tiny room.

There was barely space for two narrow beds and a small chest of drawers but the room was clean and comfortable.

A nightmare had woken Nick after barely an hour. Then sleep had eluded him for the rest of the night. Fear had kept him company and an eve of battle energy he had never thought to feel again.

It was still very early. His shirt was damp from the rain but as he stood at the window, the sunlight warmed him. He could hear the morning birdsong and the cooing of the pigeons on the window ledges. Way beneath him, two boys were rolling a barrel down the street and from an open window further up the hill, he could hear someone practising scales on a flute.

There was a soft groan from the bed and rousing himself immediately from his daydream he turned into the room. How he ached to see Catherine's beautiful face smiling up at him, to take her in his arms and kiss her and lose himself in the silky softness of her skin. This should have been their wedding night after all.

Instead, where Catherine's hair was fair and long, the figure on the bed had short dark curls and the face that turned towards him was that of a boy of no more than fifteen years.

Nick approached the bed with a low bow.

'It is morning, My Lord Prince. I hope you slept well.' The boy sat up, grimacing with distaste as he realised he was still wearing Catherine's clothes then he smiled with the honest trust of a child.

'I didn't think I would, but I did. Are we safe now?'

'Yes, My Lord,' Nick said gently. 'For the moment we are safe.'

Chapter 2
The Previous Day

Nick had never imagined that when the day came he would feel so nervous he could barely tie his boots. His hands shook as he fumbled with the laces, pulling them tight around his calf but losing his grip when he tried to fasten the knot.

Dugon, his steward stood at the door, the hint of a grin on his craggy face.

'Do you need some help with that?'

Defeated, Nick nodded his head. 'Please.'

The older man came forward took each of Nick's feet in turn and rested them on his knee fixing the laces deftly. He grinned again.

'Your father was in just such a state when he married your mother. Couldn't hardly walk he was that weak. "Dugon," he said, "I love her more than you could ever know but I'd rather face a whole company of men at arms, than face this."'

Nick closed his eyes, took a deep breath, opened them again.

'I've waited so long for this day.'

Laying a hand on his master's shoulder, Dugon looked straight into his eyes.

'You are worthy of her. You hear? You've more than proved it. Her father knows that.'

Despite Nick's nobility, Vilap the miller had not always thought him a good match for his daughter. Nick's own father had spent most of his life away at war. Though his love for his wife and son was never in doubt, he had left them to struggle on the farm without him while he proved himself a hero, loved by his men, honoured by his king. The people of his village were not impressed by battlefield heroics. Life for them revolved around the changing of the seasons, the weekly markets and the monthly fairs.

When Nick had asked him for Catherine's hand, Vilap had shaken his head wearily and sighed into his beard.

'How do I know that you'll not leave her as your father did and run off to go soldiering? You've already tasted the blood of battle and they say that you distinguished yourself. I want my daughter to have a husband at home to care for her like I've cared for her dear mother. I want my grandchildren to know their father, not just hear stories of him.'

Nick would not have dreamed of simply taking what he wanted as many noblemen would have done. He had respect for the miller. Like all the villagers, Vilap and his wife had been kind to him. They were the closest he had to family.

'When my parents died I swore I would never leave again,' Nick reminded him. Even after all this time, the weight of his loss felt heavy in his heart. 'I was very young when I went to fight. I thought it was what I wanted.'

'You are still young and you may make promises now which you will find hard to keep in the future.' The miller had sighed and shaken his head again. Then he smiled. It was the smile of a father. 'My wife and I are very fond of you, and anyone can see how much Catherine loves you.

But I will not see her deserted and lonely. I will not see her work her fingers to the bone while you go off after glory. Husband and wife working side by side, that's fine. But no woman should have to struggle the way your poor mother did.'

Nick hated to hear any blight on his father's memory, even though he knew it was the truth.

'I've worked my farm for all these years,' he insisted. 'You have seen me. I've laboured hard.'

'Yes you have, but there is still time. Like I say, you're only young. I wish you to wait two more years.'

Nick had realised that it was pointless to argue. The only way to prove his love and his commitment to Catherine's happiness was to do as he was asked.

The prospect of two more years had seemed like a lifetime but now, finally, the day of their wedding had arrived.

Nick adjusted his grey woollen tunic and shook out the arms of the shirt that Dugon's wife Ann had sewn for him. The linen felt new and crisp but also soft against his skin. He had been in the habit of wearing his hair long like the villagers but Ann had convinced him to let her cut it.

'A nobleman should look smart on his wedding day,' she had insisted.

Now Nick felt almost naked without it. He ran a hand around his neck then sighed deeply.

'Will I do, Dugon?' he said finally.

The steward nodded his head and smiled again.

'You'll do fine. Come on. We don't want you to be late.'

Downstairs the wide hall was empty and quiet but smelled of fresh herbs and flowers. For the whole of the previous day it had been a scene of feverish activity as Ann and her daughters had scrubbed and cleaned every corner of the house so that it would be a fit place for the new bride. Nick and Dugon had been shooed away to the woods to hunt boar for the wedding feast and to collect wood for the kitchen fire.

This morning, well before dawn, a band of women had arrived to prepare the food which was then piled high in carts and taken down to the village. Nick had been embarrassed by their kindness. The lives of the people were hard and he did not like to add to their burden. Cheerfully, they had waved away his protests and he had heard them laughing and singing as they worked.

The house was not grand. Nick, despite his noble birth was not a rich man but when he thought of the time and trouble that had been taken so willingly on his behalf, he felt himself rich in the things that really mattered.

Someone had groomed and saddled Ransom. The horse stood now, in the yard, his coat a gleaming black, the mane and tail combed and plaited. The saddle, though old, had been oiled and buffed and Nick could almost see his face in it. He patted the horse on his neck and with one eager bound leapt onto his back.

Ransom seemed to know that this was a special day. He stood proudly, his majestic head held high. He was descended from the great Nostarian war horses. His mother had been taken as ransom for a captured nobleman after the great victory at Hell's Mountain. Nick's father had brought her back to the farm as a present for his wife, not realising that the mare was pregnant. When Ransom was born Nick had fallen in love with the foal and claimed him as his own.

Dugon mounted his own horse and the two of them set off for the village. They trotted along the lane under the warm spring sunshine beside the field which Nick himself had sown with barley. The gentle breeze carried the perfume of spring flowers and he filled his lungs with it and began to feel calmer. Surely the Fates would finally smile on him. He would marry Catherine today and bring her back here. It was all he wanted in the world.

Within minutes the low thatched roofs of the village lay stretched out before him and closer the four-storey building of the mill and its house. He could see the window of Catherine's bedchamber and imagined her sitting on the edge of her small bed combing out her fair hair, plaiting it and coiling it neatly around her ears. He was far too familiar with that room than he had a right to be. It was fortunate that for the last year or so, the Miller had been profoundly deaf. He was unable to hear the creak of floorboards in the early morning, the opening of the window or the gentle thud of feet landing on the ground beneath.

Tomorrow for the first time Nick could wake up at the farm with Catherine beside him. He would certainly not have to leave by the window.

He was disturbed from his daydream by the sound of cheering and was touched to see that the villagers were out in the street waiting for him. They were dressed in their best clothes, clapping and waving. In front of the bakery, Todd the cooper was playing the flute. Some of the younger people began to dance.

A female voice called, 'come down and dance with us, Sir.'

'It's your last chance.' The baker beamed a toothless grin. 'There'll be no more dancing once you've done the deed. Might as well make the most of it.' His wife feigned anger and pretended to slap him but he took her in his arms and danced her along the street.

Other voices repeated the request.

'Yes Sir, come and dance.'

'Come and dance with me, Sir. See what you're missing.'

Nick glanced at Dugon and the man smiled. 'Go on. There's no harm. We've plenty of time.'

Barely had his feet touched the ground before Nick was whisked away into the crowd. The young women fought each other for a dance with him and he was passed from one to the other spinning giddily as the music grew louder and faster. At last, he had to stand still to gain his breath. Gasping, he rested his hands on his thighs and laughed.

'I'll be fit for nothing after this.'

There was no reply. He realised that the music had stopped and there was a new sound, the pounding of horses' hooves. He looked up. The villagers had stopped dancing and were staring towards the road. Three horsemen galloped into the village churning up a dense cloud of dust in their wake.

The horses stopped abruptly and one of the riders leaned forward in the saddle. He was an elderly man dressed elaborately in a long embroidered robe and despite the mild weather, a fur lined cape and hat. The other two men were younger; one no more than a boy, the other a soldier.

'We are looking for the home of Sentorman Nicholas Trayer.' The older man's voice broke up as he spoke and he seemed in some distress. Dugon pushed forward to the front of the crowd.

'Are you unwell, My Lord?'

In all the towns and villages of Subia strangers were treated with mistrust. Mainly this was to do with the Scorge. There were still many parts of the country where the odd case was reported. In this as in many other ways, these villagers had been fortunate. They were keen to keep it that way.

The old man waved a hand in irritation. 'No, no. But we have ridden hard. I need to speak to your sentorman urgently.'

Nick sighed as the sound of his title brought back all his remembered pain.

'I am Nick Trayer,' he admitted.

The villagers stood back so that he could be seen. The stranger acknowledged him with a short bow of his head.

'I need to speak with you urgently and…' he glanced around at the crowd of people who were beginning to creep nearer, '…and in private.'

Nick frowned at him. 'I'm just on my way to get married. Perhaps if you wouldn't mind waiting.'

'In that case I apologise, but it is a matter of supreme importance. I am Lord Harold Garwin, – member of the royal household and Profender to my Lord Prince …'

'I don't care who you are.' Nick said angrily. Just when he had started to believe his time had finally come he had a terrible feeling of foreboding.

'May I present…' Garwin indicated the boy with a sweep of his hand. 'My Lord Prince Rowan Garth of the Jassoir, heir to the throne of Subia.'

There was a sharp intake of breath from the assembled villagers. For all their disdain of the wider world, even they were awed to be in the presence of a prince.

The boy got off his horse and came over to Nick as Lord Garwin and the guard dismounted behind him.

'I'm very sorry to disturb your wedding.' His voice was still high, but with the rough undertone that indicated he was a child on the cusp of manhood. 'But we must speak to you now. Is there somewhere we can go?'

The miller had come out of his house and now joined them. He turned to Dugon. 'What are they saying?'

Dugon explained hastily and loudly.

The Miller shook his head. 'What's that? He's who?'

Lord Garwin frowned in irritation although the Prince seemed to find it amusing.

At last the miller's eyes widened with understanding. He bowed to the Prince. 'Forgive me, My Lord Prince. I am a little hard of hearing.'

The boy laughed at the obvious understatement. 'It's of no matter.'

'You can come inside,' the miller insisted. 'My house is just here.'

'This is Vilap the miller,' Nick explained, 'the father of my bride.'

Lord Garwin acknowledged him also with a nod of his head. 'We are grateful to you Master Miller.' He turned to the guard. 'Wait here.'

Nick had no choice but to follow them inside.

What, he wondered, were the Fates about to throw at him now?

It was a warm spring day but inside the small living room, a fire burned in the grate, surrounded by cooking pots and utensils, filling the room with smoke. A large oak table and chairs took up most of the space and on the far wall a smaller door stood open, through which a narrow staircase was just visible. There was barely enough room for the Prince, Lord Garwin, Nick and the miller. Dugon indicated that he would wait outside with the guard, but he didn't go very far and Nick knew that he would hear everything that was said.

'May I offer you some refreshment?' the miller asked.

Lord Garwin waved a dismissive hand. 'We are grateful for your hospitality but I'm afraid we don't have time.' He fixed Nick with a piercing stare. 'We have come to ask for your help. Prince Rowan is on route to Castle Baryk and we have been ambushed by one of King Tynon's war bands.'

‘A war band.’ Nick frowned. ‘Tynon would never dare to send his skirmishers so far north.’

‘A few years ago, that would have been so,’ the man agreed. ‘But much has changed recently. The Scorge has killed so many of our fighting men. To the South, in Nostaria, King Tynon knows that we are weakened. He, on the other hand, seems to have escaped the disease so far. His army grows daily in strength, while we are having to call upon reservists such as yourself. And now…’

‘I am not a soldier,’ Nick insisted. ‘I am a farmer.’

‘You are the son of Gideon Trayer. You fought with him at the battle of Highvale.’

‘I was just a boy.’

‘But you fought?’

‘Yes.’

‘Then you are a soldier.’

Nick sighed ‘But the King told me that…’

Garwin frowned in irritation. ‘I don’t have time to argue details. The Prince must reach the castle safely. The truth is, that the King is dying,’

‘My father was thrown from his horse while hunting,’ the Prince explained. ‘It looks bad for him. His physicians think it unlikely he will survive. I must return to Castle Baryk. It seems that I am about to become King.’

He did not look happy at the prospect. Though his face was still that of a child, his dark eyes spoke of strength and honesty.

King Edwell was respected as a strong leader as well as a fair and understanding monarch. Nick had met him twice. On the first occasion he had felt the King’s eyes upon him and knew himself to be subject to the deepest scrutiny. It was as if the King could read his soul, as if he were True-sighted. The True-sight though, had been outlawed since the defeat of the Valeron kings fifty years previously, and was now the stuff of legend.

When the King had satisfied himself that Nick had fulfilled whatever criteria he was seeking, he had rewarded him with a wide smile full of joy.

Later, on the second occasion, those same eyes had been gentle with compassion.

Prince Rowan, Nick could see, was very much his father's son.

Garwin waited patiently for the Prince to finish speaking although it was obvious that he wanted to hurry matters along. When the chance came, he resumed his explanation.

'There are many in this area who cannot be trusted. While our armies were strong they were little more than schemers, and we had disposed of almost all of them. But we live in a changing world. No-one expected this latest blow. Those traitors, Valeron sympathisers and Nostarian spies, who have been in hiding, are becoming bolder by the hour. The Prince must reach the safety of the castle as soon as possible.'

A floorboard creaked above them and Catherine came down the stairs and stood in the doorway, her head on one side.

Although the room was dim, what light did manage to penetrate the gloom, seemed to be drawn towards her, bathing her in a gentle glow. She was wearing a white dress of the thinnest wool which fell softly across the contours of her body and almost to the ground. Around it she had tied a belt of pale yellow silk, which Nick had bought for her from an Eastern trader. It emphasised the slimness of her waist and the gentle swell of her breasts and hips. Instead of the usual coils, her hair was left to fall loose around her shoulders in a sea of gold and she had threaded it with white and yellow flowers.

He had loved her for many years, but Nick had never seen her look as beautiful as she did now. Emotion filled his eyes and he could not drag them away from her.

'My Lords,' the Miller announced proudly, 'this is my daughter, Catherine.'

The Prince was clearly enchanted. He turned to Nick.

'This is your bride?'

Nick nodded his head dumbly.

'She is very lovely. You are a lucky man.'

'Yes,' Nick whispered, 'I am.'

'My Lord, if you please.' Lord Garwin barely glanced at Catherine before he addressed himself to Nick once more. 'This is all very regrettable but we have no time to waste. I have one guard left from a company of ten. We need your help. All we ask is that you take Prince Rowan to the city of Larock where help will be waiting. Ask there for a man called Jacob Rine. He will arrange for the Prince to be transported onwards.'

'I'm not the man you need,' Nick insisted. 'My career as a soldier was over before it began.'

Garwin took a step towards him and before Nick had a chance to defend himself, the old man grabbed hold of the sleeve of his shirt and tore it from shoulder to wrist.

Nick glared angrily at him. 'What are you doing? This is a new shirt.'

He tried to pull his arm away, but the man had a surprisingly strong grip. With his other hand, Garwin pointed to a scar at the top of Nick's arm. It was in the form of an intricate lattice circle to which a blue dye had been added to make the pattern stand out.

'You are a Warrior of the Circle of Fire. You are bound to your king's service.'

The Prince's eyes were wide with admiration. 'I've never seen one of those before. Let me look.'

Lord Garwin waved him away. 'Now is not the time, My Lord. We must hurry.'

Nick stared at the scar as if it surprised him, yet every day for nearly ten years he had lived with the fact of it. He could remember even now the agony of his branding and how proud he had felt. And every day since, he remembered the terrible cost he had paid for that pride.

'King Edwell released me,' he insisted. 'I am a farmer now.'

'There is no release.' Lord Garwin looked disdainfully at him. 'You swore to devote your life to the King's service. He may have chosen not to call upon you, and that is his right, but these are desperate times and you have no choice. Jacob Rine is another of the Warriors of the Circle. Take the Prince to him safely, and you will have done your duty.'

Before Nick had a chance to reply, there was a shout from the street.

Dugon appeared at the door.

'There are riders approaching. At least twenty. It looks like a war band.'

Chapter 3

Nick's father had been a good and thorough teacher. From sword fighting practice in the yard at the farm when Nick could barely lift the sword, to his words of wisdom on the battlefield of Highvale, he had groomed his young son to become the supreme soldier that he himself had been.

One of the first lessons Nick learned was to make a fast and accurate assessment of every situation. Now, despite the passing of nearly a decade his training did not forsake him. His priority, he could see was to protect the Prince but they would stand no chance in a fight with twenty armed men. The only other option was escape.

'Catherine.' He moved quickly across the room and took her gently by the arm. 'Take Prince Rowan upstairs and out through your window. You'll have to wade across the stream but it's not deep. Then go as far as you can into the woods, and I will find you.'

Her eyes expressed surprise. 'But you will come with us?'

'No. Dugon and I will hold them back as long as possible.' He had not yet thought how he would achieve this, but there was very little time. 'Go now, hurry. You know where to wait?'

‘Yes.’ He could see that she knew the place; a grassy knoll hidden between the trees. A place of childhood games and lovers’ trysts. Nick did not allow himself to think of those, but only to drop a gentle kiss on her lips. Then he was in charge once more.

‘My Lord if you please. Catherine will show you the way. You must hurry.’

The Prince obeyed without question. Nick lingered long enough for one last glimpse of Catherine as she disappeared from sight, then he turned to Lord Garwin. ‘My Lord I would have suggested that you accompany them but I think they will travel further without…’

The old man waved away his explanation. ‘I agree. I am too old. I will slow them down.’ He sighed, drawing himself upright, steeling himself. ‘I will speak to these men. If it is merely a ransom they seek then I may be able to do something.’

‘But Your Lordship…’ The man was out of the door and into the street before Nick could finish his sentence.

‘Let him go.’ Dugon said quickly. ‘Let him do what he has to do.’ He glanced towards the door, then back to Nick. ‘I reckon it would be best if you stay in the background? If it is a ransom they seek, you will be worth something to them. Let them think you’re one of us until we know how things stand.’

Nick agreed. He glanced at his sleeveless shirt then with a heavy heart, ripped away the other sleeve so that both his arms were bared. He tore one into strips and tied it around the brand.

Dugon nodded his approval. ‘No sense letting them know what they’ve got.’

The words were barely spoken before a man appeared in the doorway. He was tall and pitifully thin, his hair and face hidden inside an old helmet so that just his eyes were visible. These in turn were hooded by thick black eyebrows. There was something weary about the way he moved. In his hand on the end of a leather thong, the man carried a spiked mace, which he now waved in their direction.

'Outside,' he said 'All of you.'

The Miller, who had watched the entire proceedings in silence, clearly had not a clue what was going on.

'Come on Vilap,' Nick put a hand on his shoulder. 'Do as he says.'

The miller pointed to the stairs. 'But Catherine, she…'

'She's safe.' Nick assured him. 'We must go.'

The soldier followed the direction of Vilap's finger.

'Catherine. Who's she?'

Nick was surprised how quickly the lie came. 'She was his wife. She's long gone. He gets confused.'

'Who else is up there?'

'There's no-one.'

For some reason, the man seemed to believe him, or maybe he could not be bothered to search further. He hustled the three men out into the street.

Briefly, coming from the dim interior of the mill, Nick was blinded by the sunlight. He found himself on one side of the road, where the other villagers were being held, guarded by two of the raiders. These men were on foot now, their horses drinking thirstily from the trough. In the centre of the street another ten or so men were still on horseback. The man who was clearly in charge wore body armour and carried a sword while the others wore simple clothes and only helmets for protection. They were not, he realised, a Nostarian war band. These men were Subians and they all had the appearance that they had travelled far and were tired and hungry. He began to hope that the situation was not as bad as it might have appeared. The hope was short lived however, for there, lying dead on the ground was the Prince's remaining guardsman.

While some of the raiders still ran from house to house turning people out into the street, he saw Dugon in furtive conversation with the cooper who had dropped his flute and was now nodding sombrely. Nick found himself pushed gently backwards through the crowd. Though he tried to resist, wanting to see and hear what was going on, the tide took him steadily back. He knew what was happening. It was not just his imagination that his men closed in around him, forming a shield so that the raiders could not see him. It was not by chance that Ethan, the blacksmith, a giant of a man with long dark hair and beard, had positioned himself squarely in front of his master.

With the little view he had, Nick could see Lord Garwin remonstrating with the armoured leader. He could not hear what the man was saying but he watched in horror as the soldier raised his sword and brought the hilt of it down with full force onto Lord Garwin's head. A woman screamed and one of the raiders ordered her to be quiet. There was a shocked silence as the old man fell to the ground with a thud that seemed to reverberate throughout the village.

Instinctively, Nick moved to go to his aid, but felt himself restrained by several pairs of hands, one of which was clasped gently but firmly across his mouth.

The villagers stood silently as the leader removed his helmet and ran his hand through a thick mop of dark hair, shaking himself like a dog.

'I think you all know why we're here,' he said in a loud but curiously monotonous voice. He was definitely a Subian, and from his accent a nobleman. 'We have come for Prince Rowan and we know he is here. Lord Garwin by his very presence has confirmed that.'

Still there was silence. By this time, Nick estimated, Catherine and the Prince should have been across the stream and into the safety of the woods. He was not concerned therefore, when he saw the man with the spiked mace go back into the millhouse. Evidently he had had second thoughts and decided to check the building thoroughly. He came out, a few seconds later leading a woman wrapped in Catherine's winter cloak. At first Nick could not understand who she was, then he recognised the dark curls of the Prince. He made a convincing girl. To his horror, the Prince was followed by Catherine, still in her wedding dress, her golden hair shining in the warm sunshine. She looked every inch a lady.

'How charming,' the leader said with a smile, though his voice was still impassive. 'Please, My Lady, come and join us. Maybe you can tell me where they've hidden the Prince.'

The Prince was pushed roughly into the crowd and forgotten while Catherine was led towards the horsemen. Their leader said something to her which Nick could not hear and her response clearly angered him because he drew his sword again and brandished it in the air. In a voice still chillingly monotonous, he demanded 'Tell me where you have hidden the Prince or I will cut off her head.'

Nick fought with all his strength to free himself and go to her, but the hands still held him firmly. A voice spoke softly in his ear. 'There is nothing you can do, Sir. You have no weapon. You would be best to keep still for the moment.'

He strained every sinew in his body to break free, but the arms around him tightened and he could not move.

Dugon, meanwhile, had pushed himself to the front of the crowd.

‘If you please,’ he said, his voice unusually humble, ‘she is my lady Catherine, wife of my master the Sentorman. I beg of you do not harm her.’

The raider let his arm drop. ‘And who might you be?’

‘I am his steward. I can lead you to the Prince.’

‘And your master? Where is he?’

‘Castle Baryk, Sir. He is attending the King.’ The leader consulted briefly with one of his men, then he turned back to Dugon.

‘You say you know where we can find the Prince?’

‘Yes, Sir. I hid him at the farm. If you will allow me, I will show you.’

The man gave one short emotionless laugh. ‘Oh Yes. You will show me. And while we are gone, your friends will spirit the Prince away.’

‘It is the truth Sir. I assure you.’

The raider considered the matter for a moment. He spoke again to his companion, then he shouted orders at his men.

‘You four, guard the village. Do not let anyone out. The rest of us will go to the farm.’ Now he addressed the villagers. ‘If we find what we are looking for you have nothing to fear. But I urge you to think of the consequences of trying to deceive me. They will be dire. Our friend here…’ he motioned towards Dugon, ‘will guide us and her ladyship…’ he bent forward and in one movement lifted Catherine up before him. ‘She will come with us.’

Nick could feel the surge of energy deep within him as he made a supreme effort to break free. He tried to bite the hand that was held over his mouth, and to kick out at the legs which surrounded him, but there was no space to move and there were at least five men holding him. He was forced, therefore to stand and watch as the horsemen rode off, Dugon walking beside them. Catherine was hidden by the body of her captor. He could not see her face. All he could see of his bride, was the hem of her wedding dress and her foot as she was carried away.

Chapter 4

The raiders who had been left on guard, had got off their horses, and made themselves comfortable at either end of the road. They watched the villagers as they started to disperse but made no effort to interfere with them. As one man, the little group around Nick moved towards the bakery. The cooper and two other men guided him ahead of them into the building and only then did they release him.

The huge bulk of the blacksmith barred his way out of the room.

Nick looked accusingly at the cooper.

'Let me go, Todd,' he said icily.

Todd shook his head. 'We understand how you feel, Sir, but there is nothing you can do for her and I think you know that. Your duty lies elsewhere.'

Nick threw himself into a chair and rested his head in his hands. 'They will not be fooled for long, and when they come back they will kill you all.'

'Well they may and they may not,' Todd said prosaically, 'but your being here or otherwise won't make no difference. They'll just kill you too or take you prisoner and what would be the point in that. You have to take the Prince to safety, and we have to aid you.'

Nick knew that the man was right. He had known all along where his duty lay.

The living quarters in the bakery were not much bigger than those of the mill, but somehow the bodies of Lord Garwin and the guard were dragged inside and the Prince, still dressed in Catherine's clothes, followed them.

'Are they dead?' he asked of no-one in particular.

'Yes, My Lord,' Todd said. 'I'm sorry.' In Dugon's absence he seemed to have taken charge.

The Prince looked sadly at his former companions. 'I am sorry too. And I am sorry for you all. And grateful. If I do make it to safety, none of you will be forgotten.'

Todd turned to the baker. 'There's a back way out of here isn't there?'

'Yes. It comes out by the stream.'

'Good.' He looked at Nick. 'Sir, if you please, Ethan here will take your horse down to the forge. You can pick him up there and sneak out across through the woods. Some of our women'll attend to the guards. Offer them some food and drink. They look like they could use some.'

'They'll see through that in an instant.' Nick argued. Though the plan made sense, he wanted to find fault with it. He didn't want to escape to safety, even for the sake of the Prince. He wanted to be near Catherine. It was all that mattered to him. 'You'll just make them suspicious and then they'll be more alert.'

'Not if they're half as stupid as they look,' the baker insisted. 'They're all hungry and thirsty I'll wager. Don't you worry about them, Sir. You just do your duty and we'll take care of the rest.'

'Very well.' Nick tried to clear his head and think only of the task in hand. 'I need a weapon.'

Todd indicated the dead guard.

'Well he won't be needing his will he? He's lost his sword but…'

He bent down to relieve the man of his knife.

'This is an evil looking fellow. You can do some damage with this.'

He handed the knife to Nick.

'I reckon you could take his clothes as well, Sir. He's not much bigger'n you, and that leather tunic'll afford some protection.'

Without bothering to argue, Nick took off his new tunic and his ruined shirt, and dressed himself in the dead man's clothes. There was a tear in the leather just below the arm pit, and a hole and a blood stain in the shirt where the enemy's sword had found a way through to the man's heart. The clothes felt clammy and already smelled of death. They suited Nick's mood perfectly and concentrated his mind. He tucked the knife into his belt. It was strange, he thought, how after all these years, the weapon made him feel like a soldier again.

The Prince turned to Todd.

'If you can, I'd be grateful if you would bury Lord Harald. I'd like to take him back with us and give him a proper funeral, but …' he shrugged. 'He was good man and he gave his life for me. I wouldn't like to think of him becoming food for some wild animal. And the guard also. If it is possible.'

'We'll do that, My Lord,' Todd assured him.

'Now I need to find my clothes,' the Prince said. 'I left them at the mill.'

'If you please My Lord,' the cooper suggested, 'it would probably be best if you stayed in that dress. It's a fair disguise.'

The Prince made a face but he nodded in agreement.

'Yes. I suppose it is.'

‘Why did you not escape the way we planned?’ Nick asked him.

‘There was a man standing just below the window. We almost landed on him. Luckily he did not hear us. The weir is very noisy. We had to think of another plan. It was Catherine’s idea to dress in her clothes. A good idea I think? She is not just beautiful but clever also.’

Nick did not want even to think about Catherine. In his mind he could still see that fragment of her dress and her foot against the horse’s leg. He had not been able to see her face, and was therefore free to imagine how she must have looked, frightened, shocked and above all surprised that he had let her be taken in that way. Indeed, how had he? How had he allowed them to take her?

He heard someone say, ‘You must hurry now. They’ll be back soon.’

While Nicholas Trayer, Warrior of the Circle of Fire, son of the great Gideon Trayer, led the Prince out onto the grass at the back of the bakery and helped him wade across the stream in his unfamiliar skirt, Nick the farmer, thought only of what he was leaving behind.

It occurred to him that he could hide the boy in the woods and double back to the farm. He had the knife now and the benefit of surprise. Prince Rowan however, seemed to have read his mind.

‘If I were in your position,’ he whispered as they passed into the cover of the trees, ‘and they had taken the woman I loved, I would want to go after them and get her back whatever the cost. But I know that your father was a man of duty and honour and that you are a son worthy of him. I need you now. Subia needs you. I cannot imagine what the result will be if I fall into their hands.’

Nick had continued to stride purposefully through the woods though he could hear what the boy said. The prince had to run to keep up with him.

'If it helps,' he said breathlessly, 'let me tell you that I do not believe they would hurt her. She is too valuable to them. You must do what you must. You do understand that don't you?'

And he did. He could hear his father's voice in his head and there was no doubt where he would say Nick's duty lay.

For a moment he stopped and looked at the boy. There was wisdom and understanding in his young eyes.

'I will take you to Larock, My Lord. I will get you there safely.'

'Yes.' The Prince nodded. 'I believe that you will.'

They ran as swiftly as possible through the trees. The first leaves were opening as speckles of sunlight revealed the blues, yellows and whites of wild flowers. The air smelled fresh and clear. Perfect weather for a wedding.

When Nick anticipated they were level with the northernmost reaches of the village, he paused and crept forward to the edge of the trees. He could see the raiders. They had dismounted and as the cooper had suggested, they were being plied with food and drink. It occurred to Nick that the victuals they were guzzling so voraciously had been destined for his wedding feast. The pain in his heart deepened.

The blacksmith had been as good as his word and Ransom was grazing on the grass in front of the forge.

'I will call the horse,' Nick whispered. 'When he comes we must hurry.' He pointed to the raiders. 'By the time they realise what is happening, we should have a good start. My horse is fast. We should outrun them easily.' He crept a little closer. 'You will have to ride like a woman in front of me.'

'I understand.'

'Are you ready?'

The boy nodded gravely. 'I am ready.'

Nick gave a low gentle whistle. The raiders heard nothing, but Ransom's ears pricked and he turned towards his master. On Nick's second whistle he began to trot in the direction of the trees. The raiders did not notice him until he splashed into the stream. Then one of them pointed and shouted something. Nick whistled again, louder this time and more urgently. Ransom responded instantly quickening his stride. He came crashing into the trees and had barely drawn to a halt before Nick leapt into the saddle and hoisted the Prince up before him.

'Good boy, Ransom. Now run.'

They set off at a gallop, racing through the trees, taking what Nick knew was a less direct route. He did not want to break cover too soon. For a while they could hear the sounds of the pursuit, the hooves of the horses and the shouts of the two men, but Ransom was indeed fast, and by the time they had no choice but to risk the open ground their pursuers were nowhere to be seen.

Nick knew the road to Larock well. Many times, he had been to the fair that was held every month in its ancient market place. Normally it would take a whole day to get there. Today he would have to make the journey in half the time.

As the familiar villages and farms passed, he barely noticed them. Though it was a mild day, at that speed the wind stung against his face and the pain helped him to concentrate, helped him not to think but to act instinctively.

After a couple of hours, they had climbed high into the hills and came to a place where Nick remembered a lake tarn was hidden by a rocky outcrop. He slowed the horse to a trot and led him down to the water to drink. They dismounted and stretched their stiff limbs.

While the Prince went into the trees to relieve himself Nick and Ransom wandered a little way along the shore and stood looking out over the lake. Though the sun still shone, he could see dark clouds gathering in the distance and briefly he thought he saw a flash of lightning way over the hills.

When the Prince came back he looked uncomfortable.

'Well that was an interesting experience,' he observed. 'How do women manage not to piss all over their clothes?'

Despite his dark mood, Nick could not help smiling. 'I don't know. I've never thought about it.'

'When you see Catherine next, you must ask her for me.'

Nick's smile died instantly. 'You're very sure that I will see her again. She could be dead already.'

'No.' The boy shook his head. 'They will not kill her. They do not know that you are not yet married. They believe her to be your wife, a noblewoman. She is worth more to them alive.'

'There are worse things that can happen to a woman than death,' Nick said grimly.

'Yes but they won't touch her. They will kill your steward, and then they may return to the village and take the other women for their pleasure, but they will not harm Catherine.'

Nick gave him a look which said, 'Is that supposed to make me feel better?'

The Prince shrugged. 'Believe me I would wish it to be otherwise. If it were in my power to make things as they were; to see you married and happy today and your people secure in their peaceful lives I would, but I cannot allow myself to think of those things. It's a burden you know, which kings must bear.'

Nick remembered standing on the Battlefield at Highvale when the fighting was over. He had killed several men that day without a second thought. But standing on the killing field while the dead and wounded lay all around, he had been overcome with remorse. He began to think of his victims as people, some not much older than himself. They had families, wives, mothers, sisters, at home whose own lives would be devastated by their loss.

His father had put a hand on his shoulder and spoken kindly. 'You cannot stop to think of it. You must put your feelings aside and think only of your own family, your king and country. Any one of those men would have ended your life in a heartbeat. You do what you have to do. It is to your credit that you feel compassion. It makes you a man instead of a monster. Never take a life lightly, but when it is unavoidable, do not flinch from your duty.'

Nick's father's words came back to him now as he stared sadly at the gathering rain clouds.

'Where will they take her?' he asked.

The Prince shrugged. 'I do not know. These were not King Tynon's men. These men were Subians. That is very strange.' He shook his head and looked at Nick again. 'They will take Catherine to their Lord whoever he is and she will become his prisoner. Then they will demand a ransom, and when it is paid they will return her.' He shrugged his shoulders again as if it were already done, while Nick felt a cold stab of dread.

'I do not have gold enough to pay a ransom.'

The Prince smiled. 'No, but I do, and I will pay it gladly. I am not blind to the sacrifice I have forced upon you or your people. You will marry her, I promise, and I will make a wedding for you which will be remembered for many years.'

They were bold words, maybe only those of an optimistic child but the Prince's eyes were re-assuring and the panic and hysteria in Nick's gut began to fade to a dull ache.

'May I ask you something?' The Prince said.

'Of course.'

'Why did my father release you from his service?'

Nick closed his eyes. It was a time he could hardly bear to talk about.

'I think he felt responsible for the death of my parents.'

'He had them killed?'

'No, no. My father and yours were friends. They were comrades. They fought side by side many times.'

The Prince nodded. 'Yes. I understood that to be so. But why did…'

There was a fierce flash of lightning followed by a crash of thunder, Ransom whinied, but stood his ground. Nick patted him gently.

'He is a fine horse,' the Prince said admiringly. 'My brother would love that horse.'

'I think we should continue now.' Nick climbed back into the saddle. He was grateful not to have to talk about the past. The present and the future held horrors enough.

The night was closing in and a gentle rain had started to fall. Once again Nick helped the Prince up in front of him and once again he urged Ransom to go ever faster. They were still some hours from Larock and the light was fading. As he rode, Nick was constantly aware that every mile they covered, took him nearer to his goal, and further from his heart's desire.

Chapter 5

Catherine could feel the cold metal of her captor's breastplate against her back. She tried to hold herself away from him, but his hand, around her waist, pulled her fast. There was nothing disrespectful about his grip. It was merely firm and businesslike.

When she and the Prince had realised that they could not escape from the raiders he had whispered to her, 'You must pretend that you are already married. You are the wife of a sentorman. A noble lady. Remember that and it will save your life.'

Although she had always dreamed of becoming Lady Catherine, it was not the title which she coveted.

In truth, Lady Ruth, Nick's mother had never given herself airs and graces. Aware of the number of people who relied on her for their welfare, she was too busy trying to make her farm successful. With their help and with Dugon's good sense and careful management, she was able to keep the oats and barley growing and even wheat whenever they could afford it. Catherine could see no obvious benefit in being a lady except one. It would mean that she was Nick's wife. He had promised her that when he had succeeded in his dream, he would come home and marry her.

His dream of course had been to become a Warrior of the Circle of Fire, just like his father.

Nick had adored his father. Gideon was everything he wanted to be. When he spoke of him, his eyes were wide with excitement and passion.

'We could have been very wealthy, Catherine. My father could have won himself a fortune and lived a very easy existence for the rest of his life. But he is an honourable man. He has pledged himself to the service of his king and it is expensive to keep horses and armour and a company of good fighting men. His riches come from the respect that everyone has for him.'

When Catherine spoke of this to her own parents they were surprisingly unimpressed.

'Oh yes, Gideon is a great soldier,' her father agreed, 'and he takes nothing for himself of course. But I ask you, what of his family? A little wealth would do his poor wife no harm. She has barely enough to live on. If you marry that boy,' he had warned, 'you will not find happiness. He will follow his father to glory, and you will follow his mother to a life of loneliness and toil.'

'I would rather live that way,' Catherine had told him, 'than settle for a lesser man and have him always by my side.'

Nevertheless, a part of Catherine could understand her parents' concern. Lady Ruth, was softly spoken and kind, but there was a strength beneath her gentle exterior. She needed it. There was never any doubt that she loved Gideon and he, her but what use truly, was an absent husband. Lady Ruth spent what time her work on the farm permitted, in the care of her villagers. She never forgot a name. She knew of every birth and death and more than any of this, she was always prepared to share. They loved her for it.

If she is lonely without her husband, Catherine wondered, how much worse will it be when she loses her son as well?

A flame had burned in Nick from his earliest years and Catherine had shared his enthusiasm and marvelled at his bravery. When they played with the other children in the village, Nick was always 'the strongest, most bloodthirsty warrior' and of course none of the others challenged his right to that position. On the rare occasion when one of the other village children beat him in a race or in a fight, he would be genuinely shocked. He would congratulate his rival with good grace, but would practice doubly hard to make sure that it would not happen again.

When King Tynon, their neighbour in the south, threatened to invade, Gideon called for his son. It was only weeks after Nick's fifteenth birthday.

He had come to see her, his eyes shining with excitement.

'When I return, I will ask your father for your hand in marriage,' he told her.

Catherine shook her head sadly. 'My father says that Gideon will never let you marry a miller's daughter.'

'When I come back,' he insisted. 'I will be a proven warrior and I will marry whoever I wish.'

After some months, word reached the village that the battle had been won. What was more, Nick had achieved everything he had set out to do. He had fought bravely and loyally and the King wanted to reward him. It was not usual to become a member of The Circle of Fire until you were eighteen but there were no strict rules to this and Nick was to be the youngest man ever to have this honour.

The Circle of Fire, he had explained, was a branding iron. 'They put it into the fire until it is red hot,' he had told her. 'Then they hold it to your arm like that.' His fingers snapped tight across the top of her arm and she screamed. Immediately he pulled it away. 'Then they pour in the blue dye and when it heals you will bear the mark forever. You will be sworn to your king's service. My father has the mark. I have seen it.'

'But doesn't it hurt?'

'Of course it hurts Catherine. That's the whole point. It was designed as an instrument of torture. Many of the strongest men faint under the pain. Only the very bravest stand firm.'

'And you want to do this?'

'More than anything. But first I have to prove myself loyal. I have to kill many men in battle.'

It appeared that he had done just that.

A company of guards, their horses draped in red and gold was sent to escort Lady Ruth to Castle Baryk so that she could be present at the ceremony. She left amid cheers and good wishes from the villagers who loved her. Everyone was smiling. There was a party in the village with dancing in the street and every man woman and child turned out to wave her off.

They never saw her again.

On a hot and humid summer's day, a messenger arrived looking for Dugon. He was directed to the farm and Catherine waited eagerly for news of Nick.

She came down into the kitchen that evening to find the steward drinking a glass of ale with her parents. Her mother was crying and her father stood shaking his head in dismay. It seemed that Gideon and Ruth Trayer had been killed by outlaws on the way home.

'And what of the boy?' Catherine's mother asked.

'He is being cared for at the castle.'

Catherine's heart began to hammer inside her ribs. 'Is he hurt?'

‘Not from what I understand, but they say he is out of his mind with grief.’

Catherine’s mother put a hand to her mouth. ‘The poor child.’

Everything changed from that moment. Life could be hard for the people of Subia, and life expectancy was not high. War and the Scorge had ravished the country for years, but Claveham, mercifully, had been protected from most of the hardship and she had seen very little violent or premature death. She felt, looking back on those days, that if there was ever a distinct moment when she passed from childhood to womanhood, then that was it.

From that day, she stopped playing with the younger children. She began to coil her hair instead of leaving it loose, and she was more willing to help her mother and the other women of the village through the back breaking days of the wheat harvest, when all help was needed in the fields.

The warm summer turned to Autumn and the fields were ploughed ready for the whole cycle to begin again.

One morning in early November, Catherine was on her way to the bakery to collect bread for her mother. A call from the far end of the village street caught everyone’s attention.

‘It’s young Nick,’ someone shouted. ‘They are bringing him home.’

‘You cannot go calling him ‘Young Nick’ any longer,’ another voice declared. ‘He is our sentorman now.’

A company of guards, just like the one that had escorted Lady Ruth, trotted slowly into the village. In their red and gold livery, carrying the King’s banner, the men sat to attention on their horses. In the midst of them Nick, riding Ransom, kept his head down and his eyes fixed firmly on the back of the horse’s head. Villagers came out of their houses and into the street to watch just as they had watched his mother leave. There was no sound but the clip clop of the horses' hooves as they passed through the village and a growing crowd followed the sad procession up through the lane between the newly ploughed fields.

No-one knew what to expect or indeed what to do. When they reached the house, Nick sat still for a moment then got down from his horse and looked around at the people. His eyes were filled with sadness and he seemed overawed and confused by his reception.

It had been Dugon who moved first, taking him in his arms and hugging him. Catherine watched Nick lean briefly against the steward's bulk, and she saw the strength he drew from the man's compassion.

When he pulled away, Nick had fixed a smile on his face; a sad smile of gratitude. One at a time the people of the village moved to shake his hand. One at a time they mumbled their condolences. Nick thanked them all, naming each man and woman.

'Thank you, Todd. Thank you Liddie, thank you May.' It must have taken all the courage he possessed. In doing so, he earned their undying respect.

Catherine hung back. Though she wanted to be with him, the Nick she saw now was a stranger and she was uncertain of her standing with him. It had been a year since she had last seen him and the change in him was striking. She had lost her childhood playmate forever, she could see that. There was no arrogance now in his demeanour. No bravado. But he was still Nick, and it did not take long for her to fall in love with his dignified humility.

Throughout the winter she saw him only rarely. Always he smiled at her but he never stopped to speak. She wanted to go to him; to rediscover the easy friendship of the past but something held her back. Though she had never thought that it would matter, the difference in their status was a distinct barrier.

One day she met Dugon coming out of the mill. He had been discussing business with her father.

'Good Morning, Catherine,' he said brightly. 'Isn't it a beautiful day.'

She had been too preoccupied to notice, but spring had already arrived. The earth was bathed in a fresh gentle sunlight and everything looked new and bursting with promise. She looked up into the steward's face and before she could stop herself asked, 'Dugon, why won't he speak to me? Is it because I am the miller's daughter and he is now a sentorman?'

Dugon shook his head solemnly. 'No. You must know that is not true. I think he just doesn't know what to say. I think he is as shy as you are.'

Nick, shy. That was not something she had ever imagined possible.

She decided then that as soon as she found an opportunity, she would speak to him.

The chance came a few days later when she saw him cross the stream and pass into the woods. There were primroses growing between the trees, and the first few buds of leaves were starting to open. She found Nick sitting on the grass-covered knoll where they had played so often as children.

'I have not been here for years,' he said as she drew near.

'Nor me.' She sat beside him, her shyness dissolving into the warm pool of memories. 'Why have you not spoken to me since you came back?'

He stretched out his legs and began to stare intently at his feet.

‘Because…because I am not the same person as I was. I was vain and arrogant and full of swagger. I thought only of my own glory. All I wanted was this.’ He put a hand to his arm.

‘Will you show me?’

For a second he hesitated, then untied his shirt and let it fall over his shoulder. The intricate latticework of the brand stood out clearly against his tanned skin. Without stopping to think, she reached forward to touch the mark with only the tips of her fingers. He flinched at her touch and she drew back sharply.

‘Surely it doesn’t hurt still?’

‘No. It doesn’t hurt.’

His voice was rough, coarser than before. She did not understand why, until she looked into his eyes. They burned with passion, the same passion that she had known so long ago when the prize had been glory. Now, it seemed, he craved a different prize. Terrified, in case she had misunderstood, but unable to do otherwise, she touched him again. His skin was soft but firm and she felt his whole body stiffen. This time she did not pull away, instead she traced the line of the brand across his arm then rested her palm on the taut muscles of his back.

‘You promised that you would marry me.’

Against her hand she felt him tense again. He looked at her incredulously. ‘Do you still want me after all I have done?’

‘What have you done?’

‘My parents are dead because of my vanity.’

‘They are dead because a bandit tried to rob them.’

‘But …we would not have been on that road, at that time, if it were not for me. And I… fearless soldier that I thought myself, was asleep. Why would you want to marry so unworthy a man?’

‘I love you,’ she said, surprising even herself, ‘I have always loved you.’

In reply, he clasped her tightly in his arms, and when his lips reached for hers, she knew that nothing had really changed. The love they had known as children was still there. It had merely taken a different form. If anything, it was stronger now.

‘I thought the world had darkened forever,’ he whispered against her hair. ‘I thought I would never know happiness again. You do want to marry me don’t you?’

‘With all my heart.’ She sat back and looked at him seriously. ‘But my father thinks that now you have had a taste of war, you will soon go back to it, and that I will suffer the same fate as your…’ she hesitated, not wanting to cause him pain. ‘That I will be left here alone.’

‘No.’ He took both her hands in his. ‘I will never go back to war. I will be a farmer now. The house is badly in need of repair, and although my mother and Dugon worked hard there is much to do. I need to bring some prosperity back to this village, to make up for this neglect.’ He could not bring himself to criticise his father, but the criticism was implied. ‘Dugon and I have discussed it at great length. We think it will take at least five summers and the work will be hard. Will you wait for me Catherine?’

She knew the question was unnecessary. She would wait forever.

Much had happened in that time including the death of her mother which delayed their wedding even further, but she did not regret the wait.

Although she could see that Nick loved the farm as he sowed and reaped and worked for all those years, she sometimes wondered if he yearned for the excitement of the battlefield. If he did, he never let it show.

Now, sitting as stiffly as she could, with the raider's arm around her, she realised that she might never see Nick again. She took a deep breath as the farm came into view and watched Dugon as he walked firmly towards his fate.

She had thought at first that the steward had devised a plan; that he would find some way for them to escape, but on the short ride from the village, she realised that he was merely buying time.

They drew to a halt in front of the house, and the raider lifted her down and dismounted behind her. He looked around him coldly, seemingly disappointed.

'Not much of a place is it? You led me to believe that you had a wealthy husband. Perhaps you will not be worth a good ransom.'

'This is just one of my master's residences,' Dugon said hastily. 'He likes to think of himself as a man of the soil. You know how it is with these nobles.'

Some of the horsemen sniggered at this, but the leader looked at him impassively.

'Let us go inside,' he said in his deep monotone. 'We can make her ladyship comfortable while you show me where the Prince is hiding.'

Catherine did not allow herself to give way to despair as she was led inside and pushed gently but firmly into a chair.

'Please take a seat, My Lady,' the leader said with mock chivalry.

She tried not to let them know how frightened she was. She did as she was asked, but fixed her captor with an icy stare. The soldier took a rope from one of his men, and tied her to the chair.

'Forgive me, My Lady,' he said, without sincerity. 'Now that I have won such a fair prize, it would be lax of me to lose it again.'

‘How dare you?’ Catherine said in her haughtiest voice. ‘My husband will have you hanged for this.’

‘Your husband,’ the man laughed, ‘is a long way away, chasing ladies in the royal court no doubt.’

It appeared that Dugon had been largely forgotten. He had begun to edge along the wall towards the kitchen. Without warning, the man drew his sword and in one fluent movement, ran it straight through the steward’s stomach.

Catherine let out a wail as Dugon fell to his knees then to the floor, and the raider bent and pulled the sword out. She kicked out angrily at him but he merely caught hold of her ankles and lowered her feet to the ground. When she was still, he reached for the hem of her dress and wiped the blade clean.

For a few silent moments she could not believe what she had seen, then angry tears blurred her vision as the words she wanted to say were frozen in her throat by fear.

‘What are you doing?’ One of the soldiers, who appeared to be the second in command, looked at his comrade in horror. ‘He was going to lead us to the Prince.’

The leader shook his head slowly. ‘The Prince is not here. I knew that as soon as we caught sight of the place. There is nowhere to hide. He could be upstairs under the bed, or maybe in the barn but I don’t believe so.’ He shook his head again. ‘I can’t believe I let myself be fooled by this pathetic ploy.’ Angrily he waved his men away. ‘Search the place just in case.’

Catherine was terrified. She had never felt such fear in her life. Against their bindings she could feel her hands shaking. She tried to focus on the Prince’s words. You are a noble lady. It will save your life. She tried to breathe deeply; to hold herself erect and hide her fear.

All the soldiers had left the house leaving her alone with the dying man. Dugon was still alive, she could see that, but a dark pool of blood had begun to appear around him.

Softly she called his name.

There was a tiny stir from his prone body. ‘Uh.’

‘Can you move?’

She could see him try, but then he fell back with a groan. ‘Can’t move. Talk…talk to me.’

‘The Prince said that if they believe me to be the wife of a nobleman, I will be safe. Do you think that?’

‘Yes but…do not… tell this man… Nick’s name.’

‘Very well but…’

‘Make up a name but…not Trayer. It’s …ah…’

‘I’m sorry. Please, don’t try to speak. Not if it hurts.’

‘It…no…pain now.’

The tears began to flow down her face. She knew that the steward could not survive. His blood was already filling the air with the smell of death. For the whole of his life he had served Nick’s family. It was Dugon who knew what to do when they brought his orphaned master home, and Dugon who knew what was in Nick’s heart all those years ago. Without the man’s strength and his unconditional support, who knew what would have happened? Now he had sacrificed his life for him.

‘Catherine?’

She tried not to show her tears. ‘Yes.’

‘When you …are frightened. Just remember. He loves you. He…he will find you.’

Then he was still and she knew that he was dead. In some strange twisted way, his death gave her strength. For his sake she found the courage she needed to play the role of Lady Catherine to the full.

When the raiders returned, their leader crouched beside Dugon’s body, turning him on to his back. His stomach and chest were soaked in blood and his eyes were open, staring at his killer accusingly. The raider put a finger to each eye and closed the lids.

There was no pleasure, only resignation in the look he gave Catherine. She forced herself to look him straight in the eye.

'I will never forgive you for what you have done. One day you will live to regret the death of this man.'

He did not laugh at her as she suspected he might. He merely shrugged and it was a far more chilling reaction. 'That remains to be seen. The question is, what am I to do with you now?'

'You can tell me your name,' she demanded. 'So that I can arrange for your death when the time is right.'

He made a little bow.

'I am Richard of Barrow Marsh. And you, My Lady, are my prisoner.'

Chapter 6

'Are we safe now?' The Prince asked.

'Yes My Lord,' Nick assured him. 'For the moment, we are safe.'

The nightmare which had robbed Nick of his rest was one he had not had in many years. He had dreamed again of the ambush.

He had been lying hidden on the floor of a cart amongst bolts of cloth and sacks of spice. They had laid him on his back, his head resting on a pillow of silk and into his throat they had poured a dark liquid which made him gag. It had a bitter aftertaste but that was a small price to pay for the relief it brought. As the cart jolted over the rough terrain of the mountains, he wallowed in the absence of pain and let the intoxicating scent of cloves and lavender wash over him. Sleep had almost claimed him when the shouting started and the cart came to a juddering halt. He could see and feel nothing but his hearing was as good as ever. There was the clash of steel and the unmistakeable shrieks and grunts of men being slaughtered. He tried to lift himself, to reach for his sword and go to their aid but his body was numb and heavy.

The fighting ended abruptly and the silence was more telling than the sound had been. High above, a bird called as if in warning. Moments later a man spoke rapidly but he was too far away. The boy could not make out his words. Then, almost within touching distance came the one voice he loved more than any other, his father's.

'My son is not with us. He was too sick and so we left without him. Please. Kill me if you must but spare my wife, she…'

It was the last time he would ever hear his father speak. As he tried again to move, the effort exhausted him and he fell back to sleep with his mother's cries echoing in his mind.

Many days later, when finally he awoke, well meaning people would assure him that there was nothing he could have done. The potion which had been brewed to numb the pain in his arm, had dulled his mind and rendered his body incapable.

It would be no consolation that it had also saved his life

Now, in the attic room of the inn he took another wistful look across the rooftops of the wakening town. Lack of sleep had left a dull ache behind his eyes and the sunlight seemed too harsh to bear.

'What will we do now, Nick?'

During the night he had formulated a plan of sorts.

'I will go into the town and find Jacob Rine.'

'You will leave me here?'

'I think it is safest. They believe that you are a woman, my wife and that you are sick. They will not disturb you. I will make sure that Jacob is expecting you and that no-one has followed us here. When I am confident that you are not in danger I will come back for you.'

'Will you bring some food? I'm starving.'

Nick's stomach was also empty but it was the emptiness in his heart that caused him the most pain. He doubted he would be able to eat.

'I'll do my best.'

'And some proper clothes if that is possible, though I don't have any money.'

'I have only a few coins,' Nick told him. 'Enough to pay for the room and some food but not for clothes. Jacob will provide you with some, I'm sure.'

The Prince looked around him. 'There must be something we can sell. Here, this cloak is of good quality. I am sure you could barter it for a decent shirt and trousers.'

It was Catherine's cloak and he had bought it for her in this very town. He did not want to sell it. His face must have betrayed his thoughts.

The Prince sighed. 'I understand your reluctance, but she has no use for it now. When she is returned to you, you can buy her another. A more beautiful one…with a fur lining, and I will get the seamstresses to embroider it with the finest silks…and…'

Nick held up a hand to dam the flow of words. 'Very well. I will take it.'

The Prince smiled. His forthright candour was edged with a great charm and Nick could not help smiling back.

He went over to his own bed and retrieved the knife, tucking it once more into his belt. He had laid it on the floor within reach of his hand, but after the nightmare had woken him, he had not spent much time on the bed. Most of the night he had sat by the window allowing his overstretched imagination to conjure up more and more horrific fates for Catherine and the people of the village.

'Bar the door when I have left,' he told the Prince, 'and do not open it for anyone but me. I will tell them that you are still sleeping and that you are not to be disturbed.'

***

Although he was a countryman through and through, Nick loved this town.

He did not love the smell which followed him from the streets lined with excrement or the noise which thundered in his head from cart wheels and harsh voices screaming for customers.

What he loved was the bustle and the atmosphere of excitement. He had felt this way ever since he was a boy, when the biggest adventure (apart from spending time with his father) was to be taken to the market by Dugon when the crops had been harvested and ground into flour by Catherine's father, a dozen chickens had been slaughtered and baskets of eggs collected and piled carefully on the cart.

'You are not here to play, Master Nick.' Dugon would warn him as they found their place in the market, and the great bell was rung to announce that trading could begin. 'You are here to work.'

So though he caught tantalising glances of the other traders and their exotic wares, of actors playing on a portable stage, and of fire–eaters bringing forth shocked cries from their audience, Nick would work alongside the steward until everything was sold and he was free to wander wherever he wanted.

Sometimes Dugon would let him go early, knowing that if he waited too long, there would be nothing left to see. The man had been a part of his life for as long as he could remember and it was perhaps the only comfort to him that Catherine would have the strong presence of the steward to protect her.

In his childhood, Larock had been even more crowded than it was now. The population had been greatly reduced by the Scorge which had swept through the gates and carried nearly half the inhabitants to their deaths. For some years it had almost been a ghost town but gradually the recovery had begun and now it was thriving once more.

Today, as he made his way through the press of people Nick could sense that same excitement. Somehow the heady atmosphere managed to reach through the heartbreaks of adulthood and find the eager child he had once been.

It was still very early and it was only as he was well inside the marketplace that the heavy bell was rung.

He exchanged Catherine's cloak for trousers and a tunic for the Prince. Before he handed it over, he unpinned the brooch which Catherine used to fasten it. He pinned it to the inside of his shirt under the leather tunic, close to his heart. It was a sentimental gesture but one that did afford him some measure of comfort.

He rolled the clothes into a bundle and stored them in the saddle bag which he slung over his shoulder.

'Can you show me the house of Jacob Rine?' he asked the trader.

'Aye, he lives in the large house just by the North gate,' she told him. 'Though he is not often at home. You're lucky though. You see that woman over there? That's Matilda. She is Jacob's servant. She will take you to him.'

She pointed to a tall, handsome young woman, who was buying bread a few stalls away. Her thick dark hair was tied in a knot at the nape of her neck and on her hip she carried a round wicker basket.

'Matilda, hey,' the clothes trader shouted across the street. 'This young man is looking for your master.'

Matilda looked well fed and healthy, her skin was fresh and her hair bright. Her physical condition spoke of a comfortable life, but as he got close to her, her expression said something different. She did not want to meet his eye at first, and when she did, it was only for a second, but her voice was strong and deep.

'Who are you, Sir?'

'My name is Nick Trayer. I have…a package to deliver to your master.'

The woman nodded as if she had been expecting him.

'This way, Sir.' She led him away from the market square and in to the maze of streets. Each of the houses was several storeys high and the heavy wooden doors were arched. Some, he could see, led into a courtyard where carts would be kept. Some even had trees growing inside. Matilda opened an iron gate which led to a covered ally through to another street. At ground level there were wooden hatches which led directly into the cellars.

Finally they came to a narrow street which ran along the side of a small but well appointed house with a yard in the back. Through the iron fence, Nick could see a man, stripped to the waist, washing himself. He was not tall but his chest and arms were deeply muscled and his hair was cut very short. He had the look of a fighting dog.

'Is that your master?' he asked the woman. She looked through the bars and Nick thought he saw a look of distaste before she nodded.

As they came into the hall she asked him to wait, while she went to fetch Jacob.

When the man came out, he had dressed, and was tying the laces on his tunic.

'Excuse me,' he apologised. 'I was late in rising this morning. I believe I drank too much wine last night. Have I kept you waiting long?'

Nick shook his head. 'Only a few minutes. You are Jacob Rine?'

'Yes,' the man said, 'and you are Nicholas Trayer.'

'I am. I have a package for you.'

‘Indeed.’ Jacob smiled. ‘I’ve been expecting it. Sit, Sir, and have some ale with me.’ He motioned to the table where Matilda had laid a jug and two cups.

‘Did you have any trouble getting here?’ he asked as both men took their seats.

‘The Prince was pursued to my village. His escort were all killed.’ He did not feel it necessary to elaborate. The disruption of his wedding was none of this man’s problem.

Jacob shook his head sadly. ‘Do you know who they were, these raiders?’

‘No. They wore livery, but nothing I or the Prince had seen before.’

‘These are lawless times. There are many at large who should not be showing their faces at all. If this tragic accident had not befallen our king, they would not dare.’

‘Is it safe to bring the Prince through the town to you?’

‘If you are sure you were not followed. I do not think that anyone here would know Prince Rowan if they saw him. I am sure that I would not.’

Nick nodded. He was almost certain that they had not been followed. He had checked with the gate-keeper earlier this morning and he confirmed that they had been the last travellers to enter the town on the previous night.

As he walked back through the town, he looked around him to see if anything looked suspicious but no-one in the market seemed in the least bit interested in him.

Stopping only to buy some bread and a small chunk of cheese he made his way back to the inn. The innkeeper was cleaning the stones outside the front door.

‘How is your wife this morning?’ he asked with a solicitous smile.

‘She…is….recovered.’ Nick tried to make his voice sound sincere. ‘We will be leaving shortly. I thank you for your concern.’

In the room he sat in silence while the Prince ate hungrily. Then he stood looking out of the window while the boy dressed himself. The innkeeper's face when he saw Nick leave the room with a young boy, would have been funny if he had been in the mood for humour. He did wonder what the man would have thought had he known just who the boy was.

In the market place, trading was well under way and the streets were laden with people. The noise had ridden to a fearful pitch and the Prince gazed around him in amazement. Clearly he had never spent any time in a common town.

At one point he was so busy trying to look in all directions at once that he almost collided with a horse pulling a cart laden with barrels of wine.

'Oi, Lad. Watch where you're going,' the wine seller shouted angrily. He was a ruddy faced man dressed in a smock and a hat with the largest brim Nick had ever seen.

The Prince apologised and immediately his attention was caught by something else. The wine seller urged his horse on, complaining angrily of the behaviour of all children.

A small space had been cleared near to the Town Hall and a pair of acrobats were performing a graceful dance. They were not much older than the Prince. Obviously brother and sister, if not twins. Both had skin the colour of walnuts and black glossy hair. They were dressed alike in scarlet tunics and leggings and at first Nick assumed that they were both boys but as they drew nearer he could see that the girl had a slightly longer shirt and that her hair was intricately styled.

The boy pretended to drop his sister and the Prince caught his breath, captivated by the sight. Nick smiled.

Rowan showed moments of great wisdom but at other times he was still very much a child.

'Do you think they would perform at the castle for my coronation.' he asked eagerly.

'They are yours to command, My Lord.'

'That is true.' The boy nodded sagely. 'Would you find out their names for me Nick? I think the man over there is in charge of them.'

The man was as dark in complexion as the two performers, but where they were lithe and graceful, he was immensely fat.

'No fear, you see?' he pointed a flabby finger at his charges. 'And complete trust of course. You have to be trusting and fearless to be the very best.' As he spoke, his chins wobbled like bladders of water.

'Are you the leader of this troupe?' Nick had noticed other acrobats waiting at the side to perform.'

The man nodded vigorously, his head bobbing down while the chins were still coming up. 'I am Gomero. These two are my children.'

'I have a friend who is planning a banquet. He would love you to perform for him. Where can you be found?'

Gomero shrugged. 'We travel, but if you mention my name someone will know where to find me.'

Having relayed this information to the Prince, Nick was eager to continue. The boy followed him though there was a certain reluctance in his stride as though the honours that awaited him were not as attractive as the simple life he could see behind him.

'You speak of your coronation but there must be hope for your father, surely.' Nick asked him.

The Prince shook his head. 'I fear he is dead already.'

'Then I am sorry for your loss.'

‘Truly, I hardly know my father. I have spent the last few years with my mother on Iorby island.’

‘Why were you sent away?’

‘Partly for my education. There is a colony of scholars there, who are amongst the most knowledgeable in the country. Also to protect me from the Scorge.’

‘I thought the Scorge had run its course now.’

‘For the most part I believe it has but there are still parts of the country where new cases are reported.’

‘We were lucky in my village.’

‘Indeed. There are few places where that is true. We have lost a third of our population.’

Nick had not realised the extent of the problem and he was shocked. They walked the rest of the way in silence. Jacob Rine opened the door himself as they arrived. He ushered them both inside.

‘I have had a small meal prepared for you, My Lord Prince. Please eat as much as you wish. We will leave shortly. I have sent for the horses. There will be an escort of fourteen men. You need have no fear.’

Nick found that now he was actually hungry. He helped himself to a little roasted mutton and a small plate of herb salad. He glanced up before eating, and was met by the full stare of Matilda’s dark eyes. She was standing in the doorway behind her master, and though she said nothing, her eyes seemed to be pleading with him.

Looking at Jacob Rine it was not difficult to imagine him as a harsh master. There was something cruel in the thin determination of his mouth. Nick noticed once again the paradox of Matilda. She did not have the appearance of a servant yet… Maybe she was of noble birth and had fallen on hard times. Perhaps if circumstances had been different he would have been able to do something for her.

He realised that the Prince was talking to him, and tore his eyes away from hers.

'Come with us to Castle Baryk, Nick,' he demanded. 'Your steward told them that you were attending the King. That is where they will send the ransom demand.'

Nick knew that it was a sensible suggestion, but his heart told him that he must go back. 'I must go after her. I cannot do nothing. There may still be a chance.'

The Prince nodded. 'I understand. I hope that you will find her Nick but if you do not, will you come to the castle?'

'I will My Lord.'

'And if you do find her, come anyway. I promised you a wedding that would be the talk of the country didn't I?

'You did.'

'Then that is settled. I will expect to see you some time soon, whatever the outcome.'

When he had reclaimed Ransom from the stables, Nick turned his back on the town and galloped away towards home. If he rode for long enough he might be able to catch up with the raiders and rescue Catherine, though he realised that he had no idea where they would take her.

The horse seemed to sense his urgency and galloped with ease along the steep road out of the town.

Nick tried to bring to mind Catherine's face, to see if he could see into her thoughts from this distance, but all he could see were Matilda's eyes pleading with him. He could not get the thought of her from his mind. Something nagged at him; something important that seemed just out of his grasp. Then he realised what it was.

Instantly he drew to a halt. 'Damnation.'

If the horse was surprised at the sudden stop he did not show it. He merely began chewing at the long grass by the side of the road.

'Ransom, I am an idiot, a stupid fool. What have I done? I was so eager to be done with duty and get away, I just didn't think.'

For a few seconds, he gazed longingly down the road towards home, towards Catherine who despite Prince Rowan's assurances might even now be dead. He could not even bear to think what might have been done to her. If he chose to think about it, he would surely go mad.

For a few brief seconds he contemplated leaving the Prince to his fate. Even as he fought to banish the thoughts from his mind, the call of duty began to pull at him. He could almost feel the brand on his arm. And even if duty had not called him back, he had grown fond of the boy. There was no question of leaving him. Nick had made a monumental and needless mistake and only he could put it right.

In the field by his side, four black crows squawked and it seemed that they were laughing at him. Still cursing under his breath, he turned the horse around, and headed back to the town.

Chapter 7

Richard Lassall got off his horse and inspected its legs and hooves carefully for a sign of some irritant. He loosened the saddle and ran his hands gently over its back and flanks. There was no thorn or insect to explain its sudden discomfort, yet something had made the horse skittish.

Richard tightened the saddle carefully and remounted, spurring the reluctant animal forward. Ahead of him, the trail such as it was, disappeared into the forest beyond which lay the road to Barrow Marsh. He had waved his men ahead, promising to catch up with them shortly, and they had all but disappeared, taking Catherine with them. Such fools he had been given, the very dregs of the barrel.

He had hoped for a prince and had had to make do with the wife of a sentorman who, despite his steward's brave words was quite obviously poor. He should have killed her too and saved himself the trouble of looking after her. She was beautiful though, and he could not bring himself to destroy something so lovely. If her husband could not pay a ransom, he would happily find a different use for her.

Trotting slowly after his men he allowed himself to think.

His orders had assumed that the Prince and his retinue would take the straight road from the coast to Castle Baryk but instead they had turned west and taken a completely different route.

Having, therefore, avoided Richard's ambush, the Prince had had the bad fortune to come across a Nostarian raiding party who had no idea who he was, but who had killed most of the escort and stolen the wagon piled with his possessions.

Richard had then followed them into the very shabby village of Claveham. It was all a hopeless mess, though it was still possible that the man in Larock would succeed where he had failed.

Failure was not a word he could bear to contemplate. He had known it once before, and although he had been lucky to escape with his life, he had lost liberty.

Just as he reached the edge of the forest, there was a sudden shout and the horse reared again. Richard dismounted, tied it to an overhanging branch and crept forward between the trees. Just ahead of him the trail opened out into a clearing and immediately he took a step backwards. It seemed that his men had themselves walked into an ambush. He could see only two of the attackers and they were on foot, but they appeared to be in control. Two of his six men were already down and the others were struggling.

Well of course, they were the dregs after all.

It seemed that his fate had been decided for him.

Moving as quickly and quietly as he could, he went back to his horse, untied him and headed as fast as possible in the opposite direction. This task had been doomed from the start and this time it was none of his fault.

In the south, King Tynon was almost ready to attack. The Valerons, sworn enemies of the Jassoir Usurpers had taken refuge in Nostaria hoping one day to regain their throne, and as a loyal follower, Richard would, he knew, be welcomed.

Even if Prince Rowan made it safely home he was only a boy. It would take him years to build up the confidence of his people the way his father had. Subia was ravaged by the Scorge and many fighting men had been killed. King Tynon would soon be in Castle Baryk with the Valeron heir and he Richard, would be by his side.

***

The man was tall but very thin. Catherine guessed that he was around fifty, though he could easily be older. His long grey hair hung untidily around a face criss- crossed with scars. There was a new wound on his forehead which was running with blood. Wiping it away on the sleeve of his shirt the man bent towards her. His pale blue eyes were filled with concern.

'Are you hurt?' he asked softly.

As they had entered the clearing, a barrage of spears and arrows had thudded into the horses, and she had been thrown to the ground. She had banged her shoulder heavily as she fell, unable to use her hands to protect herself.

'My shoulder.' She tried to move it but the man placed a restraining hand on her arm.

'Let me untie your hands.'

He took his knife and slipped it through the chord which bound her. As he did so, she could see that he had another wound just below the pit of his arm. It caused him some pain.

Carefully Catherine moved her arm testing her injured shoulder.

'I do not think it is broken,' the man observed. 'You would not be able to move even that much.'

She pulled herself upright. The shoulder was sore but not unbearably so.

'Who are you, Lady?' His eyes found hers again and she felt instinctively that she had nothing to fear from him. Even so, she remembered Dugon's warning and ignored his question.

'Who are you?'

He took a bottle of water that hung from a strap around his neck and opened the stopper. 'It will mean nothing to you, but my name is Jacob Rine.'

'Jacob…? But that cannot be.'

'You have heard of me?' He handed her the water bottle and she took a few gulps before peering at him suspiciously.

'Jacob Rine is in Larock.'

'I live in Larock, certainly, but as you can see, I am a long way from home.'

As he took the bottle back he winced in pain and stumbled slightly.

'You are wounded.' She moved to help him but he waved her away.

'It is nothing.'

Awkwardly he sat on a fallen branch and began to strip off his shirt. He was extremely thin. His ribs stood out clearly through skin, which like his face bore the scars of many a battle. The wound under his arm was a deep gash which was still bleeding profusely.

'There are bandages in my pack.' He pointed a finger towards the roll which evidently he had been carrying on his back. 'If you wouldn't mind.'

The stiffness in Catherine's shoulder had eased with the movement and she stood up surveying the scene before her.

It had seemed when they had entered the clearing as though they were surrounded by an army, but apparently there were only two of them. Three of Richard's men and one of her rescuers lay still on the ground. The other three raiders had run off into the trees.

She retrieved a bundle of neatly folded strips and taking one, knelt in front of him. 'Here, we must wash the wound first, let me help.'

Gently, she pulled the shirt away from his arm, catching her breath as she saw the blue lattice brand. Tears sprung into her eyes. It was the same design as Nick had and on the same part of the arm.

Lord Harald had told Nick to take the Prince to Jacob Rine in Larock. He is another of the Fire Warriors

'You are Jacob.'

He looked at her quizzically.

'The Circle of Fire.' She pointed to the brand.

'What do you know of the Circle of Fire?'

Without speaking she poured a little water on to the rag and began to wash the wound. It gave her time to think.

'I cannot stop the bleeding,' she told him. She glanced at his face and he was still, clearly waiting for an answer, but he did not ask again.

From a pouch attached to his belt, he pulled out a mixed bunch of leaves. He chose three and put the rest away. Tearing the leaves in several places he packed them into the wound, holding them in place with his arm. Carefully, she tied two strips of binding around his chest.

Surely, The Circle of Fire was all the proof she needed.

When she had finished binding his wound she helped him on with his shirt then sat beside him on the branch rubbing her shoulder.,

'I am Catherine Trayer. I am the wife of Nicholas Trayer.' She did not know why she continued the lie, but it seemed the right thing to do.

'Young Nick. Gideon's son?'

She nodded, fighting back the tears. 'You know Nick?'

'Yes. I knew his father well. We were friends. We fought together at Highvale.' He gazed ahead of him as if searching for his memories. 'I was there for your husband's branding and I was also there after Gideon's murder, when they brought the boy back and decided his fate.' He shook his head sadly. 'I have always admired our lord king but I have not always agreed with him. That was a sorry decision, and a bad one. We will all live to regret it.'

'I do not understand. What decision?'

He shook his head again. 'Not now. Tell me who these men were and why they held you captive?' The wound above his eye had stopped bleeding, but the blood had congealed in an ugly mass.

'Let me wash this for you.'

She wiped away the dried blood, careful not to disturb the new scab.

'He told me his name was Richard of Barrow Marsh. Do you know of him?'

She could tell by the look of surprise on his face that he did. 'Oh yes. Though I wonder that he uses that name. What arrogance.' He flinched again as she washed the last of the blood from his face.

'Barrow Marsh is his home,' he went on as if to take his mind off the pain. 'But it is also his prison.'

'His prison?'

'It is a story too long for now. I do not understand though, why he would want you as his captive. It makes no sense.'

'It was not his intention to take me. Not at first. He does not know who I am. It was Prince Rowan that he wanted.' She explained the circumstances of her capture but did not tell him that it had been her wedding day. 'We camped last night some distance from Claveham and were to reach wherever they were taking me some time tomorrow.'

Jacob nodded slowly. 'Now it makes sense. I had a message informing me that the Prince was in need of my help and that he was hiding in the hills close to Barrow Marsh. We have spent many fruitless hours searching for him. We were on our way back to Larock when we ran into your friends here.' He took the dirty rag from her and re-stopped the water bottle which he then hung around his neck. 'Someone clearly wanted me away from home.'

Catherine struggled to understand what was happening. 'So, it is a trap. Nick and the Prince will arrive at Larock and they will walk straight into a trap.'

'I fear so.'

'We must warn them.' She stood up. 'Please. Help me get to Larock and warn them.'

'It is too late for that. We are on foot and we are both injured. It will take us two maybe three days to get there. They are on horseback and a day ahead.'

'Then, they could be dead already.' She sat down again and fought vainly to keep away the tears.

Jacob left her alone. She sensed that he did it out of discretion rather than cold heartedness. He limped across the clearing and knelt heavily in the grass beside his dead comrade.

'Poor Balloc, he was the best of soldiers. This is an ignominious end.'

He turned back to her and could see that she was weeping.

'If he is Gideon's son.' he said kindly, 'all may not be lost. After all, the Fates brought your kidnappers into my path. They may well find some way to save your husband.'

She wanted to believe that Nick could protect himself and the Prince, but she also knew that it was many years since he had fought a battle.

'Whether we are in time or not, I must return to Larock,' Jacob went on. 'My wife and daughter are there.' He looked at the dead man and sighed. 'I would have liked to bury him but… I have neither the time, nor I fear, the strength.' He smiled at her again. 'There is a village about half a day's walk from here. There I can get someone to attend my wound and find you passage home.'

'I cannot go home.' Catherine decided even though she did not know what had become of her father and the others at Claveham. 'I will come with you to Larock. I must find Nick.'

He nodded slowly.

'I cannot say that I would not be grateful for your help. This wound is not a slight one.'

She stood up and attempted to tidy the sorry rag that had been her wedding dress. 'Than let's go before it gets dark.'

Chapter 8

Of course the man was an impostor.

On the short ride back to the town, Nick had cursed himself for being so blind. What would his father, or indeed Dugon, have said if they had known how easily he had been fooled. Jacob Rine was a Warrior of the Circle of Fire, yet Nick had seen him stripped to the waist as he washed that morning, and there was no brand on his arm. Matilda's eyes had told him the truth but he had not understood, or maybe he had not let himself understand. He had been so intent on handing over the Prince and chasing after Catherine that he had allowed the boy to be led into a trap.

It was useless, he knew, to think this way. What mattered now was to get the Prince away and to the safety of Castle Baryk as soon as possible.

From the end of the street, hidden, he hoped, in the shadows of a wall, he watched the impostor come out of Jacob's house accompanied by a man armed with both a sword and a knife. Nick sank further behind the wall but they did not so much as glance in his direction.

There were three horses saddled outside, and it was clear that the rebels were preparing to leave. The impostor gave an order which Nick could not hear and the other man nodded in agreement. They went back into the house.

Nick realised that he had to act quickly and this time he had to put all thoughts of his own feelings aside, and do his duty to the Prince.

It helped that he was familiar with the city. There were two gates one to the south and one to the north. As before, Nick had entered from the south. He had made his way by the side streets, avoiding the busy market, winding down now for the end of day's trading. Even so, the town was thronged with people jostling to get to the square for their final purchases, or to get home with heavy bundles. The North Gate which was not guarded, stood open during the day but would be locked at night. It was only yards from Jacob's house. The road to Castle Baryk led to the North so Nick had left Ransom in the care of a boy who was eager to earn a few coins, and had returned to Rine's house on foot.

Of the three horses waiting outside, one would be for the Prince one for the impostor and one for an escort, but that did not tell him how many men were inside. The false Rine had promised the Prince fourteen men but that seemed unlikely. Nick had to decide whether to stage a rescue now or wait for them to leave and follow. It was likely that the Prince did not yet know he was in rebel hands. The impostor would probably keep up the pretence as long as possible to keep the boy compliant. On balance, Nick decided, it would be that much harder to get the Prince away once they were on the open road. He would have to act now before they left.

Somehow he had to get into the house without being seen.

He scanned the building for some point of entry and his eyes were drawn to the wooden hatches built into the ground by the side of the house. Earlier in the day, he had seen the wine seller delivering his barrels. The hatch would lead into the cellar, and then into the house.

Had he seen the cart again since his return to the town? He was sure that he had. Swiftly he ran back along the road. There was a chance that while he was away the rebels would leave with the Prince and then he would have to follow them across country. It was a chance he would have to take. Without knowing how many men were in the house he could not risk an outright attack. This was the only way he could think of, to get in by stealth.

The Fates smiled on him for once, and he found the cart only two streets away. He watched the man climb down and open the hatch next to a tall green painted house. He lifted a barrel from his cart grunting with the effort.

'Young Sir. If you're goin' to stand there and watch anyway, you might as well give me a hand,' the man said, although he had not appeared to be aware of Nick's presence.

Nick helped him lift the barrel and roll it into the hatch and he heard it come to rest on the cellar floor.

The man followed it inside, emerging some seconds later with an empty barrel. 'That's my last for today, thanks be.'

The plan began to take shape in Nick's mind.

'Have you delivered to Jacob Rine?'

'Not today.' The wine-seller shook his head, his ridiculously large hat flapping with the movement.

'But you do deliver there?'

'I do, Sir. He likes a barrel of the Agnes Red. It's full bodied sir, a man's wine if you know what I mean. There's just a hint of…' the man held his thumb and index finger together to form an o while he considered the subject, '…burnt oak, Sir. That's how I'd describe it.'

Nick was only half listening. He glanced northwards, the idea growing all the time. The wine-seller was still talking.

'Now for Mistress Matilda, he likes to buy a few bottles of Chateau Volle. It's not as…'

'He buys wine for his servant?'

'Ah well. I shouldn't gossip, I don't normally, but it's no secret around here that Matilda is more than just a servant to Jacob. I think he'd have married her long ago but what with him being high born and all. And then there's the little girl.'

'They have a child?'

'Oh yes. Pretty little thing she is. Sophia she's called. 'Bout eleven years old.'

Though he had carried on a conversation with the man, Nick's mind had been finalising his plan to get inside the house. But he needed something he could barter, and the only thing left of any value was the one thing he could not bear to be parted from. He reached inside his tunic, unpinned Catherine's brooch, and held it out for the man to inspect.

'This brooch is made of silver and a pearl from the Morovian Sea. It will buy you a jug of ale and some to spare. You may have it if you let me have your cart for an hour.'

The man peered at Nick from under his hat.

'Morovian Pearl , eh?'

'The best.' In truth he had no idea whether there were any pearls in the Morovian Sea, and the brooch was certainly not made of silver. But the market was closed for the day and before the man discovered its true value, he would have his cart back, and Nick would hopefully be far away.

'One hour, you say?'

'One hour. Oh and I'll need your hat and smock too.'

The man regarded Nick with distrust for a few seconds then smiled.

‘Very well. I could use a nice long drink. It’s been a hard day.’

Handing over the brooch caused him a crippling pain. It seemed that every physical trace of Catherine had been ripped from him piece by piece.

***

With relief, he saw that the horses were still waiting outside Jacob’s house. He steered the cart right up to the building and stopped against the wall. For a brief moment he thought that he had not been seen and that he would be able to get inside the house before the cart was spotted, but a few seconds later a man came out of the house. He was armed in the same way as the one Nick had seen before, but it was not the same man. That meant that there were likely to be more inside.

‘What are you doing here?’ he demanded.

Nick tried to match the wine-seller’s tone. ‘Delivery of wine, Sir. For Jacob Rine. A barrel of Agnes Red. It’s his favourite.’

‘Jacob has gone away,’ the man insisted. ‘He’ll not be coming back. Get off with you.’

‘Seems a pity, Sir.’ Nick said quickly. ‘This wine’s all paid for. Maybe you….?’

The man glanced at the barrel and then back to Nick.

‘Agnes Red you say?’

‘Indeed Sir. A full blooded wine. What I like to call a man’s wine. I can put it into the cellar for you and you can come back for it later maybe.’

The man gave a sharp nod. ‘Make it quick then.’

Nick opened the hatches then made a play of lifting the heavy barrel, even though it was empty. With a couple of groans he eased it through the opening and went to follow it down.

'Hey. Where do you think you're going?' The soldier had been watching him.

'I have to collect the empty barrels, Sir. Won't take but a moment.'

Once his feet touched the cellar floor, Nick removed the smock and hat. It took a few moments for his eyes to adjust to the dark. There were three barrels against the wall and a chair and small table. He noted that the staircase which led to the house was to his right. He took the knife from his belt then called up through the hatch.

'I'd be obliged if you'd lend a hand here, Sir. Can't seem to shift this barrel.'

'You want me to come down?'

'If you don't mind. It'd be that much quicker and then I'll be out of your way.'

He moved into the shadows but as the man's bulk filled the cellar opening, it cut out the light and he was able to creep a little nearer.

His father's words came to mind once more. Do not take a life needlessly but if you must, do it quickly and efficiently. In the end it was remarkably easy. With one stroke he cut the man's throat and dropped him to the ground. Grateful for the darkness, but aware of the smell of fresh blood, he unbuckled the dead man's sword and strapped it to his own waist. Immediately he felt the reassuring weight of it around his body. Though in some ways it was cumbersome, it felt strangely familiar, as if it belonged there. As every second passed, he realised, he was beginning to act and think like a warrior again.

He crept up the stairs as quietly as possible. The door at the top was unlocked and he pushed it gently. He was in a small pantry, the walls lined with shelves on which pots and jugs stood neatly. Through the opening which had no door, he could see into the kitchen. A square wooden table stood on the stone floor and behind it Matilda was tied to a chair. She was staring straight at him. Her eyes widened in surprise but a piece of cloth had been tied around her mouth so that she could not speak. He made a questioning gesture and pointed to the door. Is it safe?

She nodded.

As he approached, he noticed a child, tied on an adjacent chair tears running down her face. She flinched when she saw him and began to struggle.

Nick put a finger to his lips. 'I am a friend,' he whispered, and began to untie the gag around Matilda's mouth.

'Be quick,' she insisted. 'They could be back at any moment.'

'Where is Jacob?'

Matilda spoke softly as she wriggled free of the rope.

'I do not know. A messenger came. Jacob left within the hour. This other one arrived in the night. His name is Ralph Ludeck.' She spat on the ground. 'His men took Sophia and told me they would kill her if I did not do as they asked. That was three nights ago.'

'How many are there?'

'Him, and three others.'

Only two others now. Nick saw an image of the man he had killed and fought a rush of nausea.

As he untied the child, she ran to her mother and Matilda held her close.

'How did you get in?'

He explained hurriedly as they followed him back into the cellar. Stepping over the dead man, he peered out through the opening. 'There is no-one about. Find somewhere to hide until we have gone. Without the Prince they will not have a use for you.'

Matilda saw the dead man but ignored him. The little girl screamed and her mother put a hand over her mouth to stifle the sound.

'Sophia, you must run to Mary's house. Wait there for me, but do not tell her anything.'

The child pulled at her hand. 'Come with me.'

'No, but I will be there soon. Hurry.' She handed the child up to Nick who lifted her through the hatch and watched her until she was out of sight. He watched the street but no-one followed.

'You must go with her.' Nick reached down to help Matilda climb out.

'No,' she insisted. 'I am staying. I will have that man's blood.'

'It is too dangerous.'

She was almost as tall as he and as she put a hand on his arm, her grip was strong.

'I spent three nights with that man in my bed. They had my child or I would have killed him where he lay.' She squeezed Nick's arm again. 'I will kill him now.'

'What will your child do if you are killed now?' Nick said angrily. He was too unsure of himself to add a woman to his list of responsibilities. But she was already half way up the stairs.

'What will any of us do if the Prince falls into the rebels' hands?' she hissed over her shoulder, 'You need my help.'

With a resigned sigh he followed her. 'You will need a weapon, take my…'

'I have weapons enough.' From a block against the pantry wall she took two knives which she tucked into the belt of her dress and a meat cleaver which she clutched firmly. He could clearly see the white of her knuckles and the determination on her face.

The kitchen led out into a lobby across which Nick recognised the room where he had met earlier with the man he now knew to be Ralph Ludeck. He could hear Ludeck and the Prince talking. Nick drew his sword and crept out into the lobby. Ludeck was sitting with his back to them at the table where Nick had eaten earlier. From the sound of his voice, the Prince was just inside the door. He spoke softly then Ludeck answered.

'When my men have loaded with provisions we will leave, My Lord. The journey should take no more than two days.'

Nick signalled to Matilda that she should stay back but she ignored him. With a tirade of loudly uttered oaths she flicked a wrist and one of her knives flew across the room imbedding itself in Ludeck's back. The Prince moved to his defence, but stopped when he saw Nick.

'He's not Jacob Rine,' Nick shouted as he followed Matilda into the room. 'It is a trap.'

Ludeck was so surprised by Matilda's attack that he did not have time to react. Before he could even rise to his feet, she had slashed him across the face with the meat cleaver. He clutched at his eye, screaming in terror then slumped forward on to the table.

His cry brought a man to the doorway, sword in hand and before Nick knew what was happening, he was parrying a blow.

It was many years since he had fought with a sword, but he had been well taught and the movement seemed natural. The other man was not a good fighter. He soon lost his balance and Nick rammed his blade under his arm and into his chest. The man fell forward spewing blood.

The killing, it seemed. was getting easier.

‘Outside, My Lord, hurry.’ Nick ushered the Prince out to the street. He could sense Matilda following him and felt strangely reassured that she was watching his back. The last of Ludeck’s men lunged at him as he stooped to come out of the door, and he was in a sword fight once more. This time his opponent was far more proficient.

It was all he could do to block the man’s blows and he realised that he was being forced to defend when he should have been attacking. It was one of his father’s favourite rules. Never let yourself lose control. He tried to take a deep breath then ducked the next blow, throwing himself forward instead of back as the man expected. Then, before his opponent could lunge again, he swung his own sword against the man’s head. It was a poorly executed move but the man was forced to defend and the next time Nick got the timing right. He dealt a hard blow to the arm which though it caused only a minor cut, made his opponent stagger slightly.

Matilda had unleashed another of her knives and it caught the man in the leg. He fell backwards and the sword fell from his hand and landed on the road by Prince Rowan’s feet. The Prince picked it up and brandished it above his head, his usual confidence fading in a rush of indecision, but he did not need to act. The man lay still on the ground.

A family, obviously coming away from the market, were making their way up the street. When they saw Nick and the Prince with swords drawn, the parents ushered their children away.

Nick prodded the prone man with the toe of his shoe but there was no response.

‘Is he dead?’ the Prince asked, letting his sword arm sink under its weight.

Nick shook his head. 'I don't think so. He hit his head. He must have knocked himself out.'

'You should kill him, now,' Matilda said coldly, but Nick had lost his appetite for killing.

'No.' He sheathed his sword. 'When he sees that his master is dead …' he shrugged. 'We will be long gone.' The wine-seller's horse and cart were still where he had left them. He led the horse in a circle so that it was pointed back the way they had come and with a slap on the haunches sent it on his way trusting that it would find its own way back.

'He may be no danger to you.' Matilda said angrily, 'But what of Sophia and I? This is our home. We have no-where else to go. I do not know whether Jacob is alive or dead, or whether he will return.'

'She should come with us don't you think?'

Now that the immediate danger had passed, the Prince had regained his customary confidence. 'She can wait at the castle until we have news of Jacob.'

'We don't have time to waste.'

Nick untied one of the rebels' horses and began to lead it away for the Prince to ride. Matilda and the Prince followed him. Though he was concerned for her, Nick was reluctant to take on the added responsibility of the woman and her child. His face must have said as much because she put her hand on his arm forcing him to a stop.

'If it were just me I wouldn't ask. You have seen that I can look after myself, but I will not risk my daughter's safety again. Please take us with you.'

There were tears in her eyes which Nick suspected were not characteristic. She was a strong woman and a proud one. He walked on, giving himself time to think.

'Where is the child now?' he demanded.

'She is with a friend. Her house is by the North Gate. It will take but a moment to find her.'

Once again he stopped.

'We will have to spend at least one night in the open. Are you prepared for that?

'Yes.' She stood tall, looking him straight in the eye. 'May I remind you who it was that brought that man down? You may need my help again before we reach the castle.'

Looking into her clear, proud eyes, Nick did not doubt that was true.

***

The North Gate was packed with people leaving the town with empty carts and saddle bags. They had sold their goods and wanted to get home before nightfall. Nick, with the Prince at his side, led the rebel's horse through the crowd and out to the long grass where Ransom was grazing peacefully watched by the ragged boy that Nick had paid to look after him. The horse looked up as they approached and whinnied a welcome.

Within minutes, Matilda came out of the gate with Sophia. It occurred to him that the four of them would look like any other family returning from the market. It might prove to be an effective disguise.

Matilda was carrying a bundle of provisions and he was grateful for her foresight.

'You will not be sorry for my presence,' she assured him.

'We need another horse,' the Prince announced suddenly. 'We should have taken another of theirs. Do you think it would be safe to go back?'

Nick was reluctant to do so but he realised the wisdom of the boy's words. If they were to get all the way to Castle

Baryk in two days, another horse and the provisions it carried would be invaluable.

'Wait here and mingle with the crowd,' he told them, and made his way as quickly as he could against the flow of people.

At the corner of the street he stopped and looked carefully around the side of the building. His heart stood still and he leaned heavily against the wall.

The road outside Jacob's house was empty. The injured man had gone, and so had the two horses.

Chapter 9

'You should have killed him.'

Matilda's voice in his ear echoed his own thoughts. He turned to her irritably.

'You were supposed to stay with the Prince. Do you never do as you are asked?'

'I do not think the danger is so great while so many people are around.'

She pointed towards the empty street.

'Why do you think he took both the horses?'

'I don't know. Maybe he will sell one.'

'No.' Her expression darkened. 'I think…I think otherwise.'

She pulled one of the knives from her belt and began to stride across the street despite his calling to her, 'Wait, you don't know what…'

Once again she ignored him, marching straight into the house. Nick had no choice but to follow, drawing his sword again as he entered.

In the dining room the dead man still lay on the floor but Ludeck was gone. Blood had dripped on to the table and part of a handprint was clearly visible. Matilda brought her fist down on the table with a thump, which clearly hurt as she held it to her mouth.

‘I was sure that I had killed him,’ she hissed through clenched teeth. She glared at him as if he were somehow to blame. ‘We will both live to regret our weaknesses.’

‘He may be dead,’ Nick suggested, though he knew it was unlikely. ‘The other man may have removed his body.’

She shook her head. ‘No. He lives.’ She held on to the table as if steadying herself, then looked at him again her eyes clear. ‘I know that he lives just as I know that Jacob is dead.’

‘You cannot know that.’

It seemed important to him that Jacob Rine was still alive. Although it was completely irrational, he felt that the man’s fate was somehow linked with Catherine’s. If Matilda gave up hope then so, he felt, should he.

She must have seen something in his eyes because she did not argue.

‘They will come after us. We must hurry.’

Tucking the knife into her belt, she went back into the kitchen and began to search for food.

‘They have not left us much but we will need whatever we can find.’

When they had loaded themselves with provisions, they returned to the North Gate where they found the Prince and Sophia playing jacks on the grass with the boy Nick had paid to mind the horses.

He was hardly more than an urchin. About the same age as the Prince he was nearly as tall but painfully thin. His short sandy hair stood in untidy peaks around a freckled face and he wore a shirt that was too large for him and baggy trousers which had fallen into holes.

All three children were laughing as if there was nothing unusual in the day. Nick found it incredible that Prince Rowan could be so relaxed in the face of his danger.

Sometimes he seemed truly just a child, yet at others he demonstrated a wisdom far beyond his years.

I let him down, Nick thought to himself. I led him straight into a trap, yet he has put all his trust in me.

'Come Sophia, it is time to go.' Matilda took her daughter's hand and pulled her gently to her feet. Her expression was stern and unreadable. Nick wondered if he had made a mistake getting involved with this dark headstrong woman.

'She is right. We must leave, My Lo…' Nick became suddenly aware that the peasant boy was listening. He left the title unspoken. 'I think we should go.'

'Do you need someone to look after the horses on your journey, Sir?' the boy asked eagerly. 'You don't have to pay me, Sir, I'll work just for me food.'

'No. Thank you.' Nick told him. 'Go home to your family.'

'Don't have no family, Sir. They all died of the Scorge. There's only me sister and she'll be pleased to be rid o'me.'

'We could take him couldn't we Nick?' The Prince asked.

Nick shook his head. 'We have little enough for the four of us. We will have to walk most of the way as it is with only the two horses. I'm sorry but it's not possible.'

'I suppose not.' The Prince nodded his head. 'I'm sorry,' he said to the boy. 'If I had a coin or two to give you I would but…as Nick says, we have nothing ourselves.'

The boy looked at him curiously as if he could not quite understand the relationships, then he hung his head and wandered slowly away towards the gate.

***

It was late afternoon as they left the town behind and for the rest of the first day, they followed the road along the valley. They went at walking pace so as not to tire the horses, the Prince rode Ransom and Matilda and her daughter, the rebel's horse. Nick walked beside them turning from time to time to scan the road. There were many other travellers on the road at first and he was grateful for their presence, knowing that if the rebels had followed, as Matilda said, they would not try to attack with so many people about.

As night fell, they turned into the foothills of the Malbrook mountains. Castle Baryk lay in a valley on the other side. Although they had made fair progress, Nick knew that the journey through the uplands would be much harder. They would be lucky to reach the castle by the following night.

The lower part of the mountain was forested, and although the trees offered cover to any attacker, he felt that on balance they would be safer in the forest than in the open. He found his footsteps becoming heavier. He could not remember when he had last slept. Despite trying desperately to concentrate on the road ahead, he was haunted by thoughts of Catherine. She may already be dead, or she may be suffering at the rebels' hands and the image was so painful that he must have groaned aloud.

'We should stop,' Matilda said. 'There is a clearing through the trees and a stream over there. We can camp here for the night.'

Nick would have preferred somewhere a little higher; maybe a cave or at least a position with their backs to the mountain so that they did not have to worry about an attack from behind, but he did not know how much longer it would take to climb out of the forest.

The rebel horse was carrying two blankets which they laid on the ground for Sophia and the Prince. Matilda prepared some bread and cheese and they drank from a casket of ale. Nick ate because he knew he must, though he had no appetite.

Very soon, Sophia was asleep and the Prince although he tried to pretend that he was not tired, seemed about to join her.

'Get some sleep My Lord,' Nick instructed him. 'Matilda and I will keep watch.'

The boy did not have to be told twice.

'You should sleep also,' Matilda whispered, 'I will wake you in a few hours.'

'No. I would rather watch. You sleep.'

'You are too tired,' she insisted. 'The Prince said that you did not sleep at all last night. You sleep first and I will watch.'

He knew that she was right.

'If you hear or see anything, wake me. Anything. I would rather be woken for a deer or rabbit than risk another attack because you were not sure. Swear to me that you will.'

'Yes, yes, I swear,' she said firmly.

Almost as soon as he had laid himself out with his hand on the handle of his knife, he fell into a deep sleep where not even nightmares of Catherine could reach him.

***

Jacob had said that the nearest town was a half day away but already it was dark and there was no sign of civilisation. Catherine felt as if they had been walking for days. Her shoulder was hurting more than ever and blisters had begun to form on her feet. Her soft wedding slippers were no defence against the rocky path.

The old warrior could barely walk though he trudged on without complaint. When he stumbled on a stone in the road and fell to his knees, Catherine put her hand on his shoulder and insisted, 'We must stop here now. You can go no further tonight.'

It was a measure of how sick he felt that he made not even a token protest.

The path was lined with hawthorn, behind which appeared to be an orchard. Catherine found a small gap in the hedge and squeezed through. Thorns snagged at her dress and scratched her face and neck but she forced herself to ignore them knowing that it would be more dangerous to sleep on the road. She found herself on a flat area of grass between the hedge and the trees and judged it a suitable place to stop for the night.

On his back, Jacob carried his bundle wrapped in a thick riding coat. Catherine laid the cloak on the grass and amongst his possessions found a half loaf of hard bread and some cheese. The cheese, on closer inspection was covered in mould and she threw it away into the bushes. There was also a flask of water.

From the mysterious pouch which he kept at his waist, Jacob took some more leaves and tore them into pieces. He dropped them into a small bowl and added half the water.

'We must make a fire,' he instructed. 'Do you think you can find some wood? I would do so myself but I fear that at the moment I cannot move.' She could hear his breath rasping in his chest.

It was almost dark but the moon provided just enough light for her to find some large twigs and mercifully a fallen branch.

Jacob placed the bowl of leaves on the fire and let them boil until the brew began to steam and a foul smell filled the air around it. He took the bowl and drank almost half before handing it to her. 'I do not know what these herbs are,' he admitted, 'but I know that they will revive us both. It is Matilda's own recipe and she has never failed me before.'

The liquid tasted almost as bad as it smelled but Catherine forced herself to drink a few mouthfuls. She handed it back to him.

'Matilda is your wife?'

He took a few more gulps and in the firelight, she thought she could see some of the strain lifting from his face. When he spoke, his voice was stronger than it had been for hours.

'In truth no, we are not married. That was not possible. But I consider her to be my wife. I could not love her more.'

'It is the same with Nick and I,' she conceded.

He looked at her quizzically and she held her hands out to indicate her dress. 'Did you think that I was in the habit of wearing a dress like this. It is my wedding dress. We were about to be married when the Prince came to our village and… well I have told you the rest.'

'I am sorry for that,' he said kindly. 'The needs of a king are not always convenient for those of us sworn to his service.'

Catherine realised that she was hungry where before she had been merely stiff and tired. Maybe what small amount of the tisane she had drunk had worked its magic on her. She broke the bread in half and handed him a portion before biting into the other. It was stale but her stomach welcomed it nonetheless.

Jacob ate slowly but steadily. Although he was as old as her father and the strain of his injury had clearly taken its toll, she could see that he was a pleasant looking man, who in his youth might have been called handsome. He was lean but his arms were heavily muscled and she could imagine him as a soldier, leading men into battle. There was an authority in the way he spoke even now.

'Did you not say that you fought in the Battle of Highvale?' she asked.

'I did. It was a great victory.'

'And you remember Nick?'

'Of course. He was one of the finest young warriors I had ever seen. At least as good as his father. I would have predicted a great future for him if…if circumstances had been otherwise.'

'He never speaks of it.'

'I suspect he does not remember.'

For many years she had wondered about this. Whenever she tried to ask him about the loss of his parents he would shrug vaguely and change the subject.

'Do you think that he does not let himself remember? I know that he feels guilty for what happened.'

'It is possible, but also, it is likely that he has been aided in his forgetfulness.'

'How so?'

'I am sure that Matilda would know how to suppress memories. The King would have had someone with knowledge of herbs.'

'Why would Nick be made to forget his past?'

'Well, that is an interesting question,' he agreed, 'and I know only part of the answer. At the moment there is a more important question. Why is Richard Lassall a free man?'

'Lassall. Is that his name? The man who raided our village.'

'Yes. Tell me. What do you know of the Valerons?'

'I know that they were kings once but they were corrupt and cruel. They were slavers. Thomas of the Jassoir, defeated them and sent them into exile in Nostaria. That was fifty years ago.'

'Indeed. After the battle there were many prisoners taken; women and children who had followed their menfolk to the battle field. Most of the women were sold as slaves…' He raised a hand to acknowledge her cry of protest. 'Yes I know. Slavery is not acceptable these days but at the time it was the way of things.' He paused for a moment, whether to catch his breath or to gather his thoughts, she did not know. 'The children were fostered into service in Subian households or in some cases, the army. It was hoped that they would become loyal citizens.' He shrugged. 'I am sure that many did, but it is impossible to know what is in a person's heart even if they claim to be loyal.'

'But… what has this to do with Richard Lassall?'

'His mother was one of the children left behind after the battle. She married a soldier I believe and he was Richard's father, but latterly, she was one of King Edwell's favourites. He was brought up at court.'

'Was his mother still a Valeron at heart.'

He shrugged again. 'Who can say. Certainly it would appear that Richard was influenced by someone with Valeron sympathy. He committed a very serious crime. He should have been put to death but his mother begged mercy of the King.' He paused as if choosing his words carefully. 'An arrangement was made. His life was spared but he was condemned to spend the rest of it at Barrow Marsh. It is a cheerless and inhospitable place. I would have chosen death myself.'

'But he is not imprisoned now.'

'Apparently not, and that is strange, but I suppose, no stranger than some of the other things that have been happening since King Edwell had the misfortune to fall off his horse.' He rubbed at his eyes. 'Blast it Matilda, your potion would have me sleep when I need to think.' Frowning, he glared at Catherine as if forcing his eyes open. 'Too much of this is co-incidence and I do not believe in co-incidence.'

Catherine shook her head. 'I do not understand.'

'Within days of the King's fall, both the Prince and Richard Lassall came to your village. Not just any village, but the Trayers' village.' He sighed and shook his head. 'I must sleep.' He laid himself flat and rolled over onto his side. Catherine did the same.

She was used to the sound of the weir lulling her to sleep and had wondered what it would be like when she was married and tried to sleep at the Hall. Then of course she would have had Nick by her side. Closing her eyes she tried to imagine herself there, but one more question nagged at her and she pulled herself up onto one arm.

'What crime did Richard Lassall commit?'

From the edge of sleep he replied, 'That is the biggest co-incidence of all.'

Chapter 10

Matilda rested her head against the gnarled trunk of a tree. She glanced up at the branches high above. Through the leaves she could see a patch of black sky and a few bright stars, but mainly it was cloudy and what light there was, could barely penetrate into the clearing. She was no stranger to the forest. In the distant parts of her childhood she had lived on its perimeter. Her mother had known all about the trees and plants and the local people had come to her when they were sick or injured. For the first twelve years of Matilda's life, her mother had been respected, venerated even, as a healer and a midwife. Matilda had learned from an early age how to use the flowers and herbs that abounded in the forest. Officially, Herblore was frowned upon when used by women. Physicians were always men. Their neighbours did not pay this any heed however, though had they known that her mother also had True-sight they may not have been so accepting.

Then the Scorge had come, and even her mother was helpless against its relentless onslaught. Though she was able to ease some of the symptoms, nearly half the population of their village died.

All it took was one man.

He had lost his family to the Scorge and vented his anger on Matilda and her mother. Fear was a fertile breeding ground for hate. It was incredible to think how quickly the same townsfolk who had called upon her services, now condemned her.

They said she had brought the Scorge herself, dabbling in the dark ways of nature. She had a child but no husband, surely that proved that she was a wicked woman.

In fact Matilda's father had been a soldier and he had been killed when she was still a baby but memories could sometimes be short.

'Look how they have remained untouched.' The man egged the people on. 'Everyone here has lost a member of his family but not they.'

The people needed someone to blame for the Scorge, her mother realised. Soon, they would come for her and she would face the trial which no woman could ever win.

It was March, Matilda remembered, when finally they came. Her mother had sensed it. The True-sight had not let her down. She could have run, but to protect her daughter she stayed to face them.

'Go quickly into the forest,' she told Matilda, 'get away as fast as you can. Go to Larock. My brother lives there. He works for a man called Jacob Rine.'

Although she had not wanted to leave her mother Matilda was only a child and she was frightened. She spent the next weeks in the forest, sleeping in the hollows beneath the trees and living off nothing but fruit. By the time she staggered into the town and asked the whereabouts of Jacob's house she was starving. She must have collapsed on his doorstep because the first she remembered was waking in a soft bed under the concerned gaze of a man she did not know.

Jacob explained that her uncle and his wife and succumbed to the Scorge. He took her in and over the next few years she had learned to keep house for him. It was Jacob who discovered that her mother had suffered the fate of all suspected women. She was tied to her bed and her house was sealed and guarded for twenty days. If she had not died of starvation in that time it would be declared as proof that she had the protection of the dark forces and she would be killed anyway.

Jacob was more than twenty years older than Matilda but from the first, when he had looked at her with his wise gentle eyes she had adored him. When she was old enough to marry, she had confessed her love.

'I cannot marry you Matilda,' he told her.

'I understand,' she assured him. 'You are of high birth whilst I…'

'No. It has nothing to do with that. I would not care about that if I could make you my wife. The truth is, I already have a wife.'

He had married a great beauty who had always been showered with affection and attention. She resented his continual absences, and after ten years had left him for a member of the Queen's court. He had not tried to find her.

So Matilda became his mistress. When Sophia had been born, she had been a great pleasure to her father and their lives had been secure and happy. The townsfolk of Larock loved and respected Jacob and they were kind to Matilda. Although her domestic arrangements were no secret, it was rarely alluded to.

Three days previously, a messenger had arrived to say that the Prince was in need of Jacob's help. He had a letter with the seal of the Royal House.

Jacob had been gone for no more than a couple of hours before Ludeck and his men arrived. Before Matilda had realised that there was anything to fear from them, they had taken Sophia.

Ludeck seemed to enjoy his cruelty. Even now she could feel the bruises he had left her and the abuse she had endured for the sake of her daughter. At least while she was awake, she could shut out the thoughts that could have destroyed her.

Her eyes began to close. If she slept, she would dream herself back into the nightmare and it was better to stay awake.

She stood up and walked around the clearing. She went to check on Sophia. The child was asleep, nestled against the Prince's sleeping body and Matilda smiled. Sophia had taken a liking to Rowan from the first. When they had dismounted to rest the horses, she had slipped her hand into his and he had seemed not to mind. Occasionally he smiled at her and Matilda felt that he was flattered by her. It was hard to believe that a royal prince who should have been no stranger to flattery should still be touched by it.

Somehow the night passed.

At one point she very nearly fell asleep but as soon as she began to dream, Ludeck appeared to her and she began to relive the events of the previous three days and woke with a start.

The very first light of dawn seeped through the canopy of leaves into the clearing. Matilda began to see shadows, where before, the dark had been all encompassing. The shadows chilled and frightened her until suddenly she heard something moving in the trees.

It was Ludeck, she knew that. She could sense him.

Inching her way to her feet she could feel the bark of the tree grazing her back.

She pulled out her knife.

She should wake Nick, but there was no time.

Ludeck did not know she was there. She still had the benefit of surprise.

As the figure pushed past she threw herself at him, bringing them both to the ground. She grabbed at his hair, tilted back his head, held her knife to his throat.

'This time I will kill you,' she cried. 'You will die regretting you had ever seen me.'

Ludeck screamed but his screams were not those of a man. The sound confused her and she froze.

Then she heard the Prince shouting, 'No. Matilda leave him. He will not harm us. Matilda ….'

Before she had time to react, an arm caught her around the neck. She felt herself being pulled backwards and the knife was being wrestled from her hand.

'Matilda, look at him.' Nick's voice was close to her ear as she struggled against him. 'He is not Ludeck. It is the boy from Larock.'

She was suddenly still as she realised that he spoke the truth.

The boy lay as she had left him, cowering with fright.

'I almost killed him.' She fought to control her shaking body. 'Oh by all that is… I almost killed him.'

Nick supported her as she sank back onto her knees then he knelt beside her.

'I told you to wake me if there was anything. Anything at all. Why did you…?'

She pulled herself free of him. She was shocked at what she had almost done but the rage that she had felt against Ludeck was still there and now she turned it against Nick.

'I do not have to answer to you,' she hissed.

The Prince had come over to join them. He held Sophia sobbing against him. 'We understand your anger…' he started.

‘How can you understand?’ Matilda turned on him also. ‘You are just a child.’

Nick got to his feet. ‘That’s enough Matilda. He is a royal prince and you must hold your tongue.’

‘That is true.’ Rowan went on. ‘But I am not in command here. Neither are you, Matilda. I have given my trust to Nick and I will do whatever he requests. You must do the same. If you cannot accept that, then as much as we would hate to do so, we will have to leave you here.’ Sophia released herself from his embrace and went to her mother who took her in her arms. The child’s soft body was a comfort to her and she began to feel calmer. Momentarily she buried her face against her daughter’s hair breathing in the sweet familiar scent of her.

‘I am sorry,’ she said eventually to Nick. ‘You needed to sleep and I was unwilling to wake you. I thought… But the night played tricks with my mind.’ She sighed. ‘I thought it was him.’ Once again she repeated the words that still haunted her. ‘I know that he is alive, just as I know that Jacob is dead.’

The Prince squatted down beside her. ‘I may not understand Matilda but Nick does. His bride was taken by the rebels. He does not know if she is alive or dead.’

She looked at him as if to ask if it were true.

He nodded and she could see the sadness in his eyes. ‘We were about to be married.’

‘And still you came back when you realised that it was a trap.’

‘I came back,’ he confirmed. ‘I am bound to serve the King and his family. Like Jacob Rine, I am a Warrior of the Circle of Fire.’ He said the words without pride or pleasure.

‘What is her name?’

'Catherine.' It was as if he could hardly bring himself to say her name. Matilda realised that there was an understanding between them and that she could trust him.

She put a hand out to him. 'I will do as you ask. I will obey your orders. This I swear.'

'Good.' The Prince nodded his head as if the matter was settled and they could move on. 'What will we do with him?' He pointed to the boy who still cowered where Matilda had left him.

'What did you think you were doing?' she asked him. 'I almost killed you.'

'I was hungry,' he said softly. 'I saw that you had some food and…'

'But you have been following us?' Prince Rowan asked.

'Are you really a prince?'

'Yes. And very soon I will be king, so you must answer my question. Did you follow us?'

'Yes. My Lord.'

'Why?'

'I…I didn't have nowhere else to go. You seemed friendly and the little girl did and…' He gave Matilda a guarded look. 'She seemed friendly.'

'What is your name?' Matilda asked.

'Tambik, Missus. They call me Tam.'

She nodded. 'Come and have some bread. I think you are half starved.'

'We will have to take him with us now, won't we Nick?' Rowan asked.

Nick sighed. 'I think we have no choice. He will follow us anyway.' He turned to the boy and fixed him with a stern stare. 'I am Nick Trayer and it is my duty to see Prince Rowan back to the castle. You will do as you are told Tam or I will ask Matilda to take her knife to you again. You have heard her say that she will obey my orders.'

Tam glanced at Matilda warily again but the sight of the bread overcame his fear and he nodded.

'I… I too will obey you, Sir. I swear.'

He held a hand to his heart and Nick could barely suppress a smile at his solemn expression.

Chapter 11

It had been dark when Catherine and Jacob had lain down to sleep in the orchard. Now, in the light of morning, she could see a small town before them at the bottom of the hill. If they had walked for only a short time longer, they would have reached its gates.

She sighed with relief. Jacob was burning with fever, and he leaned even more heavily on his stick. Every movement seemed to cause him a great deal of pain.

The herbs by which he set such store, were gone, and his wound was heavy with pus and smelled of putrefaction.

Now, as they approached the town gates, Catherine could see that the gatekeeper was sitting on a stool in his yard playing at draughts with a younger man while a small boy watched them eagerly. The gatekeeper barely glanced at them as they made their halting progress into the town then the younger man nudged him and said something. He got to his feet.

'Wait, Mistress, is the old man sick?'

'He is wounded.' Catherine told them. 'His wound is infected.'

'He has a fever.'

'Yes. It is the poison from his wound.'

‘What is your business here?’

‘We are on route to Larock. I am looking for a physician to treat my companion’s wound. And a horse perhaps to take us further.’

‘It looks to me like the Scorge.’

The man raised the spear and made to jab at her with it. Jacob tried to draw his sword but the sudden movement unbalanced him and he staggered drunkenly. The young man covered his nose and mouth with his hand.

‘Go. We do not want you here.’

‘Please,’ Catherine begged. ‘If you will just call a physician. They will tell you that he does not have the Scorge. For pity’s sake, I can show you the wound.’

The younger man waved a hand at the boy who was still seated on the gatekeeper’s stool. ‘Fetch Josiah.’ The boy hesitated then an angry glare sent him running into the town.

‘This man, Josiah.’ Catherine began. ‘He is a physician?’

‘Yes Mistress, I suppose you could call him that. He has much experience in this area.’

Catherine sighed with relief. ‘Thank you.'

She smiled but the man still held his spear to keep them at arm's length. Jacob had now fallen to his knees and she could see by the way he swayed from side to side, that he was failing fast. She bent down beside him.

‘Try to hold on,’ she told him. ‘Help is coming. Just a little while longer.’

She was wary though as the gatekeeper shook his head sadly and went back into his house. A few minutes later she heard the sound of wheels on the cobbled street. A covered cart emerged through the town gate and she felt just a moment of relief before the sight of the driver struck fear into her.

He was wearing a long cloak and a cloth wrapped around his face so that only his eyes were visible.

Jacob opened his eyes briefly and tried to shake his head. ‘Run,’ he cried.

‘No.’ She clung on to him. ‘I’m not going to leave you.’

Roughly, he pushed her away.

‘Run,’ he insisted, ‘To save your life. Go.’

She could not identify the danger that Jacob obviously knew but she could feel the fear. Lifting her skirt she ran, all the while knowing that she had no-where to go. Then she felt an arm around her waist lifting her clear of the ground and the proximity of the cloth-wrapped head to her face. She could hear the man’s breathing echoing inside it.

Though she tried to break loose he was too strong for her and she found herself lifted higher and hoisted into the back of the cart. She landed on the wooden floor and before she had time to pull herself upright, Jacob landed almost on top of her. He groaned in pain and he was breathing heavily.

The cloth covering was pulled into place over them and with difficulty she eased him on to the floor of the cart so that he was lying more comfortably. She could see nothing in the gloom.

‘I am sorry Catherine,’ he whispered. ‘Forgive me.’

‘Why? What have you done? Who is this man? Where is he taking us?’

‘He is the fever catcher.’ Jacob wheezed. ‘He is taking us to our deaths.’

***

Although Matilda had not slept all night, she insisted that they continue and Nick could see the sense in that. After they had eaten, they loaded the horses and set off once more. The Prince rode Ransom, Sophia sitting in front of him.

Matilda rode the rebel horse. She had assured Nick that she would walk, but he could see that she was still shaken by the events of the night and he insisted. He and Tambik walked beside the horses.

The going was hard. The road was steep and even Nick was panting with the effort by the time they began to climb out of the forest.

They stopped at midday for a drink and some food but there was very little of their provisions left and he realised that they were unlikely to reach the castle by nightfall. The situation was serious. By evening the terrain flattened and they were on a pass in the mountain.

Nick was still concerned about their slow progress, but something else began to trouble him. With each step he began to feel more uncomfortable. It was late and although the sky was clear and it was a lighter night he was reluctant to stop. The pass had narrowed here and the mountains rose sheer on each side. It seemed a sensible place to spend the night but he was curiously restless and anxious. Ransom also felt something. He snorted and pawed the ground. But it was the boy, Tambik, largely forgotten until now, who seemed most affected by the place.

His eyes, in the firelight were wide with fright. Matilda looked at him then at Nick and frowned briefly to show her concern.

Nick went over to the boy and laid a hand on his shoulders.

'What's the matter?'

'This place is evil. I can feel it. It is as though someone is watching us yet... I can see that no-one is here.'

Nick nodded slowly. He was sure now that he had been here before and all the old memories began to stir.

‘They are ghosts you sense here, not men.’

He went over to the horse and stroked him gently. ‘This was the place, wasn’t it, boy? This is where they died?’

‘Who?’ Matilda asked. ‘Who died here?’

‘My parents. It is here that we were attacked.’

The Prince looked around him. ‘Are you sure?’

‘I cannot be sure. I did not see anything. It is just that I feel that it was. Ransom feels it too. He was here.’

‘I heard that your attackers were bandits,’ Rowan frowned, ‘but that makes no sense. Why were you spared if they killed your parents?’

‘I was asleep. After the ceremony, my arm was painful and I was very ill. My mother was keen to get me home and although King Edwell wanted us to stay at the castle until I recovered, we left. They gave me a sleeping draught. At least it was similar to sleep. I was aware of sounds, of some sensations, but I could not move and my body felt mostly numb.’

‘It would have been Mandrake, ‘Matilda said, ‘and possibly a little poppy. It would have deadened the pain and induced a sleep-like state. There must have been someone very capable to administer this. Too much and it would have killed you.’

Nick leaned back against a tree forcing himself to remember. It had been his mother who held the cup to his mouth and urged him to drink but there was another woman. He could hear her strangely accented voice, low and reassuring.

‘Have no fear, dear Ruth. I know my skill. In my country many women practice the Herblore.’

The shock of sudden memory made his head reel and he clutched at it, sinking slowly to the ground.

Matilda spoke sharply. ‘It is not important now. Do not let it overwhelm you.’

But now that the floodgate had been opened, it was hard to hold back the flow. He could remember lying on a bed of straw on the bottom of the cart. His father still had some of the spoils of his battles, so his mother had taken the opportunity to buy goods that she could not have got in the village. The cart was filled with them. There were bolts of cloth and jars filled with spices. The smells in themselves were enough to drug him. He was aware of a pillow of soft silk under his head, just as he was aware that they were climbing into the hills, but most of the time he slept.

At some point they had stopped and there was shouting. He was sure later, that he had heard his mother screaming, though maybe his guilt had embellished his memories. Her cries were desperate and primitive and then there was silence. They would not have killed her immediately he knew that. These were the half remembered images which had plagued him for so many years, these and the knowledge that in his young arrogance he had thought himself to be a brave and fearless warrior yet through it all, he lay sleeping in the cart, too weak to go to their aid.

Some time later there were more horses and other voices but try as he might, he remembered nothing more until he woke up in the castle, a week or so later.

'Why did the bandits not take your parents for ransom?' the Prince asked.

Nick shook his head briskly in an attempt to clear his thoughts. 'We… we had our own men though I do not think there were more than four of them. They were all killed. Maybe my father put up a good fight and that is why they had to kill him.'

'Maybe. But they did not take the cart or indeed the horses. What sort of bandits would leave such riches behind?'

‘I can only think that they were disturbed. The soldiers who found me were already close. They must have heard them coming.’

‘Hmmm!’ The Prince’s young brow creased into a frown. ‘I will find out what happened, Nick. There is something that worries me about all this.’ He sat down on a rock by the roadside and appeared to be deep in thought.

‘Do you think we should continue through the night?’ Matilda suggested. ‘We cannot be more than a few hours from the castle.’

‘I would be happy to do so,’ Nick agreed, ‘If you are all prepared to continue.’

‘Yes.’ The Prince nodded. ‘Let us continue. It is a bright night.’

Although the road now began to descend it was wide and not so steep. They made good time. By dawn they had descended into a fertile valley through which the River Constant flowed gently. In the distance, Castle Baryk was clearly visible. It was in truth more of a fortified town, sprawling around the slopes of the one piece of high ground amid the wide central plain. It was the perfect position for a castle. From its turrets the land was clearly visible for miles around.

Nick was the first to see that the flags were flying at half mast.

The Prince who had walked the last couple of hours in order to keep himself awake, sighed deeply.

Nick went down on one knee.

‘My Lord King.’

Rowan waved him to his feet. ‘No. Not yet. Let me be a prince for a while longer. Let me have a few more moments of peace.

The castle had been built on a natural mound at the point where the river forked. The main river flowed on to the north, the smaller tributary flowing beneath the castle walls, some of its flow diverted to fill the moat. Unlike Larock, there was only one entrance to the town and this was by boat or across the drawbridge. It was heavily guarded. They had of course, been spotted as soon as they joined the valley and now a man came out onto the parapet above the entrance.

'State your names and your purpose here,' he called to them.

'I am Nicholas Trayer,' Nick announced, 'and I bring with me My Lord Prince, no, King Rowan of the Jassoir.'

'Oh.' The man's mouth fell open in surprise. For a few seconds he did not move, then he roused himself. 'Right away My Lords. George, lower the bridge.'

Another man appeared beside him. 'Just one moment. How do we know it is the King. Begging your pardon Sire but, we do not know you. I think we must ask you for some proof.'

His companion punched him on the shoulder. 'You can't ask him for proof. He's the King.'

'But how do we know that?'

'Well he just told us.'

'We can't go letting anyone in just because he says he's the King.'

Nick turned to Rowan to see his reaction. The boy was trying to disguise his laughter. 'If you call for Lord John Garwin he will know me.'

They could hear voices muttering in the background. 'E says 'e's the King.'

'Why don't they let 'im in then.'

'Well no-one's seen 'im for years. Could be anyone.'

They waited some time while someone was sent to find Lord John.

‘This is ridiculous.’ Nick said eventually. ‘I’ll see if I can…’

Rowan held up a hand. ‘Please Nick. I am happy to wait.’

After some while an older man appeared on the ramparts high above them. Even from that distance, Nick could see that he was a smaller version of his brother Lord Harald.

‘My Lord, it is I John Garwin. I can see that it is indeed yourself and the sight of you fills me with joy. I will have them lower the drawbridge.’

Rowan waved a hand in acknowledgement. He turned to Nick. ‘Lord John is my father’s chancellor. I am fond of him. He is a little pompous but when you know him well you cannot help but like him. You will find that he never says yes or no. It is always. “Indeed so My Lord,” or “I believe that to be the case, My Lord. Regrettably I am unable to agree with you, My Lord.” ’

A cry of ‘Lower the Drawbridge,’ had been issued and was repeated throughout the castle. They heard the creak and groan of the drawbridge and the lifting of the huge portcullis.

Prince Rowan mounted Ransom once more and Nick led the horse forward. Behind them, Tam followed, leading Matilda and her child on the rebel's horse.

There was a gatehouse between the outer and inner walls where they stopped to be welcomed by Lord John, his entourage, and the sentries. Prince Rowan, now King Rowan got down from his horse and everyone bowed. He acknowledged their homage with a smile filled with sadness.

‘When did my father die?’ he asked.

‘Last night Sire.’ Lord John told him. ‘His neck was broken. It is incredible that he should have lasted so long.

Prince Jared was with him at the last. I am very sorry Sire. Of course we have all been most concerned for your safety. It is good to have you here.'

'Thank you. This is Nicholas Trayer. I owe my life to him and to this lady. She is Matilda, wife of Jacob Rine.'

Matilda who had dismounted at the same time as the King, started to correct him but he fixed her with a stare so regal that she merely curtsied. Only Nick heard her whispered thanks.

'You are all welcome and honoured guests.' Lord John assured them. He smiled at Nick. 'I remember well the occasion of your branding and all that followed. Your father was a great man and a dark loss to this country.'

Nick nodded his thanks.

'Let us go in.' Lord John indicated the gateway to the inner walls. 'I am sure you are all in need of rest and food.'

'Before we continue Lord John,' Nick was amazed to see how easily Rowan adapted to his position. 'I would like to see the man who questioned me at the gate.

A soldier, dressed in chain mail and the red and gold tunic of the King, bowed low.

'That was me, Sire.'

His companion interrupted. 'I told 'im it was you Sire. I told 'im to let you in.'

'What is your name?' The King ignored the second man, addressing himself to the first unfortunate guard who was bright red in the face.

'George Carver, Sire.'

'George Carver. you did not know my face or that of my companion and you quite rightly challenged us. I am grateful for your good sense. Lord John, I would like this man assigned to my private guard. I shall sleep happy in my bed knowing that he is there. Are you married, George?'

‘Yes, Sire. And I have a son and a daughter. Lovely children they are if I might say so. My eldest is…’

‘Have his family lodged in the officer’s quarters and give him a rank commensurate with that.’

Lord John inclined his head. ‘As you wish, Sire. Now, if you will all follow me please.’

They entered through the massively thick door of the inside walls. Within, all the trappings of a small town were laid out along the street which swept upwards in a spiral towards the castle proper.

A cold wind blew down towards them. Small shops which normally would be opening and bustling by this time of the morning were boarded up and everywhere there was an air of sadness and mourning.

Many of the inhabitants had come out of their dwellings as word of the King’s arrival spread. Each one bowed low as they passed.

Nick watched King Rowan with admiration and a little sadness as before his eyes, the carefree boy assumed the heavy mantle of his destiny.

Chapter 12

Catherine did not know which was more uncomfortable, the jolt that went through her shoulder every time the cart hit a rut in the road or the gnawing emptiness in her stomach.

She had no idea how long they had been travelling but it had to have been most of the day. The heat had increased and it felt airless and stifling in the cart. Jacob lay still beside her. She put a hand to his brow. The fever, it seemed, had broken but his breath was laboured and she could hear it rasping through his lungs.

'Is there anything I can do for you?'

Surprisingly he was awake and his voice was stronger than it had been. 'No. I thank you but we are both in the hands of the Fates now.'

'Where are they taking us?'

'To one of the four towns.'

'The four…?'

He waved a hand to indicate that she should wait, then took a slow breath and went on.

'When the Scorge was at its height, some towns lost so much of their population that they could no longer function.

The King designated four of them to incarcerate the sick. To…' once again he fought for his breath.

'It doesn't matter.'

'No. You should know this. The four towns were to keep the sick away from the healthy and stop the disease from spreading. There were four towns in all, hence the name, but they are known mainly as the dying towns. The plan was successful… after a fashion.'

'But we do not have the Scorge.'

'No. I am told it has run its course. However, human nature is… what it is.'

'I do not understand.'

'Perhaps that is for the best. Do we have any water?'

She took the flask which she had attached to her belt. There was a small amount of water left.

'Here?'

She held it against his lips and was pleased to see that he was able to lift himself sufficiently to drink a few sips.

'Take some for yourself,' he urged, 'but sparingly. It would be wise to save as much as possible.'

'Will they not feed us?'

He sighed and adjusted his position.

'Arrangements were made to supply the four towns so that those who were not killed by the disease could survive, but as I say, it would be wise to save some.'

'Why did you say that…?'

'Please.' He held up a hand. 'No more questions. I…I must rest.'

She sat back against the wall of the cart and a tide of hopelessness washed over her. Tears sprung into her eyes but for Jacob's sake she fought to keep them at bay and to find some hope in the situation. He seemed to think that there was nothing to fear from the Scorge but why then, did he say that they were going to their deaths.

How could it be that two days ago she had woken to the light of her wedding day and now so much had changed? She had no idea if Nick was still alive and before this day was out, she too may be facing death. Surely the Fates did not intend for it to end like this.

She closed her eyes. Earlier they had tried to break through the heavy fabric that covered the cart but it was strong and well bound. There was nothing more she could do for now.

She must have fallen asleep because suddenly she heard Jacob's voice calling. 'Catherine. We have stopped. Wake up.'

It was hotter than ever in the cart and there was a terrible smell.

'What is that?' she covered her nose with her hand.

Jacob shook his head and his eyes were fixed on hers. 'Do not think about it. Keep your wits about you. If you see any opportunity to escape, take it.'

She could hear voices outside and when the covered sides of the wagon were untied and thrown back, she could see that they had reached the gates of a walled city. For one moment she wondered if it was Larock, then a fat balding man grinned up at her.

'Welcome to Fastwater,' he announced with obvious delight.

He was dressed as a nobleman in breeches and an embroidered velvet jacket but his face was pockmarked and dirty and he spoke in the accent of a poor city man.

Josiah used his spear to prod Jacob off the cart and the old soldier fell headlong on the path. The fat man pulled open one of the heavy city doors.

Catherine got down carefully and when no-one seemed to take any notice of her, she sidled around the side of the cart and began to walk quickly in the opposite direction.

She could see that the area around the town was bleak and flat. There was nowhere to run. Realising that it was hopeless, she came abruptly to a stop and was immediately brought to the ground. Within seconds she was straddled by another strange looking man. He was as thin as the other was fat and he too was dressed as a bizarre parody of a nobleman, but he was filthy and his greasy hair hung untidily around his face. Catherine tried to fight him off but though wiry, he was very strong. Then his eyes met hers and she saw his expression soften. He stared at her with open-mouthed admiration. She wanted desperately to free herself from his grasp but something told her that she would achieve more with a smile than with a vain attempt at strength.

As if the smell that pervaded the area was not enough, the man had his own acrid smell that grew worse when he opened his mouth.

'No point in runnin'.'

He spoke slowly and deliberately as if words did not come easily to him. She nodded her assent and smiled again, showing that she would not resist.

'This is a terrible mistake,' she said softly. 'We do not have the Scorge. My companion has a wound. All we need is a physician.'

She could see the sympathy in the man's face as he helped her to her feet but he did not speak again. Keeping hold of her arm he guided her back towards the town. She stumbled once and fell against him. For one horrible moment he held her close, then released her with obvious reluctance.

'My name is Catherine Trayer,' she told him. 'My husband is with Prince Rowan. Please send word to him and he will come for me.'

Josiah prodded her through the town gates with his spear.

'His name is Nicholas Trayer,' she said again, still addressing her words to the thin man. 'Please remember that. He will reward you.'

The gates swung shut behind her and she called again. 'Nicholas Trayer. Send word to him. Please.'

'It's no use trying to get through to him,' a voice said behind her. 'That one lost his wits a long time ago.'

***

When Catherine turned towards the speaker, she found that they were in a courtyard between the outer and inner walls of the city. There was an empty arch where the inner gate had once been and in its space stood two young women and a boy of about ten years.

The woman who had spoken and from her demeanour was obviously in charge, was short and stocky, her fair curly hair cut short as if it had been hacked away. The other was dark, much taller and prettier, though her face was haggard and pale. Both wore simple homespun dresses encased with dust.

'Do you have any food?' the fair haired woman asked.

'No.' Catherine shook her head. 'I'm sorry. We haven't eaten since last night and I have only a few drops of water.'

The woman nodded sadly as if it was only to be expected.

'Take the old man to the inn,' she instructed her companions then turning to Catherine said sternly but not unkindly, 'You come with me.'

Catherine held on to Jacob's arm. 'I won't leave him.'

'They'll take care of him,' the woman assured her. 'The inn is where we look after the sick.'

‘We do not have the Scorge.’

‘No. None of us do, but some are ill nonetheless.’

There seemed nothing to be gained by insisting so reluctantly she let go of Jacob’s arm, took the water bottle and hung it around his neck.

‘His fever has broken,’ she told them. ‘He needs rest and water and he will recover. I am sure of it.’

The dark girl and the little boy led him away while the fair woman guided her through the archway. Inside, a cobbled street led to right and left and another straight ahead amid a jumble of houses.

Only twice, in all her life, had Catherine left Claveham to visit Larock. She remembered it as a busy, crowded, vibrant place, exciting but frightening after the peace of the village.

This town could not have been more of a contrast. The buildings sprawled along the streets, the upper stories jutting out across the space almost meeting in the middle but they were merely skeletal. There was no glass in the windows and where there were still wooden doors, these were hanging from one hinge or flat on the ground. The air between the houses was stiflingly hot and still everywhere was the all-pervading stench.

The woman led her to the right and alongside a wall until they came to a house which, like its neighbours, appeared completely abandoned. There was no furniture inside but on the floor was a pile of rags formed into a makeshift bed.

‘Sit here. Wait for me,’ the woman instructed. ‘I will be but a few minutes.’

She climbed the stairs to the upper storey and Catherine barely had time to sit before she reappeared with a water flask and a bundle of rags. Joining Catherine on the floor she untied the bundle revealing a few small pieces of dried meat.

'Here. Eat these.'

Catherine did not have to be told twice. The meat was tough but the act of chewing released the sharp salty flavour and she swallowed it gratefully. There was a small amount of water in the flask which helped to wash it down. Sighing, she leaned back against the wall. 'Thank you.'

The woman nodded.

'My name is Tally,' she said. 'This is my house.'

'You lived here? Before the Scorge?'

Tally nodded. 'All my life. The Scorge passed me by. I have no idea why. I am the only one left.'

'The girl and the boy, they…?'

'Fara. She was one of the first to come. She was very sick but she survived. Jostin came later, with his family. They all died.'

'How many people are here now?'

'Six. But the other three will not survive long. And now you.'

'But the others they… they do not have the Scorge?'

'No. They are dying of starvation. We have no food.'

'Does the King not send provisions? Jacob told me that he did.'

Tally smiled wryly.

'You met our esteemed custodians. The fat man is called Barch and the other is his brother Amos. It is their duty to distribute the food and water which the King is good enough to send for us. As you can probably guess, barely a scrap finds its way through.'

'The meat?' Catherine indicated the bundle from which she had just eaten.

'There are ways to get food. You can consider that a gift from me. When you have earned some for yourself you will pay me back I am sure.'

'Earned some? How?'

Tally sighed and gave her a weary look.

'You will find a way...My Lady.' She said the last words with obvious sarcasm.

'To be honest,' Catherine admitted, 'I am not of noble birth. My father is a miller. But I…' Tears came to her eyes again. 'Two days ago I was due to marry. I should be Lady Catherine now.'

Tally sighed again. 'Do not think me without sympathy but there have been too many tears shed in this town. After a while they all become as one. It will make no difference who you are or who your husband is. No-one will find you here.'

Catherine closed her eyes. 'He loves you.' Dugon had said. 'He will find you.'

But there was every possibility that Nick was dead. She had no-one to rely on but herself.

Tearfully she looked around. 'Two men, to guard a whole city. Can you not escape?'

'Originally Barch had a whole army of men at his disposal but that is no longer necessary.' Tally stood up. 'Come with me.'

She led the way out of the house and continued along the street. Catherine had not imagined it possible, but the smell grew worse the further they went.

Tally waved an arm around. 'When I was a child, this town was a thriving river port. It wasn't as large as the great seaports of course but there was enough trade to provide a living for all the people here including my father who was a cloth merchant. Then it just…died. Up river from here is the castle of Temble Deem. The Sentorman there, decided that he wanted to build a bigger mill so he diverted the water from this river and now as you can see, it runs dry. The road sloped downwards and at its end Catherine could see a small wharf and what had once been the river. There was just a trickle of water faintly visible in the distance. Here, however, the smell was so bad that she had to cover her nose and mouth, and there was a loud throbbing noise which she realised gradually was the drone of legions of flies. Overhead, silhouetted against the sun, were great birds swooping around the riverbank.

'You will learn to live with the smell,' Tally advised.

'What is it?'

'It is the dead, all the dead of this town and the others who were sent here to die. There is nowhere to bury them and besides, the ground is too dry to dig. We put them there as far away as possible from the living. I would not go any nearer if I were you. Not unless you are fond of rats and flies. They are the only creatures to grow fat here.' She smiled wryly. 'With the exception of Barch and Amos of course. But they are just a different breed of rat.'

'Can you not escape across the river?'

'No. There is nothing in that direction but barren land. Then you will reach the diverted channel and the mill. If you go that way or upriver you must pass the guards at Temble Deem. Barch will pay them for every soul they bring back. They have been known to bring stragglers who have never seen the inside of this town before.'

She pointed to the right. 'Travel down river and you will have to face the current as the river flows back into its true path. A strong man could fight the current maybe, but not a woman who has not eaten properly in weeks, and not a child or an old man, for that is all we have here. Believe me, there is no escape. If there were, we would have found it by now.'

She put a hand on Catherine's shoulder.

'I do not tell you this because I am cruel, or because I wish to enjoy your suffering. I just want you to know what lies in store for you. You can survive here, but you must be prepared to do things you have not been born to do.'

She looked at Catherine severely and sighed.

'Occasionally it rains and we are able to collect water, but that is rare. There is never enough. Food, well, we have only that which we can trade. Some folk tried to catch the rats and eat them but that is a desperate act. All who tried it died of fever.'

'Trade?' Catherine tried to ignore the nausea which the image brought. 'With what do you trade.'

'There are two commodities here.' Tally indicated that they should return and Catherine was glad to be away from the wharf. 'Anything of any worth in this town was traded long ago. You can see that even clothes have found a way on to the backs of our worthy custodians. Jostin, he is a scavenger of the greatest skill, but even he has begun to run out of stuff to offer. The other commodity only we women can provide.'

She waited for Catherine to understand, and when she saw the horrified look on her face, nodded as if to confirm what she had said.

'Welcome to Fastwater.'

Chapter 13

The narrow twisting streets of Castle Baryk were lined with men, women and children, still united in shock at their king's untimely death. As the funeral procession passed, not a word was spoken. The only sounds were that of the sombre drumbeat, the clip clop of the horses' hooves and the trundling of the cart which carried the King's body to his final resting place.

It had not been Nick's intention to stay for the funeral. He had wanted to leave for home immediately but Rowan would not allow him to do so.

'We will bury my father this afternoon and I would like you to attend the funeral,' he insisted.

Nick had tried to persuade him otherwise knowing all the while that he argued in vain.

'I must go after Catherine, Sire. Or at the very least I must go back to my village. The rebels may be there still. I am needed.'

'I understand your concern,' the young King said sympathetically. 'But I ask that you wait one more day. Tomorrow I will send men with you. The best I can find.'

So Nick had allowed himself to be feted and honoured. He ate a meal of venison and pheasant followed by soft sweet plums finding himself hungrier than he had realised, and afterwards he was shown to a chamber adjacent to the royal apartments. Bright tapestries lined the walls, depicting the great love of hunting which had proved to be the King's downfall. Over the magnificent bed hung a covering of silk and brocade, and on a couch by the window, new clothes had been laid out for him. They fitted perfectly, but he felt awkward in such extravagant garb.

Tam who had disappeared when they arrived at the castle and whom he had almost forgotten, materialised from nowhere. He too had dressed in new clothes. And he too was not comfortable with them.

'The King asked me to attend on you, Sir,' he said politely but with little enthusiasm.

Nick looked at him quizzically. 'You are not happy with that role, Tam? Am I such an ogre? Perhaps you would be happier with Matilda.'

'Oh no,' the boy replied hurriedly, his eyes so wide with fright that Nick almost laughed out loud. 'I am sworn to your service, Sir and I'm happy to do anything you ask. It's just that …excuse me for saying so, Sir but will I be allowed to take care of your horses. I don't trust those stable boys to do a good job.'

'We'll go and check on them later,' Nick promised. 'If you are not absolutely satisfied with their treatment, I will let you groom them yourself. For the moment, I am grateful for your company.'

This was true. He was acutely aware that while he languished in the safety of the castle, Catherine, Dugon and indeed all the people of his village might be suffering who knew what fate. They might even now be dead. Now that he had nothing to do, he could not escape his thoughts. Without Tam to talk to he would be alone with them.

Mercifully he had not long to wait before a page arrived to escort him to the funeral.

At the base of the castle built deep into the hillside, was the Hall of the Kings. It was a great cavern lit only by torches beneath which seven generations of Subia's rulers were buried. The hall was large enough for men to enter on horseback though today most were on foot.

Nick had followed the procession along the winding street and down into the hall where he now stood to one side with the Chancellor Lord John Garwin.

Lord John had accepted the news of his brother's death with great sadness but also with prosaic stoicism. Now his face was impassive as he watched the funeral ceremony. On Nick's other side on an ornately carved wooden chair sat Lady Maud Boderry. She was the wife of Lord Robert Boderry, the Master of the King's Treasury, and in the absence of the Queen she was the senior lady at court. Her husband stood on Lord John's right.

When they had arrived at the castle Lady Maud had immediately taken charge of their welfare, arranging for the sumptuous meal to be provided and everything they needed for their comfort. It was she who had taken Sophia to the part of the castle reserved for the court children and she who had provided Nick's clothes and the dark red dress edged with fur which Matilda now wore as she sat in a place of honour beside her.

Behind them, other members of the Royal Court stood with heads bowed as the cart came to a halt beside the grave.

Rowan of course rode on horseback behind his father's body, flanked by two other men, both in mail and armour.

One was white haired and elderly, the other very much younger. Nick recognised the older of the two. He was Felix Runmore, Commander of the King's Armies.

The younger, to Rowan's left, was the most impressive, and probably the handsomest man Nick had ever seen. He was tall and broad, his armour buffed to such a shine that each ring of his mail coat reflected the light from the torches which lined the hall. Like its owner, his horse, a chestnut stallion of a similar stock to Ransom was magnificently attired.

The man held his plumed helmet on his lap, the other hand on the reins, riding with a grace and elegance that belied his huge frame. His dark hair was cut ruthlessly short, his face set in a solemn mask that was regal almost to the point of arrogance, yet when his eyes fell upon Nick, he had flashed a smile that was friendly and good humoured. For the briefest of moments, his eyes had positively twinkled and some distant memory stirred deep within Nick's heart.

'Who is that man?' He asked the Chancellor.

'He is Prince Jared. King Edwell's firstborn son.'

'His firstborn, but…?'

'Firstborn, but fortunately illegitimate. The title of prince is one of courtesy only.'

Lady Maud glared at Lord John indignantly. 'It is also a token of his father's love. Your disdain is unfair, Chancellor. Prince Jared is a loyal and honourable man.'

'I would never question his loyalty, My Lady. That I know is beyond reproach.'

On the subject of the Prince's honour, Lord John remained silent. Nick did not pursue the matter.

The new King dismounted although his companions stayed on their horses. Despite his royal status, he appeared exactly as he was; a child at his father's funeral. Nick had once been in that same position, and it bothered him that he could not remember burying his parents. He did not even know where to find their graves. The thought nagged at him throughout the long ceremony and stayed with him during the afternoon.

Later, as evening fell, he fulfilled his promise to Tam and took him down to the stables to check on the horses. Much to Tam's relief they were also enjoying the luxury of their surroundings. They had been groomed and fed, and assigned to a larger than average stall.

As Nick and the boy approached, there was a loud chuckle and they turned to find Prince Jared striding towards them. The Prince, having removed his armour now wore a plain black tunic and dark green brocade cloak. Though his clothing was simple, his bearing was undeniably regal. He grinned again at Nick but walked straight past him into the stall.

'Ransom, my friend. It is good to see you.' He stroked the horse's head with a gentle strength, and an obvious appreciation. The animal nuzzled his hand and he laughed again. 'You have not forgotten me, I see. Which is more than I can say for your master.'

There was certainly something familiar about him but Nick could not recall having met the Prince before.

Jared turned towards him, amusement lighting his handsome face.

'You don't remember me, do you, Nick?'

Nick dipped his head in a brief bow. 'I'm sorry, My Lord, I do not.'

The Prince raised an eyebrow. 'So. You would forget an old friend so easily. It's nothing more than I would expect from a mere farm boy.'

Instantly, Nick was transported back to the battlefield at Highvale. Once again he was in the Subian camp on the eve of the battle. Before the fighting began, there were hours of simple waiting; an agony of boredom for a fifteen year old boy eager for his first battle, and for a young horse equally keen for exercise. He had taken Ransom for a run behind the Subian lines when he realised that another boy of about his own age was racing him.

'To those trees and back,' the boy shouted.

Nick called back his agreement and spurred the horse onwards.

The young soldier was obviously wealthy and he rode a beautiful black stallion but it was no match for Ransom. Nick won the race easily.

When they dismounted, his opponent was grinning widely, his face flushed with the exertion of the race.

'How does a farm boy like you, come to have such a superb horse?' he demanded.

Nick explained that his father had captured its mother some years before. The boy had shaken his head in wonder. 'I would give anything for a horse that fine. Will you sell him to me?' When Nick had refused emphatically, he continued, 'I am the son of a king. I can pay a high price.'

'There is no price high enough,' Nick had assured him.

It had been the first encounter of a friendship that lasted throughout the long days of the battle. Jared continued to call Nick 'farm boy' though it was said fondly and without malice.

At the battle's end, the friends had been parted by their separate destinies and in time the fog of his illness and his grief had erased so much from Nick's mind.

Now he smiled with delight at the firstborn son of King Edwell.

'Forgive me. I…' He shook his head. 'Of course I remember.'

The Prince slapped him on the back. 'I do understand. I was merely playing with you. I was stationed on the border after the battle so I did not see your branding, but I heard well of you. And I am deeply sorry for your loss.'

Nick acknowledged the words with a nod. 'And I for yours. This is a sad day. King Edwell was a great leader.'

'He was.' Jared agreed. His smile died and the grief was evident in his eyes. 'And he was a good father. He was not afraid to show his love.' He smiled again. 'But Rowan will be a fine king.' He put both hands on Nick's shoulders. 'I wish to thank you Nick for bringing him safely home. You have done this country a great service. Your father and mine were friends. I hope we can continue as such.'

'I have been wondering,' Nick said hurriedly to hide his pain. 'Where are my parents' graves? If I had been thinking clearly I would have asked for them to be returned home. But I was not and it…it was all arranged for me.'

The Prince nodded in understanding.

'I can take you there. Only kings are buried in the Hall of Kings. Your parents were cremated and their bones interred in the catacombs beneath the Assembly Hall. Be assured they were greatly honoured.' He pointed the way. 'Come.'

Before they left Nick turned to Tam.

'The horses are in good hands Tam, are they not?'

'They are, Sir.' The boy agreed. 'I will rest easier now I think.'

Nick smiled. 'Good man.'

Tam seemed to stand taller, revelling in his new status as Nick's personal servant. 'Do you need me, Sir?'

'No. Go and find something to eat.' Nick waved him away. 'I will see you in the morning.'

As he left, the Prince stroked Ransom's nose and patted him appreciatively.

'Will you still not sell him to me?'

Nick answered as he always had. 'I will not My Lord.'

'I will pay any price.'

'Not for any amount of gold.'

'You know that I will take good care of him.'

'I am sure of it. But still, the answer is no.'

Jared nodded and smiled again. 'Quite right. But I will continue to ask. Who knows, you may tire of him.'

'That day will not come.' Nick assured him.

***

As he had promised, Jared led the way down through the streets which were once more deserted. A mist had descended across the castle hill and the air was heavy with moisture.

'My brother tells me that he has promised you an escort for your return home. Must you leave so soon? You know that he wants you to stay.'

Nick shook his head. 'I must go. I do not know what has happened in my village, and my wife she… she was taken. I must find her.'

Jared nodded his head. 'So I was told. I thought at first that the woman who came with you was your wife.'

'Matilda, no.' He explained the circumstances which had forced him to bring her and her daughter to the castle.

'I know Jacob Rine,' Jared said. 'He is a good man. This Ludeck, I do not know his name. What of those who took your wife?'

'In truth we were not yet married.' Nick admitted. 'Our wedding was interrupted.'

'It must be hard for you my friend. I am truly sorry.' Nick nodded but could not speak. 'What can you tell me about the man who took her?'

'He carried no standard. I believe he was a mercenary. His men seemed a ragtag bunch. '

The Prince frowned and Nick had the distinct feeling that he knew more than he would say.

'Here.' They had turned the corner and arrived at the Assembly Hall; the vast building where matters of national importance were discussed and any event held which called for a large gathering of people. Had it stood in any other town, the magnificence of its white stone would have seemed overpowering. Here at the foot of the castle hill it seemed perfectly in keeping.

Prince Jared led the way inside and across the tiled floor. The ceiling was high and ornate and their footsteps echoed around the empty building. They descended a wide staircase decorated with bright tapestries depicting pastoral scenes of each of the four seasons. The catacombs led away from the staircase in a maze of dark corridors but Jared led the way to one which was wider than the others and lit by torches along the wall. It was evident that only the most honoured were interred here. They stopped in front of a stone sarcophagus engraved with the likeness of a warrior and his lady. Nick was shocked to recognize his mother and father. The mason had done a good job. His mother's face appeared as serene in stone as it had been in life, and her gentle smile spoke deep into his heart, but it was his father's noble features that caused him to catch his breath and hold onto the side of the tomb for support.

'I will leave you here,' the Prince said, touching him gently on the shoulder. 'But I will accompany you when you return to your village tomorrow. You will find your way back to your chamber?'

'Thank you, Yes.' Nick could barely tear his eyes away from the tomb. He was aware of the Prince's retreating footsteps, but his attention was riveted to the sight before him.

‘Gideon Trayer,’ he read, ‘Most honoured and loved friend of Our Lord King Edwell, and Lady Ruth Trayer his wife, forever joined in death as they were in life.’

Joined in life. Certainly, when they were together, the love they felt for each other had been evident for all to see. Yet they had followed very different paths.

He touched a hand gently to his father’s face. For the first fifteen years of his life he had longed to follow Gideon’s path. He had not truly appreciated his mother for all that he had loved her. It was only after they were taken from him that he began to see them in a different way. He began to see how lonely his mother must have been, how hard she had worked and the devotion she had shown to the villagers who depended on her. He had begun to see his father’s constant absence as neglect, the quest for glory as something less than noble and he had turned his back on all that forever, or so he thought.

Yet here he was, a very long way from home, from Catherine. Here he was on the old path once more. And he had had no choice. He could see that now. It was not just the path of glory, it was the path of duty. Although his father’s eyes in effigy were unseeing, they seemed to look right at him and for the first time he began to understand and to forgive. And maybe if he could forgive his father, he might one day be able to forgive himself.

Chapter 14

The following morning, as soon as it was light they set off for Claveham. If Nick had had his way they would have made the journey at a gallop but Prince Jared insisted on stopping at every town and village and at every farm. The prince was constantly alert, watching and making mental notes of his surroundings. He made sure that he spoke to anyone he saw, asking questions, promising to bring their fears and worries to the attention of the King, and always thanking the people for their hard work.

He also began to search out recruits for the army.

When they reached the first village where men were working on the land he stopped his horse and surveyed the fields. He pointed his finger at a young worker of sixteen or so bent over a scythe.

'You, Boy. What is your name?'

The boy straightened up and came forward. 'Jemon, My Lord.'

The Prince got off his horse and made a show of scrutinising him carefully. 'You are strong and healthy and there is something in your eyes that tells me you would make an exceptional soldier.'

The boy held himself taller.

'How would you like to be a soldier, Jemon? I am looking for men to join a special regiment? They will all be hand picked men like yourself.'

The boy was clearly confused by the unexpected invitation. 'I…I dunno My Lord.'

'Well, if you decide that it is what you want, tell your master that Prince Jared asked for you personally. Tell him that I will pay him well for you because I think you are worth it. Then come to Castle Baryk and give your name to the sergeant of the watch.' Jared tossed a coin to him. 'Here is something for your time.'

The young man caught the coin and looked at it with delight. 'Thank you, My Lord. I …I will My Lord.'

Jared favoured him with one of his wide smiles, then got on his horse again and waved the men forward.

When they came to the next village, he did the same, this time choosing two boys.

'Do you think they will come?' Nick asked.

The Prince shrugged. 'Some will. Some will chose not to. Others will not be released from their sentorman's service. The Scorge has reduced our population drastically. That is why I can only take one or two from each village.'

'Surely if you ordered them to join you they would not be able to refuse.'

The Prince nodded slowly. 'I could do that, but they would not then make the best soldiers. These men believe themselves to be chosen. They will be loyal to me and will give of their best. Besides, I cannot rob the land of all its young men. There would be no one to work the farms and the people would starve and my brother might just as well hand the country to King Tynon.' He directed his horse closer to Nick and spoke in a lower voice. 'The situation is dire, Nick. I must be honest with you. Even before my father's death the future had looked uncertain. We are so short of fighting men that if Tynon attacked tomorrow we would be virtually defenceless.

'Since you and I fought the battle at Highvale we have controlled the mountains, and therefore the border, but the Valeron heir encourages King Tynon to attack and I do not know how much longer we can hold them. Still…' He waved a hand dismissively. 'That is a problem for our return. For now we must concentrate on your village.'

They camped overnight by the river. Earlier, some of the Prince's men had caught a deer which they now roasted over the fire. Though Nick was frustrated at the slow place and anxious about what he might find, he was hungry and he enjoyed the meal.

As he finished his last mouthful he glanced up to find the Prince's eyes upon him.

'I know we are moving too slowly for you,' he admitted, 'but in truth Nick I think the raiders will be long gone. They were after Rowan. There is nothing there for them now.'

'And Catherine?'

Jared nodded slowly, the sympathy evident in his eyes. 'I think as my brother did. They will have taken her for ransom. They will not harm her I am sure. And when they are ready they will make their demands known. Whatever the price, we will pay it. I promise you that.'

When Nick did not reply he went on, 'It is of little comfort to you, I can see that. And I am sorry for all that has happened. If I could make it otherwise I would.'

***

Tam was sitting on the grass with a group of the Prince's men. They were playing Colanche by the light of the fire, their bellies full of venison, and of peaches given to the Prince by a farmer at one of their many stops.

The soldiers called him young'un or squirt and they teased him but it was mainly good natured and he felt comfortable with them. He also had Lucas, Jared's manservant, to keep an eye on him and teach him all that was required of a personal servant.

The game of Colanche required a man to bluff his way to victory. The cards had to be laid in a complicated order which depended on the number of players and other variables which were not immediately obvious.

Tam could not understand all the rules, but it did not take him long to realise that it was a game at which he could excel. Gorral, one of the mountainous footsoldiers, laid a card and claimed it was a three. Tam knew that he was bluffing. He could not see the man's face but he did not need to. The absence of truth was as clear to him as the flames of the fire. He had urged Lucas to challenge the card and the older man, though doubtful, humoured him, therefore winning the pile of cards below.

'How, by all the Fates, did you know that?' he demanded.

'It was just a guess,' Tam insisted, realising too late how close he had come to giving himself away.

True-sight. He had not at first been able to put a name to it. He just knew that from his earliest years he could see malice in the heart of a child who pretended to be a friend and fear in an adult who made light of some threat. He could not read their thoughts exactly but he had a strong sense of them.

In the beginning he had not understood that not everyone could do this. It dawned on him slowly as he began to realise how different he was. When he finally told his parents, he had been shocked at their horrified faces. It was the first time he had heard it called True-sight.

'Never speak of it Tam,' his mother had insisted. 'You will get us all killed.'

Frightened by her reaction he had fought desperately against his gift. He was aware of them watching him and he pretended that it was not there. But his family had all died anyway and though the Scorge which killed them seemed to strike indiscriminately, he did wonder sometimes if it was his fault. Was this power of his based in evil?

He tried not to use it but sometimes he just couldn't help it.

When he had seen the ghosts on the mountain they had appeared so real and he had not had time to hide it. Ransom had seen them or at least sensed them, but Nick had seen nothing, only his own memories. Afterwards Tam had felt Matilda's eyes watching him and he thought she must know though she did not speak of it.

'Come and play over here,' Gorral insisted, handing over the cards reluctantly. 'You clearly bring good luck, Young 'un.'

Lucas placed a hand on Tam's shoulder. 'You stay right here. Prince Jared told me to keep an eye on you and I guess this is my reward. I don't know how you did it, Boy. That Gorral is the most inscrutable of all.'

Tam knew that he had to divert attention away from himself so he said the first thing that came into his mind. It was a question that had been troubling him.

'Why is Prince Jared not king if he is the older brother.'

'Because he's a bastard.' Gorral declared.

'Oh.' Tam did not know what it meant although he had heard the term before. 'What is that?'

'It means that his parents were not married,' Lucas glared across the fire at the huge man.

Beside Gorral, his friend Hal, a much older man, was almost as much of a giant. 'He meant no offence Luke, you know that. We are all the Prince's men and true.'

Lucas relaxed, nodding in acknowledgement of this. He turned back to Tam.

'For some years before he was married, the King had taken a mistress. Her name was Annabelle Marchant and she was the daughter of one of his mother's ladies. Prince Jared was their offspring. They lived like a proper family, but you know that is not the way with kings. They have to marry royalty and produce an heir.'

Gorral gathered the cards. 'She was a sweet lady. Not like the sourpuss of a queen that he was forced to marry.'

Hal shook his head and waved a peach in the air. 'Queen Sybill was not a sourpuss when she first came here. I remember her. She was beautiful and she was frightened. A long way from home, she was and just fifteen years old. But from the first the King made it clear that he was in love with Annabelle and that he doted on Prince Jared.

Lucas sighed. 'The Queen insisted that they be sent away. The King sent her back to her home village, though he made sure that she had everything she needed. The Prince, and he wasn't acknowledged as such then, went with her of course.'

'Can't say as I blame the Queen for that.' Hal admitted. 'King Edwell was a good and strong ruler but he was a terrible husband.'

'She lived to regret it though didn't she?' Gorral laid the cards before them, but no-one paid them heed. They were too involved in the gossip.

'Why?' Tam was fascinated.

Hal was the only one old enough to have been at Castle Baryk at that time and he was clearly enjoying the role of storyteller. 'Well, they'd not been gone more than a year when the Scorge took Annabelle. That was the first time the sickness came to Subia. It weren't as serious that time as this last, but there were still plenty of deaths. The King was beside himself with grief. And he was angry with her, the Queen. She'd had one child still born and lost another before its time so there was still no heir, but he refused to share her bed. And he had our master brought back to the castle and gave him the title of prince. Was years before he resumed relations with the Queen.'

Gorral leaned closer to the fire and spoke quietly. 'I heard it were the King's own mother persuaded him to take his wife back into his bed. The need for a legitimate heir and all that.'

Hal turned to his friend. 'How would you hear something like that?'

'Word gets around, don't it? It's common knowledge.'

'Not to me it isn't. And there's not a lot gets past my missus.'

'Well, my brother's wife's sister is a seamstress in the Queen's household. You know the seamstresses know everything. It's all rumours though, anyway.' He laughed suddenly. 'Mind you there's no-one attracts rumours more than he does.' He nodded his head in the direction of the Prince.

'Why.' Tam asked wide eyed. 'What has he done?'

'Well that's a story for another time

Lucas bristled angrily again. 'My master is a good man. I will not allow this talk.'

'Keep your hair on.' Hal smiled good-naturedly. 'We didn't say he wasn't. He's a great commander. The best. There's not a man here wouldn't follow him to their deaths. But that don't stop us speculatin' does it. It don't stop the gossip.'

Tam watched the Prince as he spoke with some of the men who tended the horses. All three laughed loudly.

Jared seemed to laugh wherever possible, but Tam could tell that sometimes the laughter was forced and whenever he was close to the Prince, all he could feel was a deep sadness. Sometimes it came close to despair, and it made Tam feel uneasy.

'Anyway,' Hal was eager to continue his story. 'Prince Jared was 'bout eight years old when the present King was born and as soon as it's established that he's fit and healthy, the Queen upsticks and takes herself into exile. She did come back briefly, 'bout the time we was at Highvale, but she's been gone for many a year now. King Edwell, he wasn't sorry to see her go. There was a whole succession of other ladies after that but you can be sure he didn't think of them as he did Annabelle. No. She was the love of his life that one.'

There was now a general movement towards sleep and although there were nods and grunts of agreement, no-one seemed keen to continue the conversation. Tam wanted to hear more but he was grateful that attention had been taken away from him. The whole experience had scared him, and he vowed that in the future he would stay well away from card games.

Chapter 15

Barch, the Custodian of Fastwater, fastened his britches and closed the gate almost before the woman had disappeared inside. He wandered away with a bowlegged swagger. Though he was red in the face and sweating, the gap toothed grin he flashed was triumphant.

'You see?' he pointed a podgy finger at Amos. 'I told you she'd come round.'

After twenty four years, Amos did not need to be told what his brother was capable of.

'Aren't you scared o' the Scorge.' he shuddered. 'You could catch it from 'er getting' that close.' And then you could give it to me, he added under his breath.

Barch shook his head and laughed. 'There's nothing wrong with her but hunger. How many times have I got to tell you. The Scorge is long gone.'

'Then so should we be.'

As he felt the crack of his brother's hand around his ear, Amos realised he had gone too far. Barch's bad temper was never far from the surface.

He could not remember a time when there had been anyone else in his life but Barch. Sometimes vague memories of their mother appeared to him but they were not comforting. She was always drunk, and it seemed to him that he sustained as many bruises from her hand as from his brother's. Though the road Barch had taken was not an honest one, it had always been profitable. At least in his company, Amos was never hungry and there were shoes on his feet.

That road had almost led to disaster of course, when they found themselves in the dungeons of Temble Deem clapped in irons and sentenced to hang the following morning. Amos had truly believed that day to be his last, but shortly after sunset, there had been a loud rattling of keys and clanking of doors which announced the arrival of the Marshall.

'I have a proposition for you Barch,' he'd announced.

Barch grinned in that annoying way that said 'See. I told you I'd get us out of this.'

'It may be that you and that miserable specimen you call brother, will live after all,' the Marshall had continued.

It appeared that men were needed as custodians of the four towns. Obviously this position was not much sought after, which is why men such as they were offered their freedom in exchange for taking the job. When, eventually the Scorge had gone, they would be free to leave. They had been given a choice. Die on the gallows or take the job that no-one else would do. It had been no choice at all.

It did not take Barch long to realise the potential of this employment. Very little of the food found its way inside the gates of Fastwater. Only that which could be exchanged for payment or 'favours.' The inhabitants were not expected to survive, so what was the point of wasting good food and provisions on them.

Before long, with help from the unfortunates who were given no choice in the matter, Barch had stripped the town of all its valuables. The two brothers now dressed in the best clothes and their stomachs were always full. They had built themselves a shelter outside the city gates and furnished it with the best that Fastwater had to offer.

Such was human nature, that a whole business had grown up around the brothers and their rapidly increasing stock. Many traders would gladly throw scruples to the wind and buy bags of grain and dried meat, clothes and jewellery the provenance of which they never questioned. When their time here was over, Barch insisted, they would both be rich men.

Amos knew which would inevitably be the richer. He did whatever his brother told him because it led to a quieter life and fewer bruises, but sometimes he did feel sorry for the miserable group of people left in the town. Especially he felt for the girls who were so desperate for food that they would lay down his pig of a brother.

Even so, on this occasion he did question when it would be his turn and Barch cuffed him again, and laughed.

'Even death would be preferable to getting close to your ugly mug.'

Beauty did not run in their family, but at least he wasn't fat like Barch. He knew better than to say so, however.

Instead he went to find a cloth to wipe away the blood that trickled down his ear. Then he sat quietly and thought of Catherine Trayer. When he closed his eyes he could still see her lovely face smiling at him. She had stumbled and for a single, heartstopping moment, he had held her against him. He had never known such pleasure. Even just the memory brought back a measure of that sensation.

'The wagon is due in an hour.' Barch announced. 'What are you mooning about. Not that woman again.'

'She's so lovely, Barch. I ain't never seen the like of her before.'

‘She’ll look like all the rest in a week or so, and she’ll have dropped her high and mighty attitude. I told you it’s amazing what an empty stomach will do.’ Barch stuffed another hunk of bread and cheese into his face and belched happily.

‘Maybe if we tell her husband he’ll give us a reward.’

Barch looked at him almost pityingly. ‘Don’t you go causing trouble, Wormbrain. The only thing he’ll reward us with is an end to our little enterprise and our heads back in the noose.’

Amos knew that was probably true, but try as he might, he could not get the thought of her out of his mind.

The wagon arrived within the hour and he went to help the men unload the provisions.

‘We’ve had two more this week,’ Barch announced triumphantly, ‘so that’s a total of thirty three now.’

You can’t still have thirty three in there,’ the sergeant insisted. ‘Some of ‘em must have died, surely.’

‘You can go in and count em if you like.’ Barch said affecting a look of complete innocence.

The sergeant declined the offer as they knew he would and he and Barch disappeared into the shelter to attend to ‘business.’

Amos was still thinking about Catherine. Surly it would not hurt to tell someone she was there. And if her husband did come, she would know it was Amos who had told him and she would be grateful. He could not imagine that she would let anything happen to him.

The driver was dozing in the cart.

‘Woman here reckons she’s a noblewoman.’ Amos said casually.

‘Oh Yeah.’ The man laughed at him as they always did. ‘The Scorge isn’t fussy about who it bites. Don’t matter how much money they’ve got.’

‘Catherine Trayer.’ Amos said the name reverentially. ‘Her husband is Nicholas Trayer he is a sentorman. He’s with the young Prince so she says. She asked me to get word to him.’

The man laughed again. ‘Oh well. The next time I share a drink with him I’ll be sure to let him know.’

‘Catherine Trayer.’ Amos repeated. ‘Don’t forget will ya?’

Barch and the sergeant emerged from the shelter.

‘What you talking about?’ He frowned and marched purposefully in Amos’s direction. ‘What you been saying?’

‘Nothing.’ Amos cowered ready to take his punishment. ‘I was just passin’ the time ‘o day.’

‘You’ll be lucky to see out the day if you don’t stop your yackin’.’

As the blow fell, Amos brought to mind Catherine’s face and he was almost smiling as the force of it knocked him to the ground.

***

Nick did not know what to expect when, before sunset on the second day, they reached Claveham. As first the mill then the other buildings came into view, everything appeared as it always had. There was no sign of the rebels and he could see people in the village going about their business. For a brief moment, he imagined that it had all been a dream and that Catherine would be waiting at the mill to welcome him.

As they entered the village, a cry went up and before long the people were thronging around. Nick dismounted and was soon swallowed up by the crowd. Everyone was talking at once.

‘Give the man space if you please.’ Prince Jared’s voice cut through the general hubbub and the villagers turned to look at him in surprise.

After Nick had introduced him, and waited while the due courtesies were observed, he searched out the cooper.

‘They are gone, Sir.’ Todd informed him. ‘We saw ‘em off. Well that is…when they realised the Prince had escaped, they lost interest in us.’

‘And Catherine?’

‘They took her with them. Goffrey here saw them go.’

Goffrey was the cooper’s son. A plump ugly boy but one of such good nature that he was popular with everyone.

Nick looked towards Prince Jared. ‘They could be over the border by now.’

‘No, Sir.’ Goffrey said eagerly. ‘They went east, Sir, not south.’

‘East?’ The Prince frowned. ‘That is interesting.’

‘What of Dugon?’ Nick said suddenly.

The cooper looked at the ground. ‘Dead, Sir. I am so sorry. When we figured it safe we went on up to the farm. We found his body.’

Nick caught his breath and almost stumbled. Even though he had half expected this news, hearing it confirmed was a deep wound.

‘If it is of any consolation, Sir, and I doubt it will be, he would not have suffered for long. It was cleanly done.’

‘By your leave, Sir,’ another voice insisted, ’Ann and her girls, they’re at the mill taking care of Vilap. They didn’t know whether you’d want them to stay in the farm and with Catherine gone, he…he’s not so good, Sir.’

‘Of course I want Ann to stay.’ Nick was horrified that they would think otherwise. ‘Did they think I would put them out into the street. Dugon was… he was…’He took a breath to give himself some time. 'I will go and speak to them.'

Prince Jared had got off his horse and now he laid a hand gently on Nick's shoulder. 'My men and I will set up camp. We will wait for you. Take as much time as you need.'

The newly widowed Ann was stirring a pot in the millhouse kitchen. She was a short plump woman with a pretty face lined by laughter. Her blond hair was streaked with grey and pinned at the back of her head. When she saw Nick she wiped her hands and came over to him, her eyes filling with tears.

'Oh , Sir, it is good to see you. I was half convinced that you were dead as well.'

Nick pulled out a chair and motioned for her to sit, then he sat next to her, taking her shaking hands in his. 'I am so sorry, Ann. Dugon was a good man, the best of men he…' He paused. 'That is not adequate, not nearly adequate to describe him. Sometimes I think that Dugon was more of a father to me, than my own father could ever be.'

Ann seemed to draw comfort from this. 'Yes, Sir,' she said, 'and he loved you as a father would also.'

He nodded, knowing that it was true. 'Ann, if you are willing, I would like you and your daughters to stay on at the farm. I will need your help even more now. I will find Catherine and bring her home if it is possible to do so, I promise you. Dugon's death will not have been in vain.'

'Did you get the Prince to safety though, Sir?'

'I did, and he is king now, and one thing I can assure you. He will not forget the sacrifices that were made here. When he hears of your loss, I know he will grieve with you.' He could not think of anything else to say that would comfort her or indeed himself. He, after all, had stood and watched while Dugon and Catherine were taken and he had done nothing to help them.

Ann smiled through her tears. 'Do not blame yourself. You did your duty. That is all any of us can do.'

He was disarmed by her sympathy. 'I am not sure where my duty lies.'

'Oh, I think you know. And Dugon knew it too and he tried to protect you. That is why...' She sighed. 'That is why he kept something from you. Something important.'

'Dugon did?'

'It was the only thing we disagreed on in all the years of our marriage.'

'Will you tell me?'

'I will, Sir, because I think you should have known all along. Gideon and Lady Ruth, they were not killed by bandits. They were murdered, Sir, I do not know why. But I do know that they would have killed you too if you had not been hidden in the cart.'

'Who?' Nick pressed her. 'Who killed them?'

'I do not know. If Dugon knew, he did not tell me. All I do know is that the man was found, and he was punished.'

'And Dugon knew this all the time.'

'Yes. But he wanted to protect you. He knew that one day you would be called to do your duty and that you would discover the truth and he dreaded that day. But there is something else, Sir.'

'Tell me.'

'Dugon was sure that this man of whom I spoke… that he… was taking orders from someone else. Someone important. Dugon always complained that there was more went on at the court than any of us would ever know.'

'Why did he think that, Ann? Did he not say?'

'No, Sir. I'm sorry. When I tried to press him on the matter he said it were just a feeling he had. Nothing more.'

Nick saw again Dugon's kind, jovial face and knew that he could not think badly of him.

'And all the time I blamed myself,' he said softly. 'I thought that my ambition had caused their deaths.'

'I know you did.' This time it was she who took his hand and squeezed it gently.

'I cannot bring Dugon back to you, Ann,' he went on, 'and I cannot bring my family back. But I can do everything in my power to find Catherine.'

'Old Vilap will certainly be happy to hear that.'

'I am told he is ill.'

'Yes. He believes that you are both dead. It will warm his heart to see that you at least are safe.'

'Shall I go up to him?'

'Yes, Sir, if you would but if he is sleeping, do not wake him. He gets little enough sleep these days.'

As he climbed the stairs he could hear the miller snoring and was about to turn back when a thought occurred to him. It was unlikely that Prince Jared would allow him to go after Catherine alone, if at all. He and the King both believed that she would be held for ransom and the demand would come to the castle. He knew that if he had to sit around at Castle Baryk waiting for something to happen he would surely lose his mind. The only thing he could do was sneak away now, without another word. He felt bad about deceiving the Prince after his kindness but he could not see any other way.

As quietly as possible, he slipped into Catherine's room and went over to the window. He did not allow himself to linger there. The memories would be too painful and this was not the time for wallowing in the past.

The roar of the weir grew louder as he opened the window. Day in day out, the water flowed through the mill pond and back into the river. Catherine had grown up hearing that sound every night of her life. She had often joked that when she came to live with him at the farm it would be too quiet and she would be unable to sleep.

He swung himself over the window ledge and let himself drop gently. The trick was to twist slightly on the descent so that he landed on the small patch of grass to the right and not in the water.

Ransom, he remembered would be grazing on the village green. He need only whistle from behind the mill and the horse would amble over to him. Then he could get away into the cover of the trees and be far away by the time the Prince noticed he was gone.

The question of his parents' murders nagged at him and he promised himself that he would find out the whole truth one day, but for the moment, his priority was finding Catherine and bringing her home.

The Fates, however, had other plans. As he rounded the side of the millhouse, a hand grabbed him roughly around the neck and he found himself being wrestled to the ground.

Instinctively he fought back ramming his elbow into his attacker's side so that the man loosened his grip very slightly and Nick was able to twist around. He found himself staring into Prince Jared's grinning face.

Nick considered himself to be strong. He had worked his fields for many years, but Jared had a grip like iron. Nick realised that though he was fighting with as much force as he could muster, the Prince was playing with him. He seemed almost to be enjoying himself.

'Come on. Show a bit of spirit,' he bellowed. 'You fight like a girl.'

Nick dropped his arms in submission, knowing when he was beaten. 'I do not fight like a girl.'

The Prince smiled. ‘Well maybe not. But you fight like the farm boy you are.’

He pushed Nick down onto the grass and sat down beside him.

‘Did you think, that you could beat me in a fight? Have you not heard? I am this country’s greatest warrior.’

Nick stared grimly at the ground.

‘Didn’t you imagine that I would anticipate this? How did you think that you would get away?’ When there was still no reply he continued. ‘You will not find her, Nick. You do not know where they have taken her.’

‘They have taken her to the East. There are only two roads they could have taken.’

‘You cannot be sure of that. They may have turned off the road at any point. If they belong to one of our rebel lords they could be anywhere in the country. You must come back to the castle and wait for the ransom demand. Then we will pay it and you will have her back.’

‘I cannot sit on my hands and do nothing.’ Nick insisted.

‘You will not be idle I can assure you. There is much to be done at the castle. My brother wants you with him. He trusts you and it pains me to say that since our father’s death there are few that we can trust so fully.

‘We have spies everywhere. If the man who took your Catherine does not contact us, and I think he will, we will find him. Then I will take you with me and let you have your revenge.’

‘I do not want revenge.’ Nick said simply. ‘All I want is Catherine.’

Chapter 16

The grand bedchamber at Castle Baryk was familiar and yet strange to Rowan. The walls were hung, as were all the walls in the castle, with scenes of hunting and of battle. The tapestries were dim and gloomy, the colours darkened by the soot from the torches, necessary because, even when the sun was at its height, the windows were too small. The furs which covered the massive bed were no doubt shorn from the beasts that Edwell himself had killed. It was the room of a king, a soldier, a huntsman and now it belonged to Rowan.

He had slept two nights there and it seemed as if he were lodging in someone else's chamber. There was nothing here that was even remotely his. All his personal possessions had been stolen in the Nostarian ambush. Even the clothes he had worn had had to be abandoned at Claveham.

Seamstresses had been hard at work sewing a new set, but for the moment he was a king in borrowed clothes.

For the first time since his return, he had been left on his own which was a mixed blessing. It gave him a chance to catch his breath and absorb everything that had happened in the last few days, but it also allowed him time to understand the reality that had befallen him.

He had always known that one day he would be king, but that had been for the future, when he was a man and fully prepared. To find himself suddenly face to face with his destiny was at once exciting and terrifying. He did not want to think too much about it.

To divert himself, he wandered around the room trying to understand a little of his father. Edwell had not shown his heir much in the way of fatherly affection. He had looked to Rowan's welfare and spoken to him with respect but on a personal level he had held himself entirely aloof.

Beside the bed stood an oak cabinet upon which rested a book bound in the heaviest leather and sealed with a gold clasp. Rowan opened it, curious to know what his father had needed to read at night. He was surprised to see that it was not a book at all, but a painting; the likeness of a woman and a small child.

He did not need to be told who the woman was. Annabelle Marchant was the love of his father's life. He took the painting to the window so that the daylight could fall upon her. Annabelle, it appeared, had been fair haired and in fact not as beautiful as he might have thought. Certainly his mother, Queen Sybilll, was much lovelier. However the smile on Annabelle's face was so full of joy and love that he was compelled to smile back. He could not remember his mother ever smiling so freely.

The little boy was clearly a younger Jared. He had their father's dark good looks but it was his mother's smile which lit up his still chubby face.

Jared was the loved one, the golden child while he, Rowan was simply the heir. He should have been resentful of this. Surely no child could be blamed for feeling that way, but it was impossible to hate the brother who was the only person to show him unconditional love and affection.

His earliest memories were of being carried on Jared's shoulders whooping and screaming with joy while the senior members of the court frowned and tutted, and the servants smiled indulgently.

It was Jared who, with much patience and good will had taught him to ride, and Jared who, when he had returned the previous day had welcomed him with a huge bearlike hug while other members of the court could only fuss around him.

For the first ten years of Rowan's life he had lived here at the court. Having, finally produced an heir, his mother had taken herself into exile, her duty done. His father, still mourning the death of his mistress, had taken solace, not in his wife's arms, but in those of any number of court ladies and even on occasion, servants.

Rowan remembered his early life only vaguely but it seemed a happy time. Though for the most part, his father ignored him, there had been the gentle guidance of Lord John Garwin, the Chancellor, a host of masters who instructed him in physical skills such as sword fighting and archery, the kindness of the court ladies, and of course the company of the older brother he adored.

Then one day the King had called him into this very chamber.

'Your mother has asked that you visit her on the island,' he had announced. 'I think that with the new threat of disease this would be sensible.'

The ten year old Rowan could barely remember his mother. She had returned to court briefly when King Tynon had tried to invade and had been defeated at Highvale, but she had stayed only two years and had faded once more in his imagination.

'How long will this visit last?' he had enquired.

‘The details have not been discussed.’ The King was clearly irritated but it was not clear at whom this irritation was directed ‘You will remain there for the time being. I think it will be of benefit to you. The Queen has many learned scholars at her court.’

He may have been the heir, but he was still just a ten year old child and he did not want to be uprooted from the life he had always known.

Even Jared had been unable to console him.

‘They will teach you many things that you cannot learn here.’

‘I don’t want to learn those things. I want to stay here with you and learn to be a warrior.’

‘You will do that one day. But you are to be king. It is your destiny.’

Whilst the court at Castle Baryk was very much a male domain, his mother’s court was predominately female. The island itself was a most beautiful place, the climate mild and sunny. All sorts of exotic plants grew in its sheltered warmth and from the balconies of the palace high on the cliff top, you could see a million different colours, not least of all the glorious blue of an always calm sea.

The palace itself was decorated with brightly coloured wall hangings and his mother’s ladies wore dresses of almost every hue imaginable. In this colourful oasis, Rowan learned history, philosophy and mathematics, more knowledge, he often grumbled, than he could need in a whole lifetime.

The Queen herself was an enigma. She surrounded herself with such beauty, even the cooks were the very best, yet she was dour and bitter. She alternated between the same cold aloofness as his father and an almost desperate affection. On the latter occasions she would hold him fast against her as if she could not bear ever to be parted from him.

He found her moods alarming, and her bitterness upsetting so that he was never completely comfortable in her presence. During almost five years that he had spent on the island, he had frequently requested that he be allowed home, but the King insisted that he remain. He wondered sometimes if it suited Edwell to be rid of his younger son.

The news of his father's demise had, of course, taken them all by surprise. When he looked back now on that flight across the country, on the death of all his escort it brought back to him the fearsome burden he now carried. Yet...and he found this hard to believe, the last few days had been more like an exciting adventure than a flight for his life.

Wandering through the market with Nick, and later, playing jacks with Tam and Sophia and sleeping in the forest he had felt something entirely new. He could only think of it as a happy time.

There was a knock on the door and it opened inward to reveal Lord John Garwin. Rowan replaced the picture where he had found it,

Lord John had shown him great kindness when he was a child, and in his own way, love. He tried to remember the details of the Chancellor's life so that the old man would know he cared.

Lord John's only son had been killed at Highvale and there had been a grandson, he remembered.

'I am sorry for the loss of your brother, Lord John.'

The Chancellor inclined his head in a bow. 'Thank you, Sire.'

'How is Lady Garwin?

'She is as well as can be expected Sire, I thank you for enquiring.'

‘And your own wife? Lady Harriet is it not?’

‘It is, Sire. And she bears it all as best she can.’

It was an answer which raised more questions but he did not pursue the matter.

‘And your grandson? William is it?’

He was proud of himself for remembering, but was stunned to see the look of sorrow on the older man’s face.

‘That, Sire is one of the matters I need to make known to you. There are so many such things you will need to know. I hardly know where to start.’

Rowan sighed. So it was back to affairs of state.

‘Sit down, Lord John, Please.’

He sat himself in the ornate chair by the fireplace and waved the Chancellor into another. ‘I am ready to listen.’

Chapter 17

Upon his return to the castle, Nick went immediately to see Matilda who had been given a chamber in the apartments reserved for high born courtiers and guests.

The living quarters and public rooms were built at the summit of the castle hill set in a semicircle around a huge grassy courtyard, and surrounded by crenulated walls. There was no need for a keep. The hill was a fortress in itself. It was not difficult to see why the ancient kings of Subia had chosen this place for their castle. It was the only high ground in a plateau so flat and wide, that soldiers patrolling the parapet above the walls, or through the narrow slits of windows beneath, could see anyone approaching for miles.

Between the apartments and the wall was a small untidy garden, where Nick had been told he would find Matilda. At first the place appeared empty, then he caught a glimpse of her almost buried in a chaos of foliage.

She turned her head and when she saw that it was him, said excitedly.

'Look. Through here. Wolf's Bane. It's very rare in this part of the country.' She was holding a small stick which she now used to point through the undergrowth at a spear of dark blue blooms. When Nick reached out a hand she pulled his arm back.

'No, don't touch. It has powerful medicinal properties but it is extremely poisonous. That is why it is grown so deep in here I suspect.' She stepped backwards out of the greenery. 'This garden is a treasure house of herbs. I am told it was begun long ago. Some of the plants are ancient. The ladies of the court are desperate to learn some of my skills. Herblore has become fashionable once more. My poor mother would not believe it.' She shook her head sadly, then smiled. 'Truly I am unused to having nothing to do. I have my own servants now, can you believe it? And I am addressed as 'My Lady.' I fear that at any moment they will find out that I am just Matilda whose mother was killed for the Old Knowledge.'

'You are the King's friend,' he assured her. 'He is grateful to you. He knows that you are not high born but he has chosen to elevate you. Enjoy it. You have suffered greatly. You deserve your happiness.'

She sighed. 'I would gladly return to my old life if it meant that Jacob was there. I do not know if he lives or if... You must understand that Nick.'

'I do,' he admitted. 'I must sit on my hands here while Catherine is who knows where. She too may well be dead.' He paused for a moment, remembering Dugon and feeling again his loss. 'They killed my steward. My oldest friend.'

Matilda stood silently, but he knew that she understood.

'There is something I wanted to ask you,' he said eventually. 'You told me that after the ceremony I had been given a potion of what was it? Mandrake?'

'And Poppy I would imagine. It is the most effective, but only a skilled healer could prepare it. Too much, and you would have died.'

'How long would the effects have lasted?'

‘Up to a day probably. It depends on the strength.’

‘But, it was many days before I awoke. And when I did, I remembered nothing. Even now very little of that time remains to me. I was led to believe that I had been suffering from some kind of malaise of the mind.’

‘It is possible. They say the mandrake can cause madness but…’

‘No.’ He shook his head. ‘Now I believe that it was intentional. They did not want me to know what was happening.’

He told her the gist of Anne’s revelations.

She frowned. ‘There are ways to ensure that you would not remember. I could make a potion that would make you sleep for many days. I could make you see what was not there or… or not see that which was. Many things are possible.’

He nodded slowly. ‘Prince Jared claims that he knows nothing, but I suspect that he does. In fact I am beginning to suspect that everyone here is party to the same secrets and that I am deliberately being kept in the dark. I think that Lord John will know. I will ask him. Surely after all this time he will be able to tell me the truth.’

‘He has called a meeting in the council Chamber,’ she said. ‘The King was on his way there earlier. He stopped to speak to me.’

‘Yes. I was asked to attend. I am headed there now.’

‘Go then,’ she said with a smile. ‘And I hope you find your answers. I will return to my exploration of the garden.’

It was possible to walk all the way through the living quarters along the narrow stone passages, but Nick chose to take the quicker route, across the wide central courtyard. It was a beautiful spring day and on the grass ladies and children were taking a walk or playing. Sophia, Matilda’s daughter was sitting cross legged on the ground, her head bent towards another small girl. She glanced up, saw him and waved. He returned her wave with a smile but proceeded on his way. He could still hear her high, happy voice as he entered the great hall by way of the inner door. The guards recognised him and let him pass.

He walked through the hall without stopping and out into the passage that led to the council chamber. Tam was just coming out as he arrived.

'They asked me to find you, Sir. I was just coming to…'

The boy paused, frowning, as a servant in red and gold livery came along the passage from the opposite direction carrying a pitcher and a tray of silver cups. The man stopped and stood to one side to let them enter the room first.

Nick nodded a thank you, and was about to enter but the look on Tam's face stopped him and he motioned to the man to go in.

'What is it?'

Tam was clearly agitated.

'That man, Sir, he…' he sighed. 'There is something wrong. I can feel it.'

'Wrong in what way?'

'I dunno but…' The boy looked so upset that Nick was momentarily frightened. 'I can tell things, Sir. About people. Sometimes I… I just know. Something is very wrong.'

He was just a child and Nick did not understand his fear but he smiled reassuringly at the boy anyway.

'Do not worry, Tam. I will be on my guard.'

He did not have time to give the matter any more thought as he entered the council chamber.

Around the central table sat the King, Lord John, Prince Jared and Felix Runmore, the Commander of the army. It was the first time Nick had seen the Commander at close quarters and he observed him with interest.

Prince Jared had been less than complimentary about Runmore's abilities.

'At one time he was an exemplary warrior, but I fear he has slowed with age. My father allowed Felix to keep his position but he was himself the true head of the army, and I was his deputy. Now I will take over his role.' He dropped his voice. 'Out of respect I continue the pretence.'

Robert Boderry was also present. The Treasury Master had been a frequent visitor to Nick's home and he remembered the man with affection.

Here then were all the highest ranking members of the court. With Ann's words replaying in his mind, he could not help wondering if one of them had caused his parents' death and tried to kill him too. Why though? That was what he could not understand. Who would benefit from their deaths? They were not wealthy, and although his father had been a good friend of the King, he had little influence at court.

'I'm glad you are here, Nick,' Rowan said cheerfully, distracting him from his thoughts. 'Lord John has something he wishes to discuss with us but in his usual way it is taking him forever to come to the point.'

Teasing his chancellor, Nick had discovered, was one of Rowan's favourite pastimes, but he did it with fondness and Lord John seemed to understand that and did not take offence.

'This is a very difficult subject to address, Sire,' he began. 'I am not sure that…'

'Well let us drink first,' the King interrupted, 'or we will all die of thirst while we wait.'

He motioned to the servant who had been waiting by the door and the cups were placed on the table. Nick watched the man as he carried the pitcher toward the King. Tam had been very certain that something was wrong. It seemed that the man was very nervous. His hands were shaking. Maybe it was all the talk of potions and intrigue but a thought occurred to Nick.

In a flash, he stood up and in two strides, positioned himself between the King and the servant. Before the man had a chance to act, Nick grabbed the pitcher from his grasp and picked up the King's cup. In the bottom of the cup, almost invisible against the silver, were a few grains of grey powder. Nick poured a small amount of wine into the goblet, and held it in front of the man's face.

'Drink some.'

The servant shook his head. 'No, Sir, it is for My Lord King. I am not allowed to…'

'Drink it.'

'No.' The man began to back away. Nick reached for his knife then remembered that only the uniformed guards were permitted to carry weapons within the Royal Apartments. Prince Jared however, motioned to the guards who responded instantly, one of them holding the man's arms firmly behind him while the other grasped his jaw and made to pour the wine down his throat.

'No,' the servant pleaded. 'Please, please don't. I will tell you who…I will …'

The guard relaxed his grip and looked around for instructions. Felix Runmore stood up and in a surprisingly deep voice demanded.

'Why will you not drink this wine?'

'Because it is poisoned.' Nick said. 'Isn't it?'

The man shook his head. 'No, I…'

'Tell us the truth,' the Commander insisted, 'or you will be forced to drink it. You have no choice. Is it poisoned?'

The man was crying now. He nodded

'Kill him.'

The command was made and executed before anyone else had a chance to speak and within seconds the servant lay dead on the chamber floor, his head almost severed from his body.

The King sat back in his chair and looked around in disbelief. Lord John shook his head sadly, and Prince Jared stood glaring at the Commander. Nobody spoke as the guards carried the body from the room, but as soon as they were gone Jared shouted angrily.

'Why did you do that? Why did you have him killed?'

Runmore looked shocked at the words. 'He tried to poison the King. He had to die.'

'Eventually yes. But we had no chance to question him. He was just a servant. Someone must have organised this. Someone paid him or threatened him. Now we will never know who.'

'I… I did not think.' Runmore was clearly ashamed of his mistake. 'But surely he… he would have told us nothing. He was a blubbering mess.'

The Prince was about to reply but obviously saw that there was little point. Instead he paced the room angrily.

'It is an abomination that the King could be in danger in this very castle. This is a desperate situation.' He came to a halt by Nick's side and put a hand on his shoulder. 'Once again, my friend, we are in your debt. How did you know?'

Nick shrugged. 'It was the boy he… he must have heard something.'

From the throne, Rowan's voice sounded shaky. 'Well I am grateful, to you. Thank you Nick. Thank you again.'

Runmore sat down wearily. 'Since Lord Harald's death there has been no profender. I think it is more essential than ever before.' He turned to Prince Jared. 'My Lord Prince, I think you should take the position. I can think of no-one more suited.'

Jared shook his head and Nick remembered that he had intended to take control of the army. He wondered if Runmore knew that, and was trying in his own way to keep the Prince occupied elsewhere.

'I am horrified that my brother's safety has been compromised right here in the castle.' Jared said. 'By your leave, Commander. I will take charge of the Royal Guard. Nick can take on the role of protecting the King's person. He seems to manage it perfectly.'

Lord Felix intervened. 'I am not sure that Sentorman Trayer is qualified for the post he…'

'Of course he is.' The king interrupted. 'He has saved my life on several occasions just in the last few days.'

'Well maybe so, but…'

Jared had regained some of his former good humour. He grinned at Nick, throwing out the words like a challenge. 'At least do it until we find a better man. After all, you have nothing else to do.'

'I…I am not familiar with the term.' Nick admitted. 'What is a profender?'

'Because our king is so young, it is customary to appoint a profender for him.' Lord John told him. 'In common terms it is a body guard, but in effect it is much more. Apart from protecting the King's person, you would also be an advisor. Not in matters of state but ... in other ways.'

'Please Nick.' Rowan insisted. 'I would like that very much. I already think of you as my friend.'

Nick knew that the added responsibility would take his mind off his troubles. It might just keep him sane. 'I would be honoured Sire,' he said with a bow, 'though I would ask that the position be temporary. Just until…'

Rowan nodded 'Until we find Catherine. Then you wish to return to your farm.'

'I do, Sire.'

'Much as I would like to keep you here I cannot refuse you that. It is agreed.'

Prince Jared smiled at Nick. 'The position carries a new title. You will be Lord Farm Boy now.'

Chapter 18

Catherine heard the market bell ringing as she approached the city gates. It was the signal to the custodians that one of their charges wished to speak to them. She waited for the gate to open, a deep dread in the pit of her stomach. Her hands were shaking as Barch opened the gate, her legs weakening at the thought of facing him.

The heavy door creaked inwards and he appeared, grinning at her in that smug way of his. He was dressed in a red velvet overcoat which was too small for him but he rested his hands on his hips letting it stand out on each side like a peacock displaying its tail.

'What you got for me?'

Fighting her natural revulsion, she held out her hand and stepped forward to meet him.

***

Three days after their arrival in Fastwater, Jacob had finally given up his battle for life. At first, Catherine had believed Tally when she told her that he would be cared for in the inn. In fact all they had done was make him comfortable, then leave him to die with the others.

When Catherine asked for water and food for him, they had refused.

'We have little enough for ourselves,' Tally had told her. 'We cannot afford to waste what we do have on those who will die anyway.'

The old soldier and the three other invalids, lay on the floor of the inn on pallets of straw. If the air outside had been filled with the stench of death, at least there had been air of a sort. Here in the stifling heat Catherine's head thumped and she found it hard even to think clearly. Nevertheless, she had sat with Jacob during those last hours, doing what she could for him and for the others. Ignoring the pain in her head, her still unhealed shoulder and the debilitating hunger which gnawed at her stomach, she talked to him which was all she had the power to do.

On the day which was to prove his last, he had seemed briefly to rally.

'Give…give me my pack,' he instructed, reaching for his bundle.

She pulled it out for him and he fumbled inside like a blind man until he reached what he was seeking.

'They searched for food but they did not find this. It was well hidden.'

He drew out a black pouch similar to the one in which he kept his herbs. In the bag were six silver coins. Catherine looked at them in amazement.

'With these you will be able to trade,' he whispered, 'but be careful. The women here will take everything you own. There is enough to keep you for some time but not enough to share. Guard them well.'

'Why did you not show me earlier.' She was horrified. 'I could have got you water and food.'

'It is too late for me, Catherine.' His pale blue eyes held hers gently. 'But there is still hope for you.'

‘No.’ Despite her best intentions, she could not hold back her tears. ‘Please. Don’t leave me. I need you. You are all I have left.’

He shook his head. ‘You are stronger than you think. You can survive.’

‘I… I do not understand how. There is no way out of here and Nick is almost certainly dead. He cannot help me.’

‘Then you must help yourself. Use these coins wisely. But remember, do not share them. Save yourself.’

She took the bag and hid it inside her dress. The effort had clearly tired Jacob but still he struggled to speak.

‘Just rest,’ she urged, trying not to let him see her tears.

‘No. There is one more thing I must tell you.’

‘It can wait.’

‘No. There is no time. I am failing.’ He held out a hand and she took it. His grip was surprisingly strong. ‘Do you… do you remember, you asked what Richard Lassall had done to deserve his imprisonment?’

‘It doesn’t matter now. Just rest please. You must conserve your strength until I can get something with these coins.’

‘When I next rest it will be the end for me,’ he said harshly as if he were summoning all his remaining strength.

‘Nonsense.’

‘Catherine listen. If you do escape from here, it may be important for you to know.’

She held his hand as he started to speak, his voice fading with each moment and she bent towards him straining to hear. Though the story he told was shocking, it did not touch her. She heard the words and understood but all she could think about was that another good man was about to die in front of her and there was nothing she could do.

Then he was silent and his grip on her hand slackened.

She thought at first that he had fallen asleep but his eyes were fixed in a grim stare. Just as Richard Lassall had done for Dugon, she pressed his lids shut.

Her own eyes were sore and dry from the heat and the endless dust. The salty tears stung but she had no more power to hold them back, or to stop the sobs which wracked her weary body. Never in her life had she felt so alone and so tired. When the reservoir of tears was empty and the sobbing had subsided, she rested her head on the wall. She had to decide what to do with the coins she could feel inside her dress, but it was much easier just to rest. What was the point of fighting the inevitable? Even if the coins brought her some time, how long could she realistically hope to survive? Her eyes closed gratefully and she drifted into sleep.

It could have been moments or hours later when she was woken by a sharp pain in her injured shoulder. Someone was shaking her roughly.

'Catherine. Wake up. Come on we must move them.'

Tally was standing over her, hands on her hips.

'We must take his body to the wharf. If we leave him here the rats and flies will know and they will come in search of him. We do not want them here.'

Catherine could barely speak.

'If you had allowed him food and water he would have lived.'

Tally's face flushed with anger.

'Do you think I enjoy this? Do you think I want everyone around me to die? Of course I do not. But we would not have survived as long as we have, if we had wasted every morsel on the dying.'

Catherine did not move, nor did she acknowledge her words. In frustration Tally slammed a fist against the wall.

‘One day this will end and when it does I want to be alive. I want to be here when Barch and his worm of a brother are made to account for what they have done to us. You can do as you please. If you wish to lay down and die then do so, but first you must help us move the bodies.’

Her face was set in a hard line but Catherine could see the strain which lay behind the hardness. With a great effort she pulled herself to her feet. Behind Tally, Fara and Jostin were carrying another of the invalids. Evidently she too, had died.

Summoning up all her strength she took hold of Jacob’s feet while Tally took him beneath the arms. Her injured shoulder cried out but she forced herself to ignore the pain.

Somehow, though she did not know how, she managed to carry him most of the way to the wharf. When she felt she could go no further, Tally seemed to understand.

‘Rest here for a moment.’

Gently they lowered him to the ground.

Catherine’s legs weakened beneath her and she fell to her knees beside him.

‘It is just a little further,’ Tally said more kindly. ‘Take a few moments then we must go. The sooner we have done it, the better.’

Catherine knelt with her head in her hands, trying not to think too much. She was so tired in body and numbed in grief and despair that she seemed to be somewhere outside herself. Slowly she stood once more took hold of Jacob’s feet again and they began to move.

At the wharf Tally paused again.

‘It would be easier just to let the bodies fall over the edge but… somehow I feel we can at least afford them this one last dignity. She indicated the steps with her head. It will not be pleasant down there but… if you have the strength…’

‘Yes.’ Catherine had known Jacob for only four days yet he had become like a dear friend. It would be wrong to throw him to his fate when he could be carried. It was a detail but as Tally had said, it was the least they could do.

Once more she summoned her strength and together they negotiated the wooden steps. As they laid Jacob under the wharf in one of the few empty spaces she tried not to look around. It was impossible not to do so. The scene was more horrifying than anything she could have imagined. She was not afraid of rats - there were always some about in the mill and in the thatch of the village houses - but these were different. They were fat and there were hundreds of them, feasting on the flesh of the dead. Her empty stomach heaved though there was nothing to expel. Flies buzzed remorselessly and overhead the birds of prey squawked in triumph as they circled and dived.

She was almost grateful when a scream diverted her and she and Tally turned as one to see what had made the sound. Fara was thrashing about like a crazy woman. Jostin had found a piece of driftwood and appeared to be beating her with it until they realised that a rat had attached itself to her arm and the boy was trying to beat it off.

With a shriek, the animal released its hold and fell heavily to the ground.

Fara clutched her arm and when she looked up her eyes were filled not with pain, but with terror.

***

They had seen it before. The rats carried disease, not necessarily the Scorge, but other equally dangerous sicknesses and they had watched many others die from it. Within hours of being bitten, Fara was already pale and weak and bereft of energy. Catherine could not help but wonder if the girl had simply resigned herself to her fate; if the fight had just left her.

‘It is just a scratch. I am sure you have nothing to fear from this, though I wish we had water to bathe it.’ Tally wore an infuriated expression as if all this were simply designed just to hurt her but her eyes held compassion and something approaching despair. ‘Jostin, ring the bell. I will see what I can get from Barch.’

Catherine felt the coins inside her dress and knew what she had to do. Jacob had insisted that she keep them for herself, but Jacob was dead. It was true that Tally and Fara would have taken them from her if they had known, but not because they were wicked or selfish. They were merely desperate.

Tally had said that each of them had to earn their own food yet she was now willing to give herself to the odious Barch in order to help Fara.

‘No.’ Reaching into her dress Catherine pulled out the bag. ‘You do not need to do that.’

She had not been able to save Dugon or Jacob but she determined then that no-one else would die while she had the power to prevent it. She opened the coins on to the floor.

‘Jacob had these. He gave them to me today. I did not know he had them.’

The other three stared at them in amazement just as she had done.

Tally looked at her and she could see in the other girl’s eyes that she understood what it meant for Catherine to share.

‘Perhaps we can use it to bribe him to let us go.’

‘He will never let us go.’ Tally shook her head. ‘Not for any amount of silver. He cannot afford for the world to know what he has been doing here.’

She thought carefully for a moment.

'We must use these one at a time. Let him believe that we found the first, then produce the others gradually. If he knows that we have all this he will demand a higher price. Here.' She took one of the coins and put the others back in the bag. Then she held the bag towards Catherine.

'Take it and hide it where you will.'

'I need not hide it.' Catherine placed the bag on the ground between them. 'I have trust in you. They may not last as long for the four of us as they would for one, but at least if we are to die, we will do so together.'

Tally nodded her gratitude though she was not the sort to speak it out loud.

'You must take this to Barch.' She handed Catherine the coin. 'He may be more generous to one with such a pretty face.'

Now, as Barch stood before her in his ridiculous red coat, she held out the coin and though she could imagine Jacob shaking his head at her, her conscience told her that she had done the right thing.

Chapter 19

In Larock, Matilda had owned two everyday dresses and one for best, and she had felt more than satisfied with those. At Castle Baryk, as befitted her new status, she was expected to have almost a whole chest full of clothes. Consequently she had become very familiar with the seamstresses who were the main source of gossip in the court.

The girl assigned to her was called Abigail and she was always happy to share her knowledge of court matters. Generally, Matilda believed gossip to be an evil, and tried not to listen but when the subject of the conversation was Prince Jared as it was today, she could not resist, especially as Abigail described him as 'Lovelorn'

Ever since she had first seen the Prince at the funeral, she had been unable to banish the image of him from her mind.

'Why do you say that?' she enquired, with what she hoped was a casual air. 'Why is he lovelorn?'

'It is common knowledge. My Lady. He was in love with a woman who broke his heart. Ever since then, many have tried to win him but none has succeeded.'

'Who was she?'

‘I do not know My Lady. No-one seems to know. It was that nasty business with young Lord William.’

‘Lord William?’

‘Will Garwin. The Chancellor’s grandson.’

Matilda shook her head.

‘You have not heard?’ Abigail was more than happy to enlighten her. ‘Apparently they loved the same woman, and… well I don’t suppose it’s something the Prince would want to remember… but…’

‘What did he do? Tell me. Did they fight?’

‘Oh no. It was something far less honourable than a fight.’

‘Less honourable?

Lord John, she remembered, had been disdainful of the Prince. ‘His loyalty is not in question,’ he had said. But he had ignored the question of his honour.

The seamstress clearly relished the opportunity to tell what she knew.

‘It was about five years ago. Will, he was such a sweet boy. No more than … oh… twenty years old he was. His father had been killed at Highvale and he wanted so much to be a credit to him but… the poor mite was not made to be a soldier. He was too gentle. Too kind. And oh, My Lady, he was so much in love. You could see it whenever you spoke to him. I used to serve at table in those days. The other young nobles, they used to tease him I remember, but he had that dreamy look in his eyes and he never paid them any heed.

‘Prince Jared, well, you could see the tension in him. Afterwards we all agreed that he used to give poor Will the evil eye from across the room. Dark it was, that look. Dark and brooding. It was bound to come to a head sometime.

‘Then one night, Will went down to the stables and three of the Prince’s men were waiting for him. Poor boy.

He never stood a chance. Beat him they did to within an inch of his life. There was barely anything left of him.'

'But… that is terrible.' Matilda felt sick with horror. 'It's despicable. Why did the Prince not fight him honourably?'

'Maybe he did not think Will worthy of that.'

'I cannot believe it. I cannot believe him capable of such a thing.'

Abigail was clearly surprised at the strength of Matilda's reaction. 'Well I think that he regrets what he did. I think that he carries the shame with him always. You can see it in him. But he acted out of passion and… 'she sighed. ' I think Prince Jared is a passionate man.'

Matilda was just as surprised at herself. All that she had heard disgusted her yet she could see the Prince's noble features and she truly could not believe that of him.

A passionate man. She felt herself blushing at the thought.

'What happened to the woman? Who was she?'

'No-one knows who she was My Lady. That is the greatest mystery. We are not a large court here but if anyone knows anything, they are keeping it to themselves. The men who beat Will were hanged and he was sent away. They say that he can barely walk and that he is in constant pain.'

'And the Prince was not punished?'

'No My Lady. Not him. The King loved him. Loved him more than anyone or anything on earth just as he had loved his mother.'

Matilda stood in silence as the seamstress put the final touches to her dress. Surely she was not such a bad judge of character. It was true, from what she had seen of the Prince, that he showed the signs of a man burdened with guilt. But such cowardly and dishonourable behaviour? Surely he was not capable of that.

Somehow she would have to find out the truth.

***

When he had left Catherine and his men to their fate in the woods, Richard Lassall had intended to cross the border into Nostaria and join forces with the Valeron heir. He had heard that other Valeron sympathisers were doing so on a daily basis. Overnight, he stopped at Kelwin an ancient logman's town in the forested foothills of the Frontier Mountains. He knew of a rebel family who would feed him and give him news.

They were a family of some wealth so he was surprised to find that the house was small and anonymous, set away from the more substantial dwellings on a quiet side street. The head of the family, Hespian, was short and plump with a shock of white hair and a still dark beard. He greeted Richard warily at the door, his eyes scanning the street before dragging him inside and slapping him warmly on the arms.

'We live simply so that we do not attract attention,' he explained, ushering his guest into the living area which was far more comfortably furnished than the exterior implied.

When Richard explained where he was heading, the older man smiled broadly. 'No. No. My boy. You must stay with us. I will send word to the Uncle and he will find a task for you. I am sure you will be more useful to him on this side of the border.'

The 'Uncle' was not in fact a relative, except that all Valeron supporters considered themselves to be family. He had spent all his life feigning loyalty to the usurpers and had risen to become one of King Edwell's closest advisors.

From this position of trust he was able to control the rebel forces and sympathisers waiting only for a chance to see the Valeron heir back on the throne.

Hespian sent a messenger to inform him of Richard's whereabouts and they awaited instructions.

'I remember your mother,' his host declared one night as they had finished a sumptuous meal and settled to a glass of brandy. 'She was most comely.'

'Indeed.' Richard was not usually given to idle gossip, and he was certainly not one to share his own feelings, but he had drunk a little too much, and Hespian's chair was comfortable and his company congenial. It seemed good, for once to talk openly. 'If she had been plain she would always have been a servant. Her beauty elevated her. Men have always found her enchanting, not least of all my father and the usurper King.'

'And how does she fare now?'

'She died. Three or so years ago.'

'I am sorry to hear that.'

Richard shrugged as though he did not care, yet the hurt went deeper than just the loss of a parent. He had known that his mother's whole life was dedicated to the Valeron cause and whilst he had shared her aims, he could not bear to see her whoring herself to the Jassoir pretender who called himself King. He also resented his father for allowing it.

Gorben Lassall was another refugee from the war. He had been apprenticed into the army after the last battle, and had earned himself a high rank and enough gold to buy himself a hall, albeit one that was surrounded by marshland.

When he met Richard's mother, they had shared their passion for the Valeron cause if not for each other. Gorben was assigned to the royal guard when Richard was three and he moved his family to court. It was the Uncle who, realising that Mistress Lassall had caught the eye of the King could see the benefit in such a relationship. She became one of the Edwell's mistresses whilst spying for the Uncle.

When his father was killed at Highvale, fighting for a regime he despised, Richard's hatred of the Jassoirs reached a climax. He went to the Uncle and begged for a chance to avenge his father's death.

'And I failed,' he admitted under Hespian's benign gaze, 'Just as I have failed now.'

'You were very young.'

'He had faith in me and I failed.'

Sometimes he wished that he had been put to death as his original sentence demanded. Instead, his mother had used her influence with both the King and the Valerons to arrange a deal. Edwell had agreed because of his fondness for her but she had revealed her Valeron sympathies and he could no longer keep her as his mistress.

She had been sent away along with her son and in the inhospitable grimness of Barrow Marsh had wasted away until her early death some years before.

Richard had believed his sentence to be for life so he could hardly believe it when a few weeks earlier the message had arrived from Castle Baryk announcing his release. With it came a private letter from the Uncle giving him another chance to prove himself. He was to ambush Prince Rowan as he rushed to Edwell's deathbed and hold him captive.

And again he had failed.

'I believe it was a hastily formed plan,' Hespian assured him. 'You are not at fault for that.' He leaned across and filled Richard's glass. 'Rest easy. I have explained all and I am sure he still believes in you. Next time you will be equal to the task. We all learn from our mistakes.'

When word finally arrived, it did not bring much cheer. Richard was to find a company of good fighting men and await instructions.

'I have been imprisoned in my home for ten years,' he complained to his host. 'How would I know where to find men?'

Hespian smiled. 'That, I assure you, will not be difficult.'

***

The Woodfields Inn did not announce itself and most travellers followed the road without noticing the turnoff, yet its whereabouts was not a secret. It was an old timberjacks' camp; a two storey log building which had once been a dormitory for twenty men.

Richard left his horse with the ostler and approached the inn door nervously. He could hear the raised voices of men, and was assailed by the welcoming smell of meat cooking.

Inside, the ground floor was one immense hall. Long oak tables stood about the room in haphazard fashion, some hidden from their neighbours by brightly coloured screens.

The inn was not full but it was busy enough to create a hearty atmosphere.

The upper floor which contained a myriad of rooms was fenced by a wide balustrade. From here, the innkeeper kept a watchful eye on his customers while his wife and daughter served beer and food below.

Hespian had told Richard that at Woodfields, business took place and deals were struck that could not be spoken openly in the towns. The Marshalls did not know, or more likely, pretended they did not know of the inn's existence.

Rooms could be rented but many stayed at the games of Colanche which went on all night. Three types of men played at the games. There were the hard players who understood, not just the game, but more importantly, their naïve opponents. These men made a living from their winnings here. Then there were those who came to try their luck but did not expect to win and lost with good grace. They were usually young noblemen who enjoyed the excitement but had a safe home to which they could return.

Of course there were also the true gamblers; men who earnestly believed that a win was just around the corner and who lost everything they owned and more besides.

Richard found himself a place at one of the tables not devoted to the game. He nodded to the man on his right who bid him good day with an amused and interested expression.

'Are you here to play,' the man asked, 'or are you merely passing through?'

Although he had eaten a good breakfast with Hespian, Richard could not resist the smell of roasting meat.

'I have some business,' he replied. 'But first I must eat and drink.'

'Then you will need the services of our landlord's lovely daughter.' The man pointed to a young woman who was passing from table to table replacing the jugs of beer and plates of meat. Most of the men seemed to know her and they joked and flirted with her. Richard guessed that she was eighteen years or so, no more than twenty. Her light brown hair was pinned haphazardly and threatened to tumble loose as she bobbed her head. She was plump though not unpleasantly so and where her plain blue dress was tied loosely at the waist, her hips swayed gently hinting at the shape beneath.

His neighbour thumped a hand on the table and called out.

'Hey, Rosa. When you are done with those feeble oafs there are real men here who need a meal.'

Richard could not take his eyes off the girl. She turned angrily at the call, but smiled as she saw him. When she approached the table, he saw that her otherwise pleasing face was disfigured by an ugly red birthmark. It began somewhere on the left side of her breast and spread upwards, tendrils of red, burning the side of her face like flames reaching for her eyes. He was both fascinated and appalled by it.

Rosa was clearly used to this reaction. Her smile did not waver but her brown eyes looked directly into his.

'We have beef today and a good strong ale. Will that please you, Sir?'

'Yes.' Richard tried not to look at her face and found himself staring instead at her breasts. 'That…er… that will be fine. Thank you.'

As she turned away, the other man laughed again. 'You'll get used to looking at her,' he said loudly.

The girl must have heard him though nothing in the way she continued towards the kitchen betrayed that fact.

'I am Gordack.' The man offered Richard his hand. He was approaching middle age, tall and broad with long greying hair and a wide bald patch in the front of his head. There was something in the way he held himself that spoke of unflinching brutality.

'Richard Lassall,' Richard shook the hand and at once came to a decision. 'Of the Valeron.'

Gordack sat back in his seat and regarded him with interest, a smile playing about his lips. Richard pretended that he was not interested in the man's reaction.

'The food is good here, is it?'

'Oh yes. I cannot fault it.' Gordack looked around the room. 'But in many ways this place falls short of what it could be. I have a mind to own a place like this. It has…possibilities.'

Rosa returned with a tankard of ale for Richard. She smiled at him.

'Your food will be but a moment.'

'I was just saying…' Gordack addressed her in a loud voice as if she were deaf. 'I could make something of this place. Women. That's what this place needs. Whores. Your father won't last much longer if he don't learn to diversify.'

Rosa gave him a snort of disdain, but there was also fear in her eyes.

Gordack merely laughed as she turned away again. 'She's a feisty one that, for or all her ugliness, I'd make her mine tomorrow and I'd soon tame her.'

Again he had spoken so that she could hear and Richard felt sorry for her. Were it not for her disfigurement she would be a good catch for any man.

Gordack looked up at the balcony once more. 'You're wondering why he doesn't have me thrown out aren't you? It's because he owes me money.' He shouted the last words although there was much noise in the inn and it was unlikely that the landlord could hear. 'Now.' He looked at Richard again and lowered his voice. 'Master Lassall of the Valeron, what is this business you have here?'

'I am looking for men to fight for my cause.' Richard resented the fact that he felt nervous of his companion. He fought to keep his voice, and his eyes steady.

‘For your cause?’ Gordack laughed. ‘I do not think you will find many who would fight for a cause. Gold. Now that is worth fighting for.’

Hespian had provided him with a small amount but already Richard could see that it would not be enough.

‘Do you know any who might be prepared to join me?’ he asked anyway.

‘I may. Who will they be fighting?’

‘As yet I do not know. I am awaiting instructions.’

Again the mocking smile had him squirming in his seat.

‘When you have your instructions, and your gold, and your cause. I will be here.’

Chapter 20

Rowan caught a glimpse of the serving girl as she passed along the edge of the exercise yard. A sack of grain sat against her hip, lifting her skirt and revealing a shapely ankle. She glanced at him briefly then looked down demurely and hurried away. Before Rowan could drag his eyes away, Tam aimed a fierce punch at his stomach. He staggered slightly under its force then with a roar, launched himself at the younger boy, bringing him to the ground.

'Hold now. That was better.' Nick helped them both to their feet.

Tam was smaller than Rowan, and scrawny from the malnourishment of his past but he had a surprising strength and an almost instinctive feel for an opponent's intentions.

'Do not assume that your killer blow will do the job,' Nick told him. 'While you stand and admire your handiwork your opponent recovers. Always assume that he will come back at you.'

He turned to Rowan. 'Sire, you must not let your attention wander. Although you should be aware of your surroundings, all your focus should be on your opponent. He will always be waiting for just such an opportunity.'

The young King acknowledged the criticism. He waved in the direction the girl had taken. 'She was… she… em..'

‘Indeed she was.’ Nick agreed with just the hint of a smile. ‘But you must try not to think of such distractions while you are training.’

Rowan wanted to explain that at times he could think of nothing else. At his mother’s court, he was used to the women fussing over him but he had begun to find it embarrassing. Some were able to stop him in his tracks with just a look. They brought on the increasingly frequent sensation which drained the consciousness from his mind and centred it in his groin.

‘In a real fight,’ Nick went on, ‘it may lose you your life.’

‘I…?’ Nick would understand, but how could he phrase the question?

As time had progressed, Rowan had begun to surround himself with the people he liked and trusted. Nick was primary amongst those. He found his new profender’s quiet strength reassuring and he felt safe in his presence. Nick waited now for the question, but there were too many others around and Rowan shook his head.

‘It is of no matter. You are right of course and I will try to concentrate more.’

Nick gave him a friendly yet respectful smile, then turned to two much smaller boys who had also been fighting alongside the King. They were rolling around on the floor like puppies, shouting with laughter.

Nick pulled them apart and set each one on his feet as if they were indeed puppies.

These were the boys that Rowan had chosen as his pages. They were much of a size but the larger by a slight margin was Garsam, another of Edwell’s illegitimate sons and therefore Rowan’s half brother. Garsam was a smaller version of himself and despite his occasional flashes of arrogance and disobedience, Rowan liked him. The other, sandy haired and freckle faced, was Caleb son of Dominic Lowen, Prince Jared's second-in-command.

'Do you treat all your lessons with such a lack of respect?' Nick demanded of them. His expression was severe, but Rowan knew that he was fond of them both.

Garsam stopped laughing immediately and straightened his back as if the criticism were a personal affront.

'If you are to remain in the King's household,' Nick insisted. 'I suggest you take matters such as this a little more seriously.'

'If this were a real fight we would be equal to the task.' Garsam responded with an upward tilt of his chin.

'Let us hope so.' Nick turned away to hide his amusement. He signalled to a servant who had been waiting at a distance and brought a tray of cups and a flagon of water.

Garsam took the first cup and handed it to the King. He glanced briefly at Nick as if to say, 'You see. I know my duties,' then took one for himself and drunk thirstily.

Queen Sybill had always complained that the court at Castle Baryk was too informal and that Edwell allowed his subjects to get too close, but Rowan liked it that way. When Nick had taken on the task of instructing him in unarmed combat, he had agreed eagerly to the idea that Tam and the younger boys, who also needed instruction, should train alongside him. He enjoyed their company.

Tam had been very reluctant to lay hands on his King but Rowan had convinced him that he would never learn to defend himself if no-one was prepared to attack him.

Rowan was determined that one day he would be a strong warrior like his father and older brother. He worked hard in these sessions with Nick and with the swordmaster and riding instructors. But there was so much else to think about. Apart from the increasingly embarrassing effect that women had on him there were the constant day to day matters of state that required his attention and the gentle yet tedious instruction that took hours of his time with the Chancellor.

Today he was required to attend a meeting in the council chamber with Lord John and the senior members of his household, to discuss the matter of great importance that had been interrupted when the attempt had been made on his life. By the time he had changed his clothes and eaten some fruit to restore his strength, there was no time to spare before he had to go to the council chamber. He sat in his place at head of the table staring mournfully out of the window, wishing he could be riding, hunting or swimming in the river.

Around the table sat the Chancellor, Prince Jared, Felix Runmore, and Robert Boderry. Nick was also in attendance as he always was but he sat quietly at the back of the room. Sir John waited until he had their complete attention then he addressed the King.

'You may be aware, Sire, that King Tynon has several daughters. Before your father's …er…demise, we had received word that…well let us say that overtures were made and the possibility of a marriage was discussed.'

Prince Jared frowned in surprise. 'And my father was considering this?'

'The Chancellor glared at him and his distaste for the Prince was all the more evident. 'It was one possibility, yes.'

When they had arrived at the castle, Lord John's dislike of Jared had taken Rowan by surprise. He knew now, the reasons for it and he understood, but his affection for his brother was undiminished by this knowledge. It was a shocking story and Jared had not covered himself in glory by his actions but it seemed he had been blinded by love.

He was now forced to pay a heavy price. The cost was written in his eyes whenever he let down his guard. Love. It was the biggest mystery of all.

'Sire?'

He realised suddenly that they were all awaiting his answer, but he had not heard the question.

'We were discussing the match with the Nostarian Princess.' Lord John prompted.

Rowan was confused. 'How could he take a new bride while he was still married to my mother?'

The Chancellor looked at him in surprise and Prince Jared's face broke into a magnificent smile.

Lord John explained patiently. 'The match was not for himself My Lord.'

'Then, I don't understand. To whom was this woman to be married?'

'To you, Sire.'

Rowan felt as if Tam had punched him in the stomach again. It was the same, surprised, almost humiliating feeling.

'What? I cannot be married. I am not yet fifteen years of age. The last thing I need is a wife.'

'That is not entirely true, Sire,' the Chancellor explained. 'It is essential that you marry. Now more than ever it is vital that we… we ensure the succession as soon as possible.'

'That of course is true.' Jared said, enjoying his brother's discomfort.

Rowan felt as if he were about to be sick. He knew that his cheeks were burning and that everyone could see him blush. He was only grateful that they did not know of the tingling in his loins. Blind panic had him wriggling frantically in his chair. He stood up but his legs felt weak and shaky 'But surely… surely that can wait?'

Lord John considered the matter. 'Well…maybe just a betrothal would be sufficient at this stage. I understand that the youngest girl is quite a beauty.'

'I don't care how beautiful she is,' Rowan muttered to himself. 'I'm not getting married.' He took a deep breath and willed a calm into his body. Slowly he sat down again.

'I understand your reluctance, Sire,' the Chancellor went on, 'But I feel it is the only option left to us. It may go some way to appeasing King Tynon and…'

Boderry was also red in the face but this was clearly brought on by anger.

'Appeasing him? But surely it is no less than a surrender.'

The King looked at him gratefully then turned to his Chancellor.

'Quite.'

'I wouldn't use exactly such a term.'

'No, but he's right though,' Rowan insisted. 'You want me to marry Tynon's daughter so that he will not invade. Instead you want me to invite him right here into the court.'

'This is the way marriages have always been arranged, Sire. We have no alternative. We cannot hope to fight him. Our armies are too badly depleted.'

'What about our allies. Our neighbour King Ranulph. He will understand that if Tynon wins Subia, he will not stop. He will want to expand his empire and they will surely be his next target.'

'Your knowledge in these matters does you credit, Sire,' Lord John said respectfully, no doubt hoping to placate him, 'but King Ranulph is just as ravaged by the Scorge as we. We could barely manage an army between us.'

Prince Jared drummed his fingers on the table. 'Maybe…maybe that is all we need. Rather than trying to defend against his constant incursions, we should attack. Make a show of strength. One strong capable fighting force. Enough to make a first strike. Let us push them further south and secure the high ground.'

'I agree.' … Boderry slammed a fist onto the table. 'I agree absolutely.'

Felix Runmore shook his silver head sadly. 'There is no possibility that we could raise an army large enough. We would have to conscript every man in the country. Maybe if King Edwell were still alive they would…'

'I am sick of this.' Rowan rose to his feet again.

Lord John held out a placatory hand. 'Of what, Sire?'

'I am sick of being told that because my father is dead, there is no hope for us. I love this country more than I love my own life and I will not see it fall into Tynon's hands.'

'They are proud words, Sire,' Runmore said, 'but we do not have the luxury of pride or…'

Rowan turned on him angrily. 'Why not? Why should I not be proud, Commander? Why should I not show the people of this country that I have faith in them. That I believe in them.' He turned to the Chancellor. 'They think of me as just a child don't they, Lord John?'

'They understand Sire that you are the son of a great king. They know that you are well advised and that one day you will take your father's place as…'

'But would they follow me to war?'

Once more, the old man thought very carefully before he replied. 'In due course Sire, you will have…'

'No. Not in due course. We do not have time for that. By then I will have no country left to defend. Would the people follow me now?'

Lord John looked wretched. He searched vainly for the right words.

Rowan went right up to him. He was only an inch or two shorter than his chancellor.

'Do not patronise me, Lord John. Give me an honest answer. Would they follow me now?'

The Chancellor sighed. 'I doubt they would, Sire.'

'Because I am just a child.'

He nodded. 'They do not have the faith in you that they had in your father. Not yet. Given time I am sure…'

'But I do not have time.'

'I fear not.'

'Then I will have to find some way to show them that I am a worthy king. I will have to prove myself.'

'They are brave words, Brother,' Prince Jared said sadly, 'but how do you propose to do that?'

'There is a way. There must be,' Rowan insisted, 'and I will find it.'

'In the meantime, Sire,' Lord John spoke tentatively, 'Will you give me leave to approach King Tynon on the matter of his daughter?'

'No, I will not.'

'But I…'

'No.'

The Chancellor sighed. 'Very well, Sire, I will not press the matter at present.'

Rowan felt sorry for his harsh words. He sighed. 'My coronation must take place within a month of my father's death is that not so?'

'Yes, Sire.'

'If I cannot find a way to prove my strength to the people by then. I will consider the matter, Lord John. Will that satisfy you?'

The Chancellor gave a little nod of his head. 'For the moment, Sire, I will say nothing more on the subject.'

Rowan breathed a sigh of relief. His speech had been rash and ill-considered but he did not regret it. Now he had to think and he could not do that within the miserable confines of the castle. He needed air.

'I am going for a walk,' he announced and turned away before the Chancellor could speak again.

***

Nick followed the King at a respectful distance, but close enough to protect him if the need arose. The pages followed him even further behind. Rowan turned suddenly and waved the boys away, but he beckoned to Nick to walk with him.

They left the council chamber and emerged through the hall onto the courtyard which was bustling with noise. Ladies and children seemed to be everywhere. They curtsied to Rowan and there was a huge amount of giggling. Matilda had told Nick that without even trying, the young King had already won many hearts. He was, it was commonly agreed, a very handsome young man even had he not been king.

It occurred to Nick that there were a lot of children considering the amount of adults who lived in the castle. When he mentioned this to Rowan, the King smiled with a weary resignation.

'They are my brothers and sisters.'

'What, all of them?'

'Not all, but most. In fact, in some cases, the question of their parentage is not always clear. I am the only one born in wedlock. Surely you have heard of my father's second favourite sport.' Rowan screwed up his nose in distaste. 'And you must understand now why my mother spends all her time on the island of Iorby? That is the thing about these marriages that kings must endure. They are merely business contracts. A king cannot marry the woman he loves.' He looked at Nick hesitantly. 'I do not… I do not pretend to know anything about love, Nick, but…but I believe it is a good feeling. It makes you happy.'

And the absence of it is a pain almost too awful to bear, Nick thought, though he did not say so.

'It does,' he agreed.

'Sometimes…' Frowning with the effort of explaining himself, Rowan waved a hand vaguely in the direction of the women. 'They make me feel… they… it is very powerful, but it does not make me happy.'

Nick felt sorry for the boy. He was under constant instruction in how to become a soldier, and how to become a king, but there was no-one to tell him how to become a man. He though fondly of his own father and of Dugon who between them with much gentle amusement had answered all his questions.

'It is desire that you feel, Sire.' Nick wondered how he had found himself in this position. He had never imagined having to explain such things to a king. 'It is natural to feel that way. Especially when you are so young.'

'But it is not love?'

'No. Not always. It is possible to feel a strong love for someone without desire. For a friend maybe or a brother. There are also many occasions when you will feel desire without love. It is only when the two are combined that… well that is the love that you describe. If it is returned then… then that will make you truly happy.'

'And that is how you feel for Catherine?'

Catherine who could be dead, or alive and in danger, or worse. How many ways had he imagined her in the last weeks while he did nothing to save her? How could he even begin to explain?

'Nick?'

'Yes, Sire. That is how I feel for Catherine.'

The King nodded, the frown still playing on his face as if he were trying to absorb all he had been told.

'So how do I …?' the question remained unasked, and Nick was grateful for that.

Instead, Rowan smiled as Sophia came towards them carrying a tiny sand coloured puppy.

'My Lord, will you look?' she said without pre-amble. 'Isn't he adorable?'

Rowan bent so that his head was on a level with hers.

'Yes, he is.'

'Lady Maud says I can keep him. I have called him Roc because that is the old word for king isn't it?'

'It is,' Rowan agreed, 'and it is a good name. Roc, you are to guard your mistress at all times. That is an order from another king.'

Sophia stroked the puppy's head. 'His fur is so soft. Have you ever felt anything so soft in your life?'

As Rowan put out a hand the puppy bent forward and bit it.

'Ouch.' He pulled his hand away, laughing.

Sophia was horrified. 'Oh Roc, you bad dog.' She put him down on the ground and slapped him hard on the rump. He yelped and ran away.

'No.' Rowan told her. 'Do not chastise him. He was doing as I commanded. He was protecting you.'

'But your hand is bleeding.'

He looked at it as if he had barely noticed. 'It is nothing.'

'Come,' she took his other hand and started to lead him away. 'My mother will know what to do.'

‘I have my own physicians,’ he told her though he was laughing. ‘Besides it is only a scratch.’ But he followed her anyway and Nick went with them.

The wound was more than just a scratch but Matilda assured her daughter that Rowan was not going to die. From a collection of leaves that she had obviously taken from the herb garden, she chose two and broke them into pieces, securing them to his hand with a strip of linen.

‘You are very brave,’ Sophia said adoringly. ‘It must hurt terribly.’

‘I am a king,’ Rowan said with mock arrogance. ‘I have been taught to overcome pain. It is my place to…’ he paused for a moment apparently lost in thought. ‘Nick,’ he said suddenly. ‘It must have hurt tremendously to be branded with the Circle of Fire.’

Nick nodded. ‘The pain, Sire, is unimaginable.’

‘How old were you when they branded you?’

‘Fifteen years, My Lord.’

‘I am younger than you were. I am not yet fifteen.’

‘Yes, Sire, but it is not necessary for you to …’

‘No it isn’t.’ Rowan interrupted, waving his damaged hand in the air so that Matilda had to retrieve it to finish tying the binding. ‘But don’t you see, it is the perfect way to show my people that I am as strong as my father.’

Nick was so taken aback that he did not speak.

Rowan smiled eagerly at him waiting for a response. When none was forthcoming he pressed the point. ‘Don’t you agree?’

‘I…I think it is a rather drastic way to avoid marriage, Sire.’

He was joking, but he could also see that the plan was not entirely without merit.

Rowan frowned, implying that he had no time for jokes.

‘Did you stand beneath its power Nick?’

‘It brought me to my knees,’ Nick admitted, ‘But not to my back.’

‘I will stand,’ Rowan announced, ‘And every man present will see that I am no weak child. You do believe that I can do it, don’t you Nick?’

Nick looked into the young man’s eyes and saw the fire that burned there.

‘You have a great strength of purpose and a noble heart,’ he said truthfully. ‘I believe that you can.’

Chapter 21

The branding of a new warrior into the Circle of Fire required the attendance of at least four existing members. Lord John had sent word to as many as possible but for some there was insufficient time to make the journey.

There were at that time nine members of the circle including Nick and Jacob Rine. Five of those remaining were present for the ceremony.

Rowan received each upon their arrival. They bowed to him and showed him every respect but he could see in their eyes that they thought him too young and too fragile to succeed. It made him all the more determined.

Because the warriors were part of a circle, there was no leader amongst them. They were all sworn to the King, but one member had to be spokesman. As the longest standing, this position now fell to Harmon Taligat of the Frontier Mountains. His people had lived within sight and within raiding distance of the Nostarian king, and recently had suffered more than their fair share of deaths.

Taligat had been overjoyed to hear that an attack was planned, and he had been on his way already to offer his advice.

The day of the ceremony was glorious and sunny, the sky an unbroken blue. Hundreds of people crowded into the courtyard outside the royal apartments. They stood around the gravel paths held back from the grass by soldiers. Some spectators were perched precariously on the castle walls or crammed into the windows of the armoury. It seemed that every man woman and child was there. Others beside were camped out way beneath in the fields and valleys. They would have heard nothing and seen even less.

From his position on a platform high on the castle mount, Rowan had a panoramic view of the green plateau and beyond the craggy grey of the mountains. Below the castle the river meandered along the valley, disdainful of the drama that was about to unfold. On its banks a flotilla of small boats were moored or floated at anchor in its deeper water. Their occupants gazed upwards, waiting for the sign that their king had fulfilled his destiny.

Behind the platform sat the members of the royal household but this was not a royal event. It was a meeting of the Circle of Fire, and it was these men who took foremost positions.

It was by intention, the most public of occasions. If he failed in this, Rowan knew, it would be a disaster. He had no choice but to succeed. The pain would be dreadful. He was prepared for that but he could not let it beat him. The fact that he was terrified was almost irrelevant.

He tried to take his mind away from the present; to think only of his love for Subia and for its people. He imagined the country victorious after the coming battle and prosperous once more in the peace that would follow but he was too aware of the reality only yards away.

The wood sat in a portable forge shaped like a massive iron goblet. It had been lit before his arrival and now a soldier poked it with a spear sending flames leaping upwards. The smell of burning applewood filled the air.

Rowan stood stripped to the waist. Symbolically he thought it right that he should bare himself to his people, but he was aware that he still had the body of a child and he felt very much alone and vulnerable.

In a loud, slightly accented voice, Harmon Taligat had explained the proceedings but it was not a ceremony that called for speeches. The branding it appeared spoke for itself.

Nick and two of the soldiers from the personal guard stood by the forge. One of the soldiers lifted the branding iron and rammed it deep into the fire. Another moved to hold the King's arm.

'No,' Rowan offered his arm to Nick. 'You do it.'

Nick took his hand in his right and with his left, supported the arm just below the elbow. Rowan could not hide the fact that he was shaking with fear, but he turned his face to Nick's and looked him straight in the eye. The profender of all people would understand. He had stood before this same forge and felt this same terror.

The time for words had passed but Nick showed his support with his eyes and in the firm grip of his hand.

Rowan turned back to the fire.

'Let it begin,' he commanded, willing his voice not to betray his fear.

The soldier held up the iron for inspection.

In the crowd a man shouted, 'How do we know it is truly hot?'

'Any man is welcome to test its strength.' Taligat announced.

No-one took up the challenge and with a nod, the spokesman indicated to the guardsmen to proceed.

The second soldier was wearing thick leather gloves to protect his hands. He took the iron and turned to Rowan.

'Are you ready My Lord?'

Rowan felt Nick's grip tighten and he nodded. The crowd fell silent, their anticipation evident. The soldier held the iron over Rowan's arm and he could feel the heat even before the metal began to burn his skin. Every living being took a deep breath and then there was silence once more. The pain was instantaneous and all consuming. Rowan fought the urge to scream and instead let out a fierce cry. The smell of his own flesh burning made him gag.

He felt himself failing. It was as if not just his arm but his whole body was burning. The iron was removed almost instantly but the pain did not ease. If anything the rush of air against his raw flesh was even worse. He staggered beneath it but he had promised to stand, and from somewhere he knew he had to find the strength. It took all his will to pull his arm from Nick's grasp and hold his fist high in the air. Once again he cried out but this time it was a battle cry. There was an answering roar from the crowd and it gave him the strength he needed. He had prepared a speech but his throat was dry and tight and the words would not come.

Angrily he gestured to the water butt.

A page filled a cup and brought it to him. With his damaged arm still held aloft he drank thirstily, the water dripping from his chin down his bare chest. Then he threw the cup on the floor and swept the crowd with his eyes.

'I am young. I appear like a weak and feeble boy. But I am your king. Few men have the strength to do what I have done.'

The crowd roared again and began to chant. 'Long live the King. Long live the King'. But when they saw that he had not finished they fell silent.

It was so much harder than he had ever imagined, and the pain was a hundred times worse, but he forced himself to go on.

‘Subia appears weak to our enemies, but we are not weak. We will fight like the men we are. I am your leader now. I have proved my right to your loyalty. And I will lead this country to victory and to a long and lasting peace. Together we will rebuild what has fallen.’

He caught Nick’s eye and saw his nod of approval but did not know how much longer his legs would carry him. Turning away he walked briskly towards the castle door and once inside, began to run towards his bedchamber.

There he collapsed onto the bed, jarring his arm and sending fresh needles of pain throughout his body.

Lord John had followed him and now, on stiff, elderly limbs, knelt at his side.

‘Did I do well?’ Rowan whispered.

The last thing he saw were the tears in the Chancellor’s eyes.

‘You did very well,’ he said softly. ‘The spirits of your father and your grandfather and all the great kings who went before, are looking down on you, Sire. And they are proud to call you their son.’

Rowan nodded slowly. And the ghost of a smile appeared on his lips before he drifted into unconsciousness.

***

It had rained the previous day and Catherine and the others had used every container they could find to hold the water. Now they had enough to last for maybe five or six days but there was no food.

All the coins had gone.

There were only three survivors now. Despite all their efforts Fara had declined steadily until she simply gave up on life. Even now, Catherine believed that she had willed herself to die.

Amazingly, despite all this, Barch had given them a tiny spark of hope.

He had given them news.

A new king now ruled in Castle Baryk. Rowan of the Jassoir had reached safety. That in itself made little difference to the last three inhabitants of Fastwater, but the implication was clear as a beacon on the distant hills. If Rowan had survived, then Nick was probably alive. And if Nick was alive he would find her. Of that she had no doubt. It was only a matter of whether she could survive long enough.

Chapter 22

The King slept for almost three days after his ordeal and although there were plenty of physicians he would permit no healers other than Matilda to attend upon him. At one stage she worried that he would never wake. Once he did, she wished he would sleep again because he was a terrible patient.

The wound was healing and the brand stood out impressively. Despite his bad temper he was very proud of it and inspected it hourly for signs of change.

Sophia, for whom he had an obvious and touching affection, tried her best to comfort him, but even her patience began to run out.

'Will you never stop complaining?' she asked one day when he had been particularly churlish.

'You can't imagine how much this hurts, Sophia?' he muttered angrily.

'I am a king,' she said haughtily, imitating the words he had spoken when the puppy bit his hand. 'I have been taught to overcome pain.'

The look he gave her was at first thunderous, then it softened and finally he smiled.

'Well, of course that is true.'

'Your behaviour is far from kingly,' she scolded. 'My mother and all your servants want only to help you and yet you shout at them and stamp your foot and behave like a child.'

Her chiding was not in vain. From then, his manners, if not his humour improved and to Matilda he even offered a few words of apology. Of course they forgave him. Everyone did.

He was forgiven because word of his bravery had spread rapidly through the kingdom. There was a new spirit in the people now; an optimism and a lust for battle. In the towns and villages, men signed up for the new army in droves. Many of the men Prince Jared had chosen presented themselves and were initiated into a special regiment. They could be seen every day in the fields around the castle hill, drilling and practicing until they had met the Prince's exacting standards.

In the castle itself, preparations began for the coronation. Performers began to arrive from across the country including Gomero and his troupe of acrobats and in the kitchens vast amounts of food were cooked and stored ready for the feast.

Some five days before the ceremony, Nick was on his way to the King's private chamber when he met Matilda watching the activity in the main courtyard. A stage had been set up on the grass, and around it chairs were being placed in a semi-circle for the King and his court to enjoy the entertainment.

'Two days of feasting,' Matilda said almost wistfully. 'And then what, War?'

'I fear so. Though it will take some weeks to prepare for battle.'

Nick had spent the last two weeks with Prince Jared hand picking men for the King's personal guard. Every serving man, washer woman and cook was subjected to rigorous scrutiny until it could be proved that they were entirely loyal. He had barely rested because there were few occasions when he had felt confident enough to leave his young master in someone else's care.

'He will know that we are coming, surely?'

'King Tynon? Yes. He will know. He has many spies among our rebel forces. Some of them will already have joined him, but our army in the South has even now moved into the mountains and they will keep him busy until the bulk of our forces arrive.'

'The King will go?'

'Yes. He must be seen to lead the army, though others will command in fact.'

'He is so young.'

'I will take good men to guard him. We will try to ensure that he is protected for as far as that is possible.'

'Take me with you.'

He was so surprised that he did not speak.

'Teach me to use a sword and I will fight at your side as well as any man.'

'Truly,' he agreed, 'I would as soon have you with me than many of the men here.'

'Then you will?'

'If it is within my power to do so.'

'Thank you.'

'I must go,' he said. 'The King is waiting for me.'

She walked with him towards the Royal Apartments.

'Have you spoken to Lord John about your parents?'

'No. I have not had a chance. I wonder sometimes if he is avoiding me. I seem to see him only when others are present.'

'He is a kind man, I have spoken to him a little. I think also that he is very lonely.'

‘Has he no family?’

‘Yes. But as you know he has recently lost his brother. He has a wife but she is seldom seen. I am told she suffers a deep melancholy borne of a broken heart. Their son was killed at Highvale. Apparently,’ she moved closer, dropping her voice, ‘there is a grandson. He lives in exile. I have heard…’

‘When was this? When was he exiled?’

‘I do not know. Some years ago. Why?’

‘Ann told me that the man who killed my parents had connections high up in the court. You don’t think that…?’

‘No. Will Garwin did nothing wrong. Not as far as I can tell. It is frightening though, don’t you think, that there may be a traitor in the court.’

‘Or it may just have been in Dugon’s imagination. The truth though, is that everyone here knows more about my past than I do. I will do as I intended. I will speak to Lord John.’

When the guards showed him into the King’s apartment, he found a small group of courtiers awaiting him, including Felix Runmore and Lord John. They looked at him strangely and he knew immediately that something was wrong.

***

Rowan was sitting on a smaller version of the state throne, which in turn stood on a raised dais beneath the window. He watched Nick come into the room and bow in front of him making the usual greeting.

‘Your servant, Sire.’

The Chancellor had offered to speak to him on the King’s behalf but Rowan knew that he had to do this himself. He smacked the chair’s huge wooden arms with the flat of his hands. He fiddled with the lions carved on its edges. He tapped the heels of his boots on the platform. He did everything, in fact, but look Nick in the eye.

'I have to speak to you, Nick,' he said stiffly, 'and it is… it is a difficult thing to say.'

Lord John cleared his throat. 'My Lord, would you prefer that I…?'

'No.' Rowan frowned, sighed, then finally looked up at his profender. 'I have word of Catherine.'

Nick clutched at the back of a chair and Rowan was almost distraught to see the hope in his eyes. 'She is safe?'

This was hard, harder than he had ever imagined.

'She is …alive.'

'But not safe. Where? Where is she?'

The hope died as quickly as it had come. Rowan felt his own voice becoming hoarse with emotion.

'They have taken her to a village in the marshlands.'

'Taken her? The rebels?'

'No. She was apparently rescued from her abductors but…it is… it is one of the four towns. The Scorge towns.'

It was almost as if a thousand ghostly arrows fell upon Nick forcing him to his knees.

'Catherine has the Scorge?'

Rowan got up from his chair as if to go and comfort him, then he sank back again and waved a hand helplessly.

'No. That is…not as far as I am aware. But she was travelling with one who was sick and that is where they were taken.'

'But if she does not have the Scorge they will release her, surely.'

The Chancellor spoke for him, his voice soft with compassion.

'It is not possible, I am sorry. No-one can be released until it is confirmed that the village has been free of Scorge for several weeks.'

Nick was still on his knees in the centre of the room. He bowed his head into his hands. Rowan wished that there was something he could do. He looked around frantically in the hope that someone would know what to say.

In the end it was Felix Runmore who went over to Nick and touched him gently on the shoulder.

'Come, come and sit down.'

Nick allowed himself to be helped to his feet but then he shook off the Commander's hands and looked squarely at Rowan.

'You can order her release?'

'I cannot,' Rowan shook his head. 'Believe me. If I could, I would. If she were held by some human enemy I would send an army to rescue her for you but I am powerless against the Scorge. I cannot allow it to take hold of Subia again. Neither can I be seen to make exceptions for my friends. I have, only now earned the respect of the people. Much as I feel for you I cannot afford to do such a thing.'

'Then I will go and get her.' Nick turned to leave.

'No.' Rowan shook his head again. 'It is too dangerous. I cannot let you sacrifice your life to the Scorge.'

Angrily Nick turned back. 'My life is worth nothing without Catherine.'

'It is to me. I cannot let you go, Nick.'

'You cannot stop me.'

Rowan was shocked at the force of Nick's anger but there was also a hint of desperation in his friend's words as if he knew they were not true. 'You don't understand,' he went on. 'How could you. You're only a…'

‘Do not forget where you are.’ Lord John rose to his feet, ‘and to whom you speak.’

Rowan shooed away his objections.

‘It is true, of course it is. I don’t know about love. But I do know that Subia faces one of the hardest battles in its history. I must lead an army against a far more powerful foe, and I know nothing of war either. I will need every loyal friend beside me. I need you, Nick. Subia needs you. I cannot allow you to go.’

‘You are sworn to the king’s service,’ Lord John insisted. ‘It is your duty to stay by his side.’

‘I have done everything you asked of me.’ Nick shouted, pointing his finger accusingly, not just at the Chancellor but at all of them. ‘I stood and watched while they took her away. I came here to serve you at the castle when I should have gone after her. I knew it was a mistake but I let you persuade me otherwise.’

He shook his head and came closer. The guards moved to intercept him but Rowan waved them away.

Nick went down onto his knees again and when he looked up there were tears in his eyes. ‘Please. I beg of you. As my friend. Let me go.’

Felix had followed Nick forward. Now he put a hand on the Profender’s shoulder and addressed himself to Rowan.

‘For pity’s sake, can we not let the man go?’

‘The answer is no, Commander,’ Rowan insisted. ‘and that is an end to it.’

He got up from his chair again and came to sit on the edge of the dais where his eyes were on a level with Nick’s. Every part of him ached to give the man what he wanted. He wished, in a way that he could take the pain on himself. Nick had called him friend and it hurt so much to see someone he loved suffer in this way.

For just a second he glanced up at the Chancellor but the old man shook his head.

Rowan addressed himself to Nick once more.

'Believe me when I say that I know how much I owe you, but I cannot let you go. I have left instructions that although you are to be treated with respect at all times, if you try to leave the castle on your own or without my permission, you will be arrested and held in the dungeons.'

Nick glowered at him through his tears and although Rowan knew he had no choice he felt that he had in some way betrayed their friendship.

'This is for your own good, Nick,' he insisted, 'and it is for the good of the country.'

Nick stood up again but the angry words that he was about to say seemed to stick in his throat.

'That is enough.' Lord John declared in a voice Rowan had never heard before. 'Our Lord King does as he is advised to do. He has no choice in this and he does not do so lightly. I would advise you not to speak rashly and in haste.'

Nick said nothing but he dropped his eyes and Rowan knew that he was acknowledging the truth of this.

Slowly he turned away, and aware that it was against all protocol to turn his back on the King, walked towards the door.

Lord John was about to call him back but Rowan waved a hand at him.

'No, Chancellor, leave him be. Have we not hurt him enough already.'

When Nick had gone, Rowan sat down again and stared miserably at his feet.

'You did the right thing, Sire,' Lord John said softly. 'You could not have acted otherwise.'

Rowan felt himself close to tears.

‘Go away,’ he shouted. ‘All of you. Get out. Just leave me alone.’

Chapter 23

'The messenger has arrived, Richard. I think you will be interested in his news.'

Richard Lassall was in the process of tearing the meat from a leg of mutton, which the innkeeper's wife had roasted slowly on a bed of rosemary. Hungrily his teeth dug into the succulent flesh while his tongue explored its delicious juices. He looked at the man who sat down across the table from him and his appetite was instantly quashed. Ralph Ludeck's face had never been pleasant but now the barely healed scar that ran from forehead to chin was crusted with dried blood and skin. Richard dropped the meat back on his plate and sat back in disgust.

'We may have another chance to exact our revenge on the bold Nicholas Trayer or should I say the recently elevated 'Lord' Trayer.' Ludeck pulled at his leather eyepatch revealing the mutilated flesh beneath. He rubbed a fist in it ferociously and a shower of dead skin fell on to the table.

'Must you do that?' Lassall took a gulp of wine to quell his nausea.

Ludeck let the patch fall back into place. 'It itches like the blazes. When I get my hands on that woman again I'll…'

Lassall sighed irritably. 'Just get on with it. There is no point wishing for things which will never happen.

'Well, in that you are wrong.' With a rye smile, Ludeck reached across and tore a piece of mutton from the plate, then chewed it thoughtfully keeping his companion waiting. Lassall stood up and thumped the table.

'Tell me!'

'It seems that young Catherine has had the misfortune to find herself in one of the Four towns. Our instructions are to go there and hold her hostage until Trayer comes to get her. To be honest, I still don't know why you let her go the first time.'

'I did not know who she was. I've already told you that. I thought she was the wife of a poor sentorman.'

Ludeck's smile broadened into a grin and the scar on his cheek gaped revealing the barely healed flesh beneath. 'Well he is poor and apparently she is not yet his wife. It seems that you disturbed them on their wedding day. I'm surprised you didn't recognise the name. If I had spent ten years in prison I would remember the name of the family that put me there.'

Of course he remembered it. The name of Trayer had haunted him throughout the many long years of his imprisonment. No member of the Valeron family would rest while a Trayer still lived. But Richard had not known when he followed the Prince into the poor squalid little village, whose manor this was. In fact now that he came to think of it, the steward went to great lengths not to tell him. He should have realised that something was wrong.

'I was too distracted to notice at the time. I had already lost the Prince. As did you my friend. We have neither of us covered ourselves in glory over this.'

'Nick Trayer has made fools of both of us.' Ludeck helped himself to a glass of his companion's wine. 'But this time we will have him. Apparently he is besotted with the girl. When he finds out where she is he will move heaven and earth to rescue her.'

Richard saw in his mind Catherine's gentle beauty and could understand why that would be so. He berated himself again for letting her go. Turning to the window so that he would no longer have to look at the other's face, he asked, 'Do they want him killed this time or kept alive? I am hardly able to keep up.'

'Alive.' Ludeck said, disappointment evident in his voice. 'Apparently they feel he may be of use to them. A bargaining tool perhaps. Though they will kill him eventually.'

Richard sighed and shook his head. He too was disappointed. 'Do we know that he knows where she is? Can we be sure that he is coming?'

'Yes. It has all been arranged. He will come. And what is more.' Ludeck raised his glass triumphantly. 'Jacob Rine's whore is with him.'

Lassall was not interested in his comrade's private vendetta.

'How far is this place?'

'It is called Fastwater. A disused port on the Haavel river, no more than a day's journey. We should arrive some hours before them. In that we are fortunate.'

'Oh fortunate. Yes. I risk my life and my liberty for my family. Always I dream that one day I will be rewarded with a place at a Valeron court. Yet now, I must consider myself fortunate enough to spend my last days dying of The Scorge with you.'

Ludeck ignored the insult. 'I am told that there is every chance that The Scorge is spent. If not, we do not have to enter the town. We can merely keep watch for him outside.'

Lassall nodded slowly. 'Yes. That would seem to be a sensible move.'

Ludeck went on, reading from the scroll that the Uncle had sent. 'The place is guarded by a man called Barch and his brother Amos. They are paid by the King to stop the sick from leaving, but they are also supposed to distribute food and water which is sent on a regular basis. As you can imagine, friend Barch has never let a crumb into the town. He sells it all and has made himself rich. We should not have any trouble with him.'

'We?'

'I need to redeem my reputation as much as you, Richard.'

The two men had been friends from childhood. Ludeck's family, in a similar situation to the Lassalls had worked for the Valeron cause even while they paid lip service to the usurper's regime.

When Ludeck had been carried into the yard on the back of a horse like a sack of meat, he had been barely alive. His face had been sliced in two and the wound in his back was so deep that he was lucky to have kept his head. Lassall wondered if he was so lucky. Maybe it would have been better if Ludeck had died than spend the rest of his life as a mutilated freak.

He felt momentarily sorry for the man. To add insult to injury, his wounds had been inflicted by a woman. It was hardly an honourable position.

'What shall I tell the messenger?' Ludeck said now, rising to his feet. Since his injuries, he had walked with something of a hunched back.

Richard turned back from the window and watched him limp to the door. 'Are you sure you are up to this, Ralph? Have you even tried to ride a horse yet?'

'Believe me,' Ludeck's good eye burned with hatred. 'A little pain will not keep me from my revenge. Mistress Matilda will rue the day she raised a hand against me.'

'Very well,' Lassall nodded. 'Tell the messenger we will leave within the hour.'

When the other man had gone, he returned to his meal blotting out the image of Ludeck's suppurating face. He thought instead of Catherine. He might not be allowed to kill her lover, but he would take her for himself, and make Trayer suffer with the knowledge of that. The thought settled his stomach and heightened his senses so that when he bit in to the meat once more it tasted better than ever.

***

Twice, Nick had tried to leave the castle, and twice, he had been discovered and with the greatest courtesy, escorted back. Wherever he went he was aware of the guards following. They kept a distance and were polite to him but they never left him. Only in his chamber was he left alone, and even then he knew they were waiting just outside the door. Already he had looked to see if the windows allowed him escape but though they were wide enough, there was a sheer drop down the side of the hill.

There had to be something he could do.

The guards were loyal to the King and not open to bribery. He knew that. He and Jared had chosen each one of them for that very reason. Besides, he had nothing of value to offer. Although… Suddenly it occurred to him that he did have something. It was a high price indeed but for Catherine he would have given his very life.

With the spring of hope beginning to rise in his heart, he flung open the door and strode down the stone corridor and out onto the courtyard. The guards followed, but if he succeeded in this it would not matter. They would not be able to stop him.

On the newly erected stage the acrobats were rehearsing. Gomero waved to him as he passed and he felt sufficiently cheered to raise a hand in greeting.

He found Prince Jared in the armoury.

'Nick,' the Prince came towards him his handsome features creased in a sympathetic frown. 'I am pleased to see you and…'

'If you still want my horse, he is yours,' Nick said without preamble.

'Of course I do, but…' Understanding dawned on Jared's face. 'No, Nick, no. I know what you want of me but I cannot help you.'

'Not even for Ransom?'

The Prince gave an agonised look. 'You know that I cannot.'

'You should have let me go when we were in Claveham. I may have been able to find her before it came to this.'

'Most probably you would have searched in vain, or died in the attempt.'

'It would have been preferable to this.'

'I would help you if I could and I would not demand such a price to do so. But this is not the way.'

'What would you do?' Nick said the words as a challenge. 'Would you stand by and let her die if she had been the woman you loved.'

The Prince's expression darkened and he glared at Nick angrily. 'I…' it was as if he were about to say something but the words died on his lips. He breathed out heavily then shook his head and the darkness passed.

'Please,' Nick had not intended to resort to begging but he was too desperate for pride. 'You are my only hope.'

Still the Prince did not speak. He looked at Nick with sympathy this time, then he grasped him by the shoulder.

'There is always hope, My Friend.'

Chapter 24

The coronation of the new King had been a long and tedious ceremony. Matilda had been ashamed to find herself yawning. It was equally embarrassing as she had a place of honour close to the front. Even now, she found it strange to be included in the inner circle of the King's friends. She realised though that for all Rowan's undoubted bravery he must feel very much alone. For the previous year he had lived a quiet existence at his mother's court. Then the sudden and unexpected death of his father had resulted in his hurried return and there were few at Castle Baryk that he could truly call friend.

Now that the solemnities were over, he appeared much happier. To watch the entertainment he was seated on a gold throne with the rest of the court in a semi-circle around him. He was laughing uncontrollably as on the stage, a fool danced about performing outrageous antics. Matilda smiled. It was good to see him enjoying himself, the heavy mantle of his kingship for the moment forgotten.

There was a mighty guffaw from Rowan's other side and Matilda watched Prince Jared share a joke with the men behind him. The Prince looked magnificent in his state robes, not as magnificent as he did in his armour but… she pulled herself up with a start, shocked at the thought. She looked away instantly feeling a flush come to her face and a pang of guilt that she could think such a thing of a man other than Jacob, especially having heard the rumours about him.

On Matilda's left, Nick sat with his legs crossed in front of him barely watching, a picture of misery. His usually boyish face was drawn into a dark, brooding expression.

When all his attempts to escape from the castle had failed, he had taken himself to his bedchamber and remained there for three days refusing to see anyone. Matilda had decided to leave him to himself, knowing that nothing she could say would be able to help him. Also, she admitted, she could not bear to see his despair when she herself was so close to that same pain.

However, on the day before the coronation, Tam had called on her in desperation.

'He was at first in a frenzy of anger, My Lady. Now he does nothing. Neither eats nor drinks nor even speaks. I do not know what to do for him.'

She had finally found the courage to confront him. The guards were happy to let her through and she entered unannounced into his bedchamber. The room was shuttered and dark, an unpleasant mustiness testifying to the fact that it had been that way for days.

The curtains surrounding the bed were also closed. She shook her head at the unseen figure inside but did not disturb him. Not yet.

The signs were everywhere that his frustration had manifested itself in a fit of violence. One of the chairs was damaged, the wood splintered as if it had been kicked. A wall hanging had been partially ripped from its fixing, the figure embroidered on it, a maiden carrying a milk pail, hung at a drunken angle.

As Matilda approached the window she saw a tray of food standing on the window seat. He had eaten nothing that she could see but the wineglass was empty. A trail of wine stained the cushions where the cup had evidently been upset. It was damp to the touch.

She pushed open the shutters and the sunlight streamed in, together with a welcome blast of fresh air.

From behind the bed hangings came an angry tirade. Not knowing what to expect, she went across and pulled the drapes aside. She found him face down on top of the bed, still fully dressed. At first she thought that he was drunk, but as he turned to glare at her his expression showed nothing more intoxicating than rage.

'Go away Matilda,' he growled. 'I do not want your sympathy.'

'No. I can see that you already have enough for yourself.'

If it was possible for his face to darken further, it did so now.

'And what is that supposed to mean?'

'It means that you lie here indulging yourself in self pity when you should be at your duties. The King has need of you.'

He sat suddenly and she took a step back thinking that he would strike out at her, but he merely got to his feet and began to pace across the room.

'Don't speak to me of my duty. I hear of nothing else.'

She realised that for all his rage, she had nothing to fear from him. With a sigh she approached him. He tried to push her away but she held on to both his arms, forcing him to be still.

'Come. Sit with me and let us talk.'

At first he resisted then with a defeated sigh, let her lead him to a chair where he sat down heavily head in hands. Matilda retrieved the upturned goblet and poured some more wine from the jug.

'Here. Drink. Tam tells me you have taken nothing. He is worried about you.'

Still he did not speak, but he took the goblet and drank from it slowly. She laid a hand on his shoulder.

'You know, if it is true that the Scorge has all but gone, it may not be long before she is released.'

'Or she may die,' he replied coldly. 'She may die wondering why I did not come to find her. She may die knowing that I let them take her. That I did nothing to prevent it.'

She shook her head. 'You did what you had to do. You could not have done otherwise. She will know that and she will be proud of you.'

'I did my duty.' He almost spat the word. 'There it is again. How weary I am of hearing about it.'

'You are an honourable man. That is why she loves you.'

'You cannot know that.'

'I know.' She looked earnestly into his eyes. 'I am a woman, too.'

Briefly he glared defiantly at her, then his whole body seemed to soften. When he spoke, it was no more than a whisper.

'Can she survive?'

She knew better than to offer him platitudes. 'There are always some who escape it, and some who are afflicted, but survive. I cannot say to you that she will be one of those, only that she may.'

'I am assured that there is always hope,' he said bitterly.

'I would believe so.' She bit her lip.

He peered at her through reddened eyes. ‘I am sorry. I had forgotten. You also wait for news. I know I am not the only one who suffers.’

‘No, but it seems you are the only one who wallows in it.’ Immediately she regretted the words. ‘Now it is I who am sorry. That was cruel. It’s just that I cannot bear to see you like this. It is not worthy of you.’

‘Worthy.’ He shook his head miserably. ‘In… in the dark years after my parents died, when I was eating myself up with grief, she still had faith in me. She was the one good thing in my life and you cannot know how much I loved her. How much I still love her. How worthy is it of me to desert her?’

‘You did not desert her.’ She knelt beside him, taking his hands in hers but there was nothing more she could think of to say.

‘What would you have me do, Matilda?’ he asked eventually. ‘What… what would you do?’

‘I would do everything in my power to find Catherine, just as you have, but for the moment there is nothing more you can do for her.’ She paused. ‘The King needs you also. He is just a boy and he has such a burden of responsibility. It cannot have been easy for him to refuse you.’

‘I realise that,’ he admitted. ‘I do not feel proud of the way I acted and I will always be his man but this is a cruel choice to make.’

‘It is. I understand that. But you must see that he, also, is a prisoner of duty and now he believes that he has forfeited your friendship. You must attend the ceremony Nick. You must stand at his side and show him that as well as your loyalty he also has your love. It will not be easy but it will mean so much. In the meantime, if I can find some way to help you get Catherine back, I will.’

She was relieved that he had taken her advice, though her heart ached to see him this way.

It was a strange thing, she had noted, that Nick's pain seemed to make him surprisingly attractive to the women. Although he had been at court for only a few weeks, he had already made an impression. Some of the older ladies remembered his previous time here and the younger ones had heard the stories of his bravery and the tragedy that had struck at his family. She knew that they found his fresh faced good looks pleasing. There was a simplicity about him. Not in the sense that he was slow witted, but his life revolved around his farm and the changing of the seasons, rather than that of ambition and intrigue for which court life was renowned. She suspected that a few of the ladies secretly hoped that he would not find Catherine. They questioned Matilda continually about him and some even teased her that she harboured hopes of him herself.

She realised that of course she had grown to love him but it was a gentle, affectionate love, rather of the kind one would feel for a brother. Despite his boyish charm and what she thought of as his nobility of soul, he did not excite her. Prince Jared, on the other hand…

Abruptly the performance came to an end and she shook herself out of these thoughts once more. The fool left the stage to thunderous applause and whistles of appreciation from the audience. In his place the young acrobats arrived. To the accompaniment of a lutist they began to dance. The boy stood with his legs apart and lifted his sister high into the air so that she appeared to be flying.

Matilda sneaked a glance to her left once more. She caught her breath. He was truly beautiful this prince and what surely was the harm in looking. As the performance progressed she noticed that he was staring at the stage in rapt attention. She heard him muttering under his breath and caught the word, 'exquisite'. His eyes followed every movement of the young acrobat as she now stood high in the air on her brother's shoulders.

Nick must have heard him because he glanced up briefly.

'The Prince appears to be quite taken with the acrobats,' Matilda said trying to sound as if it were of no matter.

Nick looked from one to the other and the hint of a smile appeared on his face. 'So it would seem,' he said, before retreating once more into his dark reverie.

Matilda could almost feel his pain. The thought concentrated her mind and she forced herself to watch the rest of the dance and think only of Jacob.

When the entertainment was over, the celebrations moved into the assembly hall where food had been set up on long tables and the minstrels took their places in the gallery ready to play for the dancing.

'I am going to my bed now,' Nick told Matilda. 'I cannot stay any longer and listen to all this gaiety.'

'I understand.' She rested a hand on his arm. 'You have eased our young king's burden Nick. You know that, don't you? It was a noble thing to do.'

He sighed and she let him go, knowing that despite everything, he was still in a dark place where no amount of reason would reach. There must be some way she could think of to help him and she would do so gladly but she could think of nothing. In the meantime there was a feast to attend, and the vague possibility of a dance with a prince.

For a few brief seconds she allowed herself to indulge in a fantasy, which brought a deep flush to her cheeks.

'My Lady Matilda.'

She jumped guiltily, then turned to see the gentle face of Felix Runmore smiling at her. 'I did not mean to startle you forgive me. May I speak with you in private?'

***

Nick could hear the sounds of the merrymaking through the window of his room. As the King and his court danced in the assembly hall way beneath, the common people had their own party out on the meadows and on the river bank.

The sound was there but it did not touch him as he sat in his apartment nursing his depression. Tam had brought a meal for him but he had no appetite and the food sat untouched as before.

When there was a banging on the door he ignored it, not wanting any company. The banging persisted and still he did not respond. Eventually the door was opened anyway and Prince Jared stood in the doorway carrying an enormous flask of wine.

'I am not in the mood for company,' Nick told him. 'Go back to the feast.'

'I have brought some wine.' The Prince grinned, closing the door behind him as if Nick had not spoken. 'You must tell me if you like it. It was made in my father's own vineyards away to the east, which would be enough to make it fine, but this is the best vintage they have ever made. I felt it would be appropriate for you and I to sample a flask tonight.'

'Do not waste it on me. I would not appreciate it.'

The Prince took two cups from the tray and poured a measure into each. He sat in a chair next to Nick and passed the cup to him.

'I know the pain that you feel, my friend. I have felt that pain. The company of an old friend may not replace the soft touch of a lover, but it may help. I understand your loneliness, believe me.'

Nick held the cup and inspected the contents. It was evident that the Prince intended to stay whatever he said. Despite himself, somewhere deep inside he was almost grateful.

'To loneliness,' he said and drained it in one go. It was delicious.

'To loneliness.' The Prince drank his more slowly then poured them both another. 'For tonight, we have each other, we have the finest wine anywhere in Subia, possibly the world, and you, my friend still have your horse.'

Not only was the wine good, it was strong. Nick could feel the warmth of it spreading through his belly. He held up the cup again. 'To Ransom.'

'To Ransom,' the Prince agreed. 'May he live long and sire many offspring.'

Once more, the wine spread through Nick's body calming him. For some time they sat without speaking, drinking steadily until he could feel a welcome numbness take hold of him.

Outside, the sound of celebration made a noisy contrast to the silence of the two men. A woman giggled then shrieked with laughter. Then a voice slurred drunkenly. 'Long live the King.'

'To the King.' Nick held up his cup.

'To the King, indeed.' Jared nodded sagely. 'May he also live long and sire many offspring.' He poured them both another. 'I'm sure he will. Already the young women of the court are swooning over him.'

Nick looked across at his friend's handsome face. The Prince's eyes were half closed as he sipped the wine pensively, gazing at something, or someone that Nick could not see. What did Jared mean, he wondered, when he said that he understood the loneliness. Though Nick was curious, he could not bring himself to ask. Instead, he said.

'You do love your brother.'

'I do.'

'Do you not wish that the circumstances of your birth were otherwise and that you could be king?'

For a long time, Jared stared into his wine. Eventually he said simply. 'No.' He looked up, turning sad eyes upon Nick. 'I am not the stuff that king's are made of. I am a warrior, a good leader of men, but not a king.' With a flourish, he downed the cup of wine and poured yet another.

'What shall we drink to now?'

'To love,' Nick said. The numbing effect of the wine was not unwelcome and he could feel his eyelids growing heavy.

'Love is too painful,' Jared said, his expression serious for a few seconds, then he grinned again. 'We are straying too close to the pain. I came here to offer you diversion. Not to remind you of your loss.'

Nick shook his head. The wine had done what it was intended to do. His eyes were beginning to close. He smiled gratefully at the Prince and very soon he was snoring in his chair.

Chapter 25

When Nick awoke later that evening, the Prince had gone and his only companion was an insistent thumping pain in his head. The wine had left him feeling groggy, so that it was a while before he noticed the smell of burning and the sound of shouting from the corridor outside.

Stiffly he got out of the chair, went to open the door, and was immediately aware that the guards were not at their posts. The smell of burning was stronger now and looking down the corridor he could see why. The wall hangings were on fire in front of the door to the garden. His guards were helping the servants to dowse them with pails of water.

He had only just registered this fact when Matilda appeared at his side, grabbed his arm and led him in the opposite direction.

'Hurry. We don't have much time.'

'But the fire…?'

'It is nothing. More smoke than flame. Come. I will answer all your questions when we are safely away.'

They were not challenged as they came out of the royal apartments and crossed the courtyard which was darkened now, though there were still people about. From the direction of the assembly hall, Nick could hear music and loud, drunken singing. The smell of roasting meat reminded him that he had barely eaten in days.

Matilda led him past the armoury and down through the village to the outer walls. As they passed the inn the sound of merry-making filled the air, but the streets were empty. So, Nick saw with surprise, were the gate towers.

'Where are the sentries?'

Despite everything, he was horrified that the security of the castle had been compromised.

'We have only minutes,' Matilda insisted, pulling on his arm once more. 'They will be back.'

He followed her down the stone staircase into the bowels of the castle hill and to the lower door which led out into the moat. In the winter, swelled by the rains, the water would be deep enough to accommodate small boats which loaded and unloaded cargoes through this door. Now that summer had come, the door was kept locked and bolted and there was no need for a guard. Today it was open and no-one was there to stop them stepping out into the now shallow water.

Nick wondered if he was dreaming. Had his overindulgence earlier in the evening, and the lack of food made him imagine things which were not there? But when his feet splashed into the moat and the foul water began to seep in over his boots, he knew it was real enough.

There was just sufficient moonlight to guide them across. Matilda had hitched up her skirt and if she was sickened by the feel of the filthy water against her skin she did not show it. As they scrambled up onto the opposite bank she pointed ahead to the tiny clump of trees known as Harigan's Wood. It was the best part of half a mile from the castle.

'We must get to the wood on foot,' she called breathlessly. 'And pray that we are not seen.'

Nick did not stop to question as he followed her across the dry scrub of the plateau. He could barely keep up with her pace. His tired body protested, dragging the extra weight of the moat water, but he ignored the pain and thought only of escape and Catherine.

To some extent their prayers were answered as the moon disappeared behind a bank of clouds. There was no way of knowing how long it would remain there. It meant that although they would not be seen from the castle, they were running blind and had to trust their instincts that they were headed in the right direction.

Finally, just as he thought that he could run no further, Nick found himself in the cover of the trees and he allowed himself to fall on his knees and regain his breath. There was no light at all in the wood but he could hear voices, and the unmistakable sound of horses. Something wet touched his face and nuzzled against his neck and he held on to the bridle and let Ransom pull him to his feet.

The weak light of a lantern appeared gradually in front of him as did the figure of Tam, his young servant. Apart from Ransom, the boy had brought two other horses. He also had Nick's sword and dagger. The horses were laden though what they carried he could not see.

'We cannot afford to rest long,' Matilda said. 'This wood will only shield us for a short time then we must cross the open plateau. If we do not reach the mountains by dawn we will be seen.'

'They will guess where we are headed, surely,' Nick fastened the sword around his waist and secured the dagger to his belt.'

'Not until they have first searched the castle. The guards will be back at their posts. No-one will imagine that you have escaped. As long as the sentries do not see us we will have a good start on them. Here, you must drink this and eat something.'

'My stomach is truly empty,' he said and took a gulp from the flask she offered him. The cold liquid tasted foul and bitter.

'What the devil is this?'

'Drink it,' she insisted. 'It is a tisane of rosehip and raspberry to settle your stomach, and feverfew for your head.'

He looked at her suspiciously but did as she asked.

The bread and apples that she gave him were far more welcome.

'You will have to eat those as we ride,' she said. 'We must leave right away.'

'No.' He shook his head, placing his hand gently on her arm. 'I must go alone. I thank you both for your help. Believe me I will always be grateful to you but I cannot let you risk your lives for me.'

'We do not have the time to argue about this.' Matilda mounted her horse in one easy movement. 'I am coming with you. Tam must make his own decision.'

'I will come too, My Lord,' the boy said solemnly. 'I am sworn to your service and my place is by your side. You saved my life.' He glanced briefly at Matilda, as if he had still not forgiven her. 'And you have always been good to me. I will come with you.'

Nick knew that he and Ransom alone would make better time but he had no idea what awaited him, and it may well be sensible to have companions to watch his back. He nodded his thanks and climbed painfully onto Ransom's saddle.

It was difficult to eat on the gallop. At first his stomach though empty felt uneasy but soon Matilda's potion began to ease the queasiness and also the banging in his head and he could feel his strength returning. They rode throughout the night and by the time the first few fingers of light began to claw at the sky they were well inside the shelter of the mountain forests.

They found a clearing next to a small brook where they let the horses drink. Nick washed his face and neck in the clear cool water and stretched his stiff limbs then he took off his boots and washed away the foul moat water, letting the warm sun dry his clothes. He watched Matilda as she took two flasks from her saddle bags and filled them from the brook.

'This water is the cleanest I have seen anywhere,' she said smiling. 'We will have need of it I'm sure. Drink your fill now, and I will save these for another day.'

Nick shook his head in wonder. 'I have known from the start that you were a resourceful woman. It does not surprise me that you would bring empty flasks in case we found fresh water or that you would think to make a potion for my head. It does not even surprise me that you can run as fast as I. But even you could not stand down the guard. How was it done?'

'Come.' She sat on the ground with her back leaning against a tree. 'Rest awhile and I will tell you all.'

***

When Felix Runmore had spoken to her at the party, Matilda had not known what to expect. He had never so much as acknowledged her before. Now he led her to the wood panelled council chamber.

'Please.' He beckoned her to a seat then sat himself at a respectful distance. He leaned towards her, lowering his voice.

'Nick Trayer is your friend, is he not?'

'He is, yes?'

She sat back, eyeing the Commander suspiciously, wondering what this was about.

'And if you could help him to find his Catherine, you would?'

'If I could. But…the King has forbidden Nick to leave the castle.'

'Indeed and I find it hard to understand how he could be so unfeeling to a friend. One who has sacrificed so much for him already.'

She wondered if she was being tested. 'I do understand,' she said carefully. 'I'm sure it was a difficult decision, but if I were king I would probably do the same.' She sighed. 'I am not though, and if it is within my power to help Nick, I will. If you are testing my loyalty to the King, Commander, then I will say now, I am loyal. But my loyalty in this is to Nick. If that means that you will have to arrest me then…' She shrugged.

'No. no.' The Commander held up a hand to reassure her. 'I am not here to test you. I agree with you. I would like to help.'

'You would? Why?'

He shook his head sadly. 'I am not without compassion, Mistress Matilda. I feel it is cruel after all Nick has done for the King, to keep him from following his heart. Also…' He hesitated and she felt that now they were coming to the real truth. 'Ten years ago when Gideon Trayer and his family left the castle after the branding ceremony I refused them an escort. I had been led to believe that the hills were free of bandits and that they would not be molested. They had four of their own men and I thought that would be enough. I was wrong, and I have never forgiven myself for that. This is my chance to make amends.'

‘They were not killed by bandits though were they?’ She watched his reaction carefully. ‘They were murdered. By someone with connections at court. Someone who would have killed Nick also, if he had not been hidden.’

Not a muscle in his face moved as he nodded his head slowly. ‘That is true. But even so. Had I permitted the Trayers an escort, it would not have happened. The guilt is all mine.’

‘I was not entirely happy to believe him,’ she said now to Nick, ‘but in the end it was a way out. I cannot see why he would help you if it were not the truth. We formulated this plan. I arranged the fire as a distraction, and your personal guards assumed that you would sleep all night especially as you had been sampling the Prince’s wine. Felix managed to stand down the outer guard for a few minutes so that we could get past.’

‘Felix?’ Nick shook his head incredulously. ‘I too am suspicious. Though in truth he did speak his support for me earlier. Well, whatever his intentions, we are free and I am grateful for that.’

She nodded, placed her folded cloak behind her head and closed her eyes. ‘Yes, and let us also pray that we are in time and that all of this has not been in vain.’

Chapter 26

Lassall was right in his guess that Ralph would have trouble riding a horse. The injured man sat with a lopsided tilt that seemed about to unseat him at any moment. Nevertheless he clung on manfully and if he was in any great pain he did not show it.

Shortly before dawn they reached their destination. A small walled port on the river. A smell of decay became more pungent as they approached the town and by the time they reached its gates, it was almost overpowering.

The men who had been paid to guard Fastwater's inhabitants had built a makeshift fort outside the walls. As Lassall and the band of mercenaries approached, a fat bald man came out of the strange edifice. From his description, it could only have been Barch.

'What do you want?' The man growled, signalling for someone to join him from inside. His companion was as thin as Barch was fat and much younger. His dark hair hung in greasy strands around his pock marked face.

'We are looking for someone.' Ludeck got off his horse with some difficulty, but also with some relief. 'We believe this person may be incarcerated in the town.'

‘You’re welcome to look,’ the custodian said dismissively, ‘but no-one who goes through those gates comes out again. Besides, you’d probably be wasting your time. I doubt there’s anyone left alive in there. We’ve ‘eard nothing for days and not much before that. ‘eh Amos?’

The younger man grinned. ‘Nah not a word. Quiet as the grave.’ He giggled at his own joke.

‘And yet you still take the King’s money to guard them.’

Barch bristled indignantly. ‘We’ve not been told to stand down,’ he declared without fear or shame. ‘There may be others to come yet.’

Richard sighed with impatience and dismounted with far more ease than his companion.

‘This is what you are going to do,’ he told Barch. ‘You will go into the town and find anyone who is still alive. You will bring them to me. The bodies you will take away, so that my men and I do not have to look on them. We are taking this town. I have no choice but to stay in this stinking hell hole, but I do not intend to billet myself amongst the dead.’

‘By what authority do you take this town?’ Barch challenged.

Ludeck drew his sword and held it beneath the man’s chin.

‘This is all the authority we need.’

‘Maybe I would prefer to die on the end of your sword than writhing in agony from the Scorge.’

Lassall could barely hide his disdain. ‘Or maybe a purse of gold will ease your suffering.’

He was gratified to see that greed would succeed where threats did not.

‘Let me see this gold.’

He took the pouch from beneath his shirt and opened it to reveal the gold coins it contained. Then he threw it at the man who caught it eagerly.

Ludeck began to protest but Lassall silenced him with a withering look.

'You make sure that I see anyone who is left alive, and when you return there will be a second purse just like this for you.

Barch nodded curtly then thumping his brother on the back belted him towards the gates.

When they had gone, Ludeck turned to his companion. 'We do not have another purse. Neither can we spare that one. What are you doing, Richard?'

Lassall shook his head and gave a humourless smile. 'Do not fret, my friend. When they return we will relieve them of the gold and of their miserable lives.

***

Catherine lay on her pallet in the kitchen of the inn. This morning Tally had died and now only she and Jostin were left. There was nothing more she could do for him and she did not even have the energy to fight for her own life. From time to time she drifted into sleep and always she thought of Nick and prayed that he still lived.

The voices when they came might have been her imagination or they might have been real, she could no longer distinguish between the two.

'This one is weak but he's still alive,' Amos said.

There was a long pause. Then the voice that she recognised as Barch replied. 'The thing is… we don't really want him whinging to anyone about the food and such and what we been doing. T'would be better if there were none left. What say you, we help him on his way?'

The other voice was hesitant. ‘Oh I don’t know Barch. Leaving ‘em to die is one thing but…’

There was a dull thumping sound and a whimper and then silence.

‘There you are. That wasn’t too difficult was it?’ Barch said eventually. ‘I probably did him a favour. His woulda been a miserable death.’ His voice grew louder. Now it seemed to be somewhere above her. ‘Here’s your lady, Amos. The one who came the last. The one who was sure her husband would come for her. Strange how they always think that. No-one ever does come.’

‘I would if she were mine,’ Amos said. ‘She is so pretty.’ A hand stroked her hair but she did not have the energy to shake it off. ‘Maybe that’s him outside.’

‘I hardly think so. He’s not the type that women like her fall in love with.’

‘You’re not gonna finish this one off are you Barch? Even you couldn’t harm something as lovely as this.’

‘Nah. Just take her down with the others. He won’t look for her there and even if he does, he’ll be too late. She’ll not live to see another dawn.’

She felt herself being lifted and carried then some time later, Amos spoke close to her ear. ‘I’ll leave you where he can find you just in case it is him. Maybe you’ll get a decent burial at least. It’s all I can do for you now.’

When she woke again she was alone. The smell which she had thought she’d learned to live with was even worse and she knew she was lying among the bodies. The buzzing of the flies and the scuttling of rats seemed just a distant blur and she was too weak to mind.

It seemed to her that she opened her eyes and smiled. Her mother stood before her, restored once more to health, the way Catherine liked to remember her. There were other shadowy figures smiling at her. Lady Ruth, Gideon and

Dugon, Jacob and Tally and Jostin. But not Nick. Though she searched for him he was not amongst the dead. It was as she had believed. He was still alive. She would see him in heaven one day but not yet. And she closed her eyes and let the welcoming blackness take her.

***

The newly crowned King Rowan Garth of the Jassoir, rose to his feet from the magnificent throne in the great hall at Castle Baryk and glared at the three men before him.

'How did he get out of the castle?'

'We do not know, Sire,' Lord John ventured, 'I could hardly believe it myself, but we have searched the castle and the village and he has disappeared.'

Even Prince Jared looked sheepish. 'Matilda has gone, and the boy Tam, and three horses including Nick's destrier. There is no doubt that they have escaped.'

'Two men, a woman and three horses have disappeared from this, the best defended fortress in the land. How was this possible? Did they sprout wings and fly? Did no one see them and think it strange? Or was everyone too drunk to notice?' The King's eyes scanned the room as he stood hands on hips and waited. 'Well?'

'The boy took the horses earlier in the day, Sire.' This time it was Felix Runmore who spoke. 'I saw them leave. It is not unusual for the servants to take the horses out for exercise from time to time. They grow restless. He must have waited in the wood until nightfall.'

Rowan nodded. 'Very well, that part of it I can understand. But Nick and Matilda. How did they get out? It is the best part of half a mile to that wood. Someone must have seen them?'

There was no reply and he threw himself onto the throne and frowned.

'I do not blame Nick for this you know. He did what he had to do. What I would have done if I had been him. That is why…' He stood up again and shouted at them so that they all took a step backwards. 'That is why I gave instructions for him to be watched at all times. Where were his personal guard?'

'There was a small fire, My Lord.' Felix said apologetically. 'They were helping the servants to...'

'A small fire… a diversion. A trick. Are they so stupid or so lazy that they did not realise that?' Again nobody spoke and the King raised an eyebrow. He sat down again. 'There is no point in continuing this discussion. The laying of blame will achieve nothing. What we must decide is what to do now.'

'If I may say, Sire,' the Chancellor interjected, 'it is of the utmost importance that Nick Trayer returns alive.'

'Do you think I don't know that?' the King snapped, 'He is very precious to me as I told him. I…'

'No. I apologise for interrupting, but this touches on matters of which even you do not know.'

'Why don't I?'

'Because…because the manner of your accession was very sudden and I have not yet had time to instruct you in everything. I must just say that if Nicholas Trayer were to die, his death would be of great advantage to our enemies.'

'Why would it?'

'Well, em… I do not know where to begin exactly but…'

'Oh never mind. It must wait. We do not have time for one of your long drawn out explanations. The fact is, someone must go after Nick.'

Felix turned to Prince Jared. ‘My Lord Prince, may I suggest that you take a company of your best men and go yourself.’

‘Yes.’ The Prince turned to his brother, ‘With your permission, I will.’

Rowan nodded his head. ‘I agree. You must go Jared. Make sure you bring him back alive.’

The Prince bowed. ‘I will leave immediately, Sire.’

‘Felix,’ the King said now, ‘please make enquiries of your men as to how this was allowed to happen. And make absolutely sure that nothing like this will ever happen again.’

‘Yes, Sire.’

Finally he turned to his chancellor. ‘Now Lord John. We will arrange some food and wine and you will explain to me why Nick Trayer’s life is of such significance to our enemies.’

Chapter 27

It was late morning when Nick, Matilda and Tam arrived at Fastwater. They had spent the night in a village some miles away where the inhabitants were only too happy to talk about the Scorge town. They thought it most amusing that the three travellers were headed there.

'Even if it had not had the Scorge it would be all but a ghost town,' the innkeeper told them. 'No boat has stopped there in years. It is called Fastwater but since the sentorman at Temble Deem built his new water mill upriver, there's been but a trickle on the Haaval. Killed the town it did. Not that he cares.' He launched into a long list of complaints about the man and his misdemeanours. When Nick asked for directions he laughed, holding his sides as if it were the best joke he had heard for years.

'You just follow your nose. It'll soon tell you when you're near.'

And he was right. As they reached the Haaval river and kept to its path between gently rolling wooded hills they had begun to notice the stench of decay. It was a hot day and despite the early hour, the heat trapped under the grey morning mist was cloying and dense. When finally they came within sight of the walls of the port, the smell was almost unbearable.

Matilda and Tam led the horses down to the river to let them drink while Nick crept through the woods to reconnoitre the town.

'There is no Scorge,' he announced on his return.

'How can you know?' Matilda asked.

'Come. I'll show you.'

She followed him to the edge of the wood. The town was walled and the only way in, unless by boat, was through the gates. In the woods where they had stopped, the river was full and free flowing but it seemed to bend away from the town. When she asked him, Nick agreed that it was strange but his attention was on the town and she did not press him.

'There are sentries posted on the gates.' He pointed to the gate tower where an armoured head was just visible. 'Some of the men are camped outside the town but some are inside. They would not have entered if there were any fear of infection. They are not the guards we had been told about. These are trained soldiers. Someone has taken this town.'

'Why? What would they want with an empty and useless port?'

'I do not know and it worries me.' He turned to look at her, taking both her shoulders in his hands. 'Matilda, this is dangerous. It is not the danger we were expecting, but it is danger none the less. I must go in. You know I must. If there is any chance that Catherine…' His eyes told her that his hope was rapidly failing. 'I… I have no choice. But you and Tam must go back.'

She began to protest and as if he knew she would, he said, 'Well, at least wait here for me. Whatever is in there, I cannot ask you to face it with me.'

'You do not ask,' she insisted. 'You have never asked but I will come anyway.' He closed his eyes and shook his head as if he realised that it was useless to argue, but when he opened them again she could see that he was also grateful.

‘How do we get in?’

‘There is nothing for it but to walk right up to the gates. I do not think getting in will be a problem. It is the getting out that will prove more difficult.’ He frowned. ‘I do not want to risk the horses. We cannot afford to lose them. Tam must remain here to mind them and we will go on foot. I will pretend that you are sick and I am looking for somewhere to rest you. I have played that same part before.’

‘No,’ she insisted. ‘We will pretend that you are sick. They will be less guarded if they have to deal with a woman.’

‘They have not met a woman such as you,’ he said with a smile, then he was businesslike once more. ‘Even so, when we are inside, take your lead from me. Do exactly as I say.’

‘Of course.’

‘I mean it Matilda. I know you are not fond of taking orders.’

‘In this I will,’ she assured him, and she had every intention of doing so.

Returning to the river where Tam and the horses were waiting, Nick took his woollen cloak and despite the heat, wrapped it around him to hide his weapons and his expensive clothes. Matilda loosened her hair and rubbed dust into it to dull its glossy shine. She also tucked a collection of knives into her belt.

‘Where did you get those?’ Nick asked in astonishment.

‘I borrowed them from the kitchen. The armoury is too closely guarded.’

He shook his head as if he knew she would never cease to amaze him.

'Come on,' she urged, 'Take my arm. You are supposed to be sick, remember?'

With Nick hunched over and leaning on her arm, they made their way to the main gate.

***

From the window of the gatehouse, the two men watched them approach.

'Is it them?' Lassall asked.

Ludeck peered through the window. 'I cannot say.'

'You cannot say. You assured me that you would not fail to recognise the woman. You said you would know her very shape.'

'I did.' Ludeck admitted 'But I had forgotten that I have only one eye. In my mind I am still whole.'

Despite himself, Richard could not help the sympathy that he felt for this once strong and formidable soldier.

The couple approached the town slowly, the man, hunched and limping leaned heavily on the woman, who was almost as tall as he. They had emerged from the trees and were making their way across the scrubland towards the town gates.

The mercenaries had refused to billet within the town proper. Although he had assured them that the Scorge had long since gone, they had insisted on camping on the ground outside the gates. They had, however, agreed to patrol the walls and the area between the outer and inner gates. He was lucky that they had not deserted him completely. The town was all but derelict. There was nothing to loot and no women to enjoy which together with a good fight were the only things that interested them. It was only when they had killed Barch and his brother and discovered their hidden booty, that they had agreed to stay at all.

To ensure their continued co-operation, Richard had had to promise them a share of Nick Trayer's ransom. He had no idea whether he would be able to deliver on that, but he did not intend to worry about it until the time came.

Two of the twenty men that had come with him were patrolling the walls, a dozen including Gordack, were outside the town eating their midday meal. The other six were below him in the courtyard. Limkin, a tall skinny man was second in command. He polished his sword while his men were involved in a childlike contest to see how far they could spit cherry stones. The sound of their gruff laughter filled the air.

'Open the gate,' Richard called through the window, 'but do not harm them. We will come down.'

He led the way down the spiral staircase aware of Ludeck's painful progress behind him and emerged into the courtyard where the six men had the couple surrounded.

'Now can you tell me if it is them?' he asked again as Ludeck came out a few seconds later.

'I…I'm not sure that…'

With a tirade of oaths, the woman opened her cloak and from nowhere produced a knife which she threw at Ludeck missing his head by less than an inch.

'That would appear to be your answer.' Lassall called, leaping out of the way.

'Matilda, No.' Her companion straightened up and dropped all pretence of being sick. One of the mercenaries advanced towards her but Matilda produced another knife and hurled it at him hitting him in the throat He went down with a gurgling scream as the blood began to pump from his mouth.

Trayer, for Richard knew it had to be he, had drawn his sword and stood now, legs apart, daring anyone to approach.

‘I want him taken alive,’ Richard commanded. He drew his own sword but did not move forward.

So this was Nicholas Trayer. This was the man who until recently was the youngest ever Warrior of the Circle of Fire. He wore richly brocaded clothes but they did not sit well with him, he was no courtier. His sword was not simply decorative, it was heavy and businesslike and he clearly knew how to use it. Richard watched as he dispatched two of the mercenaries within seconds. One wielded a massive battle axe and was cut down by a blow to the stomach before he had a chance to use it, while the other went down from a thump on the helmet, which though it glanced off was followed by a cut to the back of the neck which laid him out.

Matilda meanwhile launched another knife at Ludeck but he moved just quickly enough so that it hit him in his foot. His scream of pain was followed by a string of oaths as he bent to pull at it. In one movement she was across the ground and shoving him to the ground. A second soldier grabbed her around the neck and pinned her in a hold that even she could not resist. He forced her to the ground and held her down with a knee on her shoulder.

While Ludeck sat on the ground nursing his foot, Trayer had engaged Limkin in a sword fight. He hesitated for a moment when Matilda was taken and the mercenary’s sword slashed into his leg. Trayer roared, whether with pain or anger was not clear and pushed forward, knocking his opponent to the ground. Limkin tried to get up but Trayer rammed his sword into his armpit and he fell back immobilised. Turning immediately he advanced toward the man holding Matilda captive.

‘Let her go,’ he shouted.

Richard was gratified to see that he was limping.

‘If he takes one more step, cut her throat,’ he commanded.

Trayer stopped dead in his tracks.

Richard glanced around at the carnage in the courtyard. ‘This is all very impressive. The very least I would expect from a Trayer.’ He forced himself to smile and not betray his nervousness.

Here, finally, was the man he had twice failed to kill.

Ten years ago, the uncle had entrusted him with the complete destruction of the Trayer family. He had been at the castle to witness the son’s initiation into the Circle of Fire and had left, as instructed, to await the procession on the mountain pass that the uncle had identified as the best point for an ambush.

The cart had arrived just as he was assured it would. Gideon and his lady rode in front of the cart. Two of Gideon’s own men rode at the rear. They had walked right into Richard’s ambush and did not stand a chance. The attack was well planned. The four men were killed within minutes. The warrior and his wife were made to suffer for longer.

Richard himself had no stomach for this needless torture but he did not stop his men. He was a young and inexperienced commander and they would have resented his intervention in what they saw as their right. Even now he cursed himself for this weakness. Not because he had any great sympathy for Gideon or his wife, but because of the delay it caused. If they had not stopped to satisfy their lust, they would have looted the cart, and if they had done so, they would have found the newly branded Nick, and Richard’s task would have been complete.

As it was, the company that King Edwell had sent belatedly to escort them, arrived before he had a chance to do so. All his men were put to the sword there and then, and Richard was taken prisoner. From that moment, and for the next ten years, his life and Nick's were inextricably linked.

Had he known, when he followed the Prince into Claveham, that his enemy was so close... There was nothing to be gained in thinking that way. Now he finally had the chance to complete the job.

'Who are you?' Trayer said coldly, then Richard could see recognition dawning in his face. 'It was you who came to my village. You took Catherine and you killed my steward. He was a good man.'

'Many a good man has fallen to the sword in this conflict,' Richard said with a shrug. 'And in answer to your question, I am Richard Lassall of the Valeron.'

'Lassall?'

'You do not know me of course, but our lives are linked in more ways than you can possibly imagine. Maybe later we can share a mug of ale together, I'm sorry that I have no wine. Then perhaps I will enlighten you.'

'I will avenge my steward's death, ere I will sit with you,' Trayer said, but not before a flicker of interest passed across his eyes

Richard smiled. 'Very honourable of you. I am glad to see you are a man of honour because it makes what we have to do next so much easier. I am instructed to take you alive, therefore what I propose is this. You will hand over your sword and dagger and any other weapons and become my prisoner and in return your friend here, she of the flying knives, will keep her life. Otherwise I will give her to my men to do with as they wish, and then they will kill her.' As an afterthought he added. ‘We can attend to your leg. I see it is causing you some distress.’

A dark red stain had appeared just below Trayer’s knee and from the way he shifted his weight, it was evidently painful. Despite this, he had positioned himself cleverly with his back to the inner door.

‘He will kill me anyway,’ Matilda said. ‘Do not let them take you. Find Catherine.’

Although he was clearly in two minds, Trayer began to back away and Richard signalled to the remaining men to follow him. They moved forward but only hesitantly.

Richard was desperate not to lose his quarry but he could not let the man know.

‘She is not there,’ he said with a shrug, ‘or if she is, you will find only her bones.’

‘Go.’ Matilda shouted. ‘He cannot be sure. There is always a chance.’

For a few seconds more, Trayer hesitated, then still holding up his sword he backed painfully through the inner gate and disappeared.

‘What are you waiting for?’ Lassall yelled at the remaining two men. ‘Stop him.’

The men looked at each other, but neither moved. The man who still had Matilda in his grip shook his head, ‘They won’t go in there. You heard what the custodians told us. No-one comes out of that town alive.’

From the outer gate, Gordack and the remaining men had entered the courtyard. ‘Enough of your superstitious nonsense.’ he commanded. ‘You will go in and you will bring him back alive and we will all grow rich on the ransom he will fetch. Is that not so, Sir?’

The eyes that met Richard’s held a clear warning of what would happen if it were not.

'It is,' he agreed. 'And the longer you leave it the further he will get.'

Gordack nodded to his men and they made for the inner door. He then sent another four after them.

Ludeck, still sitting on the ground, was trying to pull the knife from his foot.

'Leave it.' Lassall told him. 'You will make it worse. Someone will attend to it for you.' He turned to the man holding Matilda. 'Take her away. You may do with her as you think fit, but do not kill her yet.'

The man grinned and tickled Matilda under the chin. She spat at him and he grinned again.

'Wait.' Ludeck said. He looked up at Richard. 'Let me have her first.'

Richard nodded. 'But of course. I should have thought.' He turned to the mercenary. 'Find somewhere comfortable to lock her up. Comfortable for the Captain that is.' The man began to protest but Richard silenced him with a wave of his hand. He pointed to Ludeck who was still thrashing about on the ground. 'Look at him. Don't you think he deserves a little good fortune.'

The man laughed and Ludeck scowled at him.

It took two of the mercenaries to drag Matilda away and when they had gone Richard shook his head.

'Be wary of her my friend. There is little of your body left that you can afford to lose.'

Chapter 28

Nick backed through the inner gate and into the maze of narrow streets knowing that they would be following. He allowed himself a brief assessment of his situation. He needed to pick them off one by one as they entered. Aware of the pain in his leg, he darted into the nearest house, climbed the stairs and went to the window. If there had been glass in it, it had fallen out long ago and there was just room to push himself through the gap and cling on to the decaying woodwork.

Two men entered the street. He had expected more, then realised that they would have split up to cover all the town. As they passed beneath him he jumped, jarring his leg painfully but bringing both to the ground. He stabbed the first in the chest with his dagger, then as his comrade tried to stand, Nick rammed his fist into the man's face then kicked him hard with his good foot.

With great difficulty he stepped over them and ran along the street as fast as his injured leg would allow. He glanced back once but neither had moved.

Nick knew that he was losing blood rapidly. As he hobbled along the deserted streets, fighting off the nausea that came with the pain and the putrid smell, he was constantly aware of the wound. There was no breeze in the town and the heat was intense.

At first the pain was almost unbearable, but he forced himself on and it began to settle into a numbing ache. If he stopped, he knew, he would not be able to start again. Worse than the pain in his leg, was the agony that he felt in his heart. In order to go after Catherine, he had left Matilda to her fate. He knew of course, that given the same choice again, he would not have chosen differently, but Matilda was his friend. She had proven that friendship over and over again. Nothing would have persuaded him to abandon her but this. The logical part of his mind told him that twice he had told her to turn back, warned her of the danger, and twice she had insisted on coming, yet still he felt the guilt keenly.

What was more, it was becoming evident that Richard Lassall had not lied. There was no-one left alive in this sad, useless town. House after house he entered and his voice echoed in empty rooms. Not a sound, not a movement. Not a rat or a mouse or even a fly. The reason was evident. There was nothing left in the town to provide food for any scavenger. No flesh whether human or otherwise.

He leaned heavily against the wooden beam of a doorway and gradually sank to the ground. For the first time he took a good look at the wound. He realised that he had left a trail of blood to lead his enemies straight to him and it was still pumping from him at an alarming rate. If he was to survive he would need to bind it quickly.

Did he want to survive? It was clear now, even to him, that Catherine was dead. She could not have escaped from this place and there was very little chance that anyone was left alive in its empty streets. How easy it would be to sit here as the blood flowed out of his body and simply die.

Even as the thought crossed his mind, he knew he could not give up. Catherine may be dead, but Matilda was very possibly still alive. He owed it to her ten times over to go back and attempt to rescue her.

He took his knife and holding the sleeve of his shirt, made a tear in the shoulder seam. In one movement he tore the sleeve loose. It reminded him instantly of the scene in the millhouse kitchen on the day that should have been his wedding. He could see again Catherine's surprised face as she came down into the kitchen in her beautiful white dress. The image was too powerful and too painful and he suppressed it forcibly. He bound the linen around his leg, and satisfied that it was tight enough, pulled himself carefully to his feet. The wound still hurt but he could just about walk.

He decided to return by a different route just in case he should hear or see something that he had not seen before. Turning towards the river he went down to the next corner then turned east again back towards the town gates. As he reached the next house he stumbled on a small rock and the pain that shot through his leg was so great that he screamed in agony. There was a sound from his left like a stone falling and suddenly a rat scuttled out of one of the houses, ran in circles for a few seconds then headed off towards the river. Instinctively Nick followed it. The stench began to grow stronger and after a few more seconds he could hear a faint buzzing. As he drew nearer to the river, both sound and smell intensified. There were more rats now; not swarms of them but one or two every so often.

Then he was on the deserted wharf overlooking the river. Here, where he should have expected the air to be clearer it was worse than ever. The flies were everywhere and he knew what it meant. This was where the bodies had been dumped.

There was a staircase leading from the decrepit wharf down to the river. The Haavel was reduced to merely a trickle here, a few pieces of driftwood bobbing slowly downstream. The steps would formerly have led right into the river, now they just ended in a silted bank. Nick knew that he should turn away but he could not. He had to know. The stench was so bad now that he had to hold the skirt of his cloak over his nose and mouth so that he could breathe. And there they were, the corpses.

Screwing up his eyes to see better in the gloom, he looked around him. The bodies were piled in the area under the wharf, some in neat piles, some just thrown in, some more decomposed than others, some ripped apart by the rats and who knew what other creatures. Men, women and children, most unrecognisable even to their mothers.

Suddenly he caught sight of a scrap of material a tiny piece of yellow silk. Without thinking he moved through the bodies towards it.

She lay in what was probably the only empty space, slightly apart from the other corpses. One hand lay on her stomach, the other was draped on the dirt as if she had reached out for someone. He recognised the sash, and the gold of her hair and any last spark of hope died within him. Ignoring the stabbing pain in his leg he sank to his knees beside her. Oblivious now, to the smell and the dirt, he reached out to take his bride into his arms and to bury his face in the soiled fabric of her wedding dress.

Chapter 29

Matilda supposed she should consider herself lucky that Ludeck had demanded her for himself. She would have stood no chance against the mercenaries. Even if she had managed to get the better of one or two of them, there would always be another to come. Ludeck would be alone, she had no doubt of that. He had a score to settle with her just as she had with him. Of course she had no idea what would happen when she had killed him. She did not allow herself to think that far ahead. All she knew was that she would kill him. Sophia was safely within the walls of Castle Baryk and Matilda had nothing to lose. She had already made her plan.

The soldiers had led her with exaggerated courtesy into what must once have been the gatekeeper's bedchamber. There they had tied her hands and feet. They had laid her on the small bed and left. Before they closed the door, the one they called Watts had blown her a kiss.

She felt sick with fear but did not let it show and the man laughed and closed the door. She heard the sound of something heavy being pushed across in front of it.

There was no way of knowing how long she lay there, but it could not have been much more than half an hour. Ludeck would need to have his foot attended to and bound before he came, but she was equally sure that he would not delay his revenge any longer than he had to. Grateful that her hands were tied in front and not behind, she manoeuvred them so that she was able to reach inside the pouch attached to her belt. The leaves that she had brought had begun to dry. It was difficult to tell which was which until she felt the sting of the Wolf's Bane. Carefully, and painfully she brought it out, crumbling the dried leaf inside her fist. The sting of the poison against her skin brought tears to her eyes but she fought against them and soon the pain turned to numbness.

It was not long before she heard a sound outside the door. It swung open to reveal Ludeck and another man.

'Wait outside,' Ludeck instructed.

When the man had gone, he shut the door and stood for a moment looking at her. There was a chair against the far wall and he sat down facing her, playing with his dagger. He had removed his outer clothing and was wearing a simple shirt and linen trousers. His foot had been carefully bound.

He must have seen her glance briefly at the foot because he said coldly, 'It was not such a deep wound. As you can see, I can still walk. Just because I am mutilated and half blinded, do not underestimate my strength Matilda.'

She knew that he wanted her to shout and scream and threaten him but she would not give him that pleasure. She said nothing.

He stretched both arms in the air as if to loosen his muscles and despite her plans and her brave intentions the fear began to take its hold.

He smiled so that the scar on his face gaped. 'Because of you I have spent time screaming in agony on my sickbed. When I stopped screaming, I began to plan my revenge.'

She knew herself to be a stronger woman than most, both physically and mentally, but she was a woman nonetheless, and she had never known such fear as she felt now.

She forced her herself to speak calmly, not to betray herself.

'Such a powerful man, that you must have a woman trussed like a chicken.'

He smiled again. 'Oh no. Have no fear. I will untie you. I want you to struggle. Let us see how well you fight without the benefit of your knives.'

He stood up painfully then came towards her at a shuffle.

First he untied her feet. She kicked out at him knowing that he would expect her to do so and he moved aside laughing. 'Oh my dear Matilda. I am truly looking forward to this.'

He pulled her to her feet and she did not resist because she wanted to be standing. Because of his now hunched back, she was taller than he by a few inches. In her left fist she felt the reassuring sting of the monkshood as she ground it into even more pieces. With a single sweep of his dagger he released her hands and she reached up the right to claw at his face. He moved to stop her just as she had intended and immediately she opened her left fist and threw the ground leaves into his one eye. He screamed in pain and released her, bringing both hands to his eye to clutch at it, dropping his dagger to the floor. Matilda did not waste a second. She bent to pick up the dagger and as she straightened up stabbed him in the belly. She could not know how deep it entered but he, howling in pain, was disorientated, blind and unable to decide which part of himself to hold first. She pushed him forwards to the ground and he fell heavily onto the dagger. His body convulsed once then was still.

She knew this time that she had killed him.

She sat down heavily on the bed shaking from head to foot. She took two deep breaths to try and calm herself. She was not safe yet.

With great care, she placed a foot under Ludeck's body and tried to push him over onto his side. He was too heavy, so she knelt down and tried again with both arms. This time she was able to flip him over sufficiently to reach the handle of his dagger.

She gritted her teeth and pulled, feeling the shift of flesh and bone beneath the blade. It came free suddenly throwing her backwards and splashing blood on to her dress and arms. Fighting back a wave of nausea, she stood up, went to the door and thumped on it twice with the hilt of the dagger. Then she stood back against the wall.

The door was opened and the guard entered, stopping in his tracks when he saw Ludeck's body on the ground. From behind, Matilda brought the dagger down hard into the man's neck. Noiselessly, he fell forward and was still. Once again, she had to retrieve the weapon. Wiping it clean on the man's clothing, she tucked it into her belt.

She waited for a couple of seconds in case there was anyone else about to enter, then peered around the door. There was no-one. Closing it behind her she crept to the stairwell. The courtyard was empty and she could see no other windows overlooking it. Lassall, she could see, was talking to one of his men on the top of the town wall. They walked together across her line of vision, but were looking in the opposite direction.

As quickly as she could, she ran down the staircase and across the courtyard to the inner gate, wiping her hand on her dress to remove all trace of the Wolf's Bane. No-one challenged her.

She slipped through the archway and found herself in a cobbled street that led to right or left. Having no idea which route Nick may have taken, she looked around her for some clue and found on the grey cobbles to her right, a few red spots. She squatted down to see. It was definitely blood, dried now in the day's heat, but still a dull red.

'Oh Nick.'

How serious was his wound? She had not seen him take the injury and her back had been to him for most of the time. The blood was flowing quite strongly as was evidenced by the trail that he left in his wake. She prayed that the wound was less serious than it seemed. Nick did not deserve this.

Did she wish, even for a moment that he had refused to leave her? No. It was she who had insisted on coming. She could not expect him to put his quest in jeopardy because of her.

She followed the trail of blood. He had moved backwards and forwards across the street as he examined each house in turn but she was able to take the straight route. Once she came around the side of a house and almost into the arms of two of Lassall's men. They were peering through the windows of the next house and did not see her. She slipped inside and pressing herself against the wall, waited for them to pass. As long as they confined their search to looking through windows, and did not enter the room she would be safe. Within seconds she heard their voices as they stopped only inches from her and then she heard them leave. Peeping around the corner she saw their retreating backs and when they were out of sight followed the increasingly strong trail that Nick had left. The soldiers had been coming in the opposite direction. Either they had not noticed the blood, and they would have had to be stupid or blind not to have seen it, or it had not led them to their prey. Eventually she understood as the trail ended abruptly. Here there was a smudge of blood on the door post of a house and then nothing. Evidently he had stopped here and probably bound his wound. There was certainly no sign of him. She checked, in case he had gone into the house but it was empty.

Now where?

It was unbearably hot in the narrow streets, with the upper storeys of the wooden houses jutting out into the road, trapping the heat beneath. It made sense to head for the river. There at least there may be a breath of air. Not that Nick would necessarily think that way. His priority would be finding Catherine. Nevertheless she turned in that direction running silently along the street.

She was wrong in thinking that the air would improve towards the river. It was far worse. She could hear the flies buzzing and caught sight of the rats scampering down beneath the wharf. This she realised was the graveyard, the final resting place for all the poor souls who had lost their lives in this evil place.

She could not bring herself to go down there until she heard something between the wooden beams of the wharf. It was almost drowned by the buzzing of the flies but then she heard it again; a cry of pain, a primal sound, unmistakably human.

Tentatively she began to descend the staircase. 'Nick?'

There was no reply, but the cry again. It was dark here and it took a while for her eyes to adjust. She held a hand over her mouth and nose to stifle the smell then saw the first few corpses. It was a hideous sight and she tried not to look too closely. Then she saw Nick. At first she thought that he had been buried under a landfall of corpses, then she realised that he was kneeling on the ground hunched over the girl's body. She felt an almost physical pain in her heart.

'Oh no. Please, no.'

She pushed her way between the dead trying not to think about what she touched as she passed them. Kneeling down beside him she realised that it was his sobs that she could hear. Laying a hand across his shoulder she kissed him gently on the side of the head as she would if she were comforting her daughter.

'I am so sorry Nick.' Tears welled in her eyes as she looked down on Catherine's peaceful face. Though she was skeletally thin and covered with filth it was still easy to see how lovely she must have been. In an almost maternal gesture, she could not resist moving a strand of hair from the girl's face. Her skin was soft and warm and…Warm?

'Nick. She is warm.'

He did not hear her, the outpouring of his grief still too strong.

Either Catherine was still alive or she had not been dead long. She took one small hand in her own and felt at the wrist for some spark of life. It was there, a pulse, faint and tentative but a pulse nonetheless.

'Nick.' She shook his shoulder gently. 'She is not dead. Nick! She lives still. Nick!!'

Gradually she could see that he understood. His eyes, still wet with tears shone as he looked up at her. 'Are you sure?'

'Yes.' She smiled as her own tears spilled over and ran down her face. 'Yes. I am sure.'

Chapter 30

'The spark of life in her is very faint,' Matilda said. 'Perhaps we were too early to rejoice.'

They had taken Catherine to a house adjoining the wharf where the flies were less troublesome and the smell just about bearable. They were hidden from the street and there was no way in except for the door. Also, Matilda was convinced that the mercenaries would keep well away from this area. They were too superstitious to come anywhere near the dead. While she tended to Catherine, Nick had gone to find a way out of the town.

Now he returned kneeling painfully beside Catherine and kissing her lips gently. They were dry and chapped and unresponsive.

'She is not sick as such,' Matilda pronounced. 'She does not have the Scorge nor any other disease that I can see. Her body is whole and unmarked, but she is weak with exhaustion and I think starvation. She needs water, Nick, and in time food, neither of which we have with us.' She looked around her in despair. 'The Fates have forsaken this town. It has nothing for us. The dead have fouled the river and not even a blade of grass grows. I can do nothing for her here. You must get us out.'

He stood up again stiffly, taking his weight on his good leg. 'We cannot return through the gates. We would stand not a chance against armed men. We could cross the river, but the land is flat and inhospitable, we would be seen from the gatehouse. Even if we waited until dark we would never find our way, and we would be on the wrong bank of the river. Our chances of finding Tam and the horses would be too slim. The only alternative is to take the river itself. It is shallow here but further down it must deepen. Maybe there is a spring.'

'But how? 'We do not have a boat and Catherine is not able to swim.'

'There is a boat of sorts. It is barely built as though someone had been interrupted before they finished it. There is just enough room to hold her. You and I will need to swim.'

While he prepared the boat she did what she could for Catherine. Her most desperate need was for water, but she did not dare to take some from the river. There was sure to be disease there and Catherine was too weak to fight an infection. All she could do was ensure that the girl was comfortable and protected from the sun.

'Will you let me see your wound?' she asked Nick when he returned.

He shrugged though she could see that he was in pain. 'It is healing, I would not trouble yourself.'

'I doubt that is true. The binding you used is red with blood. Do you want to lose your leg?'

'I do not want to lose Catherine,' he snapped, 'and if we do not leave soon that may well happen.'

'We cannot leave until it is dark. Let me dress it properly for you. The river water will not help it, believe me.'

He let her unwrap his leg and she tried not to react too strongly when she saw how deeply Limkin's sword had cut just below the knee. The wound was a bloody mass which had begun to congeal but still oozed blood in places. She could see through the gaping hole to the bone beneath. With great care, she removed a tiny chip of bone which had lodged itself in the flesh and his whole body stiffened. She had searched the house and found a glass cup which contained the yellow liquid she now used to wash the wound. Nick peered at it suspiciously. 'What is that?'

'We do not have fresh water.' Matilda said matter-of-factly. 'It is the safest alternative.'

He looked horrified but was prevented from speaking by the pain as she pressed the sides of the wound together and packing it with comfrey leaves from her pouch and rebound it. He bit his lip and though he did not complain, the strain was evident on his face.

Her admiration and respect for him grew ever stronger. Why had the Fates singled out this, the best of men? What had he done to deserve it? The answer, she knew, lay in the endless secrets that haunted the corridors of Castle Baryk, and when and if they returned she was determined to find out.

***

At first they carried the boat between them like a litter. It was heavy and Nick, limping badly could not keep it steady, but eventually the water became deep enough to float it and soon they were able to swim. At first it was not too difficult to hold on to the boat using the flow of the water to move them along.

The ache in Nick's leg had sharpened on contact with the water but had now dulled again. He had just begun to believe that they were safely away when a rush of water from the diverted channel hit them, forcing them into a spin.

Nick fought to hang on to the boat and keep it above the water. Matilda on the other side was holding on tightly but he could he could see that she was struggling. It was all he could do to hold on as the current sent them first one way then the other. Twice he felt himself sucked under and the water entered his mouth nose and ears.

He surfaced, gasping for air but somehow still holding on to the boat.

Matilda had gone under for the third time and he knew that she would have a better chance without having to hold on. 'Save yourself. Swim to the shore,' he called, before he went under again.

Whether she heard him or not he had no way of knowing but she had gone when he surfaced again. Still clinging to the boat he forced his legs to kick against the current. His lungs were bursting and he felt the wound split open again. The pain was electrifying. If anything it helped his mind to concentrate on keeping the boat afloat and forcing it through the maelstrom.

Just when he thought he could fight no longer, the river released its hold on him and the swimming became easier, then the boat hit something solid. As he came up for air, a hand gripped him beneath the arm and helped to pull him up. He scrambled panting on to the river bank and found Tam's face smiling down on him.

'Catherine?' he gasped.

Tam hastened to reassure him. 'We have her. She is safe.'

***

Remarkably, the boat had survived the whirlpool and Catherine was unharmed. Her pulse was still faint but she lived. Matilda found the flask of fresh water and dribbled some into her mouth as Nick cradled her once more in his arms. They had wrapped her in Tam's cloak as their own clothes were still wet from the river. Although it was a dark night, it was still warm and already they were beginning to dry.

'I would like to find some milk,' Matilda said, 'and honey. There must be bees here in the woods. It would be easy for her body to take and will revive her.'

'We do not have time.' Nick shook his head sadly. 'They will come after us.'

'Yes. Of course they will.' Still, she realised, they were not safe. Escaping from the town would not be the end of it. 'Anyway I will feel happier if we get her out of this foul place. She needs fresh air and a comfortable place to rest.'

'Do you think she can survive a journey?'

From the start, Matilda had recognised the strength of Nick's love for Catherine. Now she could see it written plainly in his eyes as ignoring the pain in his leg, he held her close.

She felt the girl's pulse again. The spark of life was still there.

Gently she touched Nick's face, bringing his eyes level with hers. 'If I were Catherine and I knew that your love was the prize that awaited me, I would fight for every last chance of life.'

He smiled at her knowing that she was doing her best to reassure him, but he did not look convinced. Briefly he closed his eyes, then he turned and kissed Catherine's face with such tenderness that Matilda felt herself to be an intruder.

‘We cannot outrun them,’ he admitted, ‘but when we do have to fight, I want to be in a place of our choosing. And I want to be ready for them.’

***

Their progress was painfully slow. Though Nick would have liked to have gone at a gallop he was worried that the weak flame of life that burned beside him would be extinguished all too quickly.

He stopped every so often to feed a few drops of water between Catherine’s parched lips. Each time he did so, he kissed her and told her that he loved her in case she could hear and to give her strength. Once he thought he heard a murmur from her and once he felt her move against him but they may only have been imaginings fuelled by hope.

Eventually, when he had begun to lose track of time, Matilda drew alongside and put her hands to the reins. ‘We must stop now.’

‘A little longer,’ he said. ‘The sun is rising. She does well. Her heart grows stronger. I can feel it.’

She felt Catherine’s pulse and smiled. ‘Yes. Indeed it does. But it is not she who concerns me. Your leg is bleeding again.’

He glanced down and saw that she was right. His trousers were soaked in blood and it dripped over his boot on to the ground. He had grown so used to the pain that now he barely noticed it. He sighed and looked around him. Having climbed steadily out of the murky flatlands they had now descended into a new valley of lush trees. Here, the air felt fresher and smelled of trees and flowers instead of death and decay and to their right the river now flowed freely.

The sun was rising in the east and already it was hot. This was a comfortable heat not the enervating humidity of the previous day. A few moments ago they had passed a clearing surrounded by taller trees. It was not the place he would have preferred but facing the trail with their backs to the river it would afford them some measure of protection.

There they made a bed for Catherine amongst a pile of dried leaves. Matilda unwrapped Nick's leg shaking her head and looking at him almost reproachfully. She washed it with water from the river which she pronounced to be 'reasonably clean', and packed more comfrey leaves in the wound to help it heal.

'I would be happier if I had some Yarrow,' she announced looking around her vainly, 'It will help to stop the bleeding.'

The pain was awful and to hide it Nick frowned in irritation. 'You brought everything else,' he growled. 'Did you not think to bring that as well?'

'No,' she snapped. 'I did not expect you to get injured. I thought you were a better swordsman.'

He turned to her angrily ready to defend himself then, when he saw that she was smiling, shook his head and laughed for the first time in days.

Chapter 31

Richard Lassall turned around in the saddle to check that all his men were ready. It seemed that yet again he had allowed Nick Trayer to slide through his fingers. He cursed the orders to keep the man alive. He could have killed him, there in the courtyard in front of the gatehouse. He had him surrounded, outnumbered and injured and he had had to let him go. Again.

Shortly before nightfall, he had sent a man to check on Ralph. His friend had had ample time to taste the sweetness of his revenge and the door to the gatekeeper's bedchamber had remained firmly shut. He may not have been concerned even so, but one of the mercenaries had come to him to say that one of their comrades seemed to have disappeared. The man who had been assigned to Ludeck.

Though he could not believe that even Matilda could have got the better of Ralph this time, he had ordered the man to check. He had returned a mere five minutes later.

'Sir, please come and see.'

Ludeck lay on the floor in a pool of congealing blood. Richard saw his bandaged foot, his eye patch the scar on his face and now this new and fatal wound and he shook his head.

'Ralph, My Friend. Did I not warn you to be wary of that woman?' He turned his back and left the room. 'Bury him,' he ordered. 'He was a good soldier.'

Matilda, he was sure, had not left the town through the gates. They were firmly locked and there was no way over the wall. Besides, she had come with Trayer and would certainly have gone after him. It was worrying that Trayer had injured two of the mercenaries and the other two had returned empty handed.

'Take four more and search every inch of the town for them,' he instructed. 'Bring me Trayer alive. The woman you may do with as you please.'

The men had come back after three hours, certain that no-one remained in the town. Then one of them had come to him shamefacedly and admitted that earlier in the evening he had heard a disturbance from the direction of the river.

'It sounded like a man in trouble, Sir. I thought I heard shouting but...' He shrugged.

'Why did you not say anything before?'

'I was not sure, Sir. It did not occur to me that…'

'Stupid, incompetent fool.' A rare wave of anger gripped Richard and he lashed out, hitting the man around the head so hard that he fell to the floor. 'I do not pay you to think. I pay you to obey my instructions. Thanks to your dithering I have lost him again.' He kicked the man savagely in the ribs, then in his head, then again and again until his rage was spent. When he finally stood back he knew that he had killed him.

No-one had come to their comrade's aid. Some of the men looked shocked, others glanced nervously towards their leader. Gordack glared at Richard but for the first time he thought he detected just a hint of respect in that glare.

‘Do not mourn his passing,’ he told them. ‘You will all receive a share of his pay.’

Back in the gatekeeper's tower he found parchment and ink and wrote

My Dearest Uncle

I have followed your orders and attempted to take Nicholas Trayer alive. Unfortunately I have failed once again. Had I been allowed to kill him this would not have happened and we would today be celebrating the end of the Trayer line.

I wish you to know that I will no longer follow your instructions. I will go after Trayer and this time I will kill him or I will die in the attempt.

My only wish is to see the Trayers destroyed, the Jassoir usurpers defeated and the restoration of the Valeron throne.

To that end I remain,

Richard Lassall of the Valeron

Just as he had sealed the letter, Gordack had come into the room. He did not waste time with small talk.

‘You intend to follow them?’

‘Yes. I have no choice.’

‘And you expect my men to go with you?’

‘Of course.’ The question surprised him. ‘Why would they not? And since when have they been your men?’

‘They take their lead from me.’

‘But it is I who pay them.’

‘And there we have a problem.’

Gordack seated himself on the other side of the table and regarded Richard with the slightly amused look which had always made him nervous. ‘You have promised us gold but we have seen none of it.’

‘The custodians had much that was valuable. The men have taken it. They will all be rich.’

'But those are the spoils of war to which they are entitled. It is not the same as payment.'

Angrily, Richard rose to his feet. 'That is outrageous.'

Gordack shrugged. 'If you wish us to fight for you again, you must pay us again.'

Richard was painfully aware that the bag of gold which he had thrown so easily to Barch, now formed part of the 'spoils'. He had no means to pay the mercenaries, but he could not proceed without them.

'You will be paid.'

'By whom?'

'By me. When I show them Nicholas Trayer's body they will reward me. You will also have the woman to do with as you please.'

For some minutes, Gordack considered the matter. Eventually, much to Richard's relief, he nodded. 'Very well. But…' he stood up and leaned across the table. 'If you do not make good your promise I will kill you myself. And it will be a painful death.'

As always, with this man who frightened him, Richard fought to keep his composure. He held out the letter. 'Ask one of the men to take this letter to Castle Baryk as fast as he can. It must be handed to this man. He pointed to the name on the front. The messenger will be well paid.'

Gordack took the letter and left but as he did so, he turned back and his expression was a reminder of all that had been promised.

Now, in the first light of the new dawn, as he waited for the men to fall in line behind him, Richard tried not to think of it. He also tried to forget that he had killed one of his men. It was not the violence itself that he regretted but the loss of control. Rage was all very well when challenged in the right direction, but this time it had cost him a man and that was an unnecessary waste.

He adjusted the armour that he had taken from the dead mercenary. It was too big for him but he had lost his own armour weeks ago and it would have to do. Calmly now, he waved the men forward.

Chapter 32

'I will not let death take me,' Catherine had promised herself after she had learned that Nick still lived. 'I will live to see him again. I will fight it with everything I have.'

They had been brave words but eventually, when her stomach had been empty for some days and there was no-one left who needed her, she had begun to lose the will to fight.

'I am too tired,' she told the dead as they waited for her. 'I do not have the strength.'

Her mother's smile, the smile that had seemed welcoming had faded. 'We are not ready for you yet. There is everything to live for. Do not give up hope.'

Once she thought she heard Nick's voice in her ear. 'I love you Catherine,' he said. 'I don't want to live without you. Please come back to me.'

Then she heard another voice, one she did not recognise. 'This water is fresh and the herbs will help to revive you. Try to drink some, Catherine.'

She did as she was told although her throat was so dry that it was difficult to swallow. Gradually a face came into her vision. A smiling woman's face with dark eyes and dark hair.

'Who are you?' Catherine whispered.

‘My name is Matilda,’ the woman said. ‘I am a friend of Nick’s.’

‘Nick. Nick is alive.’ It was not a question.

‘Yes he is,’ the woman agreed, ‘very much so. I have sent him to hunt for some meat. He will be back soon. I have always found it best with men to keep them occupied. They do fuss so. Here, will you drink some more?’

She tried to drink again but the effort was too much for her and she closed her eyes.

‘I will wash your hair and your body,’ Matilda said now. ‘I will be as gentle as I can but it must be done because the lice are everywhere. The water is warmed with a little camomile. It is soothing. I promise I will leave you to rest afterwards.’

Catherine could feel the warm water against her skin and the careful removal of her clothes but she still managed to sleep through much of it. Matilda talked to her all the while.

‘I used to live on the edge of a forest such as this but when my father was killed in…’ the words became indistinct but the tone of the woman’s voice was comforting and she let herself drift away to it. From time to time the words came back and then away again until she heard something which caused her to pay attention. ‘His name was Jacob Rine and I…’

‘Jacob Rine? Jacob is dead.’

There was a pause. Then the woman spoke again.

‘Are you sure?’

Of course she was sure. ‘They are all dead.’

***

Nick held the rabbit firmly, cutting its neck with one sweep of his knife. He held it away from him to drain the blood then carrying it by the legs, made his way back to the clearing.

He had assumed that Lassall would not leave until morning and that it would take him four or five hours to reach them. There was time to prepare a meal, he was sure of that. Tam had been posted some way upriver on the high ground where he could see the road from Fastwater. When Lassall came, as Nick knew he must, they would have plenty of warning.

He did not allow himself to consider what would happen then. Only time would tell. All he did know was that they could not run any more.

Hobbling painfully, but holding on to his prize he made his way back to the clearing. This was the first chance he had had to think about Richard Lassall and the things he had said.

'Our lives are linked in more ways than you could know.'

Strangely, it was not the words but the voice that intrigued him. He had heard that wry monosyllabic voice before, but he could not think where.

Shaking his head he emerged through the trees and slowed to a halt. The scene that met him was so ordinary, so domestic, that it brought a smile to his face. The horses were grazing peacefully by the river unaware of any danger. Catherine lay wrapped in a blue cloak on the bed they had made for her apparently sleeping still. There was a small fire burning in the middle of the clearing and a pot sitting inside it presumable ready for the meat. Amazingly, as if this were any ordinary washday, Matilda herself was squatting by the river washing clothes.

He deposited the rabbit beside the fire and went to look at Catherine. Carefully he dropped to his knees. Her hair had regained its golden colour. It was fanned out behind her on the ground and when he touched it, it was slightly damp. Her lips were not as dry and parched as they had been and he bent forward and kissed her. It may have been his imagination but he thought that he saw the ghost of a smile flicker across her face. He told her once more that he loved her then got up stiffly and went to join Matilda by the river.

She stood up before he reached her and he saw immediately that she had been crying. 'What is it?' he asked, 'Catherine seems…'

'She is fine,' she assured him, wiping her eyes on the sleeve of her dress. 'She woke for a few moments. She knows you are near. I…I was merely… remembering.' She sniffed away the tears and attempted a smile. 'I have washed her clothes, look. They will dry in no time in this heat.'

He touched the thin white wool tentatively. 'It was her wedding dress.'

She nodded and squeezed his arm for a short moment before turning away to hang the dress and shift over a low hanging branch. 'Did you find us some food?'

'Yes. A rabbit. It took me far longer than it should have done. You have bound the wound so tightly that I can barely walk. This poor creature had the bad luck to stick its head out of the undergrowth just by my feet.'

'It is nothing to do with the binding,' she told him. 'You need to rest it.'

'That is not possible.'

'I know.'

They cooked the rabbit, taking the meat for themselves then boiling the bones to make a broth for Catherine. As the pot was simmering, they sat together and ate. Matilda was quiet and he did not disturb her. She was deep in contemplation. Eventually she looked up and saw him watching her.

'When they come,' she said in a whisper, 'do you think we can fight them?'

'I do not know.' He doubted that they could, but there was no alternative. 'I am wounded and you… you are…'

'I am just a woman. Is that what you were trying to say?' Her eyes flashed angrily.

'No,' he could not help but smile at her pride. 'I would never accuse you of such a thing.'

She saw the joke and relaxed immediately. 'But I am unskilled. One to one I could claim to be a match for any man, but I have never fought in a war. You do not have to say it, Nick. I know.'

He understood, and did not insult her by denying it. 'As for Tam, he is only a boy. I have taught him a little of unarmed combat but he is very much a novice. He wears a short sword but I doubt that he knows how to use it.' He sighed. 'He has courage though. "They will not take her" he told me. "They will not take her while I am still standing." I thanked him but I did not tell him that it is not Catherine they want. It is me.'

'Yes.'

'I do not know my enemy, Matilda. I know his name but nothing more. He has been told to take me alive but he very obviously wants me dead. It is hard to understand. I must fight for my life and I do not know why?'

'You are a powerful man now,' she suggested. 'You are the King's profender and his friend. He would pay a mighty ransom for you.'

'Maybe not now that I have deserted him and disobeyed his instructions. Even so I do not think it is that. We were trapped. They knew we would be coming and they were waiting for us. I do not think it was a ransom that prompted them.'

'He said that your life and his were linked.'

'He did and it makes no sense. And something else that makes no sense is that you and Tam should be involved in this. If it is me that he wants, why do I not ride out to meet him? He would be unlikely to bother with you.'

'Tam and I would follow you. You know that. We would not abandon you.'

'I abandoned you at Fastwater. I left you to your fate while I went after Catherine.'

'You had no choice. Equally, I let go of the boat in the river and swam away to save myself. I also had no choice. But in this we do.'

She wrapped the remains of the meat and stood up.

'I will take this to Tam and keep him company for a while. You stay with Catherine and rest your leg. Take this broth and feed it to her drop by drop. Do not let her take too much at first.' She rested her hand on his shoulder briefly. 'Hold her Nick. Talk to her. She will know that you are there. You need this time alone with her. Who knows what is to come.'

***

He stretched himself out beside her, snuggling against her and putting his arm around her, kissed her cheek and lips. The smell of the camomile lingered on her skin and hair. The mid-day sun, shining through the trees, dappled the ground with light and made stars of the ripples in the river. Though it was warm, they were sheltered from its stronger rays.

'Do you remember,' he whispered against her ear, 'a night as warm as this day, in just such a place? We were by the river at Claveham and you had sneaked away from the mill while your mother and father slept.'

He remembered that she had come into his arms and he had kissed her in the stillness of the woods where but for the calling of an eagle owl there was almost perfect silence. He had wanted so much more than just a kiss.

'It was your idea to swim,' he said forcing his mind to rest in the comfort of memories. 'You undressed by the side of the river and I moved away so that I would not see you. I couldn't bear to look at you, I wanted you so much.' He closed his eyes and winced, recalling again the exquisite pain of his desire. 'I was young, strong and full of energy and the woman I loved was swimming naked before me. I wished myself anywhere but there.' He kissed her lips again and caressed her cheek. 'You cannot have known what you were doing to me.'

'Of course I knew.' Her voice was faint and husky, but when she opened her eyes they were as clear and blue as ever. 'I was teasing you.'

He raised himself onto one elbow and smiled down at her. 'Were you?'

She smiled back and he was almost overcome with joy, but when she tried to speak again the words would not come. He leaned back and fetched the pot of broth then raising her head slightly, held it to her mouth. She took a few sips then shook her head. Laying her down again he replaced the pot.

'We swam,' she whispered, meaning for him to continue with the story.

'Yes. We did. I waited until you were in the water then stripped off my own clothes and dived in.'

The cool water had helped to quench his ardour but only for a moment or two. They swam separately, she out of shyness, or so he thought, and he, keeping his distance, fearing that he would not be able to control his desire if he got too close. Then while his back was turned, she had swum noiselessly towards him, slipping her arms around his waist and pressing her lips against his spine.

'I am tired of waiting,' she had whispered into his ear. 'I want to be your wife now.'

Leading him by the hand she had climbed out of the water, and drawn him down beside her onto the soft grass of the river bank. In the gentle moonlight, drops of water had glistened on her body and they felt cool against his lips as he kissed her face and neck. And it was there that he made love to her for the first time.

'We lay just as we do now,' he said, 'I think we would have stayed all night but you were soon shivering with cold. Had we been caught there would have been all hell to pay.'

He glanced down and she was sleeping again. He laid another kiss on her lips then snuggled down beside her and closed his eyes for what he thought was just a moment, then he became aware of her voice in his ear. It was stronger now.

'Nick. Wake up. I have to tell you something.'

'What?'

'Wake up.'

'I was not sleeping.'

'You were.' She smiled. 'I have been listening to you snoring for some time.'

'Nonsense.'

Her smile broadened then faded away. 'I must tell you something. It is important and it will distress you.'

'Drink some more broth first. I will have Matilda to answer to if you do not drink it all.'

When she had done as he asked she said softly.

'The man who took me.'

‘Richard Lassall.’

‘You know him?’

‘I know his name.’ His heart was full of dread as he asked. ‘Did he… did he misuse you?’

‘No. He was respectful… though he killed Dugon.’

‘Yes. I know. I have been back to Claveham.’

‘How is my father?’

He did not want her to know that the miller was unwell. ‘He will be pleased to hear that you are safe,’ he said instead.

‘L…Lassall. It was he who…who killed your parents.’ From inside the cover of Tam’s cloak she brought out a pale, thin arm and stroked his hair. ‘I am sorry. I do not wish to hurt you but, I needed to tell you in case… in case.’

He took the arm and kissed her palm. She had moved her arm. It was a sign that she was recovering. He let that thought drown out the thumping in his heart and the sinking in his stomach that her news had caused.

Gently, he placed the hand back against her body and bent to kiss her lips again. This time he felt her respond.

‘You have told me, now,’ he said. ‘Do not worry. Just sleep and get strong.’ She closed her eyes and he kissed her again. ‘I love you. That is all you need to think about.’

Chapter 33

Lassall and his men came as the sun passed its height. Matilda had left Tam at his post and begun to collect together their belongings and stow them on the horses' packs. It was so peaceful in the clearing that she had almost started to believe that they would be left to continue their journey unmolested.

Nick and Catherine lay sleeping in each other's arms, seemingly oblivious to the world around them. She suspected, however, that Nick would be ready to react instantly at the first sign of danger. She watched them with a smile letting herself share for just a few moments in the reflected glow of their love. Through Catherine's broken story she had been able to piece together Jacob's last days. The confirmation of his death had left an ache in her heart and to see the tenderness in Nick's expression even as he slept was a balm to that pain.

Despite everything she envied them. It was foolish, she knew that. There was every chance that they would all be killed when Lassall came, or worse, Nick and Tam would be killed and she and Catherine would be taken as slaves to his mercenary band. Would Catherine wish then, that they had left her to join the dead of Fastwater?

A buzzard was circling overhead and Matilda wondered if it could sense that before the day was out there would be death in this place.

From her own pack she took her three remaining knives and fastened them to her belt. She also had a dagger which she tucked in next to them. She had decided already that if Nick was killed and all chance of escape gone, she would take Catherine's life and then her own, rather than submit to an even worse fate. Settling herself in the shade by the river, knowing that there was nothing else she could do, she waited.

It was an hour later that Tam came running along the track.

'They are coming,' he called breathlessly. 'I have seen them.'

'How far?'

'Maybe two miles.'

'How many?'

Just as she suspected, Nick had woken instantly, pulling himself painfully to his feet and she now saw that he winced as he hobbled towards them fastening his sword belt.

'I counted fifteen.' Tam said. 'But… there may have been one more or less. I don't always count too good.'

Nick put a hand on his shoulder and smiled. 'You did well. One more or less will not matter.' Reaching out his other hand he drew Matilda close and looked solemnly from one to the other.

'We are outnumbered five to one, but there is still time for you both to leave. This is my fight. My path. You do not have to take it.'

Neither spoke and both held their ground. Matilda placed her free hand on Tam's other shoulder and all three stood drawing strength from each other until Nick, with a nod of his head, and a smile of gratitude, released them.

***

Nick positioned himself with his back to the river facing the trail so that they would have to approach him from the front. They had hidden Catherine amongst the trees, and Tam watched her from above, his orders to fight only if she were directly threatened.

'There is no point my giving instructions to you,' Nick told Matilda. 'You will do exactly as you please, but I would advise that you take no unnecessary risks. If you think you have a real chance then attack. Otherwise just defend yourself.'

Despite his words, as the first of Lassall's mercenaries entered the clearing, she brought him to the ground. He wore no armour, and the knife that imbedded in his breast killed him instantly. The two men who followed turned towards her. Only one made it to the trees.

More men entered the clearing and these approached Nick cautiously. Two were armed with axes and knives, the other wore half armour and carried a sword. He was vaguely aware of a fourth but this man kept his distance. When they attacked, Nick lost all sense of where he was or what was happening around him. All his instincts were concentrated on his opponents. They were fearless and experienced and he could not move easily, but eventually all three lay still on the ground.

At one point it seemed that there were fifty men at least in the clearing and they seemed to be fighting each other, but Nick did not let his attention wander. The fourth man had now approached him, and he recognised Richard Lassall. Nick knew now that this was a battle for his honour as well as his life. His enemy stood before him the look in his eye confirming that this was a fight to the death.

'If I am to die here,' Richard said. 'I will take you with me. Before long King Tynon will beat your boy king, the Valerons will regain our throne and the name of Trayer will at last be obliterated.'

Nick advanced on the man slowly, dragging his injured leg.

Richard stepped to the side, forcing Nick to change direction. I see you found your bride. I look forward to meeting her again.'

At his words Nick turned instinctively towards the trees and Lassall took the opportunity to lunge at him. 'It is a shame that we did not have time to get to know each other. She seems a most comely woman.'

It was his rage that took Nick forward. He managed just in time to parry the blow and lunged immediately. For some minutes, and he would not have been able to say how long, he put up as good a fight as he could but his leg was numb and heavy. Lassall made use of this by circling all the while. Nick could only spin round desperately and he felt dizzy and unsteady. Finally he stumbled forward taking his opponent by surprise. They fell together on to the ground and here Nick had the advantage. Lassall's armour restricted his movements whereas Nick, without having to put pressure on his leg could now move more freely. He let fall his sword and drew out his knife plunging it into the gaping sides of Richard's coif. The blade found the man's throat and a cry of pain turned to a gurgle as his mouth filled with blood. Nick pulled the knife free as his enemy's arms flayed uselessly then were still. His eyes met Lassall's in the seconds before the man died, and what he saw there was a hatred so pure that it almost turned his own blood to ice. Gradually the eyes dulled and he knew that he had finally revenged the death of his parents. He was finally free of the guilt.

He sat back allowing himself a breath of air before trying to stand.

'Rest easy, my friend, Catherine is unharmed.' Nick frowned, confused and disorientated. He thought he recognised the voice and then was sure when it bellowed. 'That was well done, Farm Boy if a little clumsy. We'll make a soldier of you yet.'

He twisted around angrily. 'How long have you been here?'

Prince Jared was leaning on his sword a few yards behind him, his face creased into his usual arrogant grin. 'Long enough to see your rather unconventional swordplay.'

'And how long were you planning to wait before you came to my aid.' The anger he felt for Lassall had not been completely abated. He now turned it on his friend. Jared seemed to understand. He walked calmly towards Nick and offered his hand to pull him to his feet.

'I would have intervened, believe me, if I had not faith in your ability. His life was yours to take. I could not deny you that.'

Nick nodded, his anger finally spent. 'Forgive me. In truth I am very pleased to see you. I had believed this day to be my last.'

'You will wish it had been,' the Prince assured him, 'when you are forced to face my brother's wrath.'

'Matilda and the boy, how are they?'

'Both alive. Tam has a small wound. It is not serious. Matilda is unhurt. I would like to see the man who gets the better of that one. Come, my men will dispose of him.' He indicated Lassall with a nod of his head.

‘I may need some assistance.’ Nick said ruefully, ‘I cannot feel my foot.’

***

Once again, Matilda unwound the dressing from Nick’s leg. She knew that it was causing him great pain but she had to ensure that it was not infected.

Jared peered at the wound and made a face.

‘You should rest that. You should not be racing around the country rescuing maidens and fighting off bands of mercenaries.’

‘Thank you,’ Nick said tartly. ‘Your advice is most welcome.’

The Prince laughed and took a piece of meat from the fire. His men had caught a wild boar in the woods and with the provisions they had brought, were celebrating their victory in one corner of the clearing. Tam and the Prince’s man Lucas, sat a little way apart watching over Catherine. She had woken for a short while after Lassall’s defeat but was sleeping again now.

For the fiftieth time Matilda glanced up at the Prince. She could hardly believe the treachery of her own body. Only hours before, she had discovered for sure that Jacob was dead. Jacob, the man she had come to think of as her husband, the man who had taken her in when she arrived starving on his doorstep, given her a home, a child, and his very heart. Yet here she was, dreaming about another man.

She had fought for her life against two of Lassall’s soldiers knowing that she could not last much longer, when suddenly they were gone. It had taken her a few moments to understand what was happening. There was chaos in the clearing as the two groups of men fought each other and then the Prince seemed to rise out of their midst like a mythical hero. As he came towards her, her legs felt weak and her face burned though whether from the exertion of her fight or the sight of him, she did not know. Fortunately, he assumed the former, and took her arm solicitously.

'Are you hurt, Matilda?'

'No, My Lord, I am just …' she waved a hand vaguely.

'Come. Sit down. Catch your breath. I must help Nick but I will send someone to take care of you.'

'That is not necessary,' she said lamely, though he had already gone. 'I will be fine.'

Tam had taken a scratch from one of the mercenaries' swords and she had gone to aid him, washing his arm and binding it while he admired it proudly.

Now, as she packed Nick's wound with the last of the comfrey, she watched Jared cut the meat from the bone with his knife and chew it before turning to her.

'Lady Matilda?'

'My Lord Prince.'

'You fought well and you showed great courage.' Her heart soared at the compliment, only to sink once more as he added. 'For a woman.'

She tugged angrily at the bandage causing Nick to yelp with pain, but the Prince paused again.

'No. That is unfair. It is most unfair. I have seen grown men fail of courage in such situations. Forgive me.'

'There is nothing to forgive My Lord.'

Jared turned and called to his servant. 'Lucas. Bring me that dagger.'

The man returned carrying a knife in a scabbard of red leather decorated with gold. He handed it to the Prince.

Jared pulled it out of its sheath and admired it.

'I took this from one of Lassall's men. These mercenaries by their very nature, acquire things which are way above their station.' He held it before him. 'The handle is inlaid with gold leaf, look. And the blade is almost perfectly balanced. It was made for a nobleman I'm sure. He replaced it, recovered it and handed it to Matilda. 'Will you accept this as a gift? It is a token of my… my admiration for your skills as a soldier.'

Matilda could not have been more surprised. She tied the bandage around Nick's leg then took the dagger, unsheathed it and held it in her palm. It was heavy and if anything so deadly could ever be, it was beautiful.

'Thank you, My Lord. I will treasure it always.'

'Treasure it, yes. Don't throw it at any one. It is not one of your kitchen knives.'

The smile which played at the corners of his mouth was awkward and shy. It bewitched her. He was in many ways so strong, yet sometimes she had the distinct feeling that he was vulnerable. Somewhere in his heart he carried the secret, the dark secret that haunted him, and that he hid beneath his arrogant bravado.

'I will not throw it,' she assured him. For just a second he held her gaze then he nodded in satisfaction and leaned forward to take another piece of meat from the fire.

Nick had been lost in his own thoughts while they were talking. Now he turned to the Prince with a frown.

'You knew that Richard Lassall had killed my parents didn't you?'

Jared studied his supper. 'I cannot deny that. And I would have told you if I could but…' He looked up at Nick guiltily. 'I could not. However, circumstances have changed. Now I will answer whatever of your questions I can.'

'He said that our lives were linked, in ways that I did not know. And though he had never met me, he hated me. Why?'

‘I will tell you what I know Nick. It may not be all.’ Jared threw the bone into the fire where it fizzled and burned as the flames caught at the fat. ‘Lassall and his men accosted your parents and killed them. As you know, they had intended that you should also die, but they did not find you. Either they did not think to search the cart or they did not have time before our soldiers found them.

‘Richard was taken prisoner, but before he was to stand trial a pact was made between his family and my father. Richard’s mother was… she was a close friend of my father’s. He agreed to spare her son’s life although he would have to spend the remainder of that life at Barrow Marsh. In return, she was to obtain an undertaking from the Valerons that there would be no further attempts on your life. If there were, she was assured, Richard’s life would be forfeit.

‘It was decided, however, that you were to be kept in ignorance of all of this. Everyone could see the merit in that. If you knew of Richard’s identity, you would be honour bound to hunt him down and avenge your family. The Lassalls naturally wanted to avoid this and my father wanted to keep you safe, as did your steward to whom he had entrusted your care. That is why the King took the unusual step of releasing you from his service. You were to remain in Claveham on your farm.

‘You were also a prisoner in your own home, Nick, though you would not have seen it that way.’

‘I knew that our attacker had connections at court,’ Nick admitted. ‘But I had convinced myself that it was the Garwins who were responsible. Lord John’s grandson lives in exile doesn’t he? I thought that he must be involved.’

Matilda’s heart gave a jolt as Jared’s eyes flashed with anger. ‘No. Will Garwin is a fool who fell in love unwisely. For that he has lost far more than just his liberty. But he is not a murderer.' There was an awkward silence as a dark cloud seemed to grip the Prince and he stared into the fire.

'What I do not understand,' Matilda asked, eager to change the subject, yet desperate to know the truth. 'Is why Nick's life is so important to the Valerons.'

The Prince shook himself as if to push away his dark mood. 'I do not know. I swear to you that is the truth. I do not know. But as soon as we return I intend to find out.'

'Felix Runmore is the key.' Matilda said. 'He has been instrumental in all of this.'

'Felix?' The Prince almost laughed. 'I hardly think so. He does not have the brainpower.'

'Are you sure?' She did not wish to argue with him but the more she thought about it the more she realised the truth. 'It was he who refused Nick's father an escort. He claims that he was badly advised but that does not ring true really, does it? And it was he who helped me to get Nick out of the castle. He arranged to stand down the guard until we were free. Also, when the messenger came to take Jacob, the message carried the royal seal.'

'Is that so?' Jared's handsome face creased into a frown.

'And we walked straight into a trap.' Nick said,. 'They knew we were coming. How else could they have known?'

'Did you not say that it was Runmore who killed the man who tried to poison the King,' Matilda added, 'before he had a chance to reveal his accomplice.'

The look that passed between the two men struck dread into her heart because she knew what they were thinking. Prince Jared stood up angrily.

'He insisted that I bring my best men to find you. He knew that Nick is my friend and that I would want to come after him. He played me for a fool. We are both here while my brother is at the castle at his mercy.' The look on his face was thunderous. ‘And Felix has command of the army.’

***

‘These are six of my most experienced men.’ The Prince told her as he prepared to leave. ‘I cannot spare any more but they will keep you safe. I have told them to travel at the pace that you think best for Catherine, and they will do as you ask.’

‘She grows stronger hour by hour,’ Matilda said. ‘Though I do not know if she will recover fully. You must go. I pray that you are in time to stop whatever he has planned.’ She glanced over to where Nick was saying his goodbyes to Catherine. ‘This is foolishness. He should stay with us and give his wound time to heal.’

‘Nick is the King’s profender,’ the Prince reminded her. ‘He has already deserted his post. He will never forgive himself if he does not go. It is his duty.’

‘Duty huh! Look where duty has got him. Please. If you are the friend you claim to be. Make him stay.’

‘You forget. Rowan is my brother as well as my king. I need all the help I can get.’

‘Then take me, and make Nick stay with Catherine.’

‘You know that I cannot.’ He paused for a moment and gave her a sympathetic look which angered her, then he smiled at her again and her heart turned to dust ‘Fare thee well Matilda.’

As he mounted his horse and rode away she whispered. ‘Take care of Nick, My Lord Prince. And take care of yourself.’

Chapter 34

The King stood gasping for breath, his hands resting on his knees.

The sword instructor smiled and gave a short bow. 'I think that will be all for today, Sire. I am very pleased with your progress.'

'By the time my brother returns I will be able to give him a good fight don't you think, Master Lambett?'

The instructor hesitated just long enough and Rowan laughed. 'Perhaps I am being a little too optimistic.'

Lambett nodded. 'Just a touch, Sire. But you are making very good progress, I have no doubt that one day the Prince will be quaking in his boots.'

Rowan laughed again and straightening up accepted a towel from his page.

'Thank you for your patient instruction and thank you also for being honest with me.'

'You are a good student, Sire. It is a pleasure.'

Wiping his face and hands Rowan made his way from the practice yard towards the armoury. As always the pages and two of his personal guard followed at a respectful distance. Joseph Padbury the Chancellor's assistant walked beside him.

‘Master Hobbs asks if he may come to see you this afternoon, My Lord. I have told him that you must talk to the chief physician first but if you will permit him to…’

‘Who is Master Hobbs?’

‘The mail maker, Sire.’

‘Oh, of course. I must try to remember names.’

‘You do that very well Sire. You cannot expect to know every member of the household.’

Nevertheless, Rowan was irritated with himself. He knew how much people appreciated being remembered.

‘Let us visit Master Hobbs in his workshop. I enjoy watching him work. We’ll go now.’

‘Master Morton, the chief physician wishes to speak with you, sire. He is waiting in your chamber.’

‘He can wait a little longer, Paddle. It is early still.’

Padbury pretended not to notice the use of his nickname but Rowan knew that he did not mind. In truth, the man was quite flattered that the King thought of him fondly enough to use one.

Instead of entering the armoury to return his sword, he went around to the back of the building where the armourer and the mail maker had their workshops.

The mail maker was bent over his bench concentrating intensely. He did not notice them until the King spoke.

‘Master Hobbs?’

‘My Lord King.’ The man arose hurriedly and bowed. ‘Forgive me. I did not see you there.’

‘Please, do not let me disturb you. How are you proceeding?’

Hobbs indicated a coat of mail hanging from a wooden cross at the side of his bench.

‘As you can see, Sire, the hauberk is almost complete. I am working on your coif as we speak. That is why I asked to see you. I would like to check that it fits.’

‘We can do that now.’ Rowan said. He came up to the table and lifted the mail hood, weighing it in his hands. ‘It is heavy.’

‘Yes, Sire. But it will not feel so when you are wearing it. If you will allow me.’

Rowan gave him the coif and allowed Hobbs to place it over his head. ‘You will have a padded hood underneath when you go to battle.’

It was true that once in place it did not feel as heavy as it had to hold but the weight was still noticeable. He wondered how uncomfortable he was going to feel with a whole suit of mail and a helmet and the plates that would cover his chest and limbs. He put a hand to his sword remembering his last lesson in the practice yard. To do all that with the added weight of the armour, seeing only what was visible through the slit of his visor, it would be very different. He imagined himself on a battlefield with enemy soldiers coming at him from all sides. It was frightening yet every warrior had to experience his first battle and though a part of him could feel the fear, there was also the part that longed to prove his worth.

The mailmaker adjusted the hood then fiddled with the edges and mumbled to himself until he was satisfied.

‘Another row at the chin, I think and that will do. Thank you, Sire.’

Without removing it, Rowan wandered over to the hauberk.

‘I hope it is to your liking, Sire,’ Hobbs inquired. ‘Each ring is twice riveted and here you see the motif of a crown that I have stamped into each one. The rings in the trimming are solid gold and I have taken the liberty of including these small discs which carry my mark.’

‘It looks very fine,’ Rowan agreed. ‘But is it strong?’

‘As strong as any armour can be, Sire.’

‘That is an honest answer, Master Hobbs.’

‘War, Sire is a nasty business.’

Rowan sighed. ‘Indeed.’

He wandered over to the far side of the workshop where another, much larger coat hung. ‘Whose is this?’

‘I am adjusting it for Robert Boderry, Sire. Peace can sometimes play tricks with the stomachs of fighting men. The food at the castle has proved his undoing and I am charged with the loosening of it.’

Rowan smiled. ‘Robert does enjoy his food, it’s true.’ He looked closely at the mail coat. ‘What are these?’ Attached to the rings of the coat above the area where his heart would be, were a cluster of what looked like makers discs only these were thicker.’

‘They each contain a lock of his wife’s hair, Sire. It is quite common for tokens such as that to be included in the armour. Even a proud fighting man likes to be reminded of the comforts of home, or the face of a fair maiden.’

Rowan thought briefly of the somewhat formidable Lady Maud Boderry and wondered that Robert would want to be reminded.

He laughed, his dark mood lifting. ‘May I take this off now?’

‘Of course Sire.’

The man lifted the coif away and Rowan felt the relief of the cool air against his head. ‘Thank you, Master Hobbs for all you have done. It is as fine a piece of work as I have seen.’

The mailmaker bowed again. ‘Thank you, Sire.’

Outside on the grass surrounding the armoury, Rowan stood to enjoy the warmth of the day. He knew that he should return his sword to the armoury and the go back to his chamber to see the physician but he liked to listen sometimes to the sounds of the castle and to the birdsong and the shouts of the children playing in the courtyard.

'My Lord,' Padbury ventured, 'the physician is still waiting.'

'Yes of course.' It seemed such a shame to go indoors and attend to such boring matters. 'What does he want? Is it not something you could do? Or Lord John?'

'I am afraid not, Sire. There is an outbreak of cattle malaise in two of our northern villages. The disease should not be serious but the villagers have requested assistance. The physician needs your permission to attend.'

'Well that is fine. As long as he returns quickly I do not have any objection.'

'Yes Sire, but… Master Morton would like to see you first just to em… to satisfy himself that you are well.'

At the armoury door Rowan paused.

'Does he think I am suffering from cattle malaise?'

'No of course not, Sire, but your health is his responsibility and…' Padbury waved an arm.

Rowan made a face. 'Will he peer into my ears and my throat and suchlike?'

'I would imagine so, Sire.'

'I can hardly wait.'

He began to enter the armoury when there was the sound of shouting from the gatehouse below. Eager for distraction Rowan ran to the wall and peered down. In the outer courtyard an armed visitor had arrived. He was surprised to see that the sentry was George Carver his favourite member of the personal guard.

'Why are you on the watch, George?' he called down.

The men in the courtyard stopped what they were doing and bowed to the King. He acknowledged them then asked again. 'George?'

'I have been reassigned, Sire.'

‘Why?’

‘The Commander insists that there be a rotation of duties, sire?’

‘A rotation of duties. What nonsense.’ He was angry that the Commander had interfered with the royal guard. He wanted the men he knew around him.

‘Who is this visitor?’

‘He comes with a message for the Commander, Sire.’

‘A message from whom?’

‘He will not say, Sire.’

‘Come up here George and bring the messenger with you. I cannot hold a conversation at this distance.’

‘Yes Sire.’

Padbury was clearly unhappy.

‘The physician, Sire.’

Rowan turned to one of his pages. ‘See that he has plenty to eat and some good wine. Tell him I am sorry for the delay but an emergency has occurred.’

‘But Sire...’

‘Enough Paddle. I want to know what is going on in the castle. I am not happy that Commander Runmore has interfered with my guard.’

He stood and waited while Padbury fretted. It was not the only strange thing that had happened over the last day or so since Jared had left. Dominic Lowen, the Prince’s second in command had come to the King the day before to complain that Felix had assigned three of his companies to duties which took them out of the castle. Lowen knew that until they left for the war, Prince Jared would never have so many men away from the castle at one time.

Rowan had suspected for a while that Felix resented Jared’s having his own regiment and that he was expected to defer to the King’s illegitimate son. Now it seemed, that in the Prince's absence the Commander was flexing his muscles.

When George Carver and the messenger arrived, the King challenged him.

'You have a message for Commander Runmore?'

'I do, Sire.'

'From whom.?

'I … do not know. The orders came from my superior.'

The King looked at his attire. 'Who's livery do you wear?'

'It is… It is a free company, Sire.'

'A free company. You are a mercenary?'

'I am.' The man looked wretched.

'I will take the message.'

'But I have been told to give it only to the Commander.'

'I'm sure you have, but I am the King. There is nothing in this land that can be secret from me. I will take the message.'

The soldier knew that he had no choice. He looked very scared. Rowan held out his hand and the man handed him the scroll. It was sealed with the Lassall seal. 'I wonder why the Lassall family hire mercenaries to deliver their letters.'

He turned to Carver. 'You are not a sentry George you are a member of my personal guard. Arrange for someone to replace you and if anyone questions you refer them to me. It is Nick who commands my bodyguard, not Felix. In the meantime, please take this man and offer him the hospitality of our guardroom. He is not to leave the castle.'

Carver bowed. 'Yes, Sire.'

Rowan looked at the message again. He was very tempted to open it there but could not quite bring himself to do so. Frowning he turned back to the Chancellor's assistant. 'Come on then Paddle. Let us see the physician.'

Striding briskly he climbed the hill between the armoury and the living quarters. In the courtyard the children were playing as usual under the watchful eye of the ladies. He caught sight of Sophia sitting by herself on a bench by the wall. Something in the way she sat bothered him and much to Padbury's frustration he went over to speak to her. Sophia got off the bench and curtsied but she would not meet his eye.

'What is wrong?' he asked.

She shook her head miserably.

'Sophia. Tell me?'

'Are you not angry with me?'

'Angry? No. Why would I be?'

'You are angry with my mother.'

'Yes. I am but only because…' He realised suddenly that everyone was listening and he did not want them to hear what he had to say. 'Come,' he insisted. 'Come with me to my chamber and we will talk about this.'

'My Lord, the physician is waiting in your chamber.' Padbury reminded him.

'That is true. We will go to your mother's room.'

Padbury held up his hands in supplication. 'Sire, please'

'That's enough.' Rowan told him angrily. 'I will see Master Morton, I promise you. But I have other things to attend to first. Not another word or I will have you locked in the dungeons.'

He led Sophia into the corridor and to the room at the far end which had been assigned to Matilda.

'Wait outside, all of you,' he instructed.

Inside, he put the Commander's letter on the table and sat on the chair, realising that he was still wearing his sword. He put out his hand to Sophia and taking it she came to stand beside him.

'It is true that I am angry with Matilda,' he said softly. 'She helped Nick to escape from the castle and I had good reason to keep him here, but that does not mean that she has ceased to be my friend. Or you. I am not angry with you.'

'Nick wanted to be with his bride.'

'I know he did and in truth I do not blame him for that but… he is a very important man and even he does not realise why. To put his life in danger for…' with a shock he realised who he was speaking to. Sophia was intelligent and she understood the implications immediately.

'Is my mother's life in danger?'

He squeezed her hand and pulled her closer, laying an arm around her small shoulders. 'I will not lie to you, it may be. However, I have sent Prince Jared to bring them back and as he is so fond of telling us, he is this country's greatest warrior. Do not be afraid Sophia. I did not mean to cause you more distress.'

She nodded but he could tell that she was still upset. He did not know what to say to comfort her and still holding her looked away so that he could not see her tears. His eyes came to rest on Felix's letter and he released the child gently and picked it up.

'This is a private letter for Felix Runmore,' he told her. 'I should not open it but… I have the strangest feeling about it. I don't know what to do.'

'I do not like the Commander,' Sophia said, sniffing back her tears.

'Why is that?'

'I do not know. There is just something about him. He scares me. And Roc doesn't like him either. He growls every time he sees him.'

‘He growls at me too,’ Rowan reminded her. ‘And he bit me.’

‘Yes but that was just playing. With Felix it is a real growl like this.’ She scowled angrily and made a loud noise through her teeth.

Rowan laughed at her serious expression. ‘Well that settles it. Roc has decided the matter for me.’

Before he had a chance to change his mind, he slipped the tip of his dagger under the seal. He opened the letter and read.

My Dearest Uncle… I have followed your orders… I will kill him or die in the attempt…

‘Uncle?’ Barely had he finished reading when there was a sharp knock on the door. He called ‘Wait,’ and attempted to refold the letter when the door was opened and Felix himself entered the room.

‘I told you to wait,’ Rowan said angrily trying not to show the fear that he felt on seeing the Commander.

Felix ignored him. His eyes darted to the letter then back to meet Rowan’s.

‘I understood there was a letter for me. A private letter. But I see it is private no more.’

Rowan stood up and called for the guards. Felix shook his head. ‘I told them to wait along the corridor and they asked no questions. I am sure you have noticed that they are not my best men.’

The letter proved that the Commander was a traitor. It answered many questions but not all. One question had played on the King’s mind from the very moment he learned of his father’s accident.

‘Was my father murdered?’ he asked.

‘No,’ the Commander replied. ‘His death was exactly as we claimed, an accident. But its timing was fortuitous.’

‘Did you attempt to poison me?’

'No. That was one of my men. He saw an opportunity and threatened your servant. I knew nothing about it, but of course I guessed.'

'And would you kill me now?'

'I assure you that I have nothing against you personally, but I cannot let you live.'

'You would restore the Valeron crown?'

'Of course. I have worked towards it every day of my life.'

'Your ancestors were cruel and corrupt. The people hated them. They did not deserve the throne.'

'And now? You think you are more deserving. You who are just a child. Your father was a womaniser who filled the castle with his illegitimate offspring. Even your own mother could not bear to be in his presence. His firstborn son is a …'

'That is enough,' Rowan commanded, drawing his sword. He glanced at Sophia who had hidden herself behind her mother's bed. He was not sure if Felix knew she was there. With his free hand he motioned to her to stay down.

Felix laughed and drew his own sword. As commander of the armies he was one of the few men permitted to carry weapons in the royal apartments.

'So you would fight me would you? Do you think that I am a feeble old man?'

'You are a traitor,' Rowan said with more courage than he felt. 'You will die for your treachery.'

'Come on then child. Let us see what Master Lambett has taught you.'

What he lacked in experience, Rowan made up for in agility and speed. Runmore had strength, but his limbs were stiff and he was clearly out of practice. Nevertheless Rowan knew he could not defeat the old man alone.

‘Sophia,’ he called, keeping his eye on his opponent. ‘Get help. Find the guards.’

As she ran for the door, Felix spun round and lunged for her and she screamed and ran back behind the bed. The movement caused the Commander’s limbs to stiffen further and the King moved in. Runmore parried the blow but not fast enough and he lost his footing and fell backwards. Rowan held his sword against the old man’s throat but could not bring himself to press his advantage.

‘Would you kill me?’ Felix asked. ‘I think not.’

He swung his knife at the King’s leg and Rowan rammed his blade home. Though it cut into the Commander’s neck it did not penetrate his windpipe and he had to push again this time with all his weight. He felt it cut through bone and sinew. The old man gasped once then was still, his eyes staring straight at him as if he could not believe what had happened.

The King stood silently staring at the body of his commander.

‘Is he dead?’ Sophia said softly. She approached tentatively her eyes wide with fear.

He knelt beside the body and felt the man’s chest for some sign of life.

‘Yes.’ He gulped, and from nowhere he felt the rising tide of nausea.

‘He was a bad man,’ she said, her voice tremulous, tears of relief welling in her eyes. ‘He would have killed us both.’ She put a hand on his shoulder. ‘You are shaking.’

‘I have never killed a man before.’ His own voice was weak with shock.

She let her thin soft arm slide around his neck. He felt tears rush to his eyes and buried his face in her small chest. Though he tried to hold them back, the sobs which wracked his body would not be contained. Sophia cried too, holding him close. After some minutes he pulled away, wiping his eyes angrily and rising to his feet.

'We must find Lord John. He will know what to do with… with him.' He halted for a moment. 'Sophia, you…you will not speak of this to anyone?'

Clearly she did not understand. She pointed to the Commander's body. 'Of this?'

'Of… of my weakness. You will not tell anyone that I cried.'

'You are not weak,' she insisted. 'You are strong and courageous. My mother says that a brave man is not one who knows no fear. It is one who moves onward despite that fear. You have done that many times and I am sure you will again.'

'Jared would not have wept like a girl. Or Nick.'

'They are soldiers. It is their duty to kill.'

'I must be a soldier. I am king. I must be all things.'

And if ever he had felt the truth of that he felt it now. There were those who would advise him, those who would see to his comfort and his health even those who would lay down their lives to defend him, but only he was the King. Every subject from Lord John to the peasants in the fields depended on him. He had never felt more alone.

As if she understood his thoughts, Sophia slipped her hand into his. Her clear dark eyes were dry now and he felt a rush of warmth at their gaze. It strengthened him.

For a few seconds he allowed himself to linger there, then he released her gently. Straightening his back as if to re-shoulder his burden, he sheathed his sword and went to the door calling into the corridor.

'Guards, Padbury, come here.'

He turned back to Sophia.

'There are many things I must do now. Will you be all right?'

‘Yes.’ She smiled and then the guards entered the room followed by Padbury and in the ensuing chaos, she slipped away.

Chapter 35

Nick knew as they came down from the mountains, that he was very ill. His body was drenched in sweat yet he was shivering uncontrollably. Pain had taken a vice-like grip on his head and the wound in his leg throbbed angrily. The fact that he was still upright in the saddle was due in the most part to Ransom's instinctive understanding. The horse could sense that his master was ailing and followed the other horses without having to be steered. When the ground was uneven, he slowed his pace so that the going would be smoother to cause Nick the least discomfort.

Tam, who had not left his side throughout the journey, was clearly worried. The Prince had set a gruelling pace and they had ridden all night and most of the day. They had stopped briefly in the early morning to rest and water the horses and take some food themselves. Tam had tried to make Nick drink from a flask that Matilda had given him.

'Mistress Matilda said that you should drink this if you looked like developing a fever and I fear that you have, My Lord.'

Nick waved it away. 'I know Matilda's potions. It will make me sleep and I cannot do that. I will not sleep until I know that the King is safe.'

Tam frowned and tried to imagine what Matilda would say.

'I will speak to the Prince. He will make you drink it.'

'You will do no such thing,' Nick shouted angrily. 'He is worried about his brother. I will not give him anything else to worry about.'

'Then let us wait here. You cannot go on, My Lord. I am frightened. I fear for your life.'

He tried to reassure the boy. 'I am grateful for your concern, Tam. But I am not dying. It is merely a fever caused by my wound. It will pass.'

Now as the mound of Castle Baryk came into view he knew that it was more serious than that. There was a fog which he sensed was not real but which his fevered brain had invented. It swirled around him, forcing his eyes to close and sending his head lolling forward.

With a supreme effort, he forced himself back into consciousness, taking in deep breaths of air and reaching for his water bottle. His hand seemed to wave uselessly in the air until he found the bottle thrust into it by the ever watchful Tam. The boy had removed the stopper and Nick held the flask above him and let the remains of the liquid cascade over him. Briefly, it revived him and as they approached the castle gates he was fully conscious once more.

The King, warned of their approach, was waiting for them on the wall above the gates.

'Runmore is a traitor,' the Prince called up to him. 'We came to warn you.'

Rowan smiled, his face triumphant.

'You are too late. I have already dealt with the Commander. We burned his body this morning.'

Nick closed his eyes with relief, then the world began to spin and he lost all sense of time. He heard Tam call his name then he felt himself falling and everything went black.

***

They stopped for the last time within a half day's ride of Castle Baryk. Matilda judged that it would be more comfortable for Catherine to rest overnight and have only the short journey the following day. One of the soldiers had ridden ahead to herald their return and to bring news from the castle.

He came back at day break informing them that all was well. They were in good spirits therefore as they approached the castle shortly before noon.

At the gatehouse Prince Jared and Lady Maud were waiting for them. The Prince greeted them with a cheerful smile, but Matilda who had studied every detail of him so carefully over the previous weeks could see the signs of strain on his face.

Catherine was still very weak but she had insisted on sitting upright in the front of the cart. The Prince went straight over and offered her his arm.

'My dear Catherine. Welcome to Castle Baryk. We met only briefly but already I see how much better you are.'

Matilda could see that even Catherine was not immune to his charm. She whispered her thanks and allowed him to lift her down from the cart. Although she was now able to take a few steps unaided, the journey had clearly tired her and when she tried to walk, her legs would not hold her. The Prince scooped her up in his arms and carried her to the litter which Lady Maud had thought to arrange. Matilda experienced a moment of envy before she frowned, scolding herself silently.

Catherine, propped now between a mound of cushions looked around her eagerly. ‘Where is Nick?’

The Prince’s smile did not diminish. ‘He is confined to his room until his wound heals. He asked me to apologise for not meeting you himself.’

‘Will you take me to him?’

Matilda knew from the tone of the Prince’s voice that he was hiding something.

‘I think you should rest first Catherine,’ she insisted. ‘It would be foolish to do too much too soon.’

Lady Maud came over to Catherine and offered her hand in greeting. ‘I am Maud Boderry and if you will permit me, I will take you to your room. I have arranged a small meal for you and a change of clothes. I am sure you will want to look your best when you see Nick again.’

To Matilda’s relief, Catherine did not object as the men lifted the litter to take her through the inner gate and up the hill, with Lady Maud fussing all the while.

As soon as she had gone Matilda turned to the Prince meeting his anxious gaze.

‘Nick is ill?’

‘Yes. He has a fever. I cannot tell you how pleased I am that you are here.’

She began to follow the procession to the castle. Along the street, all the small shops were open, the townsfolk going about their business in the spice scented air. Everywhere there was the sound of voices calling and of sacks and boxes being moved. There was a sense of bustle and expectation. It was a stark contrast to the hushed mourning of the first time she had entered the town.

‘I did consider sending a man to fetch you.’ The Prince fell into step beside her. ‘But I did not want to bring you away from Catherine. Nick would never forgive me if I put his welfare above hers.’

It was true and she was impressed by his understanding of that. There was more to him than a brash soldier's bravado.

'What of the wound? Is it still infected or does it heal?'

'I do not know,' he admitted. 'I do not have the stomach for such things. You will have to ask those who attend him.'

She stopped to catch her breath. The hill was steep and she had never climbed it so fast before. 'Will the physicians permit my interference?'

'I would like to see the man who tries to stop you.' The Prince smiled wryly. 'In truth there are no physicians in the castle. They had been called away to an outbreak of cattle malaise a day's ride away. The boy Tam has attended his master with the help of your daughter.'

They continued in silence. As they reached the castle mount, the preparations for war were immediately apparent. The practice yards and parade ground were a seething mass of men and from the armoury, came the clash of metal on metal.

Matilda and the Prince headed straight for the royal apartments and by the time she reached Nick's room her legs were aching and her breath tight. Sophia came rushing into her arms.

'Oh Mamma. I am so pleased to see you. We thought he was going to die. He is so hot and he thrashes about so and shouts and sees things that are not there. We had to bring two men to hold him down.'

Matilda held her tight, regaining her breath and enjoying one small moment with her daughter. 'I am here now. Tell me what you have done for him?'

She released the child and went over to the bed. Just a few days before she had found him here in a self-provoked melancholy. How she wished now, that a few chosen words would be all that was needed to rouse him.

He lay on his back, still for the moment as if sleeping peacefully, but his face and neck were flushed and the sweat oozed from his skin and ran into his hair and bedding.

'I knew that we should keep him cool so we had them bring ice and placed it around him. It has all gone now, though. The ice house is empty.'

'That was exactly the right thing to do.' Matilda assured her as she moved to examine the wound. It was still reddened and inflamed, but was clean and had begun to mend. 'This is good. You have done well to keep it clean.'

On the other side of the bed, Tam had been standing silently. Matilda had not noticed him until he spoke.

'We used the poultice you gave me, but it has all gone now.'

Both children showed the signs of strain. She wondered if they had slept at all.

'I am proud of you both,' she told them. 'I am sure he will recover. He is a strong man. Go, both of you. Go and get some food and some rest. I will take care of him now.' She kissed her daughter again. 'Sophia, I will find you later and you can tell me all that has happened.'

When they had gone, Prince Jared who had not left the room asked softly. 'Are you sure that he will recover?'

She sighed. 'They did everything that I would have done.' Taking a cloth and soaking it in the water, she washed Nick's face and neck carefully, 'Even so, he will need all his strength and will to live.' She placed the cloth across his forehead and looked up at the Prince. 'Thank you by the way, for not alarming Catherine. I will not be able to hide this from her for long, but...' she considered the matter. Maybe she could prepare a sleeping draft so that by the time Catherine woke, Nick would either be on the road to recovery or… She did not want to think of the alternative.

The Prince acknowledged her thanks with a nod of his head then turned to go. 'I am not the best man to have in a sick room. I will take my leave of you.' He turned back to her. 'Make sure you also get some rest, Matilda. You know, you are a very special woman and I feel honoured to have your friendship.'

'Friendship,' she said aloud when he had left. 'Is that what I want from him?' She lifted the cloth from Nick's head and soaked it again, squeezing the excess water back into the bowl. 'You are my friend, Nick. For him…' she shook her head sadly. 'For him I feel something entirely different.'

Chapter 36

Tam sat at the long kitchen table, his face flushed by the fires which burned there throughout the day. Across from him, Sophia was almost asleep where she sat, while on the table lay the remains of a meal prepared especially for them by Mistress Zira, the castle cook.

Zira was a stocky woman of middle age. She wore a plain grey dress tied around her ample waist with a wide sash which she used to carry heavy dishes and to wipe her hands. Around her head she had wound a bright red kerchief which hid the fact that she was completely hairless. Even her eyebrows and lashes were bald and the young people who worked under her liked to joke that she had been singed so many times by the kitchen fires that her hair refused to grow back. Others whispered that she had been frightened by a ghost when she was a child and the hair had fallen out with shock.

Whatever the cause, her strange appearance made Zira a figure of fear and she only had to flash her eyes to command instant obedience.

Now those same eyes were soft with concern. She ran a hand gently over Sophia's head.

'Poor little one. You should be in your bed. Get along with you now.'

Sophia sighed wearily. 'I am too tired. I do not think I can climb the stairs. Perhaps I will sleep here.' She laid her arms on the table and rested her head upon them.

'I'll call for someone to carry you.'

'Without knowing quite why, Tam leaped to his feet. 'I'll take her.'

He came around the table and began to help the girl to her feet.

'You're just a mite yourself,' Zira said, although he was almost as tall as she. 'You'll never carry her all that way.'

'Yes I will.'

Sophia put her arms around his neck and he lifted her gently. She was heavier than he expected, but pride would not let him admit it.

'See. We will be fine.'

'Don't you drop her.' Zira scowled at him. 'You'll have me to answer to if you do.'

'I won't drop her,' he assured her but by the time he had climbed the stairs from the kitchen and crossed the corridors towards the apartment Sophia shared with her mother, his legs and arms were aching unbearably. One of the guards took her from him before he could complain.

'Here, Young'un,' he insisted. 'Let me take her. You look dead on your feet.'

The relief was instant though his pride was dented. He turned away miserably. What did he have to be proud about anyway? The master he had come to love, lay dying of fever, just as everyone he had loved before had done. Anyone with half a brain could see why.

He turned towards the servants' quarters, intending to go to his bed. He could still feel Sophia's soft hair against his neck and the slight pressure of her arm around his neck, but by the time he reached his door, the pleasant thoughts had gone. He would not be able to sleep. Instead he returned to his master's room. Matilda had seemed certain of Nick's recovery but he knew the outcome was still in doubt.

As he entered the room, she was leaning over the bed holding a cup to her patient's lips. When she saw Tam she beckoned him closer.

'Here, see if you can get him to drink this. I must get some fresh water.'

She passed the cup to him and picking up the bowl of water from beside the bed, left the room.

Tam put his free arm under his master's neck and lifted his head slightly.

'Drink, My Lord,' he whispered. 'Please. I am so sorry. I try not to use it but … it is so hard not to. You must not die because of me. Please drink.'

He was surprised and relieved to see Nick's dry lips part and very carefully he let the liquid drip into his mouth.

'Well done.' Matilda's voice in his ear was unexpected. He had not heard her return. He turned to her in surprise.

'I sent a girl for the water,' she explained. 'There, it is enough. Let him lie now.'

When he had done as she asked he took his place once more on the other side of the bed. Matilda bustled about tearing herbs and pounding them in a small bowl.

She glanced at him.

'You have done well. You should not doubt that.'

He sighed. 'On the journey, I tried to do all that you had told me but … he would not take the potion that you sent.'

'That does not surprise me.' She looked at him sternly. 'You have done all he could have asked of you.'

He shook his head. 'You would not say that if you knew.'

'If I knew what? You are fond of your master aren't you?'

He nodded. 'I… When I was a small child we lived in a village like Claveham. There were farms, but they were very small, except for the sentorman's hall. It was huge. Built of stone, it was, and … and the stables… my father was assistant stablemaster and he took me with him to look after the horses. That is why I…' He realised that he was straying from the subject. 'But he was feared, our sentorman. Not that he was cruel or nothing. He was fair I think, but… he was not part of the village at all.'

'That is the way of things,' she agreed.

'But my master is different, Mistress.' He struggled to find the right words. 'When we went back to his village, it was like… like going back to family. They all loved him. Oh, they spoke to him respectful, but … but he was one of them.'

'Yes,' she glanced briefly at her patient. 'He is a good man.'

Tam nodded again. He could feel the tears starting. 'He is good to me and he cares about me. I can tell these things and…and now he will die and it is all because of me.'

'Of you? Of course it isn't. Whyever would you think that?'

He shrunk away from her. He had thought that she might understand, but now he wasn't sure. And maybe if she knew, she would also die.

'Tam. Tell me?'

The need to share his fear was now too great to ignore. 'I… I am not like other boys, Mistress.'

'I know. You are True-sighted. Is that what you mean?'

He could hardly believe it. 'You know?'

'My mother was True-sighted. It is a gift, not a punishment. Do not be afraid.'

'But… but they said that they would all die because of it and I tried so hard not to…to let it happen but I couldn't help it and they did. All my family died, 'cept my sister who lived in Larock and… and I went to live with her but she didn't really want me 'cos she knew. She knew that she was in danger because of me.'

He thought that she would be horrified and that she would have him sent away but the look she gave him was kind and understanding.

'In the past, Tam, True-sighted people were venerated. That is, they were looked up to and respected, but they were also feared as you can imagine, because they could not be fooled, or lied to. That is a powerful skill for anyone to have and it can be used for good, or for bad.

'When the Valerons ruled they used True-sighted people to question prisoners and… well all sorts of other things and they took True-sighted children and trained them to their own purposes. If the families tried to stop them they would likely be killed. That is why your family were afraid and also… when the Valerons fell, there was a backlash against the True-sighted. Do you know what that means?'

He shook his head.

'It means that the people tried to destroy them for ever. True-sight was all part of what they called The Old Knowledge. Herblore was part of that too. Only those who were trained physicians were trusted to use herbs. The Valerons had powerful potion makers also. I think that…'

She stopped abruptly as Nick began to thrash about on the bed, his arms reaching for something that only he could see.

'I can't move,' he shouted.

'Hold him,' she instructed. 'We must not let him exert himself too much.'

Tam rushed to still his master's aid while Matilda poured more liquid from the cup into his mouth. It spilled out across his chin and neck but she persevered. All the while she spoke to him softly.

'Rest now. Be still. There is no-one here but me and the boy. Quiet now.'

'I can't move.'

'You can. But you should not. Rest Nick. You need to rest.'

Gradually the shaking ceased and the voice which cried out was silenced. They let go of him and returned to their places at the bedside.

Matilda sighed deeply and rubbed her head. Tam was close to tears. He could sense in her a great fear, but also a helplessness which did not sit well with her.

'He is not improving,' he said as if it were only to be expected.

She smiled but he knew it was forced. 'There will come a point when the fever is at its height and he will either recover or… or he will not.' She looked at him gravely. 'Your family warned you about the True-sight because they were frightened that if you were discovered, you would be attacked. The fact that they died of the Scorge had nothing to do with you. Almost everyone had family who died. It had nothing to do with your True-sight. Nothing.' When he did not seem convinced she frowned at him. 'Look at me, Boy. Look into my mind. You can see that I speak the truth. You must see.'

He could, but his fear was so strong that it was hard to let himself believe. She spoke what she thought to be true. What if she was wrong?

'You should learn to use your gift for good,' she went on, ' in fact…' She stood up suddenly. 'Why did I not remember this before?' Immediately she was busy once more with her leaves and pots. 'My mother had a potion which could sometimes kill the fever, but it had to be administered just before the moment of crisis came. She had the ability, because of her True-sight, to know that moment. I can mix the potion, but I cannot know when to give it. Maybe you can.' He sensed in her the first stirring of hope. 'You can do this, Tam. You have the power to save him.'

***

Watching and waiting; Tam had done a lot of that recently, in the woods while Nick and Matilda went into Fastwater, on the hillside waiting for Valeron and his men to come, then later, in the tree keeping watch over Catherine. Now the longest scariest watch of all, at his master's bedside while the afternoon turned into night and he longed to fall asleep but dared not.

Matilda had made a bed for herself on the floor and she slept now, ready to administer her potion as soon as Tam told her the time was right. Then, she had assured him, it would be his turn to sleep.

He remembered now, how uncomfortable he had been, perched in the branches of a copper beech tree, watching through the leaves as Catherine slept below. He had heard the sound of metal clashing against metal and the cries of men as they fought, but his orders were to do nothing unless anyone tried to attack Catherine. No-one did.

One man had passed close without noticing her. The top of his head was almost bald, but he had long hair tied back from his face. It was a cruel face, one Tam did not think he would ever forget.

He watched with interest. The man headed away from the fighting, circled the area then crept back towards the road. By turning himself at a precarious angle, Tam watched him approach Valeron's tethered horses.

With another glance down at Catherine, he had pulled himself into a standing position and was just able to see as the man began taking the saddle bags from the other horses and loading them all on to one. Then he got on to the horse and road away up the road.

What sort of man, he wondered, stole from his comrades, then abandoned them to fight and die.

Now, in Nick's bedchamber, he occupied himself making up stories about the deserter but every few minutes he made sure to wash the sweat from his master's brow and try to sense when the crisis would come. There was an ominous stillness about Nick now, as if he too were waiting for something. Tam could only pray it was not death.

When the night was at its darkest, and the sounds from elsewhere in the castle had ceased, he began to notice the change. It was as if a storm were coming, somewhere in the distance. He could hear nothing, but his heart began to beat faster and in his head felt heavier. Something akin to panic began to grip him. He held hard to the sides of his chair and tried to breath deeply. His hands shook. There were no outward signs from the bed, but to Tam it was as clear as day.

'Mistress,' he called. 'Mistress Matilda. I think it is time.'

She was awake instantly and at the bedside.

'Are you sure?'

The feeling of turmoil was so strong that he was almost in tears. 'Yes. Please, Mistress, do something.'

She took the potion and poured it into Nick's mouth gently, so that he did not choke, but was forced to swallow. When she straightened up he seemed outwardly just as still then suddenly, he sat upright in the bed.

'I can't move,' he roared, 'what have you done to me?'

She spoke softly, trying to calm him, placing her hands on his shoulders. ‘It is I, Matilda. You are sick. Lie still.’

‘No! No more. I won’t take any more.’ It was as if a great rage had overtaken Nick. Although he appeared to be awake, he clearly did not know where he was. He pushed her away so hard that she fell against the wall. Then he tried to get down from the bed, and Tam rushed to stop him. Nick’s legs were too weak to hold him and they collapsed together onto the chamber floor.

Tam could hardly tell what was happening next. He was gasping for breath as he fought to free himself from beneath his master’s body. Then he was suddenly free and strong arms were gripping him and pulling him upright. There were armed men in the room and he could hear Matilda’s voice calling instructions, then he felt himself lifted from the ground and he must have fallen asleep.

When he woke, he was in his own bed, and his first sensation was that of calm. Then, although he did not know why, he realised that he was smiling.

Chapter 37

Nick had imagined himself back on the floor of the cart, his limbs immobilised by the powerful herbs, while his parents were murdered only yards away. Once again he had fought to go to their aid but each time he tried to move he was forced back and fed yet more of the hated potion.

Now, waking in his bed at Castle Baryk, he realised that it had been a dream. He felt calm and at peace. The events of the past week came back to him piece by piece, even before his consciousness returned.

Gradually, he became aware of his surroundings and then he began to hear the voices of the two women.

'I have seen the way you look at him.' Catherine's voice light with amusement. 'Matilda, do not pretend such innocence. You cannot deny it.'

He felt a gentle bump as if someone had sat on the end of his bed, then came Matilda's voice, low and secretive. 'Truly he is like a disease in me. He haunts my dreams and even when I am awake I can think of nothing else.'

'I knew it.' Now Catherine was triumphant.

'But I feel so guilty,' Matilda admitted. 'Jacob is dead and I loved him so much. How can I feel like this about another so soon.'

'Jacob was older than you.'

‘Yes. There were twenty years between us.’

‘Well that would explain it. The Prince is much younger and he is so handsome. It is a different sort of attraction.’

‘Indeed it is. I have never …ever felt this way.’

Nick had opened his eyes now and he could see the bed hangings and the outline of a tree outside his window. Carefully, he raised himself up on one elbow. The two women had their backs to him, Matilda sitting on the end of his bed, Catherine standing beside her, a hand resting on the bedpost. She turned to glance at him as she must have done many times before, then, with a cry of joy she came to kneel beside him.

‘I thought you would never wake.’

She stroked his hair, and kissed him. He noticed that she was still very thin, but her hair, tied in two braids, was shiny and golden and her blue eyes were clear and bright.

Lying back again he gazed at her drinking in the sight of her happy, smiling face.

Matilda appeared beside her. ‘You had everyone so worried,’ she said sternly, ‘and it was all so unnecessary. The King was quite safe.’

He looked from one to the other and smiled.

‘How do you feel? Do you have any pain?’ Matilda asked while Catherine held his hand.

Tentatively he tested each of his limbs. ‘My leg is still sore,’ he admitted, ‘but not as it was.’

She nodded. ‘It has finally begun to heal. You are not to move it Nick. You are not to try to stand or to put any pressure on it. I have the King’s agreement that if you do so you will be chained to your bed.’

He wanted to be alone with Catherine but needed to ask, ‘How is the King?’

‘He is well and in good spirits. I think that he is looking forward to proving himself on the battlefield.’

‘Is he angry with me? I would not blame him if he were.’

‘I think it is more that he fears he has lost your friendship. He is only a boy, Nick, don’t forget that. It was not easy for him to refuse you.’

‘No. I realise that. I always did. It was just… hard for me to say so.’

‘You must tell him that when you see him. I am sure he will visit you soon. Now. If you don’t mind, I will leave you two together. You know where to find me if you need me, Catherine.’

Catherine stood up and kissed her on the cheek. ‘Thank you, Matilda, thank you for so many things. You are a true friend.’

‘Yes,’ she said bitterly ‘I am everybody’s friend.’

When she had left, Catherine knelt beside him again.

‘How are you?’ he asked. ‘Are you fully recovered?’

‘I tire easily but I can feel myself growing stronger each day.’

‘How long have I been sick?’

‘We have been here for nearly three days. You were ill some days before that.’

He took her hand and kissed it, then held it close to his heart. ‘I can hardly believe that I finally have you back. I was lost without you. Completely lost.’

***

Nick was now allowed to walk for a while each day. With Catherine’s help he would take a turn around the courtyard then they would sit for a while in the sunlight.

The inactivity frustrated him but he understood that it was necessary if his leg was to mend properly.

Everywhere in the castle, preparations for war were at their height and he knew that soon he would be obliged to resume his duties.

'When must you leave?' Catherine asked, as if she could read his thoughts. She was sitting beside him, her hand resting in his. A week of rest and good food had done much to restore her, and her skin was soft as he held the hand to his lips.

'Two weeks,' he said eventually, stroking her hand absentmindedly as he stared into her eyes. 'We move in two weeks.'

She nodded slowly. 'Our dream of a peaceful life on the farm at Claveham was always just that, a dream. It was just that we didn't realise it.'

'Yes. There are still so many unanswered questions in my life. As soon as I find the answer to one, another appears. It is as if my fate has been written for me by some all knowing power and I for some reason, am destined to follow it blindly.' He looked out from the peace of the gardens to the practice yards and the armoury which now were the scene of constant activity. 'I did not choose this, but I must go where it leads.'

'I know.'

'Even if that were not the case, this king of ours, truly he is an exceptional young man. One day he will be a great king. Greater even than his father. But he must fight a war and I must be by his side to keep him safe. Though I would for all the world, return to Claveham and live there with you as I promised, war changes everything.'

'Of course it does, and I would not have you turn your back on him or your duty.' She took his face in her hands and looked earnestly into his eyes. 'I do not love you because of your farm, Nick or for your prowess with the plough. I love you for who you are.' Releasing him, she sat back. 'The man I fell in love with all those years ago was a man of quiet dignity and of resolve and courage. You have always strived to do everything to the best of your ability. Whether it was to become a warrior, or to make your farm profitable or to rescue me. Whatever you have to do, I will still love you. I will still marry you.'

He wondered if she realised what she was promising. They had waited so long to be married but victory in the war was by no means certain. She could be a widow within weeks.

'We may lose,' he reminded her, 'or…or I may be killed. I will understand if you wish to wait a little longer. Until the future is…is more certain. '

'Is that what you want?'

'No, but…'

She shook her head. 'Then why talk of waiting? I want to be your wife before you go. I want you to know that whatever the outcome, whatever the future, I am yours. Ask the King, Nick. Ask if we can marry as soon as it can be arranged.'

He took her into his arms and kissed her. How, he asked himself, would he ever be able to bear the pain of separation again. Then, just for a second, he saw the image of his father's face and knew that somehow the pain would be borne because it was right that it should. And for the first time he began to understand.

***

'We do not have time to organise a wedding,' the King said. 'I wanted to throw a party for you that would be remembered for all time.'

Nick and Catherine stood before him in the great hall. Nick was leaning on a stick, though if he had been given the choice he would have dispensed with it.

'We would prefer a quiet ceremony,' he insisted. 'I am grateful to you, truly but perhaps the party could wait until we all return to celebrate your victory.'

Rowan laughed. 'Nick, you sound like a courtier. I will have to send you back to the country to re-learn the art of plain speaking.'

'Then speaking plainly, Sire. I have waited far too long to make Catherine my wife. Please, I beg of you, let us be married quickly.'

'Of course,' Rowan agreed. 'I cannot refuse you that. Master Gomero and his acrobats are still in the area I hear. A little entertainment would not come amiss.'

Nick realised that this would be more for the King's benefit than for theirs but he agreed happily. 'That would be wonderful thank you sire.'

'How soon can we do this Lord John?'

'Within days,' the Chancellor affirmed, 'but before we proceed, maybe this would be a good time to…' He raised an eyebrow and indicated Nick with a nod of his head.

'Ah... yes.' The King turned back to Nick with a more serious expression. 'There is something I have to tell you, Nick. Something of great moment. It… it will change things, many things for you.'

Nick shook his head in despair. 'What now?'

The King looked around the room. 'Will someone find Prince Jared. He should hear this too.'

'Please, both of you, sit. Bring chairs for them someone. And some food and wine. This may take some time.'

When the Prince had arrived, the food had been brought and everyone was settled, the King waved his hand towards his chancellor.

'Nick, it is time for your history lesson. Lord John if you please.'

'Very well, Sire.'

'And do not spend all day about it. They are both not fully recovered. I do not want them to fall asleep before you have reached the most important part.'

'As I'm sure you know,' the Chancellor began. 'Thomas of the Jassoir defeated Henry Valeron and took over the throne, fifty years ago.

'Henry's son was also also killed, but his two granddaughters survived. The elder, Joanna, defied her family and married for love. Her husband was one of Thomas's warriors and the couple remained loyal to the Jassoir line. She was cut off by her family.

'Maria, the younger, was married to a distant Valeron cousin and her descendants have lived in exile in Nostaria ever since. They made a treaty with the Nostarians that if Subia was defeated, Maria's heirs would regain the throne. If we do not defeat King Tynon, that is what will happen.'

'But we will defeat him,' the King insisted.

'Of course, Sire. Thus far it is hypothetical. If I may continue…? Maria's descendant, Barnold Valeron is the current heir and he lives, as I say, in Nostaria.

'However, he has one problem. If hypothetically…' he glanced at the King. 'the Valeron throne is reclaimed, Maria's descendants are not the true heirs. It is Joanna's line which is in fact heir to the Valeron throne. And the true Valeron heir might well argue his right to the throne. They must wipe out Joanna's line before they can be sure of their claim. In this they have been partially successful, but one of Joanna's heirs still remains.'

It was as if a rock had been laid on Nick's shoulders a burden that had always been his though he had never known of it.

Prince Jared sat back heavily in his seat as the truth occurred to him too. 'Oh, by all that is…'

The Chancellor nodded slowly. 'Joanna's husband, the man she married for love, was Jelavan Trayer.'

'My grandfather.'

'Yes, Nick,' the King said softly. 'You are the true heir to the Valeron throne.'

Lord John nodded again. 'That is correct. You would still have been ignorant of your position had King Edwell not died before his time. When my brother Lord Harald, brought the Prince to Claveham it was not by chance. His instructions were clear. You had to be brought to the castle, to safety. I can only guess that Harald told you whatever he needed in order to bring you here. Your steward would have known what had to be done. And Jacob too, had he lived, would have ensured that you came.'

Nick shook his head sadly. 'They are all dead.'

'Indeed.'

'Because of me.'

'Not just because of you,' the King reminded him. 'They died to save us both.'

'Why was I never told?'

Lord John's eyes were kind. 'Your father had intended to tell you the truth when you recovered from your branding, but he was killed before he had that chance. You know already that your life was protected while Richard Lassall still lived, and the price for that was your continuing ignorance.'

Prince Jared nodded slowly. 'Felix was not the fool we thought him. With Richard at Barrow Marsh, and you oblivious on your farm, he could afford to wait. When King

Tynon defeated my father, as they thought he would, you would not challenge the throne, because you did not know who you were. And Richard would be released and sent to kill you before you found out. Had you known that you were a Valeron you would be always on your guard. In fact you would probably be here as you now are, to fight alongside the King.

'But our father died before any of that could happen.' Rowan explained, 'and a new opportunity presented itself. Felix sent Richard to capture me before I reached the castle. The fact that he caught up with us at Claveham was pure chance. He did not realise who you were. If he had, he would never have let Catherine go.'

'If Richard is dead,' Catherine began. 'Nick's life is no longer protected.'

'That is true. But now that he knows the truth he is in a better position to protect himself.'

The best thing you can do is to marry and have as many children as possible.' Prince Jared said. 'Thereby protecting your family line.'

Nick turned to Catherine. 'Do you still want to marry me? I am not who you thought I was.'

'Of course you are. Nothing has changed.'

'Everything has changed. I am … I am a Valeron.'

'You are a Trayer. That has not changed. It is the name I have always wanted to bear. And you are the man I have always wanted.'

'It is too late to change your mind, now, Nick,' the King insisted. 'I have already sent for the acrobats.

Chapter 38

Rowan stood with Lord John Garwin watching as Nick and Catherine were finally pronounced man and wife.

Catherine had her back to him but he could see Nick's face clearly and it was bathed in joy. Rowan was pleased for him beyond measure and yet the happiness he should have felt was kept at bay by an unexpected dark mood which had taken a grip of him since the previous day.

Nick had come to him with a request which should have pleased him.

'I would be honoured if you would stand with me at the wedding as my escort.'

For a moment Rowan had felt pleased, touched that he had been singled out in this way, then he realised the truth and his heart sank.

He had forced a smile to his face. 'Although I would be delighted to do so, I do not think that it is appropriate for the King to …'

'But My Lord…' In his usual pedantic manner, Lord John began to contradict him.

Rowan silenced him with a flick of his hand. 'I am sure that Prince Jared would be a worthy escort for you Nick.'

The Chancellor's face betrayed his disgust even before he spoke, and then his voice was laced with sarcasm.

‘Oh, a far more appropriate choice, Sire.’

Rowan turned on him angrily.

‘I know that you do not like my brother, Lord John, and I understand the reasons for it. But I would be grateful if you would keep your opinions to yourself in public.’

Lord John had bowed his head but said nothing, and Rowan felt guilty for snapping at him.

Now, as he watched Nick take his new wife in his arms and kiss her to the cheers of the many onlookers, he forced out a smile once more, applauded and signalled for the entertainment to begin.

As he took his seat, the Chancellor looked at him curiously. ‘Might I enquire, My Lord? Why did you not wish to stand as Nick’s escort? There was no reason why you should not do so.’

Rowan sighed. ‘He asked me as a courtesy. I was not really his choice of man. Jared is Nick’s friend and I am sure he much prefers to have him by his side.’

‘Would he still feel the same if he knew the truth about his… friend.’ Lord John asked bitterly.

‘Yes.’ Rowan looked the old man straight in the eye. ‘I think he would.’

***

Matilda sat next to her daughter as once again Lucilla and Titus the exotic twins performed their acrobatic dance. Sophia watched with an expression of childish wonder, clapping whenever they performed a difficult manoeuvre and clasping her hand to her mouth when it appeared that one of the performers might fall.

For all that, Matilda realised, Sophia was growing out of her childhood. In a new silk dress of pale blue, she looked older than her eleven years. Her hair was tied into a plait but a few dark tendrils had escaped and framed her sweet face. Across the room with the more senior servants, she could see Tam also watching the performance. From time to time she saw him glance in their direction. She frowned to herself. Ever since Sophia and he had nursed Nick back to health, she had noticed that he seemed to have grown attached to the child. Even Catherine had noticed and commented upon it.

Matilda had shaken her head. 'I am afraid that she has in mind a greater prize.'

Catherine's worried expression had echoed her own feelings. 'The King? I know that they are friends but…Does she know that it could never be?'

'She is very young still. You know how fickle a child's affections can be. I am sure it will not last.' Matilda had tried to sound dismissive but there was a part of her which could not help feeling that this was trouble brewing for the future.

If only Jacob were here now. As the acrobats began the finale of their act, Matilda fought back unfamiliar tears. Though she had been to all intents and purposes, his servant, he had treated her with respect, as an equal and she had loved him as much for that as for his many other qualities.

Despite these feelings, her eyes were drawn towards Prince Jared who, just as he had for the coronation, was dressed in his dark green robes and looked just as magnificent.

Though Matilda was now no-one's servant, she felt enslaved by her feelings for the Prince.

For his part, he did not so much as glance at her. He was totally absorbed following with rapt attention, the movements of the raven-haired Lucilla.

‘Mamma?’ Sophia’s voice in her ear was a welcome distraction. ‘Why is the King so sad today?’

Rowan was slouched in an ornate chair in the centre of the room, one hand supporting his chin, the other laying idly on his knee. Although he was watching the performance, his attention was clearly elsewhere. He did not seem to be enjoying himself.

‘Maybe he is thinking about the coming battle,’ Matilda suggested. ‘We leave in a few days.’

Sophia shook her head. ‘No. He is excited about the battle. He told me. He has a new horse and it is a magnificent beast. Prince Jared gave it to him as a gift.’

The germ of an idea occurred to Matilda. She had been trying to find some pretext to visit the Prince and if possible, find our more about his awful behaviour towards Will Garwin. Now an opportunity presented itself. She would ask him to find her a horse for the battle.

***

Because her rooms were in the same building as his, the guards let her pass without question. It was only as she rounded the corner into the Prince’s private corridor that she was surprised to see his servant Lucas in her way.

‘My Lord is busy, Mistress.’

With a deep breath she pushed past him and began to walk briskly towards the Prince’s door, which was barely ajar. ‘I merely wanted to speak to him fo….’

‘Lady Matilda I must insist. The Prince is not to be disturbed.’

There was a loud shout of laughter from behind the door and she stopped abruptly. Jared’s deep voice boomed out jovially.

'Twice, you have refused me. Twice. I cannot bear the shame.'

Of course he was busy. She had seen him heading towards Gomero's quarters. She had seen the look of rapt attention on his face and of course he had made no secret of his intent towards Lucilla, the exotic girl with the raven hair. How could Matilda have been so stupid?

There was another peal of laughter from within, the door was flung open, and Matilda found herself face to face with the acrobat. She could not have been more surprised. It was not Lucilla but her brother Titus who ran past her swiftly, covering his head with the hood of his cloak and slipping quietly away.

Matilda reeled with shock. Realising that she had seen something she was not meant to see, she turned to leave, walking quickly back the way she had come. Lucas barred her way inquiring over her shoulder. 'My Lord?'

'Matilda.' The Prince's voice held a shock which matched her own. 'Come back. I wish to talk to you.'

'There is nothing to say. I should not have intruded.'

She turned to him, her heart beating wildly. He was coming towards her with an outstretched arm.

'Please. Come inside.'

Despite everything, she could not resist him. Reluctantly she followed him back to his chamber. The room was unexpectedly frugal. It surprised her, but then, it was a night of many surprises.

'Sit. Please.' She heard the heavy door crash shut behind her as if to signal an end to any dreams she may have been foolish enough to harbour.

Perching herself awkwardly on the edge of the settle she waited silently as the Prince pulled up a chair and placed it opposite.

'I am sorry,' he said gently.

‘For what?’ she tried not to meet his eyes but failed. ‘It was I who…’

‘I am sorry that I could not be the man you wanted me to be.’

She was horribly embarrassed and the blood burned in her face.

‘You knew?’

‘You are not the first woman to… to be disappointed in me though, you are the first to discover why? I never cease to be surprised by you. You are very courageous.’

It was pointless to deny her feelings. ‘Not courageous. Foolish. I believed that I could win your heart. That I could succeed where…’ She shook her head helplessly.

‘You already have my friendship,’ he insisted. ‘You know it. And my admiration. I cannot offer more.’

‘The stories about you. They are all false. They say that…’ she paused as her thoughts circled alarmingly, making no sense.

‘The truth is far worse, believe me.’

Her mind raced to absorb all she had discovered. Then suddenly it made sense.

‘William Garwin. He was not your rival. He was your lover.’ He said nothing but she could see that she was right. ‘But…but you had him beaten. Why?’

‘Of course I did not have him beaten.’ He buried his face in his hands as if in shame but his voice was angry. ‘I loved him. I would not have hurt him for the world.’

‘But the men who attacked him, they were your men?’

‘Yes, they were my men.’ When he looked up at her, his eyes were wet with tears. ‘But they were not acting on my orders.’

Matilda was shocked and she knew that it was none of her business, yet she was fascinated.

‘Why? Why did they do that?’

Angrily he stood and began to pace the room as if to work off his emotion. 'Will was different. He was not a born soldier. He was very good with a bow and an excellent horseman, but he was not a warrior. The other men knew that he was different and they made his life miserable. It became a sport with them.'

'We had to be so careful,' he shook his head miserably. 'You can imagine…if I was discovered… Not just because I was the King's son but also because I commanded two regiments of the army. It would have been unthinkable.

'Everyone knew that Will had a lover but they assumed it was some young girl, a servant perhaps and no-one could discover her identity. The men thought it was a game and they became more and more determined to find out. We thought we had them fooled, but one night, they… they must have followed him. We had met in the hay loft of a deserted stable. It had always been safe before. We heard them come in and call out to him and … well there was no escape except through the window and we did not have time to climb down and get away without being seen.

'I was willing to face them. They would not have dared to harm him, but Will persuaded me that I could not risk everything by letting them discover me. He begged me to run.

'To my everlasting shame I did just that. With my boots in my hand, I jumped out of the window and ran. Matilda, they were the worst sort of soldiers. They were brutal. The sort it was useful to have on your side, but not that you would want to make enemies of. They preyed on the weak and helpless and Will was no match for them. But I ask you, which one of us was the weak and which the strong? I ran away and he stood before the window and confronted them to give me time to make my escape.

'He need only have mentioned my name and he would have been safe. But he would not betray me and they almost killed him. You have heard, I am sure, what they did to him. And finally, when they had had their fun, they threw him out of the window.'

Though Matilda had never met Will Garwin she could almost see his brutalised body lying twisted on the ground.

'But he still lives, doesn't he? I was told he was sent into exile.'

'He lives, yes. His back was broken but he lives.' He turned away so that she would not see the great pain in his eyes.

'I told my father everything. I could not do otherwise. He loved me and so he tried to understand, but I know that he was deeply disappointed, though he tried to hide it. Between them, he and Lord John acquired a house and estate a long way from here, and that is where they sent Will.'

'And the men who did this were hanged?'

'My father claimed that he had them put to death as an example, but I think he did it to stop me taking my own revenge. And I would have done. I would have torn each one limb from limb. So you see I had no-one upon whom to vent my anger except myself.'

'You did your duty to your king.'

'I did. And I have loathed myself for it ever since. I would have given everything for Will, my life, certainly, ten times over, and everything else I owned. I am not proud that I ran away that day, but I know that if I had to do it again, I would have no choice. In the end it was he who gave up everything.'

He closed his eyes briefly then looked at her apologetically. 'Matilda I have never spoken to a living soul of those days.'

Despite her shock, she felt sorry for him. She reached towards him, laying a hand on his arm and he did not pull away. 'Have you seen him since?'

'No. I do not know where he is and I promised my father I would not try to find him. It is, if you like, a self enforced punishment, but not half what I deserve.'

'How many people know the truth?'

'Now that my father is dead, only the Chancellor and…' he pointed to the door. 'Lucas, and I trust him completely.'

'What about the King?'

'I suppose Lord John must have told him, though he has said nothing to me?' Hesitantly he looked at her again. 'And now you?'

'I will not betray you.'

'You will tell no-one? Not even Nick.'

'No-one. I swear.'

'For myself, I do not care. It is not vanity or fear, you must believe me in that. But I am commander of all the armies now and we have a war to fight. The men respect me. They will fight for me. I cannot risk losing that respect.'

'I understand.'

He nodded slowly. She looked at him afresh and realised that even armed with this knowledge about him, he still moved her. Her feelings towards him had not changed and she wished that they had. To go on wanting him as she did, knowing that there was no hope of anything between them would cause her nothing but pain.

He took her hand from his arm and held on to it.

'Matilda, do…do I still have your friendship?'

'Is it that important to you?' Forgive me, she thought, but I must have this crumb of comfort.

'Very much so.'

'Then of course you do.'

He smiled at her gratefully and her heart ached.

'Anything else that I can do for you I will,' he insisted. 'What brought you here tonight?'

For a moment she forgot why she had come. It was after all just an excuse to see him. 'A horse.'

'A horse?'

'Nick has been teaching me to fight with a sword so that I can ride to battle with the army.'

'Has he indeed?'

'At least he did before he was injured. I realise there is very little time but…' she paused, 'you do not agree?'

'Of course I do. You will make an exceptional warrior. Besides, I do not believe you need my agreement. Neither I nor Nick possess the ability to prevent you from doing as you wish.'

She smiled accepting the consolation of his affectionate mockery.

'I wondered if you could find me a good horse.'

'Certainly.' There was a good deal of relief in his smile. 'That request will be easy to grant. I will find two or three that would be suitable and you can choose the one you like best. I will be happy to have you in my army although…you will have to learn to obey orders.'

'If I obeyed orders I would not have survived.'

'And for that,' he acknowledged, 'I am very grateful.'

***

On the previous night, Rowan had dreamed that it was he who was marrying Catherine. He had stood in the Hall of Kings dressed in his finest clothes as she came towards him on her father's arm, the miller having been escorted to the castle on the previous day. She had smiled at Rowan in the same way that she smiled at Nick and even though he was far too young to marry, he had felt calm and happy. But when the proclamation came that they were now man and wife he turned to her and found that she had disappeared. In her place was an ugly pockmarked girl with a painted face who leered at him and he woke up with a start in a wave of nausea. Despite all that he faced in the war, the idea that he would be forced to marry some ugly foreign princess petrified him.

This evening, following the real ceremony, he had watched an endless stream of eager young girls as they were paraded before him. Of course he was used to the flattery and the flirting which accompanied him throughout his everyday life. They unsettled him, but in a pleasurable way and he knew that there were many advantages to being king.

Tonight, however, the sight of so many girls and their parents, trying desperately to draw themselves to his notice, merely irritated him.

He told the guards to keep everyone away and sat by himself in a corner of the room while the celebrations went on around him.

Nick and Catherine had left some time ago to enjoy the wedding night they had waited for, for so long. He imagined them cocooned in each others arms oblivious to the world outside.

Jared had slipped away from the party soon after the entertainment had finished and Matilda, also, was missing.

From the corner of his eye he saw a flash of blue silk and glanced to the side imagining yet another painted bird fluttering around him. But it was only Sophia. He indicated to the guards to let her pass. At least in her presence he could relax and be himself.

'Why are you all alone?' she asked him.

‘I am not in the mood for company.

‘I am sorry.’ She turned to leave.

‘No. Don’t go. I didn’t mean…’ he beckoned her forward. ‘Your company would be welcome.’

She came to stand beside him, her hand resting lightly on the back of his chair.

Together they watched silently as the dancing began in earnest.

‘You look very pretty,’ he announced suddenly.

‘Thank you. It is the first silk dress I have ever worn. Mamma says that…’

‘You love your mother, don’t you?’

‘Of course.’

‘And your father? Did you love him too?’

‘Yes. And I am sad that he is dead, and that I will never see him again.’ He felt guilty for bringing up the subject and making her unhappy, but she did not dwell on this. ‘You must miss your father also.’

He shook his head. ‘My father and I did not know each other well enough to love. Besides, Jared was always his favourite, because Jared’s mother was my father’s true love. I was his duty child. I suppose my mother loves me, but she is… you have not met my mother. She is bitter, and that bitterness makes her cold.’ It was difficult to explain how he was feeling, because he did not even understand it himself. His words came out in a rush as if he needed to empty his mind.

‘Nick risked everything to go after Catherine. His life, his position, my patronage. And your mother, she also risked her life to go with him, out of friendship which is of course another form of love. What it must feel like to be the object of such feeling. To know yourself loved to such a degree.

‘But you are loved by everyone. You are the King.’

‘That is true, and hundreds will lay down their lives in battle for me, but it is the King they love. Not the man.’

She moved closer to him and rested her shoulder against his. Although she was only a child, he could see that she understood.

‘I love you,’ she whispered. ‘When I first met you, I did not understand who you were. Yet I loved you from the start.’

He looked up at her. She was still watching the dancers and it was as if she had not spoken, yet her words had been clear enough.

Resting his head on the back of the chair, he let this revelation wash over him. As dramatically as it had come, his bad mood disappeared and there was nothing forced about the smile that now lit up his face.

Chapter 39

Nick was woken by the geese and the peacocks who wandered the garden behind the royal apartments. Catherine slept still beside him, the fragile beauty of face bathed in morning light. It seemed that he had waited a lifetime to wake with her by his side and know that she was his wife. He watched the rise and fall of her breathing aware that she needed to sleep but longing to make love to her one more time.

The last ten years had been merely a dream; he realised that now. The knowledge of who he was and where his duty lay, may have been kept from him, but he been destined always to follow its path.

With a sigh, he climbed out of the bed and began to dress. As he fastened his belt she stirred and he went over to her and kissed her cheek.

'Where are you going?' she asked sleepily.

He stroked a few strands of hair from her face. 'I must put in some more time in the practice yard. I have been inactive for too long.'

'Will I see you before you leave?'

'We have one more night,' he promised.

She smiled. 'The last few days have been the happiest of my life. I have lost track of time.'

He kissed her again and she rolled over and was asleep before he had risen from the bed. It would take time for her strength to return, Matilda had warned him. And even then, she may never recover fully. But they would have a life together, and that was all he asked.

In the meantime there was a war to fight. Morale was high and no-one spoke of anything but victory, but the outcome was in no way certain. His own duty was not to win the battle, but to keep the young King from harm. His main problem, he knew, would be Rowan himself, who would want to fight alongside his men, but who could never be allowed to put his life in danger.

Before he reached the practice yard, Nick stopped at the stables to check on Ransom and to speak to Matilda who, he had been told, he would find there.

There were many blessings in his life, not least of all his friends. Matilda had done so much for him. Without her he would not have realised Ralph Lubeck's deception, or beaten Richard Lassall, and most importantly, he would not have been able to rescue Catherine.

He owed Matilda so much, and yet he was about to ask for more.

He found her in a stall near to Ransom's, admiring a majestic black mare.

'Is she not beautiful,' she stroked the horse's nose. 'She responds so readily to my touch. When we leave I will...' His face must have betrayed him because instantly she knew. 'Nick. Please. You promised to take me with.'

'I did,' he owned. 'And if you hold me to that promise I will still do so?'

'But why not? It is because of the river isn't it? I failed you there and now you do not think me strong enough?'

'No.' He hastened to assure her of that. 'You did not fail me. Believe me Matilda if I could choose one man to have at my side in battle it would be you.'

'Then why? Why will you not take me?'

He took a deep breath. 'You said that I had never asked anything of you.'

'That is so. All that I have given has been my choice to give.'

'I ask you now and you must believe how hard it is to do so. I ask that you stay here with Catherine.'

There was shock on her face as well as disappointment, and a tiny spark of anger.

'She is recovering, Nick. She is weakened yes, but she knows how to take care of herself and when to rest. She is in no danger.'

'From her sickness no. But she is in danger. I am the heir to the Valeron throne. There are those - I do not even know who they are - who would see me dead. Catherine is my wife now and for all they know she may already be carrying our child. Do you not see? She is constantly in danger.'

She sighed, searching for some argument that would convince him. 'I understand your fear, but Castle Baryk will be well defended. Surely she will be safe here.'

'We believed the castle to be safe before, yet twice the King's life was threatened in his own apartments. The very man who should have been above suspicion was responsible for that. Who knows who can be trusted?'

It seemed to him that her whole body seemed to admit defeat and he knew that she would stay. She nodded her head sadly. 'Very well.'

He went on, wanting to convince her further. 'The King, the Prince, even Lord John, they would not see her hurt, I know that, but their allegiance must always be to duty, not love. You are the only person living in whose care I would leave her.'

When she looked at him again her eyes were soft and her voice no more than a whisper. 'She is a very lucky woman to command such love. I will stay and I will protect her with my life.'

He shook his head. 'Of that I have no doubt, but I do not have the right to demand your life for hers. What I do ask is that you make me a promise. If ever you have to choose between her life and mine, you will choose Catherine. If you are the friend I hold you to be, you will know that it is what I would want.'

She gripped his shoulder lightly.

'Though it would break my heart,' she assured him. 'I promise.'

***

The King had gone in search of Sophia and he found her in the garden playing with her puppy.

The boy, Tam was sitting beside them on the grass. When Tam saw Rowan he stood and then bowed but Sophia smiled with delight and came over. The dog barked as if to call her back but she turned to him irritably.

'Quiet Roc. Quiet now.'

Sending a low growl in Rowan's direction the dog rested on his haunches, but he remained alert. Tam put a hand on his head as if to calm him.

'He really does not like me, does he?' Rowan shook his head. 'I do not know what I have done to upset him.'

Tam rubbed the dog's ears. 'He is jealous. He thinks you are a rival.'

'For what?'

'For his mistress's attention.'

‘Nonsense,’ Sophia said uneasily. ‘It is because he is so young. He is just a baby, Sire. He does not understand who you are.’

Rowan sighed. He was clearly missing something but there was nothing to be gained by pursuing the matter.

‘How are you?’ he asked Sophia. ‘I have not seen you since the wedding.’

She smiled again. ‘I am happy because my mother is to stay, but I think she is disappointed. It is selfish of me I know.’

He shook his head. ‘No. Of course it isn’t. You have lost so much already.’

Although he had sought her out, now that he was here, an unfamiliar nervousness overtook him. Instead of speaking his mind he turned to Tam.

‘I understand that you are now under Master Lambett’s instruction.’

The younger boy nodded. ‘I am, Sire.’

‘Then maybe we could train together. It would be good to have a real opponent.’

‘I would be honoured,’ Tam bowed his head, ‘though I am just a novice.’

‘So am I,’ Rowan insisted, ‘even if Master Lambett keeps telling me I’m not.’ He smiled with satisfaction. ‘I will arrange it then.’

Tam nodded again though he did not look overjoyed at the prospect.

Now there was no excuse not to make his request of Sophia. He put a hand on her arm.

‘Would you walk a little way with me?’

When they were far enough away that they could not be heard, he stopped.

‘There…there is something I would ask from you.’

He took out his knife and stepped towards her. Before he could speak again, the puppy had torn himself out of Tam's grip and was leaping towards them.

'Roc no.'

As he reached them, Sophia threw both arms around the animal's neck to hold him back, but she could barely restrain him. The guards who had remained at a distance came to the King's defence but he waved a hand.

'No. Do not harm him. He was defending her. Tam, take him away please.'

Once the animal had been removed, he finally found the courage to tell her what he wanted.

***

Master Hobbs was putting the finishing touches to the King's armour when the servant arrived holding a small wooden box.

'My Lord King asked me to bring you this. He said you would know what to do with it.'

The mailmaker, peered inside and his face broke into a huge grin.

'Indeed I do.'

Inside the box, curled against the velvet lining, were two locks of shiny dark hair.

***

Catherine stood with Matilda and Sophia on the walkway above the main gate. The once peaceful valley in front of the castle mount was a seething mass of troops and horses.

The sun, untroubled by the petty actions of men, shone upon the scene just as it always did. Now, it reflected off the armour of soldiers and their horses. A solitary cloud cast its shadow over one section of the Prince's men and she shivered at the thought of what that could portend.

She could hear Sophia's excited chatter and her mother's calm explanation and from the valley came loud voices, the calling of battle horns and the neighing and sneezing of horses.

She had chosen to wear a dress of the brightest red despite the fact that it made her pale features seem even paler. Nick would not see her face but he would know she was there.

Earlier that morning her honeymoon had finally come to an end. They had closed the shutters and all the curtains which lined the bed but of course the dawn had managed to reach into their bedchamber and claim her warrior husband on his king's behalf. By its light he had taken her in his arms for one last kiss and if she closed her eyes she could still imagine herself there.

As he had finally pulled away, she had felt, not fear, but a sudden dizzying certainty.

This was not the end.

He had not fought for his life against a sickness over which he had no control, only to lose it in a battle for which he had been training since his earliest days. The hope that she would see him again had helped her survive the horror and misery of Fastwater and it would help her now. He would return, and they would have a life on the farm at Claveham and raise a family.

She opened her eyes again and looked down over the waiting army.

At such a distance all the men looked alike. It was the bright red and gold of the banner that showed her where the royal party was mustered. She could just about make out the King, a figure only slightly smaller than those around him.

Next to him was Ransom and on his back Nick seemed unrecognisable. She could almost believe that the armour clad figure was not her husband. The real Nick would be beside her every night if only in her dreams.

The drumbeat started slowly and everything else fell silent. The air was heavy with expectation.

Catherine watched as Rowan lifted his arm and the sea of men parted to let him through.

One by one each company followed and the army of Subia, its young king and the hopes and fears of a nation advanced along the road to war.

Lightning Source UK Ltd.
Milton Keynes UK
UKOW051805110612

194239UK00001B/12/P

9 781907 986918